NO.1 *NEW YORK TIMES* BESTSELLING AUTHOR

SUSAN MALLERY

Desert Rogues

NO.1 NEW YORK TIMES BESTSELLING AUTHOR

SUSAN MALLERY

Desert Rogues

MILLS & BOON

Published by
Mills & Boon
An imprint of Harlequin Enterprises (Australia) Pty Limited
(ABN 47 001 180 918), a subsidiary of HarperCollins
Publishers Australia Pty Limited (ABN 36 009 913 517)
Level 19, 201 Elizabeth Street
SYDNEY NSW 2000
AUSTRALIA

MIX
Paper | Supporting
responsible forestry
FSC
www.fsc.org   FSC® C001695

CONTENTS

SUSAN MALLERY

is a bestselling and award-winning author of more than fifty books for Harlequin and Silhouette Books. She makes her home in the Los Angeles area with her handsome prince of a husband and her two adorable-but-not-bright cats.

The Princess In Waiting

Chapter One

After a long day of working in the delivery room, Emma Kennedy was ready to spend her evening with her feet propped up, the TV on and a bowl of ice cream in her hand. Okay, yes, she would probably eat something decent for dinner first but the ice cream was a must. It had been *that* kind of day.

Nothing had happened all morning, then right at noon, four women had decided to deliver. One had been a terrified teenager, and Emma had stayed with her as much as possible. At twenty-four, Emma had been closest in age of all the nurses, although a lifetime of experiences away from the streetwise, body pierced and tattooed patient.

Emma opened her mailbox, pulled out the cable bill and a flyer for a sale at Dillard's, then walked toward her apartment.

She was tired, but content. It had been a good day. A happy day. One of the things she loved about her job was the joy new mothers experienced when their babies were born. Being part of the process, even on the periphery, was all the thanks she needed. When she thought about all the— Emma suddenly stopped in the hallway. Two men in dark suits stood by her front door. They looked respectable enough—clean, short haircuts, polished shoes—but they were definitely *lurking*.

She'd taken several self-defense courses over the years, but she wasn't sure how helpful the information she'd learned would be against two large men.

Glancing first left, then right, she calculated the distance to her nearest neighbor. How long would it take her to run to her car, and what kind of reaction she would get if she screamed?

One of the men looked up and saw her. "Ms. Kennedy? I'm Alex Dunnard from the State Department. This is my associate, Jack Sanders. May we have a moment of your time?"

As the man spoke, he pulled out an ID card complete with picture. His companion did the same. Emma abandoned the idea of bolting and approached her front door.

The pictures matched the men and the cards *looked* official enough, but it wasn't as if she'd seen a State Department ID before and would know the difference.

Alex Dunnard slipped the ID back into his jacket pocket and smiled. "We have some official business to discuss with you. May we come inside, or would you be more comfortable if we met at the coffee shop on the corner?"

Emma noticed that neither option allowed her to get out of talking with them. Which was crazy. What would the State Department want with her?

She gave them the once-over and decided to let them in. Her Dallas suburb was safe, quiet and ordinary. No doubt these men had the wrong person. Once they straightened that out, they would be on their way.

"Come on in," she said, inserting her key in the lock.

They followed her into the smallish living room. It was already dusk, so she turned on both floor lamps and the light in the hall, then motioned to her sofa.

"Have a seat," she said as she plopped down in the club chair opposite.

As she set her purse on the floor, she noticed several stains on the front of her brightly patterned scrub shirt. The pale green pants were also dotted and streaked. Occupational hazard, she reminded herself.

Alex perched on the edge of her sofa, while the other gentleman stood by the sliding glass door.

"Ms. Kennedy, we're here at the behest of the king of Bahania."

Alex kept on talking, but Emma was too caught up in the word *behest*. She wasn't sure she'd ever heard someone say it in normal speech. It was more of a book word. Then the rest of the sentence sunk in.

"Wait a minute," she said, holding up her hand. "Did you say the *king* of Bahania?"

"Yes, ma'am. He contacted the State Department and asked that we locate you and then offer you an official invitation to visit his country."

Emma laughed. Oh, sure. Because that sort of thing happened all the time. "Are you guys selling something? Because if you are, you're wasting your time."

"No, ma'am. We're from the State Department, and we're here—"

She cut him off with a wave. "I know. At the behest. I got that part. You have the wrong person. I'm sure there's another Emma Kennedy floating around who has lots of personal contact with His Royal Highness, but it's not me."

She looked at her modest apartment. If only, she thought humorously. Maybe a small money grant or two could have taken care of her student loans. And she desperately needed new tires for her ten-year-old import. Oh, well. In her next life she would be rich. In this one she was just a single woman struggling to pay the bills.

Alex pulled a piece of paper out of his outer jacket pocket. "Emma Kennedy," he read, then went on to list her birth date, place of birth, her parents' names and the number on her passport. A passport she'd had since she was eighteen, young, innocent and foolish and had thought... Well, she'd thought a lot of things.

"Just a second," she said, and rose to walk into her bedroom.

Her passport was tucked in the back of her sock drawer. She pulled it out and returned to the living room where she had Alex read the number again. It matched.

"This is creepy," she said. "Look, I don't know the king of Bahania. I'm not sure I could find Bahania on the map. There really has to be some kind of mistake. What would he want with me?"

"You are to be his guest for the next two weeks." Alex stood and smiled. "There's a private jet standing by to take you to his country. Ms. Kennedy, Bahania is a valuable ally in the Middle East. Like their neighbor, El Bahar, they are considered the Switzerland of that region. These progressive countries offer a haven of peace and economic stability in a troubled part of the world. They also provide a significant percentage of our country's oil."

Emma might have only taken one political science class at college, but she wasn't stupid. She got the message. When the king of Bahania invited a young Texas nurse to vacation in his country for a couple of weeks, the United States government expected her to go.

Was she being kidnapped?

The idea was both insane and terrifying.

"You can't make me go," she said, more to hear the words than because she believed them. She had a feeling that Alex and his friend could make her do just about anything.

"You're correct. We would not force you to accept the king's invitation. However, your country would be most grateful if you would consider granting him this request." He smiled. "You'll be perfectly safe, Ms. Kennedy. The king is an honorable man. You're not being sold into a harem."

"The thought never crossed my mind," she told him hotly, even though it had. Sort of.

A harem? Her? Not on this planet. Men didn't find her especially appealing, and she… Well, she avoided matters of the heart. She'd fallen in love once and it had been a complete disaster.

"This is a great honor," Alex said. "As a personal guest of the king, you'll be staying at the famed pink palace. It is quite extraordinary."

Emma walked back to her chair and sank down. "Can we stop for a second and reflect on the reality missing from this situation? I'm a nurse. I deliver babies for a living. Unless the king has a pregnant wife or something, why on earth would he be interested in me? I'm assuming if you know my passport number, you also know I've only been out of the country once and that was six years ago. I live a quiet life. I'm boring. You have the wrong person."

Alex's good cheer didn't waver. "Two weeks, Ms. Kennedy. Is that so much to ask? Those volunteering for military service give much more."

Oh, darn the man. He was going for guilt. She really didn't like that. Her parents had been experts at it and she hated the sense of having disappointed anyone.

"I'll accompany you to Bahania," Alex continued. "To assure your safe arrival. Once you're settled, I'll return to Washington." He paused. "You're being given a wonderful opportunity, Ms. Kennedy. I hope you'll consider it. If we can leave for the airport in the next hour, we will be in Bahania by sunset tomorrow."

Her mind swirled. "You want me to go with you right now?"

"Please."

Emma glanced from Alex to his friend by the sliding glass door. She had a bad feeling that if she refused, she would be taken against her will.

Not exactly thoughts to warm her heart. It looked as if she were going on a trip.

Two and a half hours later, Emma found herself sitting on a luxurious private jet as the lights of Dallas disappeared below. She had a large suitcase in the cargo bay, a small overnight case next to her feet and, as promised, Alex Dunnard in the seat across from hers.

She still wasn't sure how it had all happened. Somehow Alex had gently ushered her through the process of calling the hospital for time off, packing and leaving a message for her parents that she'd gone away with a friend. The white lie had been his suggestion, made so that her parents wouldn't worry.

Then she'd showered, changed and found herself in a limo the size of a football field. Now she was on a plane and sitting in leather seats so soft and comfy, she wouldn't mind having the material made into a jacket.

On the bright side, if she *was* being kidnapped, it was by someone with money and style. The downside was that she'd managed to put her entire life on hold for two weeks with exactly two phone calls and a request that her neighbor pick up her mail. What did that say about her world?

Before she could decide, a uniformed young woman approached. "Ms. Kennedy, I'm Aneesa and it will be my pleasure to serve you on our flight to Bahania."

Aneesa rattled off the expected flying time, mentioned a stop for gas in Spain and offered selections for dinner.

"When you're ready to retire for the evening," she continued, "there is a sleeping compartment for your use." She smiled. "Along with a bathroom, complete with shower."

"That's great," Emma told her, trying to sound calm. As if this sort of thing happened to her all the time.

"Shall I serve dinner?" Aneesa asked. "Uh, sure. Why not?"

When the attendant had disappeared to what must be the plane's galley, Emma turned to Alex.

"Are you going to tell me what's really going on here?" she asked. "I've told you all I know."

"That the king wants me as his guest for two weeks," she summarized. "Yes."

"And you don't know why?"

"No."

Not exactly helpful.

She returned her attention to the countryside below and wondered if she would ever see Texas again. Then, determined not to wallow in unpleasant and scary thoughts, she pulled out the entertainment guide and pretended interest in the various DVDs available for her viewing pleasure.

A half hour later, the meal was served. The food was beautifully prepared and delicious, if Alex's speed of consumption was anything to go by. Emma picked at the baked chicken dish and refused wine. She studied her travel companion—a well-dressed man in his mid to late forties. Nice looking, married— if the wedding ring was anything to go by. Did Mrs. Dunnard mind her husband flying off at a moment's notice? Had it been a moment's notice for him or had he known about the trip in advance? And why on earth did the king of Bahania want to meet with *her?*

More questions she was unlikely to get answered. When she tried pumping Alex for information, he remained pleasant but uncommunicative.

One restless night in a luxury cabin, several time zones and a pit stop for gas later, Emma didn't know any more than she had when she'd stepped onto the plane in Dallas. The difference was they were coming in for landing at an airport on the edge of the desert.

She stared out the window and tried to keep her mouth from falling open. The sights beneath were so beautiful they nearly took her breath away.

Turquoise-blue water lapped up against a pure white beach. There were miles of buildings, lush foliage and sprawling suburbs that gradually gave way to the endless beige and browns of the desert. Emma could see pockets of industry, large buildings that appeared ancient and what looked like dozens of parks throughout the city before the plane banked and headed for the airport.

They landed with a light bump, then taxied to a low one-story building.

As Alex picked up his small overnight case, Emma fumbled for her purse.

She was escorted onto the tarmac where the late afternoon was warm, sunny and dry. And bright. After the confines of the plane, she found the sunlight nearly blinding. Three steps later, she entered a pleasant room where a man in uniform actually bowed when she presented herself and her open passport.

"Ms. Kennedy," he said, flashing a smile, "welcome to Bahania. May your journey be pleasant and blessed."

"Thank you," she murmured, wondering if everyone was always so polite. Not that she was going to complain. She could get used to this level of service.

The surprises weren't over. Minutes later Alex escorted her to another large limo. Inside she found a bottle of champagne sitting on ice and a small bouquet of flowers.

"For me?" she asked as Alex sat next to her.

"I doubt the king meant them for me," he told her.

Good point. Emma sniffed the roses. When Alex pointed to the bottle of champagne, she shook her head.

"I didn't sleep," she admitted. "Between being exhausted, the strange circumstances and the time change, the last thing I need is liquor."

She already felt woozy enough.

As they pulled out of the airport, Alex began to talk to her about the city. He pointed out the financial district, the old shopping bazaar, the entrance to the famous Bahanian beaches. Emma did her best to pay attention, but the longer they were on the road, the more she regretted her decision to come. Sure, Bahania was beautiful and all, but she'd just traveled halfway around the world with a man she didn't know to meet a king she'd barely heard of, and aside from her traveling companion and the king, no one on the planet knew where she was.

It was not a situation designed to make one relax.

Forty minutes later, the limo drove through an open gate, past several guards and what felt like miles of manicured grounds.

She stared out the window until she saw the first hints of the fabled pink palace.

"This is so not happening," she murmured, still unable to believe this was real.

The limo pulled up in front of the entrance. At least she assumed that was what the arched doorway and alcove big enough for a marching band were for.

"We're here," Alex said, confirming her suspicions. She glanced at him. "What happens now?"

"You meet the king."

Great. If there was a survey at the end of this, she was going to mention Alex's lack of information as one of her complaints.

The limo door opened. Alex climbed out, then stepped aside so she could exit. Emma smoothed down the skirt she'd changed into on the plane and sucked in a breath for courage. It wasn't close to enough, so she wasn't surprised to find herself shaking as she stepped out in the warm afternoon.

Several people stood by the palace: Alex, the limo driver, a few uniformed men who could have been servants, but no one who looked like a king. So did royalty wait indoors for their visitors? Shouldn't Alex have briefed her on that sort of thing?

Before she could ask him, there was a movement to her left. Emma turned and saw a man step out of the shadows. He was tall, darkly handsome and almost familiar. Then the sun hit him full in the face and she gasped in stunned amazement. It couldn't be. Not after all this time. She'd thought... He would never...

The combination of shock, lack of sleep and food, and jet lag, conspired to increase her heart rate from nervous to hummingbird speed. The blood rushed from her head to her feet in two seconds flat. The world spun, blurred, then faded completely as she collapsed to the ground.

Prince Reyhan glanced at his father, the king of Bahania, and shook his head.

"That went well."

Chapter Two

Several servants rushed toward the fallen woman. Reyhan brushed them aside and crouched beside Emma. He took her wrist in his hand and felt her pulse.

Rapid, but steady.

"Call a doctor," he said firmly.

Someone went scuttling to do his bidding.

"She didn't hit her head," a young woman told him as she gently touched Emma's forehead. "I was watching as she fainted, Your Highness."

"Thank you. Are her rooms prepared?" The woman nodded.

Reyhan gathered Emma into his arms. She lay limp, one hand pressing against his chest, the other dangling by her side. Her skin had paled and her breathing slowed.

He took a moment to study her long lashes and the fullness of her mouth. The thick, red hair he remembered hung in loose waves around her face. So much was the same, he thought. No doubt if he counted, he would find that there were still eleven freckles on her nose and cheeks.

How much had changed? Even as he silently asked the question, he found he didn't want to know. He rose and walked into the palace.

The king fell into step with him.

"At least she remembered you," his father said. "Obviously with great joy."

"Perhaps she fainted with relief that you were to be together."

Reyhan didn't bother answering. Emma hadn't seen him in six years, and from what he'd been able to find out, she'd never made any attempt to get in touch with him. He had no idea what she recalled of their brief...relationship, but he doubted her fainting had anything to do with relief.

The guest quarters were on the second floor. Reyhan went directly there, wondering if his father would mention that other arrangements could have been made. Fortunately, the king remained silent.

Reyhan swept inside the suite of rooms he'd had prepared for Emma and set her on the sofa. A maid hovered in the corner.

"Find out when the doctor will arrive," he said.

The woman nodded and picked up a phone from the small table in the corner.

Reyhan returned his attention to Emma. She lay perfectly still. She hadn't moved at all while he'd carried her.

He sat next to her on the sofa and took her hand in his. Her fingers were cold. He brought them to his mouth and breathed on them.

"Emma," he murmured. "You must awaken." She moved her head slightly and moaned.

"The doctor will be here in fifteen minutes," the maid told him. "Thank you. A glass of water, please."

"Yes, Your Highness."

"Someone else could have carried her," the king said from the seat he'd taken across from the sofa. "Someone else can care for her now."

Reyhan narrowed his gaze. "No one touches my wife."

His father rose and crossed to the door. "It has been six years, Reyhan.

Are you sure you still wish to claim the title of husband?"
Wish it or not, it was his. As was she.

Emma felt as if she were swimming against a very strong
tide. But instead of water, she was trapped by air she had to
push through to reach the surface. Thoughts formed and separated, her body felt heavy. Something had happened. She remembered that much. But what?

A cool, smooth surface pressed against her mouth as a strong,
male voice demanded, "Drink this."

She parted her lips without considering refusing the request.

Water slipped into her mouth. She drank gratefully, then
sighed when the glass was removed. Better, she thought, and
opened her eyes.

Oh, my—it was him! Her eyes hadn't been playing tricks on
her. She could feel the heat and strength of him as he sat next
to her on the sofa. His hip pressed against her thigh. One of his
hands held her own, while his dark gaze trapped her as neatly
as a cage held a small bird.

Reyhan.

She wasn't sure if she said the name or merely thought it.
Was it possible? After all these years?

She blinked and wondered if this was nothing more than a
vivid dream. Only, her luck wasn't that good. No, the truth was
he was real and she was in his presence, which didn't seem possible. It had been six years, she reminded herself again. Six years
since he'd used her and tossed her aside. Six years since she'd
hidden at her parents' house, crying for what could have been,
secretly waiting for him to come and claim her, only to find
out she'd waited in vain. He'd never come, and eventually she'd
returned to her life—older, wiser and emotionally battered.

"So you return to us," he said, his low voice rumbling like
distant thunder. "I don't remember you fainting before."

She bristled at the assumption that he *knew* things about her.
"I don't faint," she told him.

"Recent events suggest that you do. It was a long trip. Were you able to sleep at all?"

He spoke so casually, she thought in amazement. As if nothing out of the ordinary had happened. As if it had been a few days rather than years since they were last together.

Outrage blossomed into fury. She wanted to yell at him, to scream or maybe even throw something. But years of being told that a lady didn't show her anger made it difficult for her to do more than glare.

Reyhan lightly touched her cheek. "I see by the shadows under your eyes you did not sleep on the plane. At least not for long. Hardly a surprise, I suppose. You were not told why you were brought here. As I recall, you were always impatient and eager to find out things."

Her attention split neatly between his words, which annoyed her, and the light stroking of his fingers against her skin. When his thumb grazed her lower lip, she was stunned by a jolt of awareness. The sensation cut through her like lightning, heating and melting everywhere it touched.

No! She would not react, she told herself. She wouldn't feel anything. She refused to. If this man really was Reyhan, then he filled her with nothing but contempt. He was beneath her notice.

One corner of his firm mouth turned up slightly. "I see you want to spit at me like an ill-tempered kitten," he murmured. "There is anger in your eyes." He glanced at her fingers. "No claws. I doubt you can do much damage."

Then he stunned her by kissing her knuckles.

She felt the warm brush of his mouth clear down to her toes. The hot, melting sensation grew until she wanted to purr like the kitten he'd mentioned. She thought about— "Stop that right now," she said, snatching her hand back and folding her arms across her chest. The instruction was meant for both of them. In the past twenty-four hours, her world had taken a turn for the confusing, but she was determined to figure out what was going on. Which meant staying focused on the task at hand and not getting caught up in being in the same room as Reyhan.

She shifted away from him and pushed herself up into a sitting position.

When he took hold of her arm to help her, she shook off his hand.

"I'm fine," she told him, her tone as icy as she could make it. "What I need from you is information. What is going on? What am I doing here? And while we're on the subject, what are *you* doing here?"

Before he could speak, there was a blur of movement, then a longhaired cream-colored cat with nearly violet eyes jumped up on her lap. She stared at it in amazement. Cats in the palace?

Reyhan grabbed the animal and set it back on the floor. The cat glared at him, gave a sniff of disgust and stalked off.

"Are you allergic to cats?" he asked. "What? No."

"Good. The palace is filled with them. They are my father's."

His father? She rubbed her temple and tried to decide if she wanted to ask who his father was. While she would like the information, she was also afraid of it. Because crazy as it sounded, she had a feeling there was a better-than-even chance that Reyhan was somehow related to the king of Bahania.

Don't go there, she told herself as Reyhan held out the glass of water again. As she took it from him she found herself caught in his gaze.

She remembered his eyes most of all, she thought. How dark they were. How well they kept secrets. She'd once thought that if she could learn to read his eyes, she would know the man. But their few weeks together had not given them the time to learn very much about each other.

Sadness threatened. She tried to banish it by recalling what Reyhan had done to her—how he'd left and how she'd been alone and so afraid. Better to be angry. There was energy in anger and she had the feeling she was going to need it.

"I don't know what this game is," she told him, "but I'm not going to play. I wish to return home immediately. Please call Alex and have him take me back to the plane."

"Your escort from the State Department has already left the palace. He will spend the night at one of our most beautiful seaside hotels, then fly back to your country in the morning." Reyhan dismissed the man with a flick of his wrist. "You will not see him again."

Anger faded as fear took its place. Alex was gone? So she was truly alone in the palace? Alone in this country?

Emma didn't know if she should try to bolt for freedom or bluff her way through. Her head was still spinning and she didn't look forward to trying to stand up, so that left bluffing. Something she'd never been very good at.

"What am I doing here?" she demanded. "Why did the king of Bahania ask me to come here for two weeks? And what are *you* doing here? You can't have anything to do with what's going on with me."

That last bit was more plea than forceful statement.

Reyhan stared at her. His strong, handsome features could have been set in stone—or steel—for all they gave away.

"Haven't you guessed?" he asked with quiet amusement, as if she were a child who had just performed the alphabet song flawlessly for the first time. "The king is my father, and the invitation is as much mine as his."

Her mind went blank. Completely and totally. It was like losing the lights during a thunderstorm.

The man next to her rose and squared his shoulders. Then he stared down at her with a haughty expression possibly honed through a lifetime of royal arrogance.

"I am Prince Reyhan, third oldest son of King Hassan of Bahania."

She blinked. Not possible, she told herself as some semicoherent thought process began in her brain. Not possible, not likely and she refused to believe it.

"A p-prince?" she asked, stumbling over the word.

No. No. No. Emma stared at the man standing in front of her. He couldn't be. A prince? Him? But they'd met at college. They'd dated. He'd taken her away with him and…hurt her dreadfully.

"The king decided it was time for me to marry," Reyhan told her. "There was no way I could agree to any match as I was already married. To you."

He kept on talking, but she wasn't listening. She couldn't. A prince?

Married?

"But I…" She swallowed and tried again. "That wasn't real. Not any of it."

She remembered the quiet of the Caribbean island, the soft breezes, the lap of the ocean outside their hotel room. Reyhan had asked her to go away with him, and she'd agreed because she could refuse him nothing. At eighteen, she'd been more innocent than he'd realized. She'd been too ashamed to tell him she'd never dated before. He'd been her first, in every sense of the word.

Years later, when she'd looked back on the blur of hot days and long, endless nights, she'd comforted herself with the fact that she'd been too swept up in thinking she was in love to refuse Reyhan anything. She would never have considered asking him to go more slowly, to give her time to adjust. As for their marriage—her parents' lawyer had told her that had been a fake.

For a long time the realization had nearly destroyed her. She'd hated her weakness where he was concerned. Hated that she could still want him, even as he'd used and abandoned her. Time had healed her enough to give her perspective.

Reyhan's dark eyebrows drew together. "What wasn't real?"

"Our marriage. You just did that to get me into bed. Or get a green card."

As soon as she spoke the words, she realized she might have made a mistake. Reyhan seemed to get bigger and taller as his temper grew. His anger was as tangible as the sofa she sat on, but a lot more frightening. His gaze narrowed and his mouth twisted into a disapproving and scornful line.

"A green card?" he asked, his voice thick with tension. "Why would I need that? I am Prince Reyhan. I am heir to the king of Bahania. I have no need to seek asylum elsewhere. This is my country."

He spoke proudly and with the confidence of who knew how many generations of royalty behind him.

"Yes, well." She cleared her throat. At the time, him wanting a green card had made sense. But now... "So that's not why you married me."

"It was not. I was in your country to continue my education. I earned my master's degree there." His expression turned contemptuous. "I honored you by giving you my name and my protection. As for trying to get you into my bed, the effort was hardly worth the meager reward."

She shrank back into the cushions. Humiliation joined the fear. As much as she tried to block out their nights together, they continued to haunt her. She supposed her part of it could be an illustration of what *not* to do on one's wedding night and the few nights that followed.

Not that it was her fault, she told herself, trying to grab on to a little temper to give her courage. She'd been the virgin. He should have done better, too.

But if Reyhan hadn't married her to get a green card or to sleep with her, why had he?

"Are you sure the marriage was real?" she asked. "My parents' lawyer said that it wasn't."

"Then their lawyer was mistaken." Reyhan glared at her. "You are my wife. That is why you were brought here. Now that you are in my country, in my home, you will treat me with respect and reverence. Is that understood?"

The need to bolt for freedom grew exponentially. "Reyhan, I—"

But she never got to say whatever she'd been about to blurt

out. For just at that moment, a petite, curvy, beautiful young woman walked into the room.

"This isn't good," the woman said. "I heard Emma had arrived and fainted at the sight of you. Is that true?"

Reyhan turned his attention from Emma to the woman. His glare only deepened.

The woman rolled her eyes. "Yeah, yeah, I know. You're insulted. But don't forget, I gave birth to your older brother's firstborn, so you have to be nice to me."

"One wonders what Sadik sees in you."

The woman leaned close and smiled. "I'm a hottie. It's a curse, but there we are."

Emma didn't think things could get more shocking, but she was proved wrong when Reyhan actually smiled at the woman, then kissed her forehead.

"Can you fix this?" he asked the woman.

"I'm not sure if you mean Emma or the situation. If you ask me, the one who needs fixing is you." She held up her hand before he could speak. "I'll do my best. I promise. Now why don't you give us some girl time together? I'll answer Emma's questions and make her feel at home. You can go work on your charm."

Reyhan raised his eyebrows. "I'm very charming."

"Uh-huh. Just a tip here. The 'I'm Prince Reyhan of Bahania' thing gets old really fast. Trust me. Sadik tried it on me, too."

"You're a troublemaker."

"That's true."

Reyhan nodded at Emma, then at the woman and left. Emma watched him go.

"Is this really happening?" she asked, feeling both weary and more confused than ever.

"It sure is," the other woman told her. "Right down to you sitting in the middle of the Bahanian royal palace." She plopped down next to Emma on the sofa and smiled. "Let's start at the beginning. Hi. I'm Cleo."

"I'm Emma. Emma Kennedy."

Cleo looked her over. "Love the hair. My sister-in-law has red hair, too.

Is it real?"

It took Emma a second to process the question and realize Cleo wasn't asking about the hair itself, but the color.

"Yes, it's natural."

"Me, too," Cleo said, tugging on her short, spiky blond hair. "I put in gold highlights once, but was *that* a mistake. I thought I'd look more elegant and classy, which is so not going to happen. I'm stuck looking like a tacky bottle blonde for the rest of my life. No biggie. I mean I'm a princess, so now I can be royal and tacky, which I like."

Emma felt as if she'd fallen into an alternate universe. "I'm sorry. I don't understand."

Cleo grinned. "I know. I'm rambling. Plus, do you really care about my hair? So here's the thing. You're in Bahania, and Reyhan really is a prince. There are four of them altogether. Murat is the oldest and heir to the throne. Then Sadik, my husband. He's in charge of finance. Reyhan is next. He runs the whole oil thing, and let me tell you, do they have a bunch of that floating around under the sand. Then Jefri, who is putting together a joint air force with El Bahar. There's also Zara, who was my foster sister and didn't know she was a princess until about a year ago, and Sabrina, the king's daughter. She lives in the desert, but that's a whole other story."

"Oh." Emma wasn't sure what to say. Her level of confusion had just gone off the scale. "That's a lot of people." She swallowed. "And you're Princess Cleo?"

"In the flesh." Cleo leaned close. "I'm from Spokane, Washington. That's right by Idaho. I know—not exactly the birthplace of a lot of royals. I had a ton to learn—protocol and how to address everyone. I've gotten involved with some charity work, which is pretty cool, and I have a new baby. Calah." Cleo's expression softened. "She's a dream. Just three months old."

Emma wanted to ask for note cards so she could write all this down and try to keep everyone and everything straight.

Reyhan, a Bahanian prince? Was it possible? And if he was, why had he married her?

"Do you know—" Emma cleared her throat. "There was a wedding a few years back. I thought maybe… My parents hired a lawyer and he thought it wasn't exactly real."

Cleo patted her arm. "Sorry. From what I've heard, it was plenty real. You're well and truly hitched to Reyhan. And he's just like his brother. All stuffy with an 'I'm the prince' attitude. That reverence and respect stuff. Oh, please. Okay, I'll do the respect thing, but reverence? It is *so* not going to happen."

So she was married. To a prince. *Her*.

"None of this makes sense," she whispered. "I don't understand."

Why had Reyhan done any of it? Why had he married her and disappeared from her life? And why, all of a sudden, did he pick now to get in touch with her? Did he want to marry someone else? The thought of it gave her an odd squeeze in her empty stomach, but still she had to know.

"Is he engaged?" she asked.

Cleo shook her head. "It's not like that. After Calah was born, the king decided it was time for Reyhan to tie the knot and give him more grandchildren. That's when he had to fess up about his relationship with you. That there was already a Mrs. Reyhan floating around."

Emma felt the room begin to fold around the edges. She had a feeling that if she'd been standing, she would have fallen again.

Cleo grabbed her hand. "Keep breathing," she instructed humorously. "I'm supposed to be making things better, not worse."

"It's not you," Emma told her. "It's everything. I can't believe what's happening."

"Hardly a surprise. The good news is, the palace is beautiful and Reyhan is pretty easy on the eyes, too. If you can get past all that honor and tradition, he has a wicked sense of humor. Won't that be nice?"

Nice? As in Emma would enjoy spending time with him? Was that the plan?

She shook her head. This wasn't happening, she told herself. None of it.

A tall man carrying a black case entered the room. Cleo waved a greeting.

"Dr. Johnson. You're still making house calls."

The older man smiled. "Yes, Princess Cleo. As I will continue to do." Cleo leaned close to Emma. "Dr. Johnson is on call for the royal family.

He's pretty cool. You'll like him."

Emma stared into the man's warm blue eyes and felt some of her anxiety fade.

He sat on the coffee table in front of her and reached for her hand. "How are you feeling? I heard you fainted."

"I don't know what happened," she admitted. "One second everything was fine, and the next, I was falling."

"Prince Reyhan filled me in on what occurred." He released her wrist. "Your pulse is normal. Have you blacked out since regaining consciousness?"

"No."

He glanced at Cleo. "Is she speaking coherently?"

"Yup. She's a little shell-shocked, but under the circumstances, who can blame her?"

Dr. Johnson made a noncommittal noise, then pulled out a stethoscope.

Fifteen minutes later he pronounced Emma exhausted, a little dehydrated, but otherwise fit. After giving her something to help her sleep, he said he would check on her the next day.

"Everything will be better in the morning," he promised as he left.

Emma watched him go, then nodded as Cleo excused herself to return to her baby. When Emma was finally alone, she stared around at the luxurious suite and the view of the sea in the distance.

As much as she would like to believe Dr. Johnson, she had a feeling that the passage of night wasn't going to change one thing about her situation.

Reyhan did not want to speak with his father, but the request had been worded such that he'd known he didn't have a choice in the matter. So he'd appeared on time in the king's private rooms and now paced the length of the salon, all the while stepping to avoid the half-dozen or so cats milling around.

"What do you think now that you've seen her?" his father asked.

"That Emma should not have been brought here. A divorce could have been arranged without her presence."

"You defied me by marrying this young woman. Six years have passed, and you never mentioned her or spent time with her. I want to know why."

Reyhan had no answers to the questions, nor did he want to make up any. Thinking about Emma, being with her... He reached the window and stared out at the garden below. Seeing her again—it had been worse than he'd imagined.

His father stood and crossed the room to stand next to him. "You are my son and a prince," he said. "As such, you were not permitted to take a wife without my permission. Now it is done. Before I approve your divorce, I will get to know this young woman. Two weeks, Reyhan. Surely that is not too much to ask."

Reyhan knew it was not. His father's request was more than reasonable, and yet he would have given much to keep Emma away.

He nodded once and walked to the door. "Excuse me, Father. My presence is required at a meeting."

The king nodded, and Reyhan left.

As Reyhan walked toward the business wing of the palace, he wondered how he would endure the next fourteen days. There was much to occupy his time—negotiations for oil purchases, dealing with a small band of renegades, reviewing a list of potential brides. Yet he knew none of that would fill his mind. Instead he would think of a woman—the woman he had married. Emma. Their time apart had done nothing to diminish his need for her. Six years ago she had been his greatest weakness, and so she remained. He paused at the door to his office. No one would ever be permitted to know, he promised himself. Wanting her, *needing* her, had nearly destroyed him once before. That would not happen again. In two weeks the king would grant their divorce, she would be gone and he, Reyhan, would be allowed to remain strong. That he would live the rest of his life without her was of little consequence. He had survived this long. He would survive the rest of his days. Survive—not live. He reminded himself that most of the time, enduring was more than enough.

Chapter Three

Emma awoke to the not-so-surprising realization that, despite the doctor's promise, little about her situation had changed or improved during the night. Not that she'd expected either, although it would have been nice.

She sat up in the huge bed and pulled her knees to her chest. She remembered the doctor insisting she take something to help her sleep, then she'd changed into her nightgown and nearly collapsed into bed. Then nothing.

The good news was she felt more rested. The bad news... well, where exactly was she going to start? There was so much to consider. That she might really be married to Reyhan and might have been married all this time. That she was in Bahania and he was the son of the king.

She shook her head. Way too many difficult thoughts for first thing in the morning. She should take a few minutes and get her bearings, then deal with the weirdness that was her life.

Emma rose. Her toes curled in the plush carpet that was thick enough to serve as a mattress in a pinch.

The bedroom had been decorated in pale yellows and blues. Ornate, carved dark wood furniture made up the elaborate headboard, footboard and matching nightstands. An armoire stood across the room. When she crossed to it she found a large television inside, along with a DVD player and a wide assortment of movies. There was also a detailed listing of the various channels available via satellite.

"Amazing," she murmured as she touched the carved birds and flowers on the door.

The bedroom itself was about the size of the average three-bedroom house back home in Dallas. She remembered the living room had been equally huge. With two parts anticipation and one part trepidation, she walked into the bathroom.

Huge didn't begin to describe it. Her entire apartment could have fit inside, with room to spare. The long marble vanity was about twice the length of her main kitchen counter. The tub had whirlpool jets and could have served as a playground for an entire water park full of seals. There was a glass-enclosed shower, towels as big as bedsheets and every toiletry known to womankind.

Emma turned in a slow circle and tried to imagine what it would be like to live somewhere like this permanently. Was it possible to get used to this level of luxury, and would the palace continue to be a delight?

Twenty minutes later she'd showered and washed her face. After dressing, applying mascara and some lip gloss, she returned to the bedroom and put away the rest of her clothes. With that done, there was little to do but explore the rest of the suite and try to figure out what she was going to say when she next saw Reyhan.

In the light of day she knew that there was more to their relationship than her parents had told her six years ago when she'd returned home brokenhearted. But what exactly?

She left the bedroom and walked into the living room of the suite. The shutters were open and pulled back. The view was so amazing—blue sea, bright sky, the tops of several trees—that she hadn't noticed Reyhan. But when she turned, she saw him seated at the dining room table in the corner. He studied the newspaper in front of him and hadn't seen her, either.

Her first thought was to bolt for the safety of her bedroom, but before she could get her feet to move, she found herself mesmerized by the man himself.

He was so handsome, she thought, remembering how his dark good looks had stunned her the first time they'd met. His hair was cropped short, in a stylish cut. Strong cheekbones emphasized the leanness of his features. His eyebrows were pulled together, giving him a stern expression. He looked intense and dangerous, something she remembered from their past together. Being around him had always left her tongue-tied and feeling more than a little foolish. That sensation returned big-time.

She winced as she recalled accusing him of marrying her to get a green card. He was a member of the Bahanian royal family. No doubt he could come or go at will just about anywhere in the world. As for wanting her in his bed…she had her doubts. The experience had been a disaster and after those first couple of nights, Reyhan had never come looking for her again.

"How long are you going to stand there?" he asked without looking up from his paper. "I have ordered you breakfast, Emma. You didn't eat before or after you arrived at the palace. I don't want you making yourself ill."

He set down the paper and looked at her. His dark gaze seemed to see all the way inside to her quivering heart. He raised one eyebrow.

"Are you so afraid of me? I swear that I have never attacked before ten or eleven in the morning. It is not civilized."

She glanced at the antique grandfather clock by the entryway. "So I'm safe for another ninety minutes?"

"At least."

He rose and pulled out a chair. Not knowing what else to do, she settled in it then watched as he lifted the tops off several serving dishes on the sideboard.

"What would you like?" he asked.

She blinked at him. "You're going to serve me?"

"You are my guest. In the interest of privacy I sent the maid away, so there is just the two of us this morning."

The implication being she was his responsibility? Reyhan had always had the most amazing manners. Apparently that hadn't changed.

She stood and crossed to the sideboard where she studied the assortment of offerings. There were eggs and bacon, fresh fruit, croissants, Danish and a selection of cereals, both hot and cold.

"I can't eat all this," she told him.

"I'll help." He motioned to the plates stacked on the left. "Please begin."

She reached for the plate. As she leaned forward, Reyhan moved and her hand grazed his arm. The instant heat nearly made her stumble. Awareness rippled along her skin like a sudden cool breeze, making her shiver and break out in goose bumps. She found herself wanting to touch him again, wanting to move closer, to have him touch her. Erotic images sprang into her mind, and before she knew what was happening, she realized it was difficult for her to catch her breath.

All of this happened in a matter of seconds. Then she became aware of herself, of Reyhan's expression of polite interest and she quickly stepped back and turned toward the food.

This was not good, she thought frantically. Not good at all. She didn't like how her heart raced whenever he was nearby. That hadn't happened before. If anything, he'd terrified her as much as he'd intrigued her. Not that she was any less terrified, it was just now she was frightened for a different reason.

She scooped fresh fruit onto her plate, along with some eggs. After taking a biscuit and butter, she returned to the table and poured them each coffee. Reyhan waited until she was seated before claiming his chair.

"You slept well?" he asked. "Yes, thank you."

"Dr. Johnson said that your fainting was not likely to reoccur. He decided it was the combination of lack of food and sleep, along with minor dehydration and the shock of seeing me again." Reyhan's steady gaze never left her face. "Had I known you would react so strongly, I would have given you some warning. Stunning you into fainting wasn't my goal."

"Imagine what you could do if it was," she said lightly.

She noticed his single raised eyebrow again, but Emma refused to be intimidated, despite the instinct to cringe and apologize. She turned her attention to her breakfast instead and plunged her fork into a piece of mango. Sexual awareness swirled through the room like an erotic mist, but she was determined to ignore it.

Maybe she always had reacted so strongly to Reyhan but wasn't aware of it, she thought wryly. Maybe when they'd first met there had been this same powerful physical attraction between them but she'd been too young and innocent to recognize it. All she'd known back then was that she loved him and feared him with equal intensity. It was amazing she'd managed to find the strength to leave him.

Then she reminded herself that she hadn't left him. He'd left her and she'd hid out at her parents' home. Any additional contact had been through them. She hadn't even had the courage to tell him she didn't want to see him again. Not that he'd tried very hard.

"Why the heavy sigh?" he asked.

She looked up. "Did I sigh? I didn't mean to."

"You were thinking of the past."

"It's a logical place to go."

He nodded. "We will speak of it."

A statement or a command? "And if I don't want to?"

The words were out before she could stop them.

His mouth curved up in amusement. "You defy me?"

"Will that get me fifty lashes or time in the tower?"

"Nothing so boring." He sipped his coffee. "Why do you not wish to talk about our situation?"

"I do." She shrugged. "Knee-jerk reaction, I guess. My parents were always so protective. They meant well—they still do. My independence is hard-won and I get my back up when someone gives me orders."

"I see."

She had no idea what the silken words meant, nor did she want to ask for an explanation. She doubted whatever contact Reyhan had had with her parents had been especially pleasant.

"You're right," she said. "We need to talk about what happened and what's going to happen."

He nodded slightly. "If you wish."

"You're mocking me."

"I am terrified by your steely will."

Emma doubted anything terrified Reyhan. Which meant he was teasing her. Interesting. She wouldn't have thought royal princes had senses of humor.

"Do you believe our marriage was real?" he asked.

"I don't want to, but, yes. You have no reason to lie, and my presence here is more than enough proof." She shifted in her seat. She'd been married for six years and hadn't known. Talk about being a fool.

"Why did you marry me?" she asked him, knowing it hadn't been for any of the usual reasons. At the time she'd thought Reyhan had loved her, but his behavior proved otherwise.

He chewed and swallowed. "You were a virgin," he said calmly. "I would not have defiled you."

Ten simple words that made her drop her fork, push back her chair and spring to her feet.

"What?" she demanded. "You married me to sleep with me? The whole thing was about sex?"

If love was out of the question, shouldn't he have at least liked her?

Shouldn't he have pretended to care?

"Sit down, Emma. You're overreacting."

She took her seat before she remembered she wasn't going

to let anyone run her life ever again. Once seated, it seemed silly to stand up and make a fuss. She settled on glaring at him.

Reyhan looked at her. "Why are you so outraged? Do you think there are any men who marry without the thought of their wives being a sexual partner?"

"Most men think about more than just doing it."

That made him get stiff and stern. His gaze narrowed. "I am Prince Reyhan of Bahania. When I married you, I not only gave you my name and protection, but honored you by making you a princess of my country. Had you been willing to continue our relationship, I would have brought you here where you would have lived in this palace. Neither you nor our children would have wanted for anything. I would have been faithful to you until I breathed my last breath. Who and what you are would have been passed along to our children, and through that, you would have joined in the history of my people. I believe that would be defined as more than just doing it."

"But you never told me any of this," she reminded him, feeling more than a little embarrassed. "Nor did you ask me if this is what I wanted with my life. What about my plans? My dreams? Marrying you could have changed my world forever."

"Is that such a bad thing?"

She thought of her small apartment and her quiet life. She remembered her conversation with Cleo the previous night and what she'd said about the palace and the princes.

"You didn't give me a choice," she said. "Not about staying or going. You married me without telling me the truth, then you disappeared without a word."

Reyhan leaned back in his chair. "Our recollection of the events that happened are very different, but that is of no consequence. What matters is our present circumstances. We are married—something neither of us wishes to continue. The king's permission is required for a prince to divorce, and he has insisted you spend two weeks here until he will grant the decree."

Countless years of having her life run by her parents had

made Emma hypersensitive to being told what to do. Her first
instinct was to tell Reyhan that maybe she didn't want a divorce, thank you very much. Maybe she wanted to stay married.

She stopped herself before she could blurt out the irrational
statement. She didn't know the man. She didn't want anything
to do with him. Of course she wanted to go get a divorce and
go back to her life.

"You didn't need his permission to get married, but you need
it for a divorce," she said. "That doesn't make sense."

"I did need his permission to marry. I defied him."

Simple words, she thought, but stunning. He'd defied the
king? To marry her? Which brought her back to her original
question—why?

For sex? He was a handsome, wealthy, royal guy. Couldn't
he get any woman he wanted? So why her?

She had a feeling that the earth would stop turning before
she found out the answer to that one, so she chose another topic
of conversation.

"So after the divorce you'll marry someone else." A thought
occurred to her. "Have you already chosen your new bride?"
Cleo had said he wasn't engaged, but was he already in love?

Reyhan shook his head. "My marriage will be arranged."

Emma blinked at him. "You mean she'll be picked by someone else?

What if you don't like her?"

He shrugged. "That is of little consequence." It felt like a really big consequence to her. "But she could make you crazy."

"Then we will have little contact. My duty is to produce heirs
for the kingdom. I will not turn my back on my responsibility."

He had a duty? But where had all that duty been when he'd
married her?

And why would he agree to a wife he might not even like?

"Do you get to spend time with the potential brides in advance? Like *The Bachelor* for royalty?"

"No."

"But—"

He rose, cutting her off. "I have a meeting," he said politely. "Please think of your time here in Bahania as a vacation. In two weeks you can return to Texas as if nothing ever happened. In the meantime, if you need anything, please ask one of the servants. You are an honored guest of the king."

With that he nodded and left.

Emma stared after him. She might be going home, but she doubted she would ever forget what had happened here. In a matter of hours, her world had turned upside down.

She rose and crossed to the French doors that led to a beautiful balcony. When she stepped outside, she saw the balcony stretched the length of the palace, perhaps even circling around it. A nice place to take a walk, she thought as she moved to the carved railing and leaned down to inspect the wonderful gardens below.

Stone paths meandered through what looked like a formal English garden. A fountain gurgled, while birds sang from nearby trees.

Hardly what she'd expected for a desert nation, she thought, then remembered the desalinization plant Alex had pointed out on their drive from the airport. Bahania created much of the fresh water her people used. Interesting, but hardly what was on her mind.

She turned her attention from the garden to her left hand. Reyhan had placed a simple gold band there after the ceremony. He'd kissed her and promised to replace it with any ring she would like. At the time she'd thought he'd been caught up in the romance of the moment, making promises he could never keep. Now she knew he'd been telling the truth.

But why hadn't he told her the rest of it? About him being the prince and that he'd always planned to return there? And why hadn't her parents been able to find out that she was really married? Who had told them the ceremony had been a sham and why hadn't they questioned the information?

Would it have made a difference? After the fact, she could say yes. But at the time? She'd been hurt and afraid and not that interested in being Reyhan's wife. Their few days together as husband and wife had been spent in bed. He had wanted her with a passion that had terrified and confused her. While she hadn't minded him touching her, she hadn't much liked it, either. He'd been too intense, too hungry, too everything.

Now the thought of those dark eyes gazing at her with unmistakable desire made her breathing quicken. Which so did not make sense. She had no reason to be attracted to Reyhan. She barely knew him. She wasn't even sure she liked him. So why was she anticipating the next time she saw him?

Reyhan walked from the residential wing of the palace toward the business wing, moving quickly but with his thoughts still outpacing his steps.

There wasn't a part of him that was not on fire with desire for Emma. He needed her as he needed the wide spaces of the desert. She was as much a part of him, and yet as out of reach as the stars.

If only he'd been able to keep her from coming to Bahania. But his father had insisted on meeting the woman Reyhan had married and then left behind. Royal pronouncements could only be avoided for so long, and in the end he had run out of excuses. So Emma was here—haunting him. He wanted her with a grim desperation that threatened his world, and he could not have her. Not before and not now. She was, he acknowledged, the one woman on earth who could bring him to his knees. Him—a prince. A man of power and action. If she knew how he really felt…

He reminded himself she did not know, nor would she be affected if she did. She'd made her feelings clear six years ago and there was no reason to think they would have changed.

Only twelve more days, he told himself. He could survive that, especially if he avoided her.

He reached the business wing and asked his assistant to come into his office. When the young man was seated, Reyhan pulled out his schedule. He was about to find himself very, very busy.

Emma restlessly wandered around the suite. She might be an honored guest of the king, but she wasn't sure what that meant in terms of what she could and could not do. Were there self-guided tours of the palace? The maid had disappeared and she didn't know who else to ask. The last thing she wanted was to wander into some forbidden room and find herself at the wrong end of a pointy sword.

She stared at the phone and wondered what would happen if she picked it up. Did the palace have an operator? In movies, the White House always did, and the palace was at least twice as big. Wasn't an operator required?

A knock on the suite's main door saved her from finding out. For a split second, her heart fluttered in anticipation. Reyhan? Had his meeting ended early and had he decided to return to speak with her? Had...

She pulled open the door and tried not to look disappointed when she saw Cleo standing there. The petite blonde had a baby in her arms.

"Remember me?" Cleo asked. "We met last night."

"Of course," Emma said with a smile. "You came to rescue me."

Cleo grinned. "Someone had to. These princes," she said, shaking her head. "They have no idea how intimidating they can be, and between you and me, we can't ever let them know."

She walked into the suite and held out her daughter. "This is Calah. I'm going to say 'Isn't she beautiful?' and I really need you to agree with me. I know, I know. Every mother thinks her baby is beautiful. I hate being a cliché, but there it is."

Emma glanced at the sleeping baby. "She *is* beautiful. You and your husband are going to have to beat boys off with a stick."

"I suspect Sadik will just glare menacingly and that will be enough." Cleo plopped down on the sofa and held out the baby. "Are you a cuddler or do infants make you uneasy?"

Emma sat next to her and took Calah in her arms. "I love holding babies. I'm a delivery room nurse so I'm around newborns all the time. It's a great specialty and I love it, but every now and then I get the urge to move to pediatrics."

Cleo's eyebrows arched. "Ah, so you love children. Does Reyhan know?"

"I don't think so." The information would hardly matter. He might want heirs but not with her.

"Interesting. So tell me everything about your life."

Emma gently rocked the baby and breathed in the sweet scent of her. "There's not much to tell. I'm a nurse, I live in Dallas and now I'm here. But what about you? How did you come to be here, and married to a prince?"

Cleo drew her feet up and leaned back against the sofa. "Well, I already told you I'm from Spokane. I grew up dirt-poor and without much family. Eventually I went into the foster care system, which turned out to be a good thing because I got to meet Zara. She was the daughter of the woman who took me in. Anyway, we became good friends, then practically sisters. Years after her mother had died, Zara went through her things and found these letters to her mother from the king of Bahania."

Emma stared at her. "You're kidding."

"Nope. He'd met her when she'd been a dancer and he'd fallen for her big-time. Apparently theirs was a great love, but Zara's mom knew it would never last so she bailed without telling him."

"How sad," Emma said.

"I agree. I mean she could have *tried* to make it work. Anyway, Zara found the letters and the two of us headed over here to see if the king really was her father. And he was."

"That must have been a shock for both of them."

"It was. I mean voilà, instant princess. She also met Rafe,

who is American but also a sheik, and she married him—but
that is a more complicated story."

Emma laughed. "Oh, right. Because this one isn't. So you
stayed with Zara and then married Prince Sadik?"

"Not exactly. He and I—well, it was sort of spontaneous
combustion. But he was a prince and I worked at a copy store.
I mean until I'd come to Bahania I'd never been anywhere. I
knew I wasn't princess material. So I went home. But I had to
come back for Zara's wedding to Rafe, and I was pregnant and
I didn't want anyone to know. The king found out, then Sadik,
then we got married, but he wouldn't admit he loved me and
it was horrible, but he came to his senses and now we're blissfully happy."

Emma didn't know what to say. "That's an amazing story."

Cleo grinned. "I know. I can't wait until Calah is old enough
to hear the romantic bits. I won't tell her about getting pregnant
or anything." Her eyes widened. "Oh, I should warn you. Both
Zara and Sabrina are pregnant. I think there's something in the
water, so don't drink anything but bottled." She glanced at her
daughter. "Unless you want one of your own."

Emma was dealing with enough changes right now, although
a child… She shook off the thought. No point in going there.
Not now.

"I don't think this is a good time for me," she said. "Plus
there's the whole needing-a-man thing."

"Is this where I point out that you have a husband?"

One who had made it plain he'd found her anything but interesting in bed? "No, thanks."

Cleo nodded. "I understand. But that doesn't mean I won't
think it. So how did you and Reyhan meet?"

"It was at college. My first semester." Those days felt like
a lifetime ago. "I was a brand-new freshman—technically an
adult, but not emotionally. Not even close." She shrugged. "I'm
the only child of older parents. They'd given up on ever having children when I came along. I was a surprise, but a happy

one. My parents were so thrilled, they were determined to keep me safe no matter what. Which meant keeping me sheltered. It took my entire senior year of high school to convince them to let me go to a college that required me living a couple hundred miles away."

"Reyhan's older, right?" Cleo asked. "You couldn't have had a class together."

"We didn't. I was socially backward, and I would never have had the courage to talk to an actual man. I was walking home from the library when a couple of drunk guys started hassling me. I'm sure it was harmless, but I was too inexperienced to know what to do. I panicked and started pleading with them, which they found pretty funny. I was terrified and took off running. I ran smack into Reyhan. My books went flying, I'm sure I screamed and it was a mess. By the time it was sorted out, the guys were long gone and I was convinced Reyhan had rescued me from certain death."

Cleo sighed. "That sounds romantic."

Emma hadn't thought of it in that way. "I thought he was handsome and mysterious. Very attractive, of course. I was stunned when he asked me out." She shifted the baby, taking more of her weight on her lap.

"But you said yes."

"Would you have said anything else?"

"Probably not. The rescue would be really tough to ignore. It's very princely." She laughed. "I say that so calmly, but I'm used to Sadik being royal now. At the beginning it was a big deal to me."

"Do you miss your old life?"

"Not even for a minute. Not just because this is so much nicer—which it is. But because of Sadik. I love him." Her dark blue eyes glowed with affection. "He makes me insane, but that's okay. I drive him crazy, too. Besides, being different keeps things interesting. And he loves me." She glanced at Emma.

"Handsome, arrogant prince types may be hard to tame, but when they love, it's with every part of themselves."

Emma fought against a surge of envy. She had always wanted to be loved like that by a man. It wasn't that her parents hadn't cared for her, they had. But their love had been about protecting her from a difficult and frightening world. She'd always wanted just to be loved for herself.

Cleo shrugged. "Okay, I get carried away. That's part of my charm. So enough about me and my past. Are you excited about living in the palace?"

"It should be an interesting vacation. At least that's how I'm trying to look at it."

"Your one chance to be a princess?"

"Something like that."

Cleo grinned. "What if you find you like it so much, you want to stay?"

"Not an option. As soon as my two weeks are up, I'm heading back to Dallas." And her regularly scheduled life. There was nothing for her here in Bahania. She ignored the little voice inside that whispered there wasn't much for her back in Dallas, either.

Chapter Four

Reyhan had hoped the large palace would provide enough room for him to avoid Emma, but he had not taken his father's need to meddle into account. Now that the king had passed control of much of the day-to-day details of the country on to his sons, he had far too much free time to plan ways to torment them. His newest strategy began with an invitation for both Reyhan and Emma to join him for dinner.

Reyhan studied the casually worded email and knew the phrase "if it's convenient" was there for show. Should Reyhan protest it was not convenient, his father would change the request to an order. Defying one's father was easily accomplished. Refusing the king was another matter, especially when Reyhan needed the monarch's agreement to the divorce.

Which was why he found himself walking toward his father's private quarters that evening, trying not to think about how he would survive several hours in Emma's company.

Before she had arrived, he had nearly convinced himself that everything was different. That he no longer had feelings for her, and even if he did, that she was not the same woman. But a few minutes with her had told him that not only did she still have that ultimate power over him, she had somehow retained the gentle sweetness that had first drawn him to her.

When he reached his father's suite, he squared his shoulders. He was Prince Reyhan of Bahania. Royal, powerful and without weakness. He would survive this meeting and any others. He would endure and in the end, Emma would be out of his life forever.

"My son," his father said happily as Reyhan walked into the main salon. "How good to see you."

"And you, my father."

The king's cheer warned Reyhan that his father might have a trick or two coming during the dinner and that he would be wise to stay alert.

He crossed to the wet bar and poured himself a Scotch, then walked to the large sofa facing the French doors leading to the balcony. Only one cat lay on a center cushion. Reyhan avoided it as he sat down.

"Emma should be here shortly," his father said, stroking the large Persian draped across his lap.

Reyhan had offered to escort her himself, but the king had said he preferred to speak with his son privately first. Now Reyhan waited patiently.

"Your wife is a very pretty young woman," his father said.

Reyhan nodded. He never thought of Emma as "his wife." If he had, he would have claimed her, despite her wishes to be as far away from him as possible. He would have wanted to have her, take her, *be* with her. It had been safer for them both to be on opposite sides of the planet. Literally. He'd forced himself to think of her only on rare occasions, usually at night, when he couldn't sleep and the sounds of the Arabian Sea had echoed with her soft voice.

"I arranged tonight's dinner so I could get to know her," his father said.

Reyhan didn't like the sound of that. "She will be leaving in a few days."

"Until then, she is my daughter-in-law. A relationship of some importance."

Reyhan wasn't sure if his father meant that or was trying to make trouble. On the king's side were his close ties with Cleo, Sadik's wife. She was a favorite and spent much time in the king's company. If that happened with Emma, as well, his father might not want to agree to the divorce. Reyhan knew he could not stay married. Not to her. Not with his need burning so hotly inside.

Before he could come up with a reason to keep them apart, there was a knock at the main door. He rose, bracing himself for the impact of seeing her again.

"Come in," the king called.

A young woman pushed opened the door, entered and bowed her head.

Emma followed her, pausing uncertainly just past her escort.

Reyhan set down his drink, then crossed to her. As he approached, he took in the emerald-green sheath that clung to her sensual curves, the elegant upswept way she'd styled her dark red hair and the makeup emphasizing her eyes and mouth. She needed no artifice to make her more beautiful, yet he appreciated the effort...and the results.

Wanting flared, as did heat. He ignored both, concentrating instead on the excitement and apprehension battling in Emma's green eyes. A tentative smile tugged on the corners of her mouth, as if she wasn't sure which emotion would win.

When he stopped beside her, he reached for her hand. The second his fingers closed around hers, the ache inside of him increased to unbearable. Still, he dismissed the painful need and settled her small hand in the crook of his arm. He urged her toward his father, who had put down the cat and risen.

"Father, this is Princess Emma, my wife. Emma, this is King Hassan of Bahania."

He felt her stiffen at "Princess" and wondered if she'd considered her position here. As long as they were married, she

was a member of the royal family. Bahania was a long way
from her life in Texas.

"Enchanted," the older man said as he took her free hand
and lightly kissed the back of it. "Would you like something to
drink? Champagne? We should toast the moment."

"No. I—I'm fine."

The king drew her from Reyhan and settled her on the sofa,
next to the sleeping Siamese. He took the opposite side of the
couch, leaving Reyhan the chair.

Not difficult duty, Reyhan thought as he sat. Emma was in
his direct line of vision. He could visually trace her profile, the
line of her neck, the length of her bare arms. And while looking at her, he could remember their few nights together. How
she'd felt when he'd touched her. How she'd tasted when he'd
kissed her. The tight dampness of her virgin body when he'd
first claimed her as his own.

The images had an expected result, and he was forced to
shift slightly in his chair. Stop, he ordered himself. Thinking
about what had once been and never would be again offered
torment but little else.

"Tell me about yourself," the king said. "You are from
Texas?"

Emma nodded. "The Dallas area. I've lived there nearly all
my life.

Except when I was at college."

"Do you have brothers and sisters?"

"No. My parents had actually given up on ever having children when I came along." She smiled. "I was a surprise."

The sweet pull of her lips hit Reyhan like a punch in the gut.
He consciously relaxed his muscles and sucked in a breath.
Soon she would be gone and then he could forget she had ever
lived, he told himself.

"A happy one," his father said.

Emma laughed. "You're right. My parents have made it very

clear how much they adore me." Her humor faded slightly. "They are extremely protective."

"As they should be. A daughter such as yourself is a rare treasure."

"Thank you," she murmured as she bowed her head.

Reyhan caught the light flush on her cheek. So she still blushed. When he had first met her it seemed that everything he did caused her to blush. A compliment, a kiss, a whisper of desire. She had been the most innocent woman he'd ever met.

"Treasure or not, they made it difficult to have a life," she said. "Not that I don't love them dearly. But there were things I wanted to do." Her voice had turned wistful. "They were very strict about things like school dances and dating."

His father raised his eyebrows. Reyhan stepped into the conversation. "Many Western high schools offer chaperoned dances for the students,"

he said.

"A dangerous practice," the king said. "Now you know why I sent you to England for much of your education."

"An all-boys school," Reyhan said dryly. "It was thrilling."

Emma glanced at him and smiled. For that second, there was a connection between them. He could nearly see the sparks arcing across the room and feel the temperature increasing.

"Where did you meet my son?" the king asked, breaking the spell.

Emma returned her attention to the monarch. "At college. It was my first year there. I'd had to beg my parents to let me go. I was very excited, but scared, too."

"And did he sweep you off your feet?"

She swallowed, blushed, then nodded. "Yes. He was very charming.

Very…worldly."

Reyhan thought of the young man he'd been at twenty-four. Hardly worldly, except in Emma's inexperienced view. He'd wanted her and he'd pursued her with a single-minded focus that had left her nowhere to escape. He'd been determined to have her, and, upon discovering she was a virgin, he'd married her.

"Yours was a brief courtship," the king said. Emma glanced at Reyhan. "I…we…"

"She knew nothing of who I was," Reyhan said, interrupting her hesitation. "I alone defied you, Father. The blame, the responsibility, is mine."

Emma's eyes widened slightly, but she didn't say anything. The king nodded.

"You stayed together only a short time." The king's words were more statement than question.

"You know this," Reyhan said as he stepped in again. "I was called home because of Sheza's death." He glanced at Emma. "My aunt."

"But you did not return to your wife."

He had tried, Reyhan thought bitterly. He had called and attempted to see her, but she refused to have anything to do with him. Eventually her father had ordered him to stay away. No explanation save that Emma regretted the marriage and never wanted to see him again.

He'd told himself the sting he'd felt was little more than wounded pride.

That he hadn't actually cared about her. Loved her.

He shrugged with a casualness he didn't feel. "The past is finished.

What value is there in discussing it now?"

"I wish to know," his father said. He looked at Emma. "So after things did not work out with Reyhan, you returned to your parents?"

Reyhan didn't save her from that probing question mostly because he wanted to hear her answer.

"I, ah, stayed with them until the new semester started, then I returned to college. By then, Reyhan was gone."

True enough. Once he'd realized he'd lost her, he'd finished the requirements for his master's and had gone back to Bahania. He'd never tried to see Emma again.

"And what do you do now?" the king asked. "How do you spend your days?"

Emma looked confused, as if she expected them to already know this. "I'm a delivery room nurse. I received my RN and went to work in a Dallas hospital." She shifted in her seat and smiled. "It wasn't easy, let me tell you.

My parents really hated the idea of me living on my own, but I knew it was time. I have a good job. I can support myself."

Reyhan stiffened. "You what?"

His father glared at him. "You abandoned your responsibility?"

"I did not." He turned to Emma. He wasn't surprised that she worked. Many women preferred to fill their day with a job, especially when there weren't small children to tend to. But that she acted as if she *needed* the money. "You do not need to work to support yourself."

She stared at him. "Excuse me? How would you know what I need and don't need?"

"I left you financially provided for."

Emma leaned back in the sofa, trying to put a little distance between herself and an obviously furious Reyhan. She wouldn't mind his temper so much if she knew what he was so mad about. Nothing made sense. He hadn't left her a dime.

"You didn't do anything when you left," she said, then winced when he seemed to puff up and get even madder.

"After we were married, I opened a checking account for your personal use. Two hundred and fifty thousand dollars were put in a checking account. When the balance reached below a hundred thousand, the account was to be replenished."

Two hundred and fifty *thousand* dollars? He'd left her money? "I don't understand," she whispered.

"What is complicated about the information?"

Good point, she thought. But her head was spinning and nothing made sense. "Why would you take care of me?"

Wrong question, she thought as he stiffened even more.

"I am Prince Reyhan of Bahania and you are my wife. You are my responsibility. When you did not use the money, I assumed it was out of pride and anger. I sent a letter requesting you reconsider, and then funds were withdrawn, as they have been ever since."

Now it was her turn to get all huffy. "Wait a minute. I didn't know about any money and I sure didn't spend it."

"You knew. When you refused to see me, I spoke with your father. I gave him the account information."

Her father? "You came to see me?"

"Of course."

No. That wasn't how it happened. Emma distinctly remembered being curled up on her bed back in her parents' house, praying for Reyhan to contact her. But he never had. Not a note, not a phone call and certainly not a visit.

Unless he'd shown up while she'd been...ill.

"I was sick for a while," she said, telling herself it wasn't exactly a lie.

There'd been a sickness of spirit.

"I came by several times, in fact."

Had he? Was it possible her parents had kept the information from her?

She thought they might not have wanted to tell her that Reyhan had been by to see her, but they never would have kept information about that kind of money from her. They loved her. They were devoted to her.

"I don't believe you," she said. "Not about the money. If I don't know about it, who withdrew funds? Not my parents. They would never do that. This doesn't make sense. You disappeared from my life for six years, only to drag me over here and tell me you want a divorce. Why should I believe anything you say?"

"Because I do not lie."

She glanced at the king, but he seemed more amused than upset by the argument. Which was fine. She was upset enough for two people. She turned back to Reyhan. "Liar or not, you've insulted my parents and for no good reason. I don't know what this game is, but I'm done playing it."

She stood and walked out of the room.

After fifty feet down the hall she had the unsettling thought that it was probably considered a very bad thing to walk out on the king of Bahania. She paused, not sure if she should go back and apologize, or keep going. Before she could decide, she heard footsteps, then Reyhan rounded the corner and stopped in front of her.

He was obviously furious—tight-lipped and hard-eyed. Without speaking, he took her by the arm and led her away. She didn't recognize the twists and turns they took, even when they ended up in front of her suite. Reyhan opened the door and hustled her inside.

When he released her, she had the strangest urge not to move away. For a split second she thought about throwing herself into his arms and begging him to hold her. As if his embrace would make things right.

Not in this universe, she thought, taking a step back and bracing herself for whatever he had to say.

His gaze narrowed. "Why do you question what I tell you?"

"Why shouldn't I?"

"Because there is proof of everything. For weeks I kept vigil outside of your parents' home. I called or came by every day. I returned to claim you as my wife only to be told you refused to see me. I left when I received your letter."

Emma didn't understand any of this. "What letter?"

"The one you wrote telling me you regretted meeting me and everything about our marriage and that you only wanted me to disappear."

He spoke stiffly, as if the words were difficult to say. "That's crazy," she told him. "I never wrote that."

She hadn't thought it, either. Not at the time. She'd longed to see Reyhan, but he'd abandoned her.

"You used me," she continued. "I don't know why, but you got it in your head you wanted to sleep with me, so you pretended to care about me." She couldn't say the word *love*, not even now. "You took advantage of me for a long weekend, then took off. No explanation, nothing."

It took a lot to get her angry, but once she was on a roll, she liked to keep going. She remembered the pain and humiliation of being tossed aside like a broken toy.

"You promised me things," she said, her voice rising. "You talked about our life together and I believed you. I trusted you and you just took what you wanted and walked away."

"I left because a beloved aunt died."

"Did the funeral take six weeks to prepare? Did you ever once call me?

Did you think to tell me what was going on?"

He frowned. "Of course. I phoned nearly every day."

She rolled her eyes. "Oh, right. And I just happened to be out."

"That is what I was told."

She turned her back on him and walked to the floor-to-ceiling glass wall. None of this mattered, she told herself, trying to cool her temper. Soon it would be behind her. She had to remember the big picture.

Reyhan spoke into the silence. "If you think so little of men, you must be pleased to be rid of me. Just a few more days and the marriage will be over. As if it had never existed."

Fury surged. "Right. Because you can dismiss what happened. Because it didn't matter." She spun back to face it. "It mattered to me. Do you have any idea how innocent I was? I'd barely kissed one boy in high school. And then there was you. You didn't just seduce me, Reyhan, you took what you wanted, without regard for my feelings. I'll never forgive that."

His expression turned menacing. "You were more than willing."

"I was terrified. Now I'd know better. Now I'd tell you no."

"Are you saying I had you against your will?"

He hadn't, not exactly, but she was mad. "Yes."

"You were a child, only interested in chaste kisses and expensive presents. A child who couldn't please a man."

That hurt. She tried not to remember how embarrassed she'd been, how awkward and unsure.

"You were a man who couldn't be bothered with seducing his bride.

Instead you just took."

They were both enraged, breathing hard and glaring at each other. A part of her was terrified, but she refused to back down. Not even when he moved closer still. Not even when he reached behind her and grabbed her by the hair and pulled her up against him.

"If that is who I am," he said with frighteningly soft menace, "a liar and a defiler of women, then there is no point in holding back now."

He kissed her. Not the soft kiss of seduction or coaxing, but a kiss of power. He was a man with something to prove. His firm lips pressed hard against her own, claiming her with passion.

She wanted to protest, to scream, to pull back, but she could not. They touched everywhere. Her body pressed against his, their legs tangled. She put up her hands to push him away, but when her palms brushed against the hard planes of his suit-covered chest, she found herself unable to protest...or even breathe.

Fire consumed her. Hot and hungry, it swept through her, melting her resolve, her reason. Against her will, she found herself moving her hands from his chest to his shoulders. She clung to him because letting go would mean collapsing at his feet. Worse, she kissed him back.

She couldn't explain it, and given the choice, she would probably deny it, but there it was. A need that grew. Wanting was alive inside of her. In that moment, with his mouth against hers and his hands moving from the back of her head to her shoulders, then to her hips, she couldn't get close enough.

Emma wanted to surrender, to crawl inside of him. When his kiss gentled and he stroked her lower lip with his tongue, she parted for him and anticipated his more intimate kiss.

At the first stroke of his tongue against her own it was all she could do not to scream. At the second, she ceased to have a will of her own. And with the third, she clamped her lips around him, greedily holding him in place, wanting him to kiss her forever.

She ached. Her breasts, between her legs, all over. Her skin felt hot and too tight. She wanted to strip her dress off and have him touch her everywhere. She wanted to be naked, vulnerable, offering herself to him.

She rubbed one hand against the back of his neck. He held on to her hips and then dropped his hands to her rear where he squeezed the curves. She surged against him, wanting to rub like a lonely cat. But before she could put her plan into action he broke the kiss and stepped away.

They stared at each other. Loud breathing filled the silence. Emma was pleased to note that Reyhan looked as swept away by passion as she felt.

Perhaps they should call a truce, she thought. Start over as friends.

Friends who could bring about the end of the world with just a kiss.

"You have learned much in my absence," Reyhan said, his cold voice contrasting with the fire in his eyes. "Before you accuse me of more sins, you should look at yourself. A wife who takes lovers. Isn't there a name for that?"

Her mouth dropped open, but before she could snap back at him, he was gone.

Emma glared at the shut door and yelped in anger and frustration.

"That is not fair!" she yelled into the empty room. "I didn't know we were married and you know it."

Besides, there hadn't been any other men. Not seriously. And she'd never allowed any of them into her bed. If she kissed better now, it was because she was older, and because kissing Reyhan had made her feel things she'd never felt before. Not even *with* him.

Emma slowed her breathing and tried to calm down. She was shaking and not just because she was mad. She was shaking in reaction to what had happened when Reyhan had kissed her. She'd wanted him. Funny how she'd started to worry that there was something wrong with her because none of the guys she went out with had made her want to get naked and do the wild thing. Just her luck that the first one to push all her buttons was an arrogant prince who just happened to be a man trying to get her out of his life as quickly as possible.

"I don't think I can handle any more," she said quietly as she stepped out onto the balcony. "By the time I get home, I'm going to need a serious vacation."

She crossed to the railing and glanced down into the beautiful gardens. The peaceful setting began to ease her tension and she felt herself relaxing. After a time, she heard voices and searched until she found a couple walking into the gardens.

Even from two stories above, she recognized Cleo. The tall, handsome man at her side must be her husband. Emma couldn't make out the words, but she heard the affection in their voices. Sadik turned to his wife and held out his arms. Cleo willingly stepped into his embrace and they kissed.

Not wanting to intrude on an obviously private moment, Emma stepped back and returned to her suite. Alone in the silence, she paced the length of the living room as she tried to figure out what happened next.

Should she say anything to Reyhan? To the king? Could she just leave?

The musical chimes of a grandfather clock caught her attention. She stared at the face and calculated the time difference with Texas, then crossed to the telephone and pressed zero, hoping to get an operator. Less than a minute later, she heard her mother's voice on the phone.

"Emma! How lovely to hear from you. Where are you, darling? George, it's Emma. Pick up the other phone."

Emma waited until she heard her father's familiar "Hello, kitten," before sighing in relief. The tension fled her body and for the first time in three days she knew everything was going to be all right.

"Are you enjoying your vacation?" her mother asked. "I've heard spring in San Francisco is very beautiful. Are you getting a lot of fog?"

Emma winced as she remembered the lie she'd told her parents. Alex from the State Department had made the suggestion and she'd gone along. Now she wondered if the original idea had been Reyhan's.

"I'm not in San Francisco," she told them.

"What?" Her father's voice turned worried. "Was there a problem with the plane? Do you need us to come and get you?"

"No. I'm fine. I'm in Bahania."

"The Bahamas?" her mother asked.

"No. Bahania. It's next to El Bahar. In the Middle East. I'm here because of Reyhan."

Her mother gasped. "I knew that horrible man wouldn't stay gone. Oh, George, he kidnapped her. We have to call the police. They'll know what to do."

"Now, Janice. Don't jump to conclusions. Kitten, are you all right? Did he hurt you?"

"No, Daddy. Reyhan has been very polite." She had no intention of mentioning the kiss they'd just shared. "Why did you say you didn't think he wouldn't stay away, Mom? You told me he never bothered to come see me."

There was a long silence. Finally her father spoke. "He might have stopped by a time or two."

Deep in her heart Emma wasn't surprised. Her parents loved her and wanted to protect her from everything. That would include what they saw as a dangerous man intent on using their daughter. The problem with them admitting guilt in one area was that now she had to doubt them about everything, involving her pseudo marriage and the time following it.

"Just come home," her mother pleaded. "Emma, you don't belong there with those people. We'll come get you if you like. Wouldn't that be nice? Then we could all go to Galveston together. I'll bet that nice house we used to rent is available. It's not too close to summer. I could call and check and we could—"

"Mom, no. I'm not coming home just yet and I don't want you to come get me. I'm fine. I'm just..." How to explain what she was doing?

"That man is going to bewitch you," her mother said. "Just like he did before. It's not right. He should be in jail."

"For what?" Emma asked. "He married me and provided for me." Sadness overwhelmed her. Sadness for what had happened and what she'd believed. Sadness that her parents couldn't have believed in her enough to tell the truth.

"He abandoned you," her father pointed out. "What kind of man does that? He tried to turn your head, the way he's doing now."

"Emma, you've never been strong enough to take care of yourself," her mother said, her voice pleading. "You can see that, can't you? Oh, darling, come home. You belong here, with us."

Emma ignored the pleas and the claims. She'd been plenty strong—she should know. Her independence had been hard-won.

"He didn't abandon me, Daddy," she said. "He came to see me every day. He called when he was in Bahania for his aunt's funeral, and as soon as he got back to Texas, he practically camped out in front of the house, didn't he?"

"Is that what he told you?"

"Yes. Is he lying?"

Her father was silent for a long time. "He came by a few times."

She clutched the phone tighter. Reyhan had told the truth about everything. "You told him I didn't want to see him. You decided *for* me."

"Kitten, you were in no shape to deal with him. Have you forgotten what you went through?"

No. She would never forget. The pain would be with her always.

"Mom, did you write the letter telling him I never wanted to see him again?"

"I… Oh, Emma. It was for the best."

She closed her eyes and wondered how her life would have been different if she'd known. She'd loved Reyhan as much as her childish heart had allowed, and she would have gone with him in a second. Had her parents realized that? Had they not wanted to see their only child living half a world away in a foreign land?

If she had only known…

"What about the money?" she asked, more resigned than angry. "Why didn't you tell me about that?"

"We thought it was best for you not to worry about that," her mother said primly.

Not to worry? "I have student loans and a ten-year-old car," she said. "You had no right to keep that information to yourself. Spending it or giving it back was my decision to make."

"You were so young, kitten," her father said. "Too young." For all of this, she thought.

"Reyhan said he sent a letter telling me not to let pride get in the way of the money. After that, some has been withdrawn regularly. What did you do with it?"

"We didn't spend it," her mother said, sounding outraged. "We simply moved it into a money-market account. It's all there, darling. I'll show you the bank statements when you get home."

She felt drained and weary. It had been an evening of too many emotions.

"Were you ever going to tell me the truth?" she asked. "Of course," her mother said.

"We love you," her father added.

"When? Oh, let me guess. When you thought I was old enough."

"Exactly."

She was twenty-four and living on her own. She had a job, an apartment and something closely resembling a life. What rite of passage had her parents been waiting for?

She was sure in their hearts they had planned to tell her what had happened, but they would have put it off as long as possible. Partly because they wouldn't want to make her angry and partly because they wouldn't want her returning to Reyhan. She was beginning to suspect they would have done anything to keep her close. Even lie about her marriage.

"Why did you tell me the marriage wasn't real?" she asked.

"We weren't sure," her mother said. "That lawyer we hired couldn't verify it one way or the other. Best to be safe."

"By telling me I wasn't married when I was? What if I'd fallen in love and had gotten married again? I would have been a bigamist."

"If you'd gotten serious about someone, we would have said something," her father told her. "Emma, you have to understand our position in all this. We only want what's best for you."

Words she'd heard her entire life. For a long time she'd believed them, but now she wasn't so sure. Did they want what was best for her or for themselves?

"I need to go," she said. "I'll call when I get home."

"Emma, no!" Her mother sounded frantic. "You can't stay there. It's so far away."

"I'll be back in two weeks. Don't worry. Everything is fine."

"But, Emma—"

She cut them off with a quick "I love you" then hung up.

Alone, confused and weary to her bones, she curled up in a corner of her sofa and wondered when exactly her life had become so messy and what she was going to do to get things in order.

Chapter Five

The next morning Emma awoke with a brain full of questions and an achy feeling low in her belly. She knew the latter came from a night of erotic dreams with her and Reyhan as the stars. In her sleep he'd taken her over and over again and she'd been a willing participant. She'd pleaded and wanted and touched and surrendered happily.

Uneasy and more than a little apprehensive, Emma decided to ignore whatever not-so-subconscious message might be lurking in her dreams. Right now she had bigger problems—namely, what she'd said to Reyhan and how he'd told the truth about everything.

After showering in her Montana-size bathroom and dressing, she skipped breakfast. She owed Reyhan an apology and the nerves clog dancing in her stomach were unlikely to go away until she'd delivered it.

After getting directions to his office from the young woman cleaning the suite, Emma stepped out into the main corridor and walked toward what she hoped was the business wing of the palace. Ten minutes and three more sets of directions later, she walked into what looked like a very busy, very upscale office facility. She crossed to the middle-aged man sitting at a reception desk.

"I would like to speak with Prince Reyhan," she said.

The man's neutral expression didn't change but she thought she caught him eyeing her inexpensive dress and dismissing her.

"Do you have an appointment?" he asked. She shook her head.

He reached for the large phone console on his desk. "I will call his assistant and check his schedule. May I ask who you are?"

She'd been about to say "Emma Kennedy" but her pride had been bruised. It wasn't her fault that she couldn't afford nice clothes. Besides, she was clean and tidy and she'd taken extra time with her makeup, and did Reyhan think she was badly dressed, too?

She raised her chin slightly and looked the man in the eye. "His wife."

The man raised his eyebrows, color fled his cheeks and his jaw dropped. "Of course, Your Highness." He nodded deferentially and quickly pushed several buttons on the phone. When he was connected, he announced her and then hung up.

"This way, Princess Emma," he said, rising, then bowing.

Emma felt kind of small and petty for claiming a relationship that barely existed, but it was too late to call back the words.

She was led into a large open area. There were alcoves leading to private offices. The man apologized for making her wait even a second, then scurried off. Emma entertained herself by studying a color-coded map on the wall. She saw the capital city of Bahania and the sea. El Bahar was also outlined and there were small markers at random intervals.

She moved closer to get a better look, when she felt a tingling at the back of her neck. Turning, she saw Reyhan striding toward her.

If her heart had not been trapped in her chest, it would have taken flight. He was so tall, she thought foolishly. And handsome. A powerful man who ruled an empire. Emotions flashed in his dark eyes but they were gone before she could catalog any of them. Then Reyhan was standing in front of her, staring, and Emma couldn't think. She could only breathe in the scent of him and silently wish he would kiss her again.

"Emma," he said, his voice low and sensual.

That was all. No more than her name and she found herself swaying toward him.

"Reyhan."

"Now that we have established our respective identities, perhaps you would like to tell me the reason for your presence in my offices."

"What? Oh." She glanced around at the people working. They were trying not to pay attention while hanging on every word. "Could we please speak in private?"

"Of course."

He took her arm and led the way into a massive office. A carved wooden desk dominated the center of the room. An exquisite Oriental rug outlined a conversation area, while bookcases lined one entire wall.

She saw another detailed map opposite the window and three different computer systems.

"What is that for?" she asked, pointing at the map.

"It details the placement of the oil wells and pumping stations here and in El Bahar."

"There are a lot of them." He smiled slightly. "Yes."

She'd heard Bahania was a rich nation—now she could see why.

"Our oil production is my area of expertise," he said. "That is why I was in Texas getting my master's degree."

She thought of all the oil in her own state. "I guess we're experts, too."

"Yes."

He led her to the sofa grouping and motioned for her to sit

down. When she'd done so, he settled across from her and assumed a patient expression.

Funny how he looked so remote and distant, she thought. As if he hadn't kissed her the previous evening. As if he hadn't reacted with desire, breathing hard and wanting her. Or had she imagined his reaction? Had he kissed her to show he still had power over her, while not reacting himself?

She didn't have enough experience to be able to tell which it had been —a disadvantage she didn't enjoy because there was no doubt in her mind that Reyhan had known exactly what was going on inside of *her* body.

"What did you wish to speak to me about?" he asked.

She twisted her fingers together on her lap and shrugged. "I spoke with my parents last night."

She waited to see if he would say anything, but when he didn't, she continued.

"You were right…about everything. The marriage, the money, that you tried to get in touch with me."

She glanced at him. He looked neither surprised nor annoyed. "I'm sorry I doubted you," she whispered.

"Why would you not?" he said. "You have known your parents your entire life. We had been together only a few weeks. I disappeared after the wedding without giving you any information. Your parents would have been suspicious. No doubt they thought the worst."

"They're good at that," she said, surprised he was being so magnanimous. She would have expected a little gloating on his part—he'd more than earned it.

"I should have questioned them," she said. "I wanted to, but I was afraid."

"That I sought you?"

"That you didn't. That I'd been far too forgettable."

He looked at her. "You are many things, Emma, but not that. I, too, could have put more effort into getting in touch with you. I suspected some subterfuge on the part of your father, but I walked away. I assumed that in time you would learn what had occurred and get in contact with me."

There was more to it than that, she thought. Reyhan was a proud man.

He wouldn't beg. Not for her. Probably not for any woman.

"I should have been more curious," she told him. "Instead I took the easy way out and I believed them."

She studied the strong lines of his face. Who was this man who had married her and then walked away? If only she hadn't been so young and inexperienced. If only they'd met more as equals. Six years ago she might have intrigued him initially, but in time he would have tired of her childish ways. And now?

She didn't have an answer to that, although she was more than willing to try the kissing again. Not that Reyhan seemed to be offering.

"So all this time after the fact, we make peace with the past," she said. "And in a few days the king will authorize a divorce."

"Yes."

Ouch. His agreement stung a little. Foolish, she told herself. She couldn't possibly have any interest in him. Better to get this all behind her and start over. She would find someone else— someone more like her—and settle down. Have kids. That was her destiny—not a handsome prince from a foreign land.

She stood, and he rose, as well.

There was so much so say, and yet nothing. What could have been would stay a mystery.

"I was wondering about palace tours," she said. He frowned. "What do you mean?"

"I'm unlikely to get back to Bahania anytime soon. I would like to take advantage of my remaining time here to see something of the palace and the city."

"You may go anywhere you like in the palace."

She laughed. "Gee, thanks, but wandering around lost isn't my idea of a good time. I'm interested in hearing about the palace itself. Maybe some of the history. Is there a regular tour offered? I could join that."

"I will take you anywhere you would like to go."

"That's really nice of you, but unnecessary. I know you're busy."

Not that she would mind spending time with Reyhan. Being around him made her insides flutter—a new and thrilling experience. But he had responsibilities that didn't include her.

"Until the divorce, you are my wife. I will show you the palace and the city. We will begin today after lunch."

"That sounds like more of an order than a request."

He smiled. "You were the one to mention the tour. I am accommodating you."

Hmm, if he said so. Emma figured there was no point in arguing. Not only would Reyhan likely win, but having the argument would prove her to be a complete idiot. She wanted to spend time with him, which he was offering. A smart woman would smile and say yes.

"I look forward to it," she said brightly. "What time?"

"Two o'clock. Is that convenient?"

She laughed. "It's not like I have a full social calendar. I'll be ready."

He reached out and took her hand, then drew it toward his mouth. At the last second, he turned her fingers and pressed his lips against the inside of her wrist.

The hot, damp contact sent shivers zipping up her arm. Tension invaded her body and she would swear her knees were within seconds of buckling.

"Until two," he said, and released her.

Emma left quickly while she could because the alternative seemed to be throwing herself at him and begging him to never let her go. A feeling she couldn't deny, nor could she explain.

Reyhan showed up promptly at two. While he still looked hunky and appealing in the suit he'd been wearing earlier,

Emma had agonized over her clothing choices. She'd wanted to look sexy and glamorous and enticing. All a challenge based on the contents of her suitcase. Not that her closet back home would have been that much help. She spent her workdays in scrub pants and brightly colored shirts and her evening attire pretty much consisted of khaki pants or long skirts and casual tops. Not exactly the fashion-forward clothing she would need to catch the eye of a prince.

A prince very interested in divorcing her, she reminded herself as she smoothed the front of her skirt and smiled brightly. Reyhan had made it more than clear he was intent on getting her out of his life. Not exactly the actions of a man prepared to be overwhelmed by her modest charms.

"What interests you most?" he asked as she stepped into the hallway and shut the door of her suite behind her. "There is an impressive display of centuries-old jewelry in a few of the public rooms."

"I'm sure it's lovely," she told him, "but I'm more of an antique furniture and tapestry kind of girl."

Reyhan raised one dark eyebrow, but didn't comment on her statement. Maybe he didn't believe her, which wasn't her problem. Sure, she liked sparkling things as much as the next woman, but they weren't her world.

"Very well," he said. "We'll begin in the older section of the palace. The original structure was built in the late 900s. Since then, the pink palace has been updated and enlarged several times. Once, during the reign of Elizabeth the first, the daughter of a wealthy merchant was captured and held for ransom by the bastard son of the king. After a time, instead of returning her, he fell in love with her. They married and lived happily together. For their tenth anniversary, he presented her with a chapel—a miniature representation of a cathedral she'd seen once in France. We'll begin there."

Emma walked next to him, trying not to get caught up in

the heat his body generated. "Were many women captured and held against their will?"

Reyhan smiled. "It is a time-honored tradition for sheiks to take that which they admire."

How comforting. "So there's a harem here in the palace, too?"

"Of course."

She wasn't sure if she wanted to see it or not. Imagine a place where women were held simply to offer pleasure to one man. Of course there would be a lot of free time. She could catch up on her reading.

She glanced at her estranged husband and wondered what it would be like to be captured by him. Would he be kind? Demanding? She shivered at the thought of either. The wanting that was always just below the surface when he was around, burst into life. Her body ached to be close to his. She wanted him to pull her against him, kiss her, caress her. Instead she had to be content with the occasional brush of his arm against hers.

"Do men in Bahania have more than one wife?" she asked.

"No. That practice died out long before it was outlawed. Men quickly came to realize that keeping one wife happy was a full-time job."

"I've never understood why the multiple-wife thing was so popular," she said as they stepped out into a beautiful formal garden. She recognized it as the one she could see from her balcony. Where Cleo and her husband had come to be alone.

"It would be easy for a woman to be with more than one man in an evening, but after men, um, have their way, they're sort of out of it for a while."

Halfway through her sentence, she realized she'd stepped into some very dangerous territory. Did she *really* want to be having this conversation with Reyhan?

He stared at her, his expression unreadable but not the least bit friendly. "You know this from personal experience?"

"No. I've just…heard."

"It is not about pleasure," he told her, his voice slightly

strained. "It is about children. A woman is with child for nine months. In that time, a man can continue to impregnate other women, while she can only bear him one son at a time."

"Oh. That makes sense." She spoke brightly, as if this conversation was no big deal. "Good point. What's that?"

She pointed at a large statue of a horse rearing. It was life-size and pure white.

"A gift from the king of El Bahar some years ago. We have always had close ties with our neighbor."

"I remember hearing that."

Reyhan led the way down a narrow path. Lush plants grew on both sides and tall trees offered shade. It was early April and still pleasant but she was sure by mid-July the temperature, even in morning, would be unbearable.

"Here we are," he said, pointing to a small but exquisitely built chapel.

Spires reached toward the heavens. All of the windows were stained glass and looked ancient. Stone steps led into a darkened and cool interior.

Emma walked inside and instantly felt at peace. Half a dozen pews flanked a wide center aisle. In front, more stained-glass windows stretched up to the arched ceiling.

"Master craftsmen were brought in from France," Reyhan told her. "They worked for three years on the chapel, all in secret. While they were here, they trained many local masons who incorporated the designs in their own work."

Emma touched the carved wood pews. The finish was thick and glossy, obviously well cared for. What a private treasure, she thought.

"Are services ever held here?" she asked. "On special holidays."

She fought a sudden longing to attend one, knowing she would be gone and forgotten before the next occasion.

Reyhan led her back into the palace. They walked down

several flights of stone stairs, until she was sure they were underground.

"Long-lost treasures were recently returned to us," he said, pushing opening a massive wooden door. "Tapestries and statues, along with jewels and pieces of furniture. Local experts are restoring our history to us."

He showed her a wall-size tapestry in a frame. Two women matched threads and carefully repaired a large tear. It took Emma a second to see the scene—four men galloping across the desert. Their expressions were intent and fierce, their faces slightly familiar.

She glanced at Reyhan, noting the similarity in the shape of the eyes and build of the bodies.

"Relatives?" she asked.

"Ancestors. This dates back to the 1200s."

She wanted to touch the cloth, but knew too much handling could damage the delicate treasure.

He showed her shelves of statues and stacks of carved furniture. "Pieces are moved around in the palace," he said. "Some things are on display here in the city museum. Others are sent on tour around the world."

"I can't imagine what it would have been like growing up here," she said as they left the storage area and climbed stairs to the main level.

"As a young child, I had little use for the past. It was simply information I needed to learn to please my tutors."

"I suppose. We never appreciate what we have when we're young. Not unless we lose it."

He glanced at her. "What did you lose?"

She thought of her childhood. Loving, if overly protective. "I'm not sure there was anything. I was speaking in general." She glanced around at the city-size rooms they passed. "I think my entire house could have fit in there. You and your brothers must have had a good time playing hide-and-seek in here."

"We were not permitted to play games in the main rooms of the palace."

"Probably just as well. You could have gotten lost for days."

"Our tutors would have come looking for us."

Tutors. Not exactly a reference she could relate to. "You didn't go to the local schools?"

"No. When I was eleven I was sent to boarding school in Britain."

"It's that whole prince thing, huh?"

He glanced at her. One corner of his mouth curved up. "Prince thing?" She grinned. "You know. Being royal. It made you different."

"We were given many unique opportunities."

"I suppose you would have to learn things regular kids didn't. Like how to behave in certain situations, and rules about running a country. Of course I'll bet each of you had your own horse. I guess it's a tradeoff. There are advantages and disadvantages to most circumstances."

They walked into a huge reception room. The ceilings had to be three stories tall. There were carved poles and an intricately inlaid marble floor. Floor-to-ceiling beveled windows let in light. A raised stage stood at one end of the incredible room.

"My apartment doesn't even have a foyer," she murmured, and wondered again why he'd bothered with her all those years ago. "I was little more than a country mouse."

"What?"

She motioned to the gold light fixtures. "I'm going to guess that color isn't just a really nice paint job. Those are real gold."

"Yes, but it is of little consequence."

"Perhaps to you." She turned in a slow circle.

Reyhan's leaving her was for the best, she thought sadly. There was no way she could have fit in here then. No way she fit in now.

"Is there another man?" he asked abruptly.

She stared at him. "What? You mean am I seeing anyone?" He nodded.

"No. I'm not dating anyone right now. I've never been very good at the whole boy-girl thing, but you would know that better than anyone."

Memories crept in of their three nights together after their wedding. How he had taken her over and over and how she'd been unable to be anything but afraid.

Things would be different now, she thought with regret. She was sure she could respond, even hunger for him. But a man intent on getting a divorce was unlikely to be physically interested in the woman he was leaving behind—passionate kisses aside.

"Once you are no longer married, you can change that," he said. "As can you."

But she didn't want to think about him being with another woman.

"It's scary to think what could have happened," she said to distract herself. "I really didn't know about the marriage being real. If I'd gotten serious about someone and we'd wanted to get married…" Would her parents have told her the truth? She would like to think so, but she was no longer sure about anything.

"I would have been in touch to let you know we were still married."

"How would you have known?"

He stared at her without speaking, and then realization sank in. "You've kept track of me." It was a statement, not a question. She wasn't sure if she was pleased or creeped out.

"At first, I received monthly reports," he told her. "Now, yearly. You are my wife. It is my duty to watch over you."

As he hadn't known about her job, the last report must have been sometime last summer, after her graduation but before she'd started work at the hospital.

"If I'd known we were still married, I would have contacted you," she said. "I mean, being married all these years and being apart doesn't make any sense." She realized how that sounded. "Not that I'm suggesting we *should* have been together."

"I understand. Divorcing is the most sensible plan."

"Right."

Sure. It wasn't as if she knew anything about Reyhan, save the fact that being within ten feet of him reduced her to a quivering mass.

"I wonder what would have happened if I'd known you'd come back for me," she said. "Would you have brought me here?"

"Of course. As my wife, your place is at my side."

"What about my education? I wouldn't have been able to go to college here."

"Should we argue about what never was?"

"Probably not."

But everything would have been different. They would have had children by now. She'd always wanted children, she thought wistfully. And with Reyhan as their father, they would be stronger than her. More able to stand up for themselves.

Would she have been able to keep him happy? Would their marriage have flourished or would her youth have worn on his affections?

Had he loved her, even a little? More questions she wouldn't be asking. "Reyhan…"

She spoke his name, then paused, not sure what she wanted to say or ask.

He stared at her, his dark eyes narrowing slightly. "Stop," he ordered.

"What?"

Her chest tightened as it became difficult to breathe. Awareness flickered through her body, making her tremble. Her mouth went dry, her fingers tingled and wanting swelled until she thought she would burst.

Then she was in his arms with no way to understand how

she'd come to be there. He held her tightly, possessively and she reveled in belonging to him even for that single moment.

She had less than a heartbeat to anticipate the kiss before he pressed his mouth against hers and claimed her.

She parted instantly, wanting the intimacy, needing to make him desire her. The melting began, in her chest and between her thighs. At the first brush of his tongue against hers, she closed her eyes. At the second, she held in a sigh of contentment. Passion flooded every part of her body, making her squirm to get closer.

She touched his shoulders, his arms, then ran her hands up and down his muscled back. His fingers tangled in her hair. Their tongues stroked and circled and danced before he pulled back slightly and kissed her jaw.

He nibbled his way to her ear where he drew the lobe into his mouth and sucked gently. Her breath caught. He dropped his hands to her hips, then to her fanny where he cupped her curves before pulling her hard against him. As her stomach nestled against him, she felt a bulge.

Fierce gladness flashed through her. Reyhan was aroused. She excited him as much as he excited her. The thought thrilled her then was lost as he licked the sensitive skin under her ear, and she was unable to think about anything other than the exquisite sensations he created.

Heat was everywhere. His fingers burned, his body warmed. She found herself wanting to strip off clothing and bare herself. The large room and hard marble floors offered neither privacy nor comfort, but she didn't care.

She breathed his name, and when his mouth returned to hers, she was the one to slip her tongue against his lower lip before dipping inside.

He tasted faintly of coffee, with a little sweetness she couldn't explain. He continued to press against her, rubbing his arousal against her belly. She wanted to raise herself up on tiptoe so he could rub her *there* and pleasure them both.

One of his hands moved from her rear to her hip, then traveled higher. Her breasts swelled in anticipation of his touch. She wrapped both arms around his neck and clung to him so that when he reached his destination, she would not collapse at his feet.

Closer and closer and closer until she nearly begged him out loud. At last he cupped her right breast and brushed his thumb against her tight nipple.

Pleasure jolted her like lightning. She gasped, then nipped at his lower lip while he continued to stroke her. She could feel tension building between her thighs, the dampness of her panties and the trembling in her legs.

And then he was gone. He stepped back and stared at her. His breath came in rapid pants. Passion brightened his eyes and tightened the lines of his face. She didn't have the courage to glance lower, to *see* that he wanted her, but she knew.

They stared at each other for what seemed like an eternity. Emma wished she knew what to say, or even how to ask why he'd stopped when they were both so obviously willing. But nothing in her life had prepared her for such a reaction, so she couldn't find the words.

"I must return to my office," Reyhan said at last. "You will find your way back to your rooms."

It was a statement rather than a question, and Emma wasn't sure she could speak, let alone argue. She watched him walk away, then she staggered a few feet to one of the columns and leaned against it until her heartbeat slowed to normal.

She didn't understand what was happening with Reyhan. She hadn't seen him in years. Why was he getting to her? And why did he have to be the only man who made her *want* with such incredible intensity?

"Too many questions," she whispered when she could finally think and breathe like a normal person. "No answers." Just a man who made her burn and a ticking clock that reminded her it would soon be time to leave.

* * *

Reyhan didn't return to his office right away. He detoured through the far end of the palace, walking briskly in an attempt to burn off the passion and need that Emma had created.

Nothing had changed. Emma's pull over him remained absolute. She could bring him to his knees with just a glance. When she touched him—he would capture the moon if she so requested.

He could never let her know the power she had over him, could never let her know his weakness for her. He paused by a window and stared uneasily out at the view. He *would* control this, he told himself. He would *stay* in control.

In a few days she would be gone and there would be relief. But instead of anticipation, he felt only pain at the thought of his world without her. The ache inside of him deepened.

So much time had passed, he'd hoped that he could face her and not care, not need. But he'd been wrong. Worse, she responded to him with the wants and desires of an experienced woman. She was no longer the frightened child he'd married.

Who had taught her to kiss so expertly? he wondered grimly. What man had tutored the woman who belonged to *him?* Passion blended with rage as his hands curled into fists. Were that man here now, Reyhan would rip him apart.

No! Control. He had to get control. Emma might be the color in his world, but she was also dangerous. Better to live in shades of gray than risk everything. Just a few more days. Then she would be gone and he would be free.

Chapter Six

The main marketplace was so filled with light and color, it was like stepping inside of a kaleidoscope. Emma didn't know where to look first. Wooden stalls lined the wide stone street and everywhere she turned there were more wonders to be seen. Bright silks puddling like quivering gems, copper pots of every shape and size, fruits, vegetables and rich, supple leather goods tempted her to step closer and touch.

In addition to the visual display, there were also strange and intriguing scents—sandalwood, coconut, exotic flowers and spices blended with wood smoke and the underlying musk of perfumes. A hundred conversations blended into a unique musical accompaniment with the call of the merchants, the barking of dogs and the laughter of the children racing through the back alleys.

"It's wonderful," she breathed, pausing to stare into the eyes of a camel tied up at a corner. "Like something out of a movie."

She smiled at Reyhan, who nodded.

"There are few sights that compare with an open-air market," he told her. "We have one of the oldest and largest in the world."

She smiled at a young woman holding a baby. The woman ducked her head and slowly backed away. Emma knew it wasn't because of her—no one knew her from a rock. Instead it was the presence of a prince, and the three large and hostile-looking bodyguards that were assigned to accompany them. The well-dressed and well-armed men kept the other shoppers at least an arm's distance away and discouraged casual conversation.

Emma wanted to protest, saying they would be fine on their own, but who was she to judge? Besides, Reyhan had explained that the accompanying men were as much for crowd control as protection.

She'd been surprised when Reyhan had offered to take her to the local market. After their last encounter she'd been sure he would want to avoid her, what with how he'd stalked away without saying anything. Yet two days later he'd shown up at her door with the invitation.

She'd been delighted to accept.

"Local dates," Reyhan said, stopping by one of the stands. "Try some."

The merchant, a tiny wizened man with a huge smile, held out a tray of plump dates. When he nodded encouragingly at her, she took one and tasted.

"They're good," she said.

The merchant beamed. Reyhan reached into his pocket and pulled out a few coins.

"No, no." The old man backed up and shook his head. "It is my honor.

My pleasure."

Reyhan smiled. "Such is the power of a beautiful woman."

Emma was so startled by the offhand compliment, she laughed. "Oh, sure. He's overwhelmed by my beauty, not by the fact that you're a prince and traveling with enough muscle to start your own wrestling federation."

His dark gaze settled on her face. "You don't think you're attractive?"

"I'm okay." Passably pretty, she thought. No one had ever

looked at her and then run shrieking in the opposite direction. "But I've never overwhelmed anyone."

He continued to study her, then looked away without saying anything. The merchant pressed a bag in her hands. She could feel the soft fruit inside.

"Thank you," she said. "You're very kind."

As they walked away, Reyhan said something in a language she couldn't understand. One of the bodyguards made a note on a small pad he'd pulled from his jacket pocket.

"What was that about?" she asked when they'd drifted down another aisle in the market.

"Someone from the palace will visit the old man's stall later in the week," Reyhan said in a low voice. "A large quantity of dates will be purchased at a premium price." He jerked his head back the way they'd come. "The old man offered a gift he can scarcely afford to give. Respect from my people shouldn't come at the price of starving."

"It was just a few dates."

"He has nothing else to sell."

An interesting point, she thought, studying Reyhan from the corner of her eye. She would have said he was firm and intelligent. Remote and stern with a hidden well of passion. But she would never have guessed he had a compassionate heart for those in need. One more item on the long list of things she didn't know about her soon-to-be ex prince-husband.

Two young boys ran past them, laughing and yelling as they went.

Emma turned to watch them go.

"Did you come play in the market when you were a child?" she asked. "Were you allowed out and about?"

"Sometimes," Reyhan said. "With my brother Jefri." He shrugged. "Once we were playing with more abandon than usual and knocked a cooking pot off an open fire. In our hasty effort to retrieve it before the large and mean-looking owner noticed, we bumped a burning log into the corner of a stall. It was old, dry wood and went up in seconds."

She covered her mouth with her fingers. "Was anyone hurt?"

He shook his head. "No, but three stalls were completely destroyed before the fire was brought under control. Jefri and I were in trouble for a long time. Our father refused to let us simply pay for the damage out of our pocket money. Instead we had to rebuild the stalls and then work in them for several weekends. In the end, the owners came out ahead as people shopped to see the young princes up close."

"So it was a fitting punishment?" she asked, even as she thought it sounded a bit harsh. Not the rebuilding. That made sense, but the working in public where the boys would be stared at like zoo animals.

"My father wanted us to learn," Reyhan told her, not really answering the question. "Jefri and I were more careful on our next trip to the marketplace."

They stopped in front of a stall displaying silver jewelry. The merchant nodded exuberantly and held out dozens of silver bangles. They were large and beautifully carved.

"Something to remember the day by," Reyhan said, selecting several and offering them to her.

She wouldn't need a reminder. Everything about this time with him was burned onto her brain. But the bracelets *were* pretty. She reached for one made of linked hearts and slid it on.

He took the bag of dates from her and passed them to one of the bodyguards, then held her hand out in front of her. When he turned her wrist, the light caught the shiny bangle.

"Very nice," he said, and gave the jeweler several folded bills.

"Is it terribly expensive?" she asked, feeling a little guilty. "I can pay you back. I have my checkbook in my purse."

Reyhan didn't speak, nor did he turn away. His dark gaze did the talking for him as she remembered who he was and all the money he'd left in her account. No doubt a silver bracelet wasn't going to be a blip on his financial radar.

"Thank you," she said softly. "It's very beautiful."

"You are a woman who deserves beautiful things."

That compliment nearly made her stumble, but she managed to stay upright. *Fake it until you believe it*, she told herself. Even if the faking lasted right up until the moment she walked into her apartment back in Dallas.

She wanted to ask what made her deserving of beautiful things and if he meant it when he looked at her with fire in his eyes. Did he feel the sparks between them? Did the heat draw him? Had he relived their kisses, as she had, longing for more, for every intimacy?

Rather than risk a potentially embarrassing line of conversation, she went for something safer.

"Did you attend school locally?" she asked.

"No. Just the tutor, then to a British prep school, then an American university."

He placed his hand on the small of her back and urged her down another crowded aisle. Several people bowed and smiled when they saw him. From what she could tell, Reyhan was very popular with his people. Probably a good thing when one was a prince.

"My father thought it was important for his sons to have a diverse education and contact with the West. Much of our business is conducted with American and European interests. Familiarity with mindsets and customs helps the process."

She thought of her own small life. Aside from now, and except for their brief honeymoon in the Caribbean, she'd never been out of the state.

"I would imagine both Britain and America were different for you," she said.

"I knew some of your ways from watching movies. I'd been raised speaking English as well as Bahanian, so I was comfortable with the language. But there were still lessons to be learned."

She stopped and touched his arm. "Like what?"

He glanced at her. "When I first arrived at my university, I told a few people who I was. Word quickly spread and my time there became…difficult."

"Everyone wanting to rub shoulders with a real, live prince?" she asked sympathetically.

"Something like that. Some young women were enthusiastic in their effort to get to know me."

She could imagine. "You would have been something of a catch."

One corner of his mouth curved up. "So I was told. When I went to Texas, I decided not to tell anyone who I was. A few recognized me from various articles in magazines and reports on television, but for the most part I was able to simply be myself."

"I had no clue," she said, more than a little embarrassed by the fact. "I guess I should have paid more attention to current events."

He started walking again and drew her along with him. "Not at all. Your interest in me was about who I was as a person, not who I was as a prince."

"The whole royalty thing would have overwhelmed me," she admitted. "Actually, I would have run in the opposite direction."

"And I would have chased after you."

"Really?"

She glanced at him, wondering if he was teasing or telling the truth. Would Reyhan have pursued her? She wanted to believe he had been that interested, but was it really possible? She'd just been a very shy, inexperienced eighteen-year-old. Hardly the sort of woman to catch the interest of a sophisticated man of the world.

He took her hand in his and squeezed lightly. "You wanted to be a nurse. I know you graduated with honors, but I'm not that familiar with your work. Tell me what you do."

It was difficult to concentrate with his fingers rubbing against hers. When his thumb brushed against her palm, she nearly moaned. Wanting burned low in her belly, making her ache and need.

So many physical reactions, she thought. Why was her body coming alive now? With him?

Better not to ask, she told herself and focused on Reyhan's question. "I'm a delivery room nurse," she said.

His expression tightened with surprise. "You assist with births?"

"Pretty much." She smiled. "It's so wonderful to spend my day helping babies being born. It's a time of joy and happiness for everyone involved."

"I suppose that is more fitting than you dealing with men."

"That's not why I chose my specialty. I went into it because I love children and babies and I thought it would be very gratifying. I was right."

"My sister-in-law recently had a baby. My sisters Zara and Sabrina are also pregnant."

"I'd heard. Cleo told me."

As she spoke, she raised her face toward his. Sunlight turned strands of her hair to the color of copper. Humor brightened her eyes and made her skin glow as if lit from within.

Beautiful, Reyhan thought desperately. She had always been beautiful.

Not that her being ugly would have helped, for if he closed his eyes when he was with her, he still wanted her. The sound of her voice was as musical as the rush of the tide. The scent of her body teased and enticed him. Her gentle spirit called to him, as did her intelligence and humor. Blind, deaf and mute, he would have burned for the lightest brush of her touch.

His need for her grew every second he was in her presence. Soon it would be as uncontrollable as a wild animal, and like that animal, he was in danger of devouring her. He had to get away from her but not just yet. One more day, he told himself. Then he would retreat to nurse his wounds and wait out her remaining time in his company.

"What will you do when you return to Dallas?" he asked. "What do you mean? I'll go back to work."

Amusement tempered his growing desire. "Because you have bills to pay?"

She laughed. "Yes. All the usual things like rent and utilities, plus my student loans."

She was still so innocent.

"I am Prince Reyhan of Bahania."

She blinked at him. "Actually, I know that."

"You are my wife."

She shook her head. "I suppose technically, although not really."

"Legally you are."

"Okay. I guess. But you want a divorce."

"And after the divorce, do you think you'll leave with nothing?"

Emma's green eyes widened in surprised. "I don't want anything. I'm not your responsibility, and I'm perfectly capable of taking care of myself."

How like her, he thought. Other women of his acquaintance would be trying to squeeze out every dollar they could.

"I will provide for you," he told her. "Arrangements will be made for you to purchase a house, then I will set up a checking account as I did before."

"You really don't have to do this."

"I know."

"But we were only together for a few days." It should have been for a lifetime.

The thought came unbidden. Reyhan did his best to chase it away, but it stayed in place. Stubborn, real and tempting. So much would have been different if he'd simply insisted on her returning with him. When his aunt had died, he'd left Emma behind, to spare her the trauma of finding out who and what he was. He didn't want to thrust her into royal life without some time to get used to the idea, nor did he want her meeting his family at a funeral. But by leaving her behind, he'd lost her.

How would their lives have been different if he'd brought her home right away? She would be a mother by now. His wife in every sense of the word. How would she have handled the responsibilities, the traditions? Would she have grown into them or chafed at the restrictions?

He would never know—about any of it. She could not be his wife; he had chosen a different path. But perhaps they could pretend for a single day. "All the women I've ever met love to shop," he said. "Are you different in that, as well?"

She smiled. "I don't mind spending an afternoon or two at the mall. Are you trying to tempt me into accepting your more-than-generous offer of a settlement?"

"Not at all. The money will be provided. You don't have a choice in the matter."

She shook her head. "You're pretty high-handed."

"Yes."

She laughed. "That's it. Just a yes? Aren't you going to protest?"

"I get what I want one way or another."

"Must be nice."

"It is."

Except when he wouldn't allow himself what he wanted.

"This way," he said, taking her arm and leading her through the marketplace. The bodyguards trailed along behind.

Emma knew there was no point in protesting or asking where they were going. Reyhan would tell her when he was ready. Besides, she was enjoying her time with him to the point that it didn't much matter to her what came next.

She glanced down at the bangle on her wrist. Something to remember him by, she thought fondly. Not gold and expensive jewels, which weren't her style. Just a simple, silver bracelet.

They turned a corner onto a main street, then stopped in front of a plain storefront. She glanced at the sign that read Aimee's before Reyhan moved inside.

The cool interior was a contrast to the warmth of the afternoon. Emma took in the cream-on-white decorations, the elegant displays of clothing and shoes and instantly felt frumpy in her outlet-sale clothing.

A tall, painfully thin woman approached. "Yes, may I—" The woman touched her perfectly coiffed hair, then smiled. "Prince Reyhan. A pleasure. How may I serve you?"

"This is Emma," he said. "My wife."

The woman's dark eyes widened as she nodded graciously. "Princess. I am Aimee. Welcome to my shop."

Emma offered a smile even as she wondered what Reyhan was doing. It was one thing to tell people they were married in the palace, but why would he do it in public? No one had known they were married and they were going to be divorced very soon. Why bother with the hassle of explaining?

"She needs a complete wardrobe," he continued. Emma turned to him. "What?"

"Indulge me."

"But…" Aware of the older woman's obvious interest in what was going on, Emma lowered her voice and leaned in close. "I don't need a new wardrobe. Mine is fine. I'm not saying her clothes aren't lovely, but they've got to be really pricey and they don't fit into my regular world."

"You're not in your regular world now, Emma. You're in mine. You're also a beautiful woman who deserves beautiful things. It pleases me to buy these for you."

Protesting too much seemed both ungracious and stupid. Instead she nodded. "Thank you for your kindness."

How bad could it be? she thought as she followed the well-dressed store owner into the dressing room area. A couple of dresses, maybe a pair of jeans or two and she would be done. Reyhan didn't strike her as the kind of man who would enjoy waiting while a woman tried on clothing.

Or was he?

Two hours later Emma was less sure about everything. Reyhan had been remarkably patient as she'd been dressed in everything from simple sundresses to suits to elegant evening wear. Whenever something looked especially nice on her, Aimee urged her to step out into the main salon for him to see. Much to her chagrin, he'd been the one to make the decisions on what to buy and what not to.

"These are supposed to be *my* clothes," she said as he shook his head over a dark pants suit she quite liked.

"Too severe," he told her. "The cut is too loose."

"I can't spend my day flashing cleavage at the world."

"No. That you save for me."

Instinctively she pressed a hand against the vee neck of the suit. Was he talking as the powerful husband and prince or as a man? Were they different? She stared at him, trying to figure out what he was thinking and what he wanted from her. The strong, handsome lines of his face gave away nothing.

But his words had made her *aware* of him again. While she'd been busy trying on outfit after outfit she'd been able to forget the tension lurking just under the surface. She'd managed to forget how much she liked being close to him and how he'd made her feel when he'd kissed her. Now she remembered everything.

"This will be fabulous," Aimee said when Emma returned to the dressing room. The older woman held out a strapless beaded gown in bronze. "The color will bring out the fire in your hair. Perhaps the prince will buy you a necklace of yellow diamonds to complete the look."

Yeah, right. Like that was going to happen. Emma didn't think that soon-to-be divorced wives rated rare gemstones. Of course she hadn't thought they rated new wardrobes, either.

After stripping off the pants suit, she studied the dress. No way was she going to be able to keep on her bra. Aimee stepped outside to give her privacy, so Emma continued undressing until she stood in just her panties, then she stepped into the elegant gown.

It fit her perfectly, sliding over her hips as if it had been made for her. Aimee returned with a pair of strappy sandals and some combs to hold back Emma's hair.

"Excellent," the woman said approvingly. "You look exactly like the princess you are."

Emma glanced in the mirror, then did a double take. She *did* look royal, or at least elegant in a way she never had before.

"I guess clothes really do make the woman," she murmured as she walked out into the salon.

Reyhan looked up from a newspaper, then rose to his feet and nodded. "Yes. That is exactly right. You are stunning."

"Thank you. The dress is amazing and I know it fits great, but there's no way I'm going to keep it."

"Why not?"

"Reyhan, where will I ever wear it? I really appreciate your interest in my wardrobe, but be serious. This isn't me."

He dropped the paper onto the small table by his chair and walked toward her. When he was less than a foot away, he stopped and looked into her face.

She met his gaze and felt the impact of his intense stare. Heat grew until she felt uncomfortable in the strapless gown. She wanted to tug down the hidden zipper and let the dress pool at her feet. She wanted to be naked before him. Naked and vulnerable and slick with wanting. Need made her ache deep inside. Her thighs trembled.

"It pleases me to buy you these things," he said, his voice hoarse. "Why do you object?"

Why, indeed. At this moment, she could deny him nothing. If only he would say that he wanted her. If only he would touch her. Anywhere. Her arms, her face, her breasts. She felt her tight nipples rub against the soft lining of the gown and wished the contact to be against Reyhan's palms instead.

Take me.

She didn't speak the words, but somehow he heard. Fire erupted in his eyes. His muscles tensed and his breathing quickened.

When his gaze shifted to the entrance to the dressing room, she knew what he was thinking. That they could be alone there. Right now. No waiting, no wondering if it was right. Just a man and woman taking pleasure in each other.

It was insane to even consider such a thing, but she wanted to. Desperately. They could— The click of heels on the tile floor cut through the erotic silence. Before Emma could object, Aimee came out of the back room and Reyhan turned away. It was as if the moment had never been. Reluctantly she returned to the dressing room and took off the dress.

Later, when their limo was filled with boxes and bags from the boutique, and Reyhan sat so carefully at the opposite end of the long leather seat, she tried to figure out what was going on between them.

Six years ago, after their brief marriage ceremony, they'd retired to a hotel suite and spent three days together. Emma remembered the intimacy of making love with him. There had been little desire on her part. Mostly she'd felt embarrassment, fear and occasionally pain. The more Reyhan had wanted her, the more scared she'd become. When he'd been called back to Bahania, she'd been grateful.

Back then she'd simply endured his desires, whereas now she shared them. What was different? Her? Had she grown up to the place where she could meet Reyhan as an equal? Had he changed? Was it chemistry or timing? Was it a quirk of fate that she would find herself falling for a man who planned on divorcing her then have her disappear from his life forever?

Emma paced the length of her suite. She'd already unpacked her beautiful clothes and admired them while trying not to look at the price tags. Some of her evening gowns cost as much as a good used car. She had no idea where she would wear them, but that was really the least of her problems. Instead there was the pressing matter of Reyhan.

What was going on between them? Was acting on their mutual attraction a good thing or would it make her a nominee for idiot of the year? Should she say something to him? Ask him if he'd changed his mind about the divorce? Ask him if he just wanted her for sex? Ignore the whole thing and count the hours until she headed back for Dallas?

"If you were the least bit brave, you'd talk to him," she murmured to herself. "Put it all out on the table and see what happens."

A sensible plan.

She crossed to the phone, intent on calling him at his office, but before she could there was a knock on her suite door.

Reyhan? Her heart pounded at the thought. She replaced the phone and hurried to the door.

But instead of her handsome husband, a young maid stood in the hallway. The girl handed her a note, nodded and left. Emma closed the door, then unfolded the piece of paper. As she read, her chest tightened and her spirits sank.

Disappointment swelled inside of her. He was gone and she might not see him again until it was time for her to go back to Dallas. Not exactly the actions of a man overwhelmed by passion. Had she misread him completely?

She hadn't been very good at understanding Reyhan when they'd first met. Apparently time and distance hadn't changed that fact.

"It's for the best," she whispered, crushing the note in her hands. "I'll go home and this will all be forgotten. I'll get on with my life. Find someone else and get married."

Although she had no idea who that someone else might be. Reyhan was going to be a tough act to follow.

Chapter Seven

"For a woman with a brand-new wardrobe, you're pretty down in the mouth," Cleo said the next morning.

Emma nuzzled baby Calah's sweet-smelling head and sighed. "It's guilt.

Reyhan spent too much on me. The clothes are beautiful, but…"

Cleo rolled her eyes. "What? You don't deserve them? Emma, we're talking about the royal family. They've been rich for about a thousand years. Trust me. Your shopping spree didn't even count as pocket change."

Emma wanted to mention that the trip to the boutique hadn't been her idea, but she thought it might sound like she was making too big a deal of things. Cleo didn't think anything was out of the ordinary. Reyhan hadn't minded. He'd wanted her to buy more than she had. The guilt was hers and she should deal with it by herself. Except…

"I didn't really need them."

Cleo laughed. "That's your mother talking. It's a very parental thing to say. Isn't it fun to buy things you *don't* need and not have to worry about cost? Think of this as the fulfillment of your every-female shopping fantasy. Besides, I know you made Reyhan happy. From what I can tell, all the princes like to take care of women. It can be occasionally annoying but for the most part it's pretty nice."

"So you're saying I went shopping just to keep *him* happy?"

"If it helps with the guilt, sure."

Emma smiled. "I'm going to look pretty silly wearing a beaded gown in the grocery store on Saturday morning."

"Not if you're over in the imported foods section. Tell everyone you're European."

"That might work." Emma thought of the beautiful evening gowns sitting in the suite's large closet. "Are there a lot of formal functions here at the palace?"

"Two or three each month. I've only just started attending them, what with being pregnant and all." She rubbed her baby's arm. "But now that Calah is here and I've had a chance to recover, I have social obligations, not to mention charitable ones."

"What do you mean?"

Cleo blew her daughter a kiss, then turned back to Emma. "I'm in a unique position to help people. In a way, that's a bigger dream fulfillment than the shopping. I've spoken with Sadik and the king, and I'm getting involved with homeless children. There aren't very many in Bahania and El Bahar, but it's a big problem in other countries. I had something of a twisted upbringing for my first few years and I know what it's like to be alone and scared. Sabrina and Zara, the king's other daughters, each have their causes. Sabrina's seriously into finding antiquities and returning them to their rightful countries so people can enjoy their heritage. Zara is a former professor. She's working on a network of scholarships for girls who want to go to college but can't afford it."

"Sounds exciting," Emma said, hoping she didn't sound as wistful as she felt. Cleo was right. The chance to help people by using nearly unlimited resources would be a wonderful way to spend her life.

What would she have done if she and Reyhan had stayed together? She'd always loved children, especially babies. Maybe something with prenatal care. Not that she was going to get the chance to find out.

"How much longer do you have here?" Cleo asked. "I was hoping we could fit in a field trip so you could meet Sabrina and Zara. They live in a very interesting place."

"Not here in the city?"

"Not exactly."

When Cleo didn't seem willing to say anything else, Emma considered her question. "I was told I would be here two weeks, but I don't have an exact date for my return. I guess that's up to the king."

Not that she was all that anxious to head out, she thought. Spending time with Reyhan had been exciting and fun and something she wouldn't mind doing more. But with him gone... She sighed. Her simple life had sure had gotten confusing.

"How are things with you and Reyhan?" Cleo asked. "Or is that too personal? I just meant it's been a long time. Is he the same guy you remembered?"

Emma chuckled. "Are we allowed to refer to a Bahanian prince as a guy?"

"Hmm, good point. We might be risking a beheading. Fortunately Calah is too young to turn us in."

Emma bounced the baby on her lap. "She would never betray us, would you, honey? You're one of the girls. We have to stick together." She looked at Cleo. "As for Reyhan being the same or different... Honestly, *everything* is different. When we met, I was a freshman, away from home for the first time in my life. He was a sophisticated older man who swept me off my feet. I spent most of our time together trying not to sound too young or stupid. That took most of my energy. I can't say I *did* ever know him."

"And now?"

Interesting question. "He's terrific. Not just those handsome dark good looks, either."

Cleo sighed. "Agreed. Sadik would be a catch even if he were a brainless fool. I could happily suspend my life simply looking at him. But there's a genuine person buried inside. I'm guessing Reyhan is the same."

"Yeah. He's smart and serious, but funny, too." And sexy. Too sexy, she thought remembering their almost close encounter in the boutique. She would have sworn he'd wanted her as much as she'd wanted him. So why had he just up and disappeared without seeing her to say goodbye?

"So the girl in you was overwhelmed the first time around," Cleo said. "How does the woman feel the second time around?"

"She's impressed," Emma admitted.

"Which doesn't make you sound like a woman who's hot for a divorce."

"Of course I am. Maybe not eager, but it's why I'm here. Reyhan is ready to get on with his life and his plan doesn't include me."

Cleo's blue eyes widened slightly. "You don't have to blindly agree, you know. You could take some time, see where things go."

Emma blinked at her. Could she? Was that an option? "I never thought I had a say in things."

"Arrogant princes prefer the world to do their bidding, but it doesn't always have to happen that way. You're half of the couple. You get a vote." She touched Emma's hand. "Seriously. If you're not sure what you want, tell the king. I'm sure he'd be more than willing to hold off the divorce for a while."

Tempting, Emma thought a half second before she shook her head. "No.

There's no point. I don't belong here."

Cleo arched her eyebrows. "Oh, and I did? When I met Sadik I was the manager of a copy shop. Not exactly princess material." She waved her fingers at the room. "It's not about the trappings, or even tradition. The king wants his sons to fall in love. Prince Jefri has decided on an arranged match, but he's the only one."

Cleo was wrong, Emma thought sadly. Reyhan wanted one, as well.

He'd told her.

"Maybe if things had worked out differently when we'd first met," Emma said firmly. "But that time is past. We're different people. I have my own life back in Texas."

"Sure," Cleo said. "If you're not falling for Reyhan, there's no reason to stay. So tell me about your work in the hospital. You work in the delivery room, right?"

"Yes, it's wonderful."

Emma talked about a typical day, if there was such a thing, and how she loved what she did. But in the back of her mind, she kept hearing Cleo's words over and over again. *If you're not falling for Reyhan.*

She wasn't, she told herself firmly. She hadn't and she wouldn't. Falling for him after all these years apart would be just plain stupid. The fact that she enjoyed spending time with him was interesting but not significant. She wouldn't let it matter. She couldn't. Because Reyhan had made it clear he was only interested in moving on.

"They're making threats again," Will O'Rourke said quietly. "The usual?" Reyhan asked from his place by the fire.

"Death and destruction. Interruption of oil production. The usual."

Reyhan kicked at a small rock in front of his chair. "I would have more respect for these boys if they had a genuine complaint. We have neither taken their lands, nor displaced them."

"They want something for nothing. A share of the oil money or they make trouble. They're kids—seventeen or eighteen. To them this is a game."

"Extortion is a time-honored tradition all over the world." Reyhan turned his attention to the sky. It took a few seconds for his eyes to adjust to the total darkness, then he saw the thousands of stars twinkling in the heavens.

Beautiful, he thought. Mysterious. Distant. A world unto themselves.

Much like Emma.

He shook his head. The point of his trip to the desert had been to avoid her, but if he was going to spend all his time thinking about her, then he might as well torture himself by being in her presence.

"I doubt they have a plan," Will said.

It took Reyhan a moment to remember what they'd been talking about.

The teenage renegades.

"They imagine themselves to be characters in a movie," he told his security chief. "They will ride their purebred Bahanian stallions to victory." Reyhan had no more patience for these boys. He'd listened to their grievances and investigated their claims. They had not been pushed off their lands, nor injured in any way by the oil production. Most of them were bored second sons from hardworking nomadic families. Unable to inherit, they didn't want to work to acquire their wealth. Instead they sought to take that which belonged to the people.

"Watch them," Reyhan said. "In time they will grow bored and go home."

"You hired me to keep the peace, then made it impossible for me to do my job."

"To date there have been threats, but no actions. They are afraid of you.

I consider that doing your job."

Will was a former army ranger who had grown up on oil rigs in the Gulf of Mexico. His unique combination of knowledge and skills had made him a find. Over the past three years he'd worked his way up from the person in charge of security to Reyhan's second-in-command. There were those who disapproved of an American holding such a high position, but there was no one else Reyhan trusted at his back.

"The royal family has a centuries-old relationship with the nomads," Reyhan said. "Under normal circumstances, I would agree to your plan to simply round them all up and let them rot in prison for a decade or so. But the majority of these boys are sons of chiefs, and I have given my word that I will not endanger them without cause. Threats are not cause."

"As you wish."

The tall, blond American rose to his feet and headed to his tent. Reyhan watched him go. Will was frustrated, but he wouldn't say any more. Instead he would do his job. He would focus on the task. Did he know a way to keep a man from going insane?

Reyhan closed his eyes and tried to see nothing, but instead Emma filled his mind. Being apart from her had only made him want her more. She was like water to a man dying of thirst. Her light filled his day and without her, he was blind.

Not much longer, he told himself, looking for comfort and finding none. Just a few more days and Emma would be gone. Then he would be free to marry someone else. A sensible woman who would bear him fine sons. A woman he could respect and never love. A woman who was not Emma.

Emma found use for one of her fancy dresses two nights later when she was invited to dine with the king, Cleo and her husband, Prince Jefri and Murat, the crown prince of Bahania. Nerves rode a roller coaster through her stomach as she carefully applied her makeup, and she wished Reyhan was going to be around. With him at her side, she would find it a whole lot easier to make casual conversation with everyone else at the table. But she hadn't heard from him since he'd left and she was beginning to think she wasn't going to.

What if the two weeks ended while he was gone and she had to leave Bahania without seeing him again? She briefly closed her eyes and told herself not to think about it. If she had to leave without seeing him again, she would survive. Maybe it would even help her get over him more quickly.

Not that she had anything to recover from. It wasn't as if she was falling for him or anything.

After checking the mirror one last time and smoothing the front of the peach-colored cocktail dress she'd pulled on, she walked out of the suite toward Cleo's rooms. Cleo and her husband had offered to escort her to the dinner so she wouldn't get lost on the way.

"This is Sadik," Cleo said a few minutes later as she introduced her husband.

Emma wasn't sure if she was expected to curtsy or what. Wishing she'd asked Cleo in advance, she held out her hand and tried to look more impressed than nervous. "Your Highness."

Sadik—tall, darkly handsome and more than a little intimidatingsmiled. "As you are a member of the family, I suspect first names would be allowed." He bent slightly and kissed the back of her hand. "Welcome, Emma. I'm not sure how you have been able to put up with my brother these past few days, but the fact that you have is a testament to your character."

She'd been expecting to shake hands, so the kiss startled her, although not as much as the gentle teasing. Were all the princes *nice* as well as goodlooking and powerful? Was it possible?

"He's been very kind," she murmured.

"But a fool. Any man who leaves such a beautiful wife on her own takes his chances."

Cleo, lush and amazing in a dark blue low-cut gown, raised her eyebrows. "Sadik, are you flirting?"

He turned to her. "I am making our new sister feel welcome. You know there is but one woman in my world."

He spoke with an intensity and love that made Emma feel she'd stumbled into a private moment. She turned away, but not before she saw the way Cleo smiled at her husband. It was a smile of true contentment and security. In that moment Emma vowed she would find a man who would love her as Sadik loved his wife, and she would give her whole heart to him.

The three of them walked into the hallway.

"Jefri's fun," Cleo said, linking arms with Emma. "He's the youngest and has a great sense of humor. Murat is more stuffy. I guess it's the whole crown prince thing."

"Murat has many responsibilities," Sadik said firmly. "The weight of the country rests on his shoulders."

"He's also still single," Cleo told her. "Imagine marrying him."

"No, thanks. I'm having trouble dealing with being a princess, however temporarily. I wouldn't want to think about being queen."

"Someone's going to have to," Cleo said. "The king has started talking about Murat needing an heir. Not that there aren't hundreds of women lining up to volunteer."

"She will be the mother of his sons," Sadik said. "Not a choice to be made lightly."

"Exactly," Cleo said with a grin. "Now, if he was going to only have daughters, then he could pretty much marry anyone."

Sadik sighed. "You mock me, wife."

"Pretty much every chance I get." She looked at Emma. "It's a hobby."

Emma was still chuckling when they walked into the formal dining room. This was not the same dining room she'd been in on her second night in Bahania. That room had been impressive, but small and intimate. This one was much larger, with arched windows and elegant tapestries.

The table itself would seat at least twelve, and judging by the chairs lined up along one wall, could expand to seat many more. The inlaid wood gleamed in the soft light of crystal and gold chandeliers. The floor was marble, the flatware gold and the plates appeared hand painted and antique. Equally impressive, there wasn't a cat to be seen.

Despite the warm temperature outside, the room was cool and

a fire crackled in a massive carved fireplace. The king stood beside it, a drink in his hand. Two men stood next to him. They were both tall and dark, with strong features and lean bodies.

Do they know how to grow handsome princes here or what? Emma thought, trying not to give in to her nerves and panic. She just had to get through the dinner, then she could escape back to her room. No biggie. Besides, if Jefri and Murat were as well mannered as Reyhan and Sadik, she would be made to feel welcome. There was nothing to worry about. Really.

Emma had nearly convinced herself when the king turned and saw them. As he approached, she felt her knees begin knocking together. Telling herself over and over that he was just a man didn't help. Not even a little.

"Emma," King Hassan said as he approached. "How lovely to see you." He squeezed her arm lightly, then turned to Cleo, whom he kissed, then Sadik. The two men shook hands.

"I heard you went to our marketplace earlier this week," the king said as he led her to the other princes. "Did you enjoy it?"

"Very much. The people were gracious and kind."

"A Bahanian trait," he told her, then he introduced her to his sons.

They were much like Reyhan, yet different. Murat was taller and more serious. Jefri smiled easily. Both welcomed her.

When a servant approached to take her drink order, Emma chose white wine because she didn't want to appear out of place, but she had no intention of actually drinking any liquor. Not under these circumstances. Back home her friends teased her about being a complete lightweight, which was true. One drink and she was giggly, two and the world got blurry. Better to keep her wits about her tonight.

"It is unfortunate Reyhan couldn't be with us," Murat said a few minutes later.

Emma noticed the king in conversation with Sadik and Cleo while Jefri had excused himself to take a quick call from America. Something to do with the new Bahanian Air Force. She smiled at the crown prince.

"Another familiar face in this impressive gathering would be helpful," she admitted. "But he has responsibilities and I understand that."

"Many women do not."

"I can't imagine why not."

"They find reasons." He sipped his drink as he studied her. "Is it true you knew nothing of who he was?"

"Absolutely. I didn't completely believe it even after I was brought here.

The whole prince thing isn't exactly a part of my regular life."

"The life you will return to in a few days?"

She nodded. "Regrets?" he asked.

She considered the question. "One or two foolish ones."

"Why foolish?"

She motioned to the room. "This is fifteen light-years from where I belong. Reyhan needs to find a wife who will fit into his world."

"You let him go easily."

Was Murat criticizing or stating the obvious? "It's what he wants."

"And what do you want?"

Emma thought of her time with Reyhan. How he'd made her laugh and made her ache. Of how her heart fluttered when he was in the room. Of how innocent she had been all those years ago and how she'd let him walk away.

"I would like to go back and do things differently."

"Not possible," he told her. "Not even for a prince." Jefri returned just then and dinner was announced.

Emma found herself seated on the king's left, with Prince Jefri next to her. Murat was across from her. She felt the sharp gaze of the crown prince settle on her more than once as the appetizers were served. She longed to ask what he was thinking and if he would say anything to Reyhan when he returned.

Were the brothers close? Did they confide in each other? Did Murat know something of Reyhan's heart, and if he did, would that information please her or hurt her?

"The planes are being delivered next week," Jefri said, sounding satisfied.

"All that training will finally pay off," the king said. "Are they being delivered to El Bahar, as well?"

Jefri nodded. "The people from Van Horn will be here by the end of the month to start the integration process."

Cleo leaned toward Emma. "Okay, you look confused. El Bahar and Bahania are starting a joint air force to protect the oil fields. Jefri, who has been a flying fool for years, is in charge. He bought a bunch of really fast planes. F-somethings. Anyway, Van Horn Enterprises is a private firm that trains fighter pilots."

Sadik sighed. "I'm not sure where to start, Cleo."

She straightened. "What? Did I get any of it wrong?" Jefri looked at her. "You called me a flying fool."

"And?"

One corner of his mouth twitched. "Never mind."

King Hassan looked indulgently at Cleo. "She has given me my first grandchild. Little else matters."

Cleo winked. "You gotta like that, right?"

Emma nodded, thinking that they might be royal and rich and live in a palace, but at heart this was a family like every other. The knot in her stomach untied and faded away.

Conversation turned to current events and how they impacted Bahania. Emma had long known that Bahania was an American ally, but she was surprised by the close relationship the king and Murat obviously had with the president and several leaders in the Senate.

They had just been served a delicious chicken dish when one of the servants approached the king and spoke into his ear. The monarch listened, said something back, then looked at Emma.

"It seems there has been a slight plumbing problem in your suite," he said. "A pipe cracked and flooded the room. Nothing of yours was damaged, but you'll need to spend the night somewhere else." He smiled. "I think we can find a spare bed."

She thought of the dozens of rooms in the guest section. "I'm not concerned about it."

"Good. I have asked for your belongings to be packed and moved. After dinner I'll escort you to your new quarters myself."

"Thank you."

The meal lasted another two hours. When it was over, Emma felt so full, she could barely move. The king made good on his word and walked her to her new room.

"I hope you're enjoying your stay in my country," the monarch said as they turned a corner and started down a long corridor.

"Very much. What I've seen is so beautiful. And everyone has been so kind."

"Even my son?"

She glanced at him. He was tall, with a slight graying at his temple. In his dark suit he looked both regal and powerful.

"Especially Reyhan."

"I was sorry he could not dine with us tonight."

Emma agreed, but didn't want to say that. "He has responsibilities."

"He takes them seriously," King Hassan said. "As do all my sons. But in Reyhan's case, perhaps too seriously."

She wasn't sure what he meant, but before she could figure out a polite way to ask, they stopped in front of a large door.

"You will be staying in here," her host told her. "I hope you will find the room to your liking." He smiled and left.

Emma opened the door and stepped inside. The quarters were larger than her own had been, but more spartan. There were no overstuffed sofas and lush paintings. Instead the room was filled with simply designed pieces in muted earth tones and the artwork leaned more toward sculptures with a few boldly colored abstracts for contrast.

She turned on several lamps and walked around the living room. Something about it made her feel…not uneasy, just odd. The room was almost familiar. How strange. Had she seen it when she and Reyhan had toured the palace? She didn't remember any guest rooms being on their tour. Had she seen one similar?

She walked into the bedroom. The huge bed rested on a platform. Massive pieces of furniture filled the space without crowding her. Again the colors were muted but not— She froze in place. There was a book on a nightstand. An open book. Quickly she crossed to the closet and pulled at the double doors. Dark suits lined one side of the closet. Built-in shelves were home to shirts, sweaters and shoes. Her own newly purchased wardrobe filled the other side of the closet. She fingered the sleeve of the closest suit and knew exactly who owned it.

Reyhan.

The king had moved her in with her husband.

Emma sighed, not sure what to do with the information. Should she protest? Request another room? Was King Hassan testing her? Testing them? Even with Reyhan gone, she felt that she didn't belong in his rooms. They had never lived as man and wife. This felt too…intimate.

In the bathroom she found her cosmetics on the same counter as his shaver. Two bathrobes hung by the large glassed-in shower. As if they had always been together.

Not sure what to do, Emma decided she would stay the night, then speak with Cleo in the morning. Perhaps the other woman would know what was going on and what Emma should do about it. In the meantime, she would simply pretend all this was real and that this was where she belonged.

Reyhan arrived back at the palace shortly after midnight. The same demons that had driven him away had forced him to return. He had to see her, touch her, breathe the same air she breathed. The need inside of him had grown until he couldn't eat or sleep. He could only *want*.

He took the stairs two at a time. When he reached the second floor, he walked toward the guest wing. But as he approached her door, he slowed his step until he stopped several feet away.

What was he going to do? Break down the door and take her? He closed his eyes and shook his head. No. He would be strong. Just a few more days and she would be gone. He was back in the palace now. Within a few feet of her. That would be enough. He would retreat to the safety of his own rooms and figure out a way to survive until she was gone.

Retracing his steps, he made his way to the other side of the building and let himself into his suite. He shrugged out of his jacket and left it on the back of the sofa. As he loosened his tie, he walked into the bedroom, only to come to a complete stop.

He was not alone.

A woman lay in his bed. In the moonlight streaming in from the open French doors he could see a bare arm, the curve of a cheek and dark hair tangled on a white pillow.

His heart stopped for a full second, then resumed at a thundering pace. His body heated as blood raced down to his groin. He was instantly hard and ready to take.

Emma was in his bed.

Chapter Eight

Reyhan told himself to leave, to back out of the room before she awoke. As much as he wanted her, he couldn't have her. Not now, not ever. But he couldn't move. The passion was too strong. He could only stand in place and drink in her beauty.

He must have made a sound, or perhaps she sensed his presence, because she stirred, turned over then opened her eyes.

"Reyhan?" she asked, her voice sleepy. She pushed her hair out of her face and raised herself on one elbow. "What time is it?" She glanced at the clock, then back at him. "I've only been asleep for a couple of seconds. I thought…" She blinked. "Wait. What are you doing here?"

"This is my room."

"What?" She glanced around. "Oh." Her breath caught. "*Oh!* Right. I, ah, I had dinner with the king and your family and while we were eating someone came and told him that a pipe had broken in my suite. So he said he would put me somewhere else. Which turned out to be here. I thought it was weird, but it was late and I figured I would just stay here until morning, then straighten it out. I didn't think you'd be back tonight."

Of course she didn't. He hadn't told her when he would return. But he'd told his father who had most likely arranged for him to find Emma sleeping in his bed. While he was curious as to why his father wanted to tempt him with Emma, he was more concerned about the temptation itself. He had to get out of here before he said or did something he would regret. Before he gave in to the hunger consuming him.

"I'm sorry," she said, sitting up and drawing her knees to her chest. "I should have said something right away. I can go find somewhere else to sleep."

She started to climb out of the bed. He caught a glimpse of semitransparent fabric and sensuous curves.

"Don't," he said, turning away and staring blindly out the French doors. "Just stay there. I'll leave."

"But this is your room."

"Tonight it is yours."

Tonight and always, he thought, knowing he would never forget seeing her there. In the morning, when she was gone, he would haunt the rooms, searching for some hint of her presence, some clue that she'd been there at all.

"How were your meetings?" she asked. "They went well."

"Did you really have to go, or were you just avoiding me?"

The softly worded question surprised him. The Emma he remembered would never have been so bold. He returned his attention to her and found her sitting cross-legged, staring at the sheets.

"I was avoiding you, but not for the reasons you think." Her chin lifted and her eyes widened. "I don't understand."

Perhaps it was the night. Perhaps it was the ache inside of him, an ache that grew and fed on his soul. Perhaps it was the hint of sweetness in the air, the scent of which could only come from Emma. Perhaps it was madness. Regardless of the reason, he decided to speak the truth.

"I cannot be around you without wanting you," he said. "Rather than give in, I went away."

Understanding dawned slowly. The soft light of the moon

didn't allow him to see her blush, but he imagined it. She swallowed, then shrugged.

"Oh. I, ah…" She cleared her throat. "You mean sex."

Her acceptance nearly made him smile. He wasn't sure if she was trying to act casually or if she was truly unsurprised by his admission. What had she learned in their six years apart and who had been her teacher?

"I prefer to think of it as making love, but, yes."

She tucked her hair behind her ears. "I guess it's a guy thing," she said. "I never understood all the fuss."

He did his best not to react to her words, not to hope too much. "Your lovers have not pleased you?"

Her nose wrinkled. "I've sort of avoided the whole man-in-my-bed thing. It's not my style."

Two warring thoughts invaded his brain and produced two very different reactions. First was pleasure and relief that she hadn't been with anyone else. That she was still only his. The second was stung pride that he hadn't satisfied her when they'd been together. He knew now that he'd been too intent on his own release, on claiming her over and over. He hadn't taken the time to pleasure her.

"Not that it's your fault," she said, interrupting his internal battle. "I was too young. We went from kissing, to, well, you know, too fast for me. You were right about what you said before, that I wanted a schoolgirl's courtship with kisses and presents."

So hard that he thought he might explode, Reyhan forced himself to walk to the chair close to the bed and sit down.

"You were a virgin," he told her. "That fault lies with me. I was young and eager to take my bride. Too eager."

She ducked her head again. "Yes, well, it happens."

"It should not have happened that way. The women I had been with before had been older and more experienced. They had been the teacher and I the student. With you…" He clenched his teeth. "I should have been more patient, more understanding.

I should have seduced you with slow kisses and soft touches. Only when you were begging for more should I have taken you."

A shudder rippled through her body. "That sounds nice," she whispered. The slight quaver in her voice told him she was not unaffected by his words. The knowledge nearly propelled him to his feet and across the room to the bed. What would happen if he slid in beside her? Would she welcome him? Want him? Respond to him? Every cell in his body screamed for him to find out.

No! He could not. He knew the price of being with her again. A single moment of exquisite pleasure followed by a lifetime of wanting what he could not have. Better to not have her at all.

He forced himself to stand but not approach, and nearly shook with the intensity of his feelings. "Good night, Emma," he said as he turned away. "Sleep well."

"Reyhan, wait."

A rustle of sheets told him she had slid out of the bed. Her footsteps made no noise on the thick carpet but he *felt* her approach.

His blood boiled, his erection throbbed. It was more than he could bear and yet he did not turn around. He would not do this. No matter how much resisting cost him.

"Before," she whispered, her voice low and husky. "When you kissed me. It was different."

He thought of her passion, of how she'd clung to him, demanding as much as he. They'd fit together perfectly. Everything about her had called to him, yet he'd forced himself to pull back.

"It *was* different," he agreed. "I'm not that child anymore."

Five simple words—an invitation to paradise. He heard them and was nearly afraid to believe.

It doesn't matter, he told himself desperately. Taking her now, making love with her, would be a disaster. How would he let her go? How would he marry someone he didn't care about and live with her for the rest of his life? What of his future, his plans? What of being strong?

What of Emma?

Without thought, he turned slowly and stared at her. She stood only a few feet away, naked except for the diaphanous silk nightgown skimming her curves. Her long auburn hair tumbled over her shoulders; the curling ends lightly teased the tops of her breasts. Her eyes were bright, her lips slightly parted, her breathing rapid.

He told himself he could still resist her, and he nearly believed himself. Until she walked closer, raised herself on tiptoe and pressed her mouth to his.

The soft, gentle, chaste pressure undid him. It was as if the savage beast inside had been set free to prey upon the world. He grabbed her and pulled her close, wanting to touch everywhere at once. As his mouth settled on hers, he rubbed her back, her hips, then her fanny. He could feel the smoothness of her skin under the thin gown, but it wasn't enough. He needed more.

Tilting his head, he swept his tongue across her lower lip. When she parted for him, he plunged inside, stroking, exploring, needing. At the same time he tugged on the fabric of her gown, pulling it higher and higher until it bunched in his left hand. With his right, he stroked the now-bare skin of her hips, then slid up her back. She shivered and wrapped her arms around him.

He ground himself against her, rubbing his arousal against her belly. She flexed into him and moaned softly.

He let the nightgown fall back to her ankles and raised his hands to her shoulders. The thin straps slid down easily. He moved from her mouth to her jaw, then her neck, tasting her skin, licking, sucking, nipping. He bathed her long, slender neck with sensual attentions that made her shudder and cling to him. He bit her shoulder, then licked the wound.

The silk clung to her breasts, but one quick tug drew the fabric over her tight nipples so that it fluttered to the floor. Then she was naked.

Torn between looking and touching, he bent down and took her nipple in his mouth. He circled his tongue around the hard peak and she groaned her pleasure. She wrapped one arm around his shoulders and the other around his neck. Her fingers tunneled through his hair.

"Reyhan," she breathed. "It's too good. All of it."

Her words were like icy water thrown in his face. Reality crashed in on him as he realized what he was doing. Taking her hard and fast. They weren't even in bed. He was still fully dressed. Had he learned nothing?

Reyhan swore under his breath, which didn't bother Emma nearly as much as when he stopped what he'd been doing. He straightened, leaving her nipples damp and achy. Everywhere he'd touched, she burned. Tension tightened her muscles and made her tremble. She didn't even mind that she was naked— not as long as he kept touching her.

"I'm sorry," he breathed.

She stared at him, at his dilated dark eyes and the firm set of his mouth. "For what? I liked it."

One corner of his mouth pulled up in a smile. "I'm glad you liked it but my plan was to seduce, not take."

"Taking works. Really."

"That is because you haven't been seduced. Come. I will show you the difference."

He led her to the bed and urged her to lie down. While she made herself comfortable, he quickly stripped out of his clothes, leaving only the briefs covering his arousal. Her interest in the long, hard bulge dissipated when he slid in next to her and pulled her close.

"You are so beautiful," he whispered into her ear right before he took the lobe between his teeth and nibbled.

Shivers rippled across her skin.

"You're soft," he continued as he kissed below her ear, then down her throat. One of his hands lightly stroked her belly.

"The scent of your skin drives me wild with passion. I ache

to be inside of you. Filling you slowly, deeply, until your pleasure makes you scream your delight."

Scream? She didn't consider herself the type. But under the circumstances, she was willing to give it a try. Just the feel of his hand on her belly made her want to squirm. Up or down, she thought as he kissed her jaw. He needed to move that hand either up or down. Having it right there in the middle was making her crazy.

"The color of your nipples," he whispered. "Like a fully ripe peach.

Open your eyes."

The unexpected request took a second to sink in. Emma opened her eyes and saw Reyhan lean over her breasts. As she watched, he touched the tip of his tongue to the tip of her left nipple. The combination of seeing and feeling was the most erotic experience of her life. She cried out in delight.

He circled her nipple, then drew it fully into his mouth. The gentle sucking had her arching against him. At the same time, his hand finally dipped south, slipping through her curls and between her legs.

She parted for him, catching her breath as he rubbed against her slick center.

This was nothing like before, she thought as tension filled her body. She ached with every fiber of her being. When he shifted his fingers slightly and found a single spot of pleasure, she nearly rose off the bed.

"Reyhan," she breathed. "Don't stop."

Thankfully, he didn't. He continued to touch her, stroking her, teasing, circling, as he worshiped her breasts. The combination made her mind go blank, her legs go limp and her breathing come in fast pants. She couldn't bare herself enough to him. She wanted to be more naked, more exposed, more intimate.

Her wish was granted when he shifted so that he knelt between her legs and kissed his way down her belly. Part of her suspected what he was going to do while the rest of her couldn't believe it was really happening. She'd heard...she'd read...but before, he'd never...

He kissed her between her legs—an openmouthed kiss that made her tremble. Tension exploded inside of her as muscles tensed and collected. He found that one spot and licked it over and over until all she could do was dig her heels into the mattress and clutch the sheets with her hands. She tossed her head from side to side, tried to catch her breath, then gave up air completely as her release claimed her.

She hadn't known, she thought hazily as her body released and muscles contracted, that this much pleasure existed in the world. That she could feel so good, so right, so everything.

Her climax rippled through her and still he touched her, gentling the contact until the last drop had been wrung from her body. She opened her eyes and stared at him.

"I can't believe you did that." He smiled. "Better than before."

"Miraculous. I've never..." She wiggled, feeling more than a little selfconscious. "You know."

"Yes, I know."

He sat up and removed his briefs. She barely had time to gaze at his arousal before he settled between her legs and kissed her breasts. She felt a shivery kind of ache all over. Suddenly there were more possibilities than she'd ever realized and she wanted him inside of her.

"Yes," she whispered, as he raised his head and stared at her. "Be in me." She reached between them and guided him inside.

He was large and stretched her in the best way possible. She felt filled, yet the need for more grew.

He wrapped his arms around her, drawing her close so they pressed together everywhere. She clung to him, urging him deeper.

"More," she breathed as he withdrew only to fill her again.

The rhythmic thrusting made her pulse against him. She couldn't get enough and she couldn't seem to keep control. She strained toward him, reaching, needing, wanting. She dropped her hands to his hips to pull him closer.

"Take me," she begged. "Oh, Reyhan, yes."

In and out, in and out. Tension grew again. She couldn't focus on anything but what they were doing. And then her body convulsed in release and she could only hang on as he took her to heaven and back. At the very end, when she was sure there couldn't be anything else, he shuddered in her embrace and called out her name.

Later, when the moon had set and they were both lying naked under the covers, Emma rested her head on Reyhan's shoulder. He was warm and relaxed next to her. She had the thought that things could have been awkward between them, but he'd made everything so easy and right by simply pulling her close. As if he never planned on letting her go and this was exactly where she belonged.

Emma awoke to a bright sunny day and the feeling that she could quite possibly fly. As she lay in the large bed and relived her night with Reyhan, she felt herself smiling, tingling and fighting the urge to break out in song.

So *that* was what all the fuss was about, she thought happily as she rubbed her hand against the sheets where Reyhan had slept. Amazing how she'd missed the whole point before. Now she got it completely. Her only regret was that he hadn't taken her again and again, as he had on their honeymoon. For the first time, making love several times a day made perfect sense.

"We'll have tonight," she said as she tossed back the covers and stood. She was still naked, but there wasn't anyone around to see. After grabbing her robe from the foot of the bed, she walked into the bathroom and turned on the shower.

As she stepped into the steaming spray, she had the thought that night was really far off and maybe he wasn't doing anything for lunch. Or there was that massive desk in his office.

The surface might be a little hard, but the space had possibilities. She was still laughing when she began to shampoo her hair.

Forty minutes later she made her way through the hallways of the palace. She found Reyhan's office with only a single wrong turn and practically beamed at the man in the foyer.

"Princess Emma," he said, leaping to his feet. "I'll tell your husband you're here."

"Thank you."

Emma continued to smile at no one in particular and practically floated into Reyhan's office. He hung up the phone as she entered.

"Is there a problem?" he asked, sounding both distant and stern. "No. Of course not." She paused expectantly and waited.

He stared at her. A grandfather clock in the corner ticked. The silence grew.

She felt some of her happiness bleed away, and with the sensation came the chilling thought that he had regrets about what had happened.

After a few seconds, he rose and circled around his desk. "I'm very busy, Emma. Is there something you need?"

He spoke almost coldly, as if she were an assistant who had lingered too long. Trepidation clutched at her chest and she took a step back.

"I thought…" She swallowed. "I was just…" Mentioning her fantasy of a lunch break on his desk seemed impossible.

Who was this distant stranger? she wondered frantically. Where was the hotly passionate man from the previous night? What had happened?

He waited, watching her, giving nothing away. She remembered then that he'd tried to leave the bedroom and she'd been the one to stop him. Had she kept him against his will? Had he not wanted to make love with her? Had he done it out of obligation?

Her eyes began to burn but she refused to give in to tears. She was all grown up now, and she'd known what she was doing when she'd invited him into her bed. She'd *wanted* to make love with him. If there were consequences, they were her responsibility.

Pride squared her shoulders and raised her chin. She met his dark gaze.

Maybe this was the moment to get answers to her questions.

"Why did you ever marry me?" she asked. "And once you decided to return to Bahania, why did you *stay* married to me? I don't believe it was because you were afraid to tell your father what you'd done. You fear no man."

"It doesn't matter."

"Maybe not to you but I want to know what's going on. You disappeared from my life for years, then you dragged me back here, played the charming host, then disappeared. Last night—"

A knock on the closed door interrupted her. Reyhan frowned. "What is it?" he called.

His assistant stepped into the room. "I'm sorry, sir. I wouldn't have disturbed you except you and Princess Emma have been summoned by the king. He wishes to see both of you right away. It seems her parents have arrived at the palace."

"They can't be here," Emma murmured as she and Reyhan walked through the maze of corridors. "They don't like to fly. They never wanted me to. All our vacations were by car."

But here they were. As she followed Reyhan into a large reception room, she saw her parents standing with the king in an obviously awkward moment of silence.

When she came to a stop, Reyhan paused beside her. So far, he hadn't said anything, and she was grateful. This was going to be difficult enough without him taking on her family for withholding significant information from her for years.

In the second before they looked up and saw her, she studied them. Her mother was small and a little bent, her thick hair more gray than red, her father much taller and spare. They looked old, frail and out of place. Funny how all her life they'd seemed so powerful. She'd been afraid to defy them, to question the rules. Her only act of rebellion had been to fall in love with Reyhan and then run off with him, and she'd paid for that several times over. Now she saw they were just people. Older, out of their element and afraid for her. They had acted out of love, however misplaced, taking control because she'd never told them they shouldn't.

"Emma!" her mother shouted as she saw her. Both her parents rushed over and hugged her fiercely. Reyhan moved away.

"Are you all right?" her father asked. "Have they hurt you?"

"What? I'm fine. Everyone has treated me exceptionally well." She thought about last night. *Well* didn't begin to describe it.

"You shouldn't have left Dallas," her mother said as she brushed at Emma's sleeve. "You know you're not strong. Situations like this confuse you."

"I would think finding out you're a princess would confuse anyone," Emma said, trying to step back, but they held on tight.

Flanking her, they turned to the king. "We've filed an official complaint with the State Department protesting our daughter's kidnapping," her father said.

"Dad, no. I wasn't kidnapped. I'm here as the king's guest to deal with my marriage to Reyhan. You're seriously overreacting."

"Am I?" He looked at her. "You up and disappeared, you lied to us about where you'd gone. For all we know, they're brainwashing you."

From the corner of her eye she saw Reyhan take a step forward. Outrage darkened his features. She didn't want to think about how much her father had just insulted the king.

"I'm not being brainwashed," she said, then realized it was a foolish argument. If she was, would she know?

"As your daughter's husband, it is my duty to care for her," Reyhan said stiffly. "I assure you, her safety and well-being are my primary concern."

"Some concern," her mother said tartly. "You're the reason she's here in the first place. If you hadn't carted her off back then none of this would have happened. She was just a child."

"I was eighteen," Emma reminded her. "I loved him."

"You don't know what love is," her mother told her, still glaring at Reyhan.

"You seduced her and then ran off," her father added. "What kind of concern is that?"

Reyhan glared at the older man. "I attempted to contact her on several occasions. You're the ones who kept me from her."

"Good thing we did. Who knows what would have happened if we hadn't?"

She would have come to Bahania, Emma thought. She would have been Reyhan's wife. They would have had children.

"This isn't accomplishing anything," she told her parents. "I married Reyhan and now we all have to deal with it. I don't want you interfering. You already got between us once. It won't happen again."

Her mother stared at her. "You said you were here to get a divorce."

"I am, but—"

"Then there's nothing to get in the way of, is there?"

"No, but—"

Her mother narrowed her gaze. "We'll be taking our daughter with us this afternoon. If you would have someone pack up her things."

"I'm not leaving," Emma said. "Not yet."

"Why not?" her father wanted to know. "You can't possibly plan to—"

"Silence," the king said.

His voice wasn't especially loud, but something in the tone got everyone's attention. They all turned to him.

He smiled at her parents. "You are my honored guests for as long as you would like to stay in Bahania. Or you may leave at any time, as may your daughter."

That surprised her. Reyhan also looked startled. "The divorce," he said.

His father nodded. "That is a separate matter." The monarch paused.

Emma felt her insides clench in panic. Suddenly she didn't want to hear what King Hassan had to say. Was he granting the divorce a few days early? It made the most sense, but she didn't want him to. Things were too unsettled between herself and Reyhan. She needed to understand what last night had meant and why he'd been so cold this morning. She wanted to know what the fluttering when he was near meant. Was it just about sexual attraction or was there more?

Time. She needed time.

The king looked at her and it was as if he could read her mind. His kind eyes seemed to tell her that everything would be all right. To trust him. She took a deep breath and tried to relax.

"Despite Reyhan's request for a divorce, I am not convinced it is the right course of action," the king said.

"No!" her mother protested.

"This is an outrage," her father said.

Reyhan was completely silent and Emma felt only a sense of relief.

"It is my decision that Reyhan and Emma must get to know each other again. Something drew them together enough for them to impulsively marry. Was it a youthful prank or true love? Only time will tell. Therefore they must spend two months in each other's company. Not a day or a night apart. At the end of that time we will speak again. If they still both wish to divorce, I will grant it and their marriage will disappear as if it had never been."

Chapter Nine

Emma felt both relief and panic at the king's proclamation. Two months in Reyhan's company. If there were more nights like the previous one, that would hardly be difficult duty.

She glanced at the man who had married her. It was as if his expression were made of stone. She couldn't tell what he was thinking, nor could she see anything friendly or welcoming in his dark eyes. One thing she *was* sure of—he didn't look happy.

Without saying anything, Reyhan turned and left the room. Emma watched him go and tried to ignore the knot that returned to her stomach.

Beside her, her parents continued to protest.

"There has to be some legal court we can take this up with," her father said heatedly.

The king appeared more amused than insulted. "Mr. and Mrs. Kennedy, please." He opened his arms in a gesture of welcome. "You are honored guests in my country. I would ask you to stay here in the palace as long as you would like. Visit with your daughter. Get to know my people. You will find things very pleasant. As for your daughter—" he smiled at Emma "she is a charming young woman. You must be very proud."

Her mother sniffed. "Of course we are. She's a very good girl."

Emma felt like a wayward puppy who had finally been pronounced housebroken.

"I do not wish to be unreasonable." The king turned to her father. "You are right—there are courts and laws. They state all royal marriages must be approved by the king. Reyhan defied me when he married your lovely daughter. Having met Emma, I can forgive his impulsiveness. Who could blame him?"

While she appreciated the compliment, she thought he was laying it on a little thick.

"This isn't her world," her mother said. "She belongs home, with us."

"She is a grown woman. Perhaps it is time for *her* to say where she belongs. In two months she will have that opportunity."

He beckoned someone from the rear of the room. Emma saw several servants approaching.

"Show the Kennedys to their quarters," he said, then nodded and left.

Emma's mother huffed. "Just like that. You have a life. Has he forgotten that? Responsibilities. A job."

Emma blinked in surprise. Honestly, she'd forgotten all about that. Her world back home. Funny how it had faded from her memory so quickly.

"You're right. I'll have to take a leave of absence."

"They won't like that," her father told her. "You've not even been working there a year."

Good point. "I'll have to explain things," she said, not sure how she was going to. Would anyone believe her? "If I do get fired, I'll find another job when I get home."

"A very cavalier attitude," her mother said. "You were raised better than that."

"Mom, I know you're worried. I appreciate that, and I know you only came here because you care about me. But I'm twenty-four. It's time to let me live my life my own way. If I make mistakes, then I'll recover from them."

Her mother's mouth dropped open, while her father seemed equally surprised. She took advantage of the silence and smiled at one of the servants.

"Okay," she said. "Lead the way." She linked arms with her parents. "You two are going to love this place. The rooms are amazing. And the views, even better than when we went to Galveston my senior year of high school."

Her mother sighed. "I don't like any of this, Emma. It's not you."

"I know. But from what I can tell, I don't have a choice. The king has to give his permission for a prince to get a divorce. So I'm stuck here until that happens."

Two months with Reyhan. What would that time bring? Would she learn to understand the man she'd married so impulsively? Would she be eager to leave when the time was up? Or would she find herself falling in love? And if it was the latter, would he love her back or would he still want to get rid of her so he could marry someone else?

Reyhan didn't return to his offices. Instead he walked to the garages where he took the keys for a Jeep and drove out of the city. An hour later, surrounded by desert, he stepped out into the warm afternoon and raised his face to the sky.

He wanted to yell his frustration, to rip and tear something. Anything. He wanted to travel north, deep into the inhospitable land and become someone else.

Two months. It was an eternity. How could he survive spending his days and nights with her? How could he be close to her and not reach for her?

Last night had been paradise. A miracle. When he'd left her bed this morning all he'd been able to think about was how much he wanted her. Having her had only increased his need. When she'd walked into his office, he'd held on to his control with every ounce of will he possessed. Just a few minutes longer and he would have snapped.

"I am Prince Reyhan of Bahania," he yelled to the heavens. "I am a man of power, of substance."

Yet in the presence of a mere woman he was weak. He would travel any distance, complete any task, risk life, limb anything, just for Emma.

He clutched the side of the Jeep. There had to be a solution somewhere. An answer, a trick, a way to survive two months around her without going mad. He couldn't give in and take her into his bed. If he did, he would never let her go. And if she stayed...

He sucked in a breath as he considered the possibility. To have her stay was to love her. To give her his very soul. Then he would be nothing but a shell of a man. A spineless creature—a parasite.

No! That could never happen. Somehow he would conquer this. He would find the strength to turn away from her. To resist her. When the time was up, he would let her go. It was the only way. The alternative was unthinkable.

Emma went with her parents to the guest suite. It was similar to the one she'd had and even the ever sensible and conservative George and Janice Kennedy were impressed.

"You can see the ocean," her mother said as she stared out the large French doors.

"It's the Arabian Sea," Emma told her. "Bahania has some beautiful beaches. Tourism is an important industry."

Her father opened the suitcase one of the servants had left on the bed. "I can't believe they wanted to unpack for us. Like we're invalids or something."

"It's not that they thought you were incapable," Emma said. "It's part of the service."

"I've always done my own cooking and cleaning," her mother reminded her. "I never did understand those women who pay someone else to come in and clean their dirt. It's not right."

Her mouth pressed together as tears filled her eyes. "None of this is right."

Emma took her hand and led her back into the large living room. Her father followed. When the two of them were seated on the sofa, she curled up in the wing chair across the glass-topped coffee table.

"We have to talk about it," she said.

Her mother pulled a lace-edged hankie out of her sleeve. "There's nothing to say. That man was trouble before and he's trouble now."

"Don't distress yourself, Janice," her father said gently. "We're here now and we'll make sure our girl is safe."

"I know. It's just… This place. It's so big and fancy."

"The palace is amazing," Emma said, trying not to get sucked into a familiar pattern of panic when she upset her parents. Knowing she made her mother cry was enough to give her a stomachache for three days. But she couldn't keep giving in. King Hassan had been right when he'd said it was time for her to make some decisions about her life.

"All this is happening now because we didn't straighten things out six years ago," she said.

Her father sighed. "We went over this, kitten."

The familiar name made her stiffen. For years she's loved that he called her that, but now she wasn't so sure. A kitten was hardly a force to be reckoned with.

"You should have told me what was going on," she said quietly. "I had the right to know that Reyhan had tried to see me."

Her mother started to speak, but Emma held up her hand to stop her. "If I was old enough to get married, I was old enough to know the truth."

"But you would have gone away with him," her mother wailed. "We would never have seen you."

"Is that what this was all about? Keeping me close?"

Her parents looked at each other, then at her. "We only wanted what was best for you," her father said. "We love you."

Why had she been afraid of defying them for so long? she wondered. They were just people. Misguided, maybe. She might not agree with their decision, but she believed they'd done what they thought was right. Their motivation had been selfish, but only because they cared about her.

"Emma, we should have said something about the money," her mother admitted. "It was such a large amount. It's not that Reyhan was bad, it's just that he wasn't like us. You were so sad. When you were happy again, we wanted to keep you that way."

Emma didn't know what to feel. Loss for what could have been. Although would she and Reyhan have had a chance all those years ago? At eighteen she'd barely been able to take care of herself. How would she have handled a husband, and maybe a child?

"It's done," she said, wanting to move on. "We can't change it and now we have a different situation to deal with."

Her mother sighed. "I can't believe the king is going to insist you stay here two months. That's barbaric."

Emma smiled. "You can call living in the palace a lot of things, but not that. Besides, I want a chance to get to know Reyhan again."

Her parents exchanged a look of worry and panic. "Is that such a good idea, kitten?" her father asked.

"I don't know. I loved him once."

"You were just a little girl."

"Legally, I was an adult," she said, silently admitting that on the inside she'd been a child. "But that's not the point. As King Hassan said, there's a reason the two of us ran off."

Her mother pressed her lips together. "We all know what *his* reason was.

He was little more than an animal."

Emma thought of what had happened the previous night. A little more animal-like behavior would be fine with her.

"You two have loved each other for nearly fifty years. Don't you want that for me?"

"Not with him," her father said. "Can't you find a nice boy back home? Emma, you're only twenty-four. You have years before you have to settle down and get married."

"I'm already married. I'm staying the two months, and I'm going to take the time to get to know Reyhan again."

Her mother's eyes welled with tears. "But what if you fall in love with him?"

Would she? "It's a chance I'm willing to take."

"Oh, Emma. He broke your heart before. What's to stop him from doing it again?"

Good question. "I have to risk it. I'm sorry. I know you want to protect me but this time you can't. I have to do it on my own. So I'm going to ask you to trust me."

Her elderly parents stared at her. She sensed their misgivings and fear.

Then they looked at each other and nodded.

"All right, kitten," her father said. "If this is what you really want, we'll stand by your decision."

"When he destroys you, we'll be here to pick up the pieces," her mother added. "We'll take you home and you can move back into your own room." Talk about motivation to make things work with Reyhan, Emma thought. Still, she wouldn't let her parents sway her one way or the other.

The king had granted her the gift of time and she intended to take advantage of it.

Emma spent the afternoon with her parents. She took them on a tour of the palace, the gardens and the chapel. They seemed to enjoy the dozens of cats more than anything. An hour before dinner, she returned to the room she now shared with Reyhan and called her supervisor back in Dallas. Fifteen minutes later she found herself on indefinite leave and accepting good wishes that it all work out for the best.

If only, she thought as she hung up the phone.

She leaned back on the sofa and tried to figure out what to

do next. She was having dinner with her parents. There would be a more formal event with the king and several ministers the following evening, and a party later in the weekend.

"A whirlwind of social events," she murmured to herself, trying not to feel nervous as she watched the clock and waited for Reyhan to return. However much he might want to avoid it, they *had* to talk, and the sooner the better.

Thirty minutes later, she'd given up trying to read her book. Sixty minutes later she was pacing the room with the intensity of an athlete training for an Olympic event. When the main door of the suite finally opened, Emma nearly stumbled in shock.

Elation, excitement and trepidation coiled together in her stomach as she searched Reyhan's face, hoping for a clue as to what he was thinking. There wasn't one.

"Good evening," he said when he saw her. "Are your parents settled?"

Not the words of a man overwhelmed by passion and desire, she thought sadly as she fought her own visceral reactions to being in the same room as the man who had taught her what all the fuss was about.

"Yes. They love their rooms." A slight exaggeration, but he was unlikely to press her. "How are you?"

"Fine."

He walked past her into the bedroom. She trailed after him, wishing he'd said a little more. "I'm having dinner with my parents tonight," she said. "You're welcome to come, but you don't have to. I know they probably make you uncomfortable."

Reyhan shrugged out of his suit jacket. "I would think the situation would be the reverse."

That he made them nervous? Probably. "Would you care to join us?" she asked. "Do you have to because of what the king said?" Days *and* nights together. She still wasn't sure what that meant.

He loosened his tie. "My father's statement was meant to

keep me from taking an extended business trip. We are not required to spend every waking second in each other's company."

Too bad. She twisted her hands together. "I didn't know what to do about staying here. Should I? Do you want me to move to one of the guest rooms?"

Reyhan pulled his tie free of his shirt collar. "No. Stay here. I'll sleep in the second bedroom."

Supreme happiness crashed in and burned in a tenth of a second. "There's another bedroom?" she asked, because the alternative was to ask why he didn't want them to sleep together.

"I have a small office at the other end of the suite. I'll have a bed brought in. We'll have to share the living quarters and the bathroom, but I'll make every effort not to get in your way."

"But I… But we…" She swallowed and took a step toward him. "Reyhan, what's going on? Why are you acting like this?"

He pulled his shirttail out of his trousers. Her gaze dropped to his belt and she had the sudden fantasy that he was going to get naked in front of her. Wouldn't that be a treat?

His expression turned weary. "It is only two months," he said. "Surely you can endure my company that long."

"Enduring your company isn't the problem. Last night…" She cleared her throat. "Reyhan, we made love."

He turned away and crossed to the French doors. "It will not happen again."

Stark words that clawed at her heart. "Because you don't want me?"

Because it wasn't good? Hadn't she pleased him? Last night she'd been so sure, but now…

Her throat tightened, as did her chest. Her legs felt heavy and thick, as if they belonged to someone else.

He bowed his head briefly. "Two months, Emma. That is all. At the end of that time, you can return to Texas where you belong."

And he would stay here, marry another woman and have children with her.

* * *

"But I thought…"

He turned to her. She'd never seen such coldness in a man's eyes before.

Such rejection. "You thought wrong."

"I swear, there should be a law allowing wives of princes to lock their husbands in chains once a month. Just to keep them in line," Princess Sabrina said, grinning.

"Would you want to beat him, too?" Cleo asked as she reached for a slice of cantaloupe.

"Only when he really makes me crazy. Probably every third month."

"Works for me," Princess Zara said cheerfully. "Not that I'd ever want to hurt Rafe, but threatening him from time to time would make me really happy."

The three women laughed with delight. Emma smiled, knowing however big they talked, none of them was anything but completely in love with their husbands. She'd sensed it from the first moment they'd met.

Cleo had arrived that morning to invite her to lunch. "Without your folks," she'd insisted. "Not that they're not great, but you need a break."

Sabrina and Zara, both daughters of the king, although by different mothers, had been charming as they'd welcomed Emma.

"So you're the mystery woman Reyhan married," Sabrina said as she passed around a plate of tea sandwiches. She was seven or eight months pregnant and a beauty with dark eyes and lustrous red hair.

Zara, equally pretty but in a more quiet way, looked like her sister but with dark auburn hair. She was pregnant, as well, but not so far along.

"I don't consider myself a mystery," Emma said, which was true.

Compared with being a princess, her life was pretty boring.

"Reyhan never said a word," Sabrina told her. "Not that any of my brothers are the chatty type. But a wife. That's a big secret to keep." She tilted her head and smile. "Then you appear out of the blue. Are you completely freaked?"

"Pretty much."

"I would be, too," Zara told her. "Sabrina grew up with all this, so she's used to it, but for the rest of us it's been a challenge."

Cleo laughed. "It's true. Zara resisted being a princess for the longest time."

"So did you," Zara reminded her.

"For different reasons. You were one by birth. Sadik wanted me to be one by marriage."

Emma was confused. "Didn't you want to marry him? You're so in love."

"It's complicated," Cleo told her. "A story for another time." She leaned over the back of the sofa in her suite and checked on Calah. "This is the best baby in the universe. She never cries, she sleeps like a dream and I swear she has an IQ of about two hundred."

Sabrina and Zara rolled their eyes. Emma laughed.

"She's *very* smart," Cleo said, sounding huffy. "You guys wait until your babies are born. You'll see what I mean."

"Sure, Cleo," Sabrina said. "I'm guessing we'll all be as goofy as you about our children."

"You mock me now, but just you wait."

"Watch yourself," Sabrina said to Emma. "There's something about this palace. It's pregnancy central. Be careful or you'll catch a baby of your own."

The three women laughed and Emma tried to join in, not that she was very successful. It was hard to joke when she'd just realized that she and Reyhan hadn't used protection when they'd made love.

She sucked in a breath and tried to stay calm. It had only been one time, she reminded herself. A quick calculation told her the day had been safe, relatively speaking. So she was unlikely to be pregnant. Based on how he was avoiding her, she wasn't going to be in a position to have a second chance at getting pregnant, either. Which was good. Right?

She *was* happy not to have to deal with an unexpected baby. Except she could easily picture herself with Reyhan's child. Holding him or her and overwhelmed by love. That would be wonderful.

She knew Reyhan wanted children, just not with her. Which made her wonder why. He'd been willing to marry her before. Why was he so determined *not* to be married to her now? She didn't think there was anyone else in his life. He'd said he would accept an arranged union. So she— "Earth to Emma," Zara said. "Are you still with us?"

Emma blinked and saw all three women looking at her. "Sorry. I was lost in thought."

"I bet I know who was starring in that fantasy," Sabrina said teasingly. "It would be romantic if it wasn't my brother."

Emma felt herself coloring. "No, really. It was nothing."

As she'd never been a very good liar, she wasn't surprised when they didn't buy her story.

"Maybe there's more going on than we know about," Cleo said. "Which could be interesting."

"We'd love to have you as part of our princess sisterhood," Zara told her. "Think about it."

"Thanks."

She appreciated the invitation more than she could say. She'd always wanted a sister. But staying or not staying wasn't just up to her. Reyhan had a part in it, and based on what she'd seen so far, he couldn't wait to have her gone.

Chapter Ten

Two days later Emma accompanied her parents down to the stable. The king had suggested Reyhan take them out into the desert to show them some of Bahania's natural beauty. She was relatively sure her husband had agreed to the outing because he didn't have a choice. Ever since they'd shared that one night, he'd made it more than clear that spending time in her company was about as pleasant as root canal surgery.

What hurt her was that her feelings were so different. Since sharing a bed, she couldn't stop thinking about being with him in other ways. She wanted to talk to him, get to know him, laugh, tease, make memories. She wanted him to hold her close instead of stiffening every time she was near.

"Are you sure this is safe?" her mother asked as they crossed the stone courtyard leading to the stable. "Aren't there robbers and pirates in the desert?"

"Pirates are on the ocean," her father said gently. "However, we're going to have to deal with robbers."

Emma held in a sigh. She loved her parents very much but in the last couple of days they'd really started to get on her nerves. They weren't open to any new experiences and, despite the wonders of the palace, they kept talking about how much they wanted to go home. When she encouraged them to make plans they refused, telling her they wouldn't leave without her. The thought of two months in such close quarters made her teeth ache.

But that was a problem for another time. Right now she had to worry about the fact that Reyhan stood by the front of the stable, and upon seeing him she felt her heart rate quadruple while her thighs began to quiver.

"Good morning," Reyhan said as they approached.

He wore riding boots, dark slacks and a loose white shirt. Despite the short hair and freshly shaven face, Emma had the thought that he looked as dangerous as the pirates her mother feared.

But as appealing as she found him, he didn't seem to return her interest. He neither looked directly at her nor acknowledged her personally. He motioned to a large open vehicle—part roofless SUV, part topless van. There were three rows of seats.

"You'll be comfortable for our trip out to the oasis."

"Is it safe?" her mother asked. "Are there a lot of wild people and robbers on the loose?"

Emma winced. "Mom," she said quickly, "Bahania is a very civilized country."

Reyhan's expression didn't change. "The laws of the desert offer hospitality to all who enter. You will be welcomed by my people and treated as an honored guest." He motioned to the vehicle.

Emma's parents exchanged a glance before cautiously stepping inside. She hung back, wanting more than an impersonal trip with a man who was doing his best to become a stranger.

"I thought we'd be riding," she said.

He looked at her for the first time that morning. She felt the impact of his gaze all the way down to her already-curling toes.

"Do you know how?"

"I've had a few lessons." When she was twelve. "I'm a whiz on horses made of wood, but I can probably handle the real thing if he or she is gentle and doesn't think tossing me would be good for a chuckle."

Reyhan's dark eyes didn't flicker, nor did his mouth even twitch. When exactly had he turned into a man of stone?

"Wait there," he said, and walked into the stable.

"Emma, what are you doing?" her mother asked fretfully.

"Reyhan and I are going to ride."

Both of her parents shrank back in their seats. "You can't."

"Sure I can. It will be fun."

Her father frowned. "When did you get so adventurous?"

She considered the question. "I can't give you an exact date," she admitted, knowing her change of heart had something to do with finding out nothing in her life was as she had first thought. Her parents weren't perfect. In fact they'd lied and kept the truth from her. Sure their actions had been in the name of keeping her safe, but she'd been an adult. The decisions hadn't been theirs to make. Not only that, but she'd been married for the past six years and hadn't had a clue. Information like that was bound to produce a change.

Reyhan returned, leading a beautiful white stallion. Emma might not know much about horses, but she'd heard rumors.

"Isn't he going to be too much for me to handle?" she asked, trying not to back up as Reyhan and the horse approached. Up close the animal seemed extremely large.

"He can have a temper, but he's very fond of the ladies."

The horse in question tossed his head, then seemed to give her the onceover. He looked large enough to pound her into the ground with just one hoof—the thought of which didn't exactly give her a warm fuzzy feeling inside.

"Great," she murmured. "A sexist horse. What's his name?"

For the first time in days, Reyhan smiled at her. "Prince."

"How appropriate."

She approached the powerful horse and tentatively stroked his nose. Prince stepped in close and rubbed his head against her arm, then bumped her side and exhaled.

"Is he flirting with me?" she asked, not wanting to know what the big animal would do if he lost his temper.

"Yes. He likes you. We'll ride out and take the Jeep back."

Reyhan murmured something to the horse, then moved to its side and made a step by lacing his fingers together. Emma remembered enough from her long-ago lessons to know she was expected to jump right up in that saddle. She sucked in a breath for courage and put her foot in his hands.

Not only was Prince's back about four hundred feet from the ground, the English saddle she settled in offered about as much protection as a handkerchief.

"There's nothing to hang on to," she said rather desperately as Reyhan handed her the reins.

"You'll be fine."

She would be maimed and possibly crippled, she thought, fighting fear.

Reyhan disappeared into the stable, presumably to get his own horse. "Emma, you can't ride that beast," her mother said. "It's not safe. Come down right now and sit with us."

The order gave her the impetus to stiffen her spine and smile brightly. "I'll be fine. We aren't going to go all that fast."

At least she hoped they wouldn't. It was a long way to the ground. Reyhan returned with an even bigger gray stallion and mounted easily. "The Jeep takes a longer route using the main road," he told her. "We'll cut across the desert and meet your parents at the oasis."

"Works for me," she said, thinking time alone with him might give them a chance to talk.

He waved off the driver and the Jeep pulled out. Reyhan gave her a few instructions, then watched her ride in slow circles. She found that her lessons from long ago came back to her and she quickly settled into the horse's rhythmic gate. After a few minutes, Reyhan led the way off the stable grounds and into the wild beauty of the open desert.

The morning was warm and brilliantly sunny. She was grateful for her hat and the sunscreen she'd slathered on her face. The hard-packed trail was easy to spot. She and Prince walked along behind Reyhan and his mount. When they went faster, Prince also picked up the pace. There were a couple of minutes of bone-jarring trotting before they settled into an easy canter. Reyhan pulled his horse to the side of the trail so they could ride next to each other.

The wind tugged strands of hair free from her braid. She tossed her head to get them out of her face and nearly slid off her horse. Reyhan shot out a hand and grabbed her arm. She managed to stay in the saddle, but only just. The slick leather seat suddenly felt smaller and more precarious.

"We will walk the rest of the way," Reyhan called as he tugged on his reins.

She slowed Prince, then glanced at the man next to her. "Sorry to be a bother."

"The fault is mine. You took to the riding so easily, I thought you were more experienced."

They walked side by side. Emma chose, then discarded several possible conversational openings. They all sounded forced and stupid, so she settled on the truth.

"I know you didn't want to do this today. Be with me and my parents, I mean. I appreciate you arranging everything and then coming along."

"It is important that you all enjoy your time in Bahania." Before they left, she thought glumly.

"Seeing the desert will help you understand our ways," he said. "The desert is filled with tradition. For centuries nomads have wandered through the vastness of these lands. Thieves preyed on those using the silk road."

"Great. My mother was worried about being robbed."

He raised his eyebrows. "Those times are long past. Today those who live in the desert protect the oil fields to earn their living. A combination of the old ways and the new."

"Sounds like a good plan."

He shrugged. "There are those who do not wish to work. They want to take—much like the thieves of old."

She glanced around at the rolling dunes, the few clusters of scrubby plants. "Take what?"

"Money. They threaten our oil fields with disaster if we don't pay them off."

She caught her breath. "That's illegal, isn't it?"

"Yes. We know who these boys are. Most are second and third sons of nomadic chiefs. As they will not inherit, they are locked out of the family wealth. Instead of earning a living, they seek something more profitable and to their minds, easier. They play at being men."

"Are you going to have them arrested?"

He shook his head. "I have given my word to their fathers that I won't lock them up without cause. Mere threats are not considered cause, not out here. So we wait and watch. Sometimes angry young men grow up. Sometimes not."

"I don't understand," she admitted. "Why wouldn't their fathers want them to go to prison? What they're doing is wrong."

"To a man of the desert, there is no greater torture than to be locked away from the sun. I won't arrest anyone until he gives me a reason. This information does not make my head of security very happy."

"Hardly a surprise."

This was the longest conversation they'd had since they'd spent the night together. Emma wondered if Reyhan was thawing toward her or simply making the best of a bad situation.

"I'm sorry this is so difficult for you," she said. "Having me stay.

Having my parents here. All of it."

"The time will pass."

Not exactly words to warm her heart. She wanted to remind him that a few days ago he'd wanted her with a passion that had thrilled them both. That he had kissed her and touched her. Remembering their time together made her stomach clench and her body burn.

"What if I just left?" she asked.

He continued to look straight ahead. "Nothing would change. When you returned, the ticking clock would continue. My father can be most stubborn."

She thought about how Reyhan avoided her as if she had some disease he didn't want to catch. How he barely spoke to her and never laughed anymore. The stubbornness seemed to be an inherited trait.

They arrived at the oasis about an hour later. Emma's parents were already there and rushed to greet their daughter. Reyhan watched them, wondering at their anxiousness. She had been with him and he would have died to keep her safe. Not that her parents had ever trusted him.

He dismounted and moved beside Emma's horse. Her mother glared at him as he helped Emma down. Even with her parents watching and disapproving, he noticed the warmth of her body and the way she leaned against him while she regained her footing.

"So I have a way to go before I'm an accomplished horsewoman," she said with a smile. "At least I survived."

He wanted to smile back at her and tell her that he would be happy to teach her to ride. He wanted to put his arm around her and draw her closer against him. He wanted to kiss her and touch her and be with her. Instead he stepped back and turned away.

"This oasis is not considered large. There are others deeper in the desert that cover several acres. But many families travel here because they can be close to the city while maintaining their old ways."

"Is it safe for us to wander around?" Emma asked. "Are there any things we shouldn't do? I don't want to offend anyone."

"You are an honored guest. You will be welcome." He looked at the small campsite set up around the pond of water. Children played with each other. The women talked together over the open fires, while the men tended the camels. Their arrival had been noticed, but his people would wait for him to make the first move.

"You have nothing to worry about," he said. "Are you sure?"

He nodded, not surprised by her concern. One of the things he'd liked about her when they'd first met had been her soft heart. She cared about others—an unusual characteristic in the women he generally met.

Emma linked arms with her parents. "Isn't this fabulous?" she said happily. "Let's go introduce ourselves."

"They're strangers," her mother said. "We don't know if they speak English."

"Most do not," he confirmed.

"Then we'll have to fake it," Emma said, and pulled her parents toward the women.

He resisted the need to walk with her and claim her as his own by staying close. His presence was enough protection, he reminded himself. Even though she didn't need any.

He looked at the men hovering by the pen of camels. When he nodded, they approached, then bowed and offered greetings of respect. He recognized the oldest man, the chief of the small tribe, as someone who had ridden the desert with his father.

"Bihjan," he said, returning the bow. "I bring greetings from my father."

"I return those greetings and wish blessings on you and your family."

"And to yours."

The old man looked at Emma and her parents. "She is as beautiful as the sunrise."

Pride filled Reyhan. "My wife."

The old chief showed no surprise. "I see your blessings have already begun. You care for her."

Reyhan nodded rather than speak the truth—that *care* didn't come close. She was his life, his breath, and he wasn't sure he would survive without her.

"She will give you fine sons."

"If it is to be," he said simply, ignoring the tightness in his chest when he thought about children. He and Emma had made love without protection. He'd been so caught up in the moment, he'd never thought, never considered the consequences. If she was pregnant...

He cast the worry away. She couldn't be. If she were pregnant, she would stay forever, and being with her would destroy him. But to have a child with her...

He returned his attention to the chief. "You have been blessed with many sons," he said.

Bihjan nodded, his eyes dark with worry. "My youngest son, Fadl, leads the renegades," he said quietly. "I know what they do, what threats they make."

"I have given my word," Reyhan reminded the old man. "If their threats remain empty, then I will do nothing. Perhaps in time, they will grow up enough to rejoin their people and become honorable men."

Bihjan sighed with relief. "I had heard it was so, but I wanted to ask for myself. I know these young men try your patience."

"My security chief's, as well. He believes they should be arrested and put in prison. I have explained that to be so confined is a form of death for men of the desert." He narrowed his gaze. "But be warned. My patience has limits. If any of the renegades acts in the smallest way, if their talk becomes action, my retribution will be swift and severe."

The old man nodded. "As it should be, Prince Reyhan. As it should be."

Emma loved everything about the oasis. The people were charming and at least two of the women understood a little English—at least enough for them to attempt to communicate. The children were beautiful and friendly and fun. She adored the dogs and the baby camels and the clever way the camp itself came together after being carted across miles of desert. Even her parents seemed to be having a reasonably good time, asking questions more than complaining. Maybe there was hope for them after all.

"They have invited us to dine with them," Reyhan said as he came up to stand next to her. "I have accepted."

Emma instantly glanced at the pen holding the camels and swallowed. "So, uh, what will be on the menu?"

Reyhan smiled. "Fear not. It's chicken."

"That's a relief. I don't think I could chow down on something I'd just petted and cooed over."

"I would not expect you to." He took her arm and pulled her away from everyone. "I told them you were my wife, without mentioning the pending divorce."

"Okay. That makes sense. The situation is complicated." She didn't know how to tell him she didn't mind him claiming her as his wife with no "but" tacked on.

"I wanted you to know," he said. "Thank you."

They were called to dinner. Everyone sat around in a circle. Dishes were passed from person to person. Emma sampled spicy rice casseroles and tender chicken. There were flat breads and grilled vegetables. Two teenage boys played three-stringed musical instruments and a young girl with bells around her wrists and ankles danced for them.

"Can they afford to feed us like this?" Emma asked after a tray of honey-coated dates were offered. "I don't want them to starve or anything because they played generous host with us."

His dark gaze lingered on her face. "I appreciate your concern for my people. Do not worry. I have taken care of things."

She trusted that he had. Reyhan was a good man, a man she could admire. What would he say if he knew that she wanted these people to be her people, as well? That the more time she spent in Bahania, the more she liked the country and was confident she could have made a home here?

After the meal, several of the women rose and disappeared into one of the tents. A few of the men wandered off toward the camels. Emma started to rise, but Reyhan put a hand on her arm.

"There's more to come," he said. "I'm pretty full."

"It's not food."

Sure enough, a young girl walked up and knelt in front of Emma. She held out her hand, offering a beautiful blue and red enameled necklace. Emma looked at it, then at him.

"I can't take that."

"You have to. You're their princess and they want to show respect." He leaned close and lowered his voice. "Don't worry. All that is expected is that you are enthusiastic and love everything. When we leave, the gifts stay behind."

"Good thing," she murmured as she noticed a teenage boy leading several camels toward her.

Still caught up in how Reyhan's warm breath had tickled her skin, she accepted the necklace, kissed the girl on both cheeks and thanked her warmly. Reyhan slid the necklace over her neck.

There were more pieces of jewelry offered, several bolts of amazing silk, four adult camels and one baby camel. The only gift she had trouble returning was a sweet puppy who licked her entire face and wiggled to get closer.

When she'd thanked everyone and carefully left all the smaller gifts on a blanket by the fire, she walked toward the SUV with Reyhan.

"They were wonderful people," she said. "Do the children go to school?"

He nodded. "They attend several months at a time, then return to their families. We are fortunate in that we can afford excellent teachers and modern schools that can meet the needs of children from the city and from the desert."

Emma thought about what Cleo had said—how she did charity work in her free time. Would that have been available to Emma, as well? Although she loved her job and knew she helped through one of life's greatest miracles, she was willing to admit to wanting to help on a grander scale.

Not likely, she told herself. Not when she was leaving and Reyhan was marrying someone else.

By the end of the week, Emma's parents had settled into life in Bahania. Emma was pleased to watch their attitudes slowly change from hostile mistrust of everything to pleasant acceptance. She would have loved to discuss the surprising transition with Reyhan but he continued to avoid her. So much for spending their days and nights together, she thought as she leaned close to the mirror and applied mascara to her lashes. They might physically be in the same palace, but they rarely spoke anymore. Reyhan worked impossible hours then disappeared into the guest room. The only time she saw him was at command dinners by the king.

At least tonight would be different. There was a large formal state occasion that was doubling as a welcome party for her parents. Reyhan had already informed her he was to be her escort. She would have been a lot more excited if he'd at least pretended to be happy about spending the evening with her. Instead he'd looked about as thrilled as a man facing the loss of both legs and an arm. She was determined to change his mind.

After finishing with her makeup, she pulled the hot rollers out of her hair, then fluffed the ends. After bending over at the waist, she sprayed her hair from underneath, then flipped her head to let the curls fall back into place.

"Not bad," she murmured as she finger combed a few wayward strands.

Next up was the bronze beaded evening gown. She slipped it on and pulled up the zipper, then stepped into her high-heeled sandals.

She studied her reflection and knew this was as good as it was going to get. If she couldn't dazzle Reyhan like this, it wasn't going to happen.

"Good luck," she whispered to her reflection, then walked out of the bathroom and into the sitting area.

Reyhan was already there. She nearly stumbled when she saw him in his well-tailored tux. His shoulders were broad and strong, his features lean and handsome. Her heart swelled with an affection she didn't want to name.

"You look beautiful," he told her. "Thank you. You look great, too."

He held out a velvet-covered box, about ten inches square and only a couple of inches deep.

"For you."

She hesitated before accepting the gift and opening it. When she saw the contents, her breath caught in amazement.

A yellow diamond necklace lay on a bed of white silk. The graduated diamonds had to be at least three carats each in front, and nearly a carat in back by the clasp. Two clusters of yellow diamonds formed earrings and there was a white and yellow diamond bracelet.

Emma reached for the necklace only to find she was shaking too much to pick it up.

"I can't," she told him. "It's too much."

"You are my wife," Reyhan said, taking the box from her and setting it on the table. He removed the necklace and placed it around her neck. "Who would wear these if not you?"

"The next woman you marry," she said as he handed her the earrings. "You'll want these things passed down to your children."

As she spoke, she looked at him. Some emotion crossed his face but it was gone before she could read it. Awareness crackled between them and when he held out the bracelet to her, she wanted desperately to toss it aside and fling herself in his arms instead.

But she didn't. She let him fasten on the bracelet, then admired the fiery stones. She would wear these lovely things tonight but with the intent of leaving them behind. They were a part of his heritage and she had no right to claim them. If things had been different... But they weren't.

"Reyhan—" She touched his forearm, feeling the warmth of him and the tension of his muscles. "I want to mention something. About when we were together."

He didn't speak but a muscle twitched in his jaw. "There is nothing to say."

"Yes, there is. We didn't…" She cleared her throat. "When we made love…" She stopped and gathered her thoughts. "We didn't use any protection. I wasn't sure if you were worried about consequences. There aren't any. I wanted to reassure you that I wasn't pregnant."

"I see. You're sure?"

More than sure. Three days ago she'd gotten her period. "Positive."

He didn't say anything else as he led her to a large mirror in the dining room. He placed her in front of it and stood behind her with his hands on her shoulders.

"The jewels complete you," he said.

She looked at the elegant stones glittering at her ears and around her neck. They were lovely, but they didn't complete her. Only he could do that. She wanted to know what he'd thought about the possibility of her being pregnant. Had he even considered it? Had he worried? Wondered?

Had he hoped?

She had. Now that she knew for sure she wasn't pregnant she could admit that there had been times she'd thought it would be a good thing. That having a child together would be what they needed to connect. The truth or a schoolgirl fantasy? Now she would never know.

"Are you ready?" he asked, holding out his arm.

She nodded and slipped her hand into the crook of his elbow. They walked out of the suite together.

Emma had seen the formal ballroom on her tour with Reyhan but standing in the large empty space hadn't prepared her for the reality of seeing it filled with elegantly dressed people, sparkling lights and a full orchestra.

There were about five hundred guests, including several prime ministers and heads of state. A film crew working on an action movie in the desert had been invited, along with a former American president and a Nobel Prize winner.

Reyhan introduced Emma to many of the guests. She smiled, said little and reached for a second glass of champagne from a waiter circulating with a tray.

"Are you doing all right?" Reyhan asked quietly.

"Considering this is my first official function as a princess, I'm doing great. We'll ignore the butterflies in my stomach, my knocking knees and the nearly overwhelming urge to bolt for the gardens. I have to admit I'd feel a lot more comfortable with the king's cats."

Reyhan smiled. "You're charming and well-spoken. Everyone is impressed."

His compliment made her beam. Just then her parents walked up. They were actually smiling. Could this evening produce any more surprises?

"Kitten, you look beautiful," her father said. "Nearly as lovely as your mother." He kissed his wife's cheek.

Emma's mother dimpled. "Oh, George, you're just saying that." She leaned close to her daughter. "Isn't this party wonderful? We met that action star your father likes so much. Jonny Blaze. He was very pleasant, although his girlfriend looks thin enough to need Third World aid. And did you see the former president? He was very nice, too. Oh, and the king told us he's sending us on a cruise on his private yacht. We're going to explore the Mediterranean for a couple of weeks."

Emma nearly dropped her champagne glass. "You're going?"

"Of course. It's a once-in-a-lifetime opportunity. He said the boat's captain knows all the best places to take us."

Her father winked. "It will be like a second honeymoon."

Janice Kennedy actually giggled, then waved at Emma and

Reyhan. "You two kids enjoy yourself. We have more famous people to meet."

Emma watched them walk off. "That was pretty amazing. I owe the king big-time. Not that I don't love my folks. I do. But they can be—"

"Oppressive?"

She smiled. "Absolutely. And a little judgmental. I hope they enjoy their cruise."

"I'm sure they will."

And she and Reyhan would be able to spend time together without her parents hanging around. The only trick would be getting him out of his office and paying attention to her. For that she would need a plan—and she would come up with one, just as soon as the champagne-induced fuzziness wore off.

The orchestra struck up another song, one that made her want to be in Reyhan's arms. She looked around and saw several of the guests dancing. They swayed to the music and laughed.

"You are more easy to read that usual," Reyhan said, taking her glass from her and setting it on a table in the corner. "Come. I will dance with you."

She was so pleased, she didn't bother to worry that he was doing her a favor. Not when he pulled her into his arms and held her close. If only the song could last forever, she thought happily.

Reyhan rubbed his hands against Emma's back and wished they were alone. Rather than dancing to music he wished to move with her in other ways. Perhaps it was the night, or how she looked or the invitation he saw in her eyes, but for some reason his resistance to her charms was weaker than ever.

He wanted her. More frightening than the desire was the truth that he wanted her in and out of his bed. He wanted to be with her, talk with her. He wanted to learn her secrets, discuss the future, name children and grow old with her. He wanted her to be his wife in every sense of the word.

He had the answer to his question about the baby. There wasn't one and he couldn't risk creating one with her. Yes, there was protection and it could be used, but that wasn't the point. He had escaped the possibility and he would be a fool to risk a pregnancy.

But he had always been a fool where Emma was concerned. From the first moment he'd met her that night on campus. She had smiled at him and he had been lost.

She swayed with him, sighing softly and snuggling close. She belonged, he thought. Whether laughing with his people in the desert or conversing with heads of state. She fit in. She made people feel at ease and never expected to be the center of attention. She was smart, kind and a woman of honor.

The fire always lurking below the surface flared to life and began to consume him. The need grew until he had no choice but to give in. He took her hand in his and pulled her toward a small alcove behind on of the decorated pillars.

"But the dance isn't over," Emma said. "Can't we finish the dance?" Instead of answering, he drew her close and kissed her.

She melted into his embrace, parting her lips instantly and clinging to him. She stroked his tongue with her own and moaned softly. Her hands slipped under his jacket where she rubbed his back.

"Better than dancing," she whispered when he pulled back to kiss her jaw, then her neck. "I'll give up dancing for kissing you anytime."

He nibbled the sensitive skin below her ear and made her groan. She reached for his hands and brought them to her breasts.

As he cupped her full curves, he stared into her eyes and saw an answering passion there.

"Make love with me," she pleaded.

He knew how right it would feel. How good things would be between them. He knew she was wet to his hard, yielding and aroused. He knew he could claim her, mark her, make her his. And he knew the price he would pay if he did.

Without saying a word, he dropped his hands to his sides,

turned and walked away. Emma's soft cry of pain made him pause, but only for a second. Then he resumed his stride and left the ballroom without looking back.

Chapter Eleven

Emma couldn't tell how much of the ache in her body came from her champagne hangover and how much came from humiliation. It wasn't just that Reyhan had left her alone at the party, it was that he'd kissed her and touched her, making her think he wanted her, and then he'd walked away. She felt both hurt and bruised, as if he'd been playing kick ball with her heart.

She curled up in the dining room chair and tried to work up some interest in the breakfast laid out there, but it wasn't happening. She'd taken a walk on the balcony encircling this level of the palace and that hadn't helped, either. Maybe she should shower and see if she could wash away the sense of having been a fool for a man who hadn't even noticed.

She stood and stretched. The good news was her parents were heading off to have a good time. The cruise was leaving that afternoon. As far as she could tell, they hadn't witnessed her humiliation, so she wasn't going to have to talk about it with them. But that didn't mean she was going to stop thinking about it.

She headed for the bathroom. What had gone wrong? One second Reyhan had been kissing her as if he'd really enjoyed it. He'd been the one to pull her into the alcove, he'd been the one touching her. Except she'd brought his hands to her breasts. Had he disliked her being aggressive? Did *he* need to be in charge?

She didn't want to think that was true. He'd never been weird about having to "be the man." Not that she had a whole lot of sexual experience with him or anyone. Had she freaked him out when she'd— Emma had been so deep in thought she hadn't noticed the steam and heat in the bathroom. It was only as she came around the corner and saw Reyhan stepping out of the shower that she realized she wasn't alone.

He was wet and naked. Water dripped from his arms and legs, from his hair. Droplets ran down his cheeks. Her gaze met his and she found herself unable to turn away.

In less than two seconds, she went from hurt and hungover to hungry. She wanted to touch him all over and have him touch her back. She was aware of his arousal growing, thickening. As if he was getting as turned on as she was.

She licked her lips. "What are you doing here? You're usually gone long before I wake up."

"I went riding at sunrise and came back to shower."

He was now fully erect. The sight of him made her midsection clench.

He obviously wanted her, so why was he just standing there?

He reached out his arm. For one brief heartbeat, she thought he was going to pull her close. Instead he grabbed a towel and turned his back on her.

"I'll be done in a few minutes."

It was a very polite invitation to leave.

Emma dropped her head, realized the sudden burning in her eyes came from unshed tears and fled to her bedroom. She closed the door behind herself and leaned against it.

Ten days ago she'd considered the king's insistence that she stay for another two months a stroke of good fortune. Now it was torture—a prison sentence that trapped her with a man who wanted nothing to do with her.

* * *

Reyhan read his email without understanding what any of it said. Instead of words he saw Emma's hurt eyes and the tears that had filled them as she turned away from him and fled the bathroom. Two hours and three meetings later, he hadn't been able to erase the memory of her confusion and pain.

He'd caused her that pain. No matter how much he wanted to escape the truth, it remained. He'd never meant to hurt her and the need to make it up to her was strong.

He instantly thought of returning to their room and offering her what they both wanted. That would ease the throbbing inside of him and hopefully bring her pleasure. But he couldn't risk it for himself and he wouldn't make her promises he did not intend to keep.

Determined to lose himself in his work, he returned his attention to his email. An hour or so later, his phone buzzed and his assistant announced that Will was on the phone.

"There's been a change in circumstances," his head of security said as soon as Reyhan came on the line.

Reyhan swore. "What?"

"I'm holding Fadl."

Fadl was the son of a prominent chief. "What happened?"

"He was caught stealing drilling equipment. Two other men were with him."

Reyhan frowned. "Did he say why he wanted it?"

"He's not talking. I have a few theories of my own. He could sell it on the black market and make a few bucks."

"That sounds like too much work for him and his friends."

"Agreed. He could also sabotage it somehow and then return it to inventory. When the replacement parts were put into service, we could have a pretty impressive disaster."

Reyhan shook his head. Was that possible? Had the boys decided to act on their threats? "We're going to have to inspect all parts in inventory and anything put into service in the past few months."

"I've already got men on that. I'm also rounding up the rest of his buddies. They've scattered so it may take a while."

"Keep on it. I'll be there in a couple of hours."

"Good. Maybe Fadl will talk to you. I'm getting nowhere."

"I'll see what I can do. As the prince, I can make certain threats to his family he wouldn't believe from you. I'll be there shortly."

"We'll be waiting."

Reyhan hung up the phone and considered his options. While he had been willing to keep his bargain with the chiefs up to a point, the rules had now changed. If Fadl was stealing—or worse, sabotaging—then he and his friends had to be stopped. Being young and sons of chiefs would not protect them anymore.

He called his assistant into his office and made arrangements for his meetings to be rescheduled. Once he'd reserved the helicopter and told the pilots where they were going, he walked to his father's offices. The guards there waved him inside, where he found the king on the phone.

"Reyhan," his father said cheerfully when he'd hung up. "What brings you to me this fine morning?"

"Will has detained Fadl, Bihjan's son." He quickly recounted what his security chief had told him.

King Hassan didn't look happy. "Have they moved from making threats to acting on them?"

"That's what I plan to find out. Will is going to invite Fadl's friends to join him in custody. We'll send a team in to search their camp. If they've already sabotaged replacement parts we should find evidence. Regardless, all the equipment will be inspected."

"Which means shutting down production for a few days."

Reyhan had already done the calculations. "We'll be back on-line at the end of the week." He shook his head. "There is also the possibility this was Fadl's plan all along. To get caught in such a way that we would have to shut down. But I won't take the risk. All the wells will be inspected."

"What are the international ramifications?"

"Minimal. We'll issue a statement saying we're running scheduled inspections, and production for the next month will be increased to make up the difference."

The king raised his eyebrows. "But the inspections aren't scheduled."

"They are now."

"Good point. When do you leave?"

"As soon as we're done here."

"I'm sure Emma will enjoy the trip."

Reyhan stared at his father. "You can't be serious. I am not taking her with me."

"Of course you are. You already have their leader in custody and will soon have the rest of his men. She won't be in any danger. If you're truly concerned about her standing out, have her put on native dress. I'm sure she'll look especially fetching."

Reyhan glanced at the sleeping tabby on the sofa in the corner and thought about throwing the creature at his father. But he recognized the stubborn look in the king's eyes and knew he didn't have a choice. Take Emma. It was a ridiculous request, and he refused to acknowledge the sudden pleasure he felt.

He left his father and headed for his rooms. At least Fadl's activities had been more passive than violent. Reyhan wouldn't have to worry about Emma walking into the middle of a gunfight.

He steeled himself, vowing not to react when he saw her. She sat on the sofa, reading and looked up when he entered.

"I have to go into the desert," he said. "I'll be gone a day or two. The king has suggested you accompany me."

Her green eyes were wide and unreadable. She looked both hurt and broken. As if her spirit had received one too many mortal blows.

That was his doing, he acknowledged shamefully. He'd been the one to reject her over and over. He reached for the phone and pressed three buttons. As he waited for his call to be answered, he wondered if there was some way he could explain so that she would understand and see this wasn't about her. Not really. His actions were about himself. Then he admitted he doubted that information would be of much comfort to her.

He made his request, hung up and returned his attention to her.

She hadn't moved, except to close the book. "Are they for me?" she asked, referring to the traditional garments he had ordered.

"Yes. I'll need you to wear them while we're at the camp. I don't expect any trouble, but regardless, they'll keep you safe."

"You don't want me to go with you," she said flatly. "What I want isn't important."

"It is to me."

He stood behind a club chair and rested his hands on the back. "This is business. There has been an arrest. I'm confident everything will go smoothly but as I am not completely sure, I would prefer you not be there."

"So this is only about keeping me safe?" He nodded.

"I don't believe you. Wanting me to stay is about more than that." She rose and faced him. "I want to speak to the king and tell him you find my presence intolerable. There's no reason for me to stay here and both of us to be tortured. I don't believe that's his purpose. Once he knows there is no hope for a reconciliation, then he'll agree to the divorce and you'll be free of me."

As she spoke, she squared her shoulders and met his gaze with a confidence that impressed him. The frightened little girl she had been was completely gone and in her place was a self-sufficient woman.

She stood before him, offering him his freedom and all he wanted was to pull her close and claim her as his own forever. He longed for her with a need that defied description and still he would let her go.

"When we return," he told her, "we will both talk to the king."

Light faded from her eyes, as if the last flame of her spirit had been extinguished. Reyhan wanted to move closer, to touch her and tell her his reasons were not what she thought, but he stayed where he was and dug his fingers into the back of the chair.

"I guess I should pack a few things," she said tonelessly. "What do I wear under the robes?"

"Whatever will be most comfortable. The days are hot, the nights cool.

Jeans or slacks will give you freedom of movement."

She nodded and headed for her bedroom. He retreated to his quarters where he quickly collected a few belongings. By the time he returned to the living room, the traditional robes had been left on the sofa.

Emma didn't recognize the woman in the mirror, but she didn't know how much of that had to do with the yards of fabric that covered her from head to toe and how much had to do with her bleeding to death from the inside out.

Reyhan wanted her to leave.

She supposed she'd known there were problems and that he didn't want to sleep with her again, but that was a far cry from having him practically jump with joy at the thought of never seeing her again. She'd hoped to shock him with her suggestion that she speak with the king and ask to leave sooner. Instead he'd agreed with her plan. He was going to get everything he wanted and she would spend the rest of her life in love with a man who didn't want to be with her.

Emma didn't know exactly *when* she'd fallen in love with him, or if it had been with her, buried for the past six years. Did it matter? More important than the how or when was the reality of losing Reyhan for a second time.

He escorted her to a helicopter. Nervous excitement at flying in one for the first time eased some of her heartache. She strapped herself in and picked up the headset Reyhan pointed to. When the engine roared to life and the rotors began to move, she understood that the headset was the only way they would be able to communicate.

"We're going about a hundred miles into the desert," he said into his microphone. "To the western edge of the central oil fields."

She could see his lips moving and hear the sound coming through her speakers. The helicopter rose.

Emma clutched the armrests as the aircraft zoomed up and forward, moving dizzyingly fast. The sensation was very different from a plane, but not unpleasant. She watched the edge of the city disappear under them, then there was only the vast stretches of nothing.

"A young man was arrested today," Reyhan said. "He was stealing replacement parts for the oil rigs. We're not sure if he planned to sell them on the black market or sabotage them and put them back into inventory."

"Faulty parts could create an economic and ecological disaster."

Reyhan nodded approvingly at her grasp of the situation. "Exactly. His friends are being rounded up and will also be arrested. The man we caught, Fadl, has been unwilling to tell us what he's up to. I want to talk to him and see if I can convince him to cooperate."

She remembered what Reyhan had said about the nomads' need to be free. "Will he go to prison?"

"Probably. It depends on the seriousness of his crime. In this case, simply stealing would be a relief to everyone."

"An odd reality."

He smiled. "How true."

She turned away because she didn't want to smile back. She didn't want to feel that things were once again well between them. How could he act as if nothing was wrong?

She stared out the window and reminded herself that he had

made it clear from the beginning that he *wanted* her out of his life. She'd been the one to forget that and try to change the rules. Was it his fault he hadn't agreed?

"There is a small camp of nomads by the oil station," he said. "They are friendly and you will be safe in their company. Even so I will assign two men to stay with you. Just in case."

"That's fine. Are there any cultural rules I should keep in mind?"

"No. Simply be yourself and they will adore you."

As I do.

He didn't speak the words, but Emma heard them. They hung in the silence between them as loud as the engine. She looked at Reyhan, but he was staring out of his window and she couldn't see his expression.

A trick of her own imagination, she told herself. Nothing more. Her feelings for him weren't going to change anything and she had to remember that.

They touched down about an hour later. Emma saw the low buildings clustered together and the oil rigs beyond. To the left, a dozen or so tents were pitched close to the bubbling oasis. Reyhan had told her the pool was fed by an underground spring.

He climbed out of the helicopter first, then held out his hand to assist her. She took it and instantly felt the warmth of his fingers. Weakness invaded her, a weakness she had to learn to control and eventually conquer.

In time, she promised herself. She would heal in time.

Reyhan entered the interrogation room and stared at the young man sitting there. Fadl was all of eighteen, slightly built and sullen looking. The youngest son of a powerful chief. While he would not have inherited all his father's wealth, he could have made a good life for himself with the tribe. Instead, he'd chosen to take what he wanted.

"You have crossed me," he told the young man. "You knew that your father didn't want you harmed or arrested. He thought you would come to see the error of your ways. But I am not a foolish old man who still indulges a spoiled child. I am Prince Reyhan of Bahania and now we will play by *my* rules."

Fear flickered in Fadl's eyes. "That's a load of bull. You can't hurt me.

You promised my father."

Reyhan allowed himself a small smile. "I agreed to let you run around and play at being a man until you broke the law. Which you did by stealing parts. Now the deal doesn't exist and you are mine."

The young man squirmed in his seat. "I don't believe you."

"Good. I will enjoy putting you in prison. Because of you, the oil rigs must be checked for sabotaged parts. That will cost my country hundreds of thousands of dollars. As I know you have no funds of your own to compensate me, I will take what I can out of your hide."

Fadl visibly paled. "How did you know that's what we were going to do?"

Reyhan kept his expression impassive. He'd guessed correctly. Now he simply had to get the details from the boy and let Will deal with damage control.

"What made you think you could succeed?" Reyhan asked. "You know nothing of the oil equipment. You certainly haven't worked the rigs."

Fadl shifted in his seat. "I don't want to go to prison."

"You don't have a choice. The question on the table is for how long. Please me and I will make sure your time there is almost pleasant. Annoy me and I will find a particularly uncomfortable place for you to call home."

There were several seconds of silence. In the end, fear won.

"It wasn't us," Fadl admitted. "Not really. A bunch of us were at a bar in El Bahar and we were trying to come up with a plan. This guy approached us. He said he'd been listening and that we were amateurs. If we wanted to make some big money, we needed to hire professionals. So we did."

Reyhan's blood ran cold. He crossed to the door, pulled it open and yelled for Will to join them.

Fadl told them everything. The name of the man whom they'd hired, how many associates he'd brought into Bahania and how much Fadl and his gang were to pay them.

"We haven't put back any bad parts," Fadl said frantically. "They're all in our camp. You have to believe me, Prince Reyhan. I swear. We were just after the money and this seemed like an easy way to get it."

Reyhan stared at him with loathing. "See if you feel that way after your stay in prison."

Emma wandered around the oasis. Her bodyguards kept far enough away that she was able to forget about them. As she'd seen before on her outing with her parents, there were children playing and filling the afternoon with the sound of laughter. Several small dogs tumbled over each other in a game only they could understand. Women clustered together sewing and cooking and sending glances her way.

A little girl of about seven or eight ran up to her and offered a plate of dates. Emma smiled her acceptance and bit into one. Soon another little girl joined them, then another and another.

"I can't eat all these," Emma said with a grin as she touched the closest girl's smooth dark hair. "But thank you for offering."

A little boy tugged on her sleeve. She bent down to his level and he pulled on her head covering. She reached up and slipped it down to her shoulders. All the children gasped at the sight of her red hair.

"I know. Not the usual thing," she said happily.

A girl reached out to touch it, then shrank away. Emma laughed.

"It's all right. It doesn't burn." She stroked her hair herself, then took the girl's hand in her own and brought it to the side of her head. The child touched her lightly, giggled and touched her again. The other children crowded close.

"My, my, my. Aren't you a pretty lady?"

At the sound of the male voice, the children scattered. Emma stood and turned, only to come face-to-face with two tall, armed strangers. Her bodyguards were nowhere to be seen.

"You're American," she said, trying not to betray her nervousness.

The man closest to her grinned. He had close-cropped blond hair and a tattoo of a snake on his forearm.

"Good guess," he said and stepped behind her. Before she could make a move, he had grabbed her and pulled her close, then pressed a knife to her neck. "And you're our prisoner."

"What the hell were you thinking?" Will demanded as he paced in front of Fadl. "You hired a man you met in a *bar*. Didn't it occur to you that he wasn't just a military consultant? Didn't you think you were getting in over your head?"

Fadl looked miserable, young and scared. "He said if we didn't do what he wanted, he'd kill us."

Reyhan stared at the boy. "You *wanted* to get caught," he breathed. "You need our help to get out of this mess."

Fadl nodded frantically. "Prince Reyhan, please. They're out of control. You have to help me. Help all of us. We're sorry. We didn't mean for any of this to happen."

"Of course you did. But now you've got a tiger by the tail and you don't know how to keep it from eating you." He looked at Will. "This is your area of expertise."

"I'm on it," his security chief told him. "I'll call in a team from El Bahar and—" he glanced at Fadl "—elsewhere."

Reyhan knew Will meant the City of Thieves, a secret city in the middle of the desert on the border with El Bahar and Bahania.

"I know the head of security there," Will continued. "Rafe Powers and I have worked together before."

"Good."

Will started to leave, but before he reached the door, a man burst into the room. He ran to Reyhan.

"She was taken by two Americans. They shot one of the men guarding her and knocked out the other. They have Princess Emma."

Reyhan went very still and very cold. He looked at Fadl. "If she is harmed in any way, the desert will run red with your blood."

Chapter Twelve

"So how many millions are you worth, sweetheart?" the man with the tattoo asked as he pushed Emma into the back of a truck.

The gag in her mouth made it impossible to speak, so she could only glare her rage.

"I didn't know Prince Reyhan was married or I would have planned this better," the man said with a grin. "Guess I just got lucky today. Don't worry. No one wants to hurt you. I thought those unhappy kids would be our ticket to the easy life, but they turned out to be all talk. When it came right down to doing the dirty work, they got scared. Said they didn't want to blow up any oil wells. So I figured I'd wasted my time. Then you came along."

Emma wanted to shriek her outrage. She couldn't believe this was happening. If she could just get her hands loose she would claw her kidnapper's eyes out.

Her anger pleased her. It meant she wasn't going to be immobilized by fear. She had to stay strong so that when the time came she could escape.

The man fingered a strand of her hair. "I'm guessing your old man is going to pay through the nose to get you back in his bed."

A knife flashed. Emma jumped back but not before her captor sliced off a lock of her hair.

"Just so he knows I'm not bluffing," the man said, and slammed the door.

She found herself alone and in darkness. The hum of a motor and cool air blowing over her told her there was an air-conditioning unit. At least she wouldn't die of heat exhaustion.

Don't give in to the fear, she told herself. She had to stay strong. She had to be prepared. The men who had taken her weren't going to kill her.

She was too valuable for that. They wanted money, and lots of it.

Feeling her way along the inside of the compartment, she found a bench seat and lowered herself onto it. Her hands were tied behind her. Ropes cut into her wrists and as she struggled to loosen them, her shoulders began to ache.

How long would it all take? She knew that however much Reyhan might want her gone, he wouldn't ever just leave her like this. She knew he would rescue her. But when? And how could she hang on until then?

Fadl shrank back in his chair. He looked far younger than his eighteen years. "I swear I didn't know," he said as tears filled his eyes.

Reyhan didn't care. "You are responsible. I should kill you now." Will grabbed his arm. "Killing him won't help. We have a situation." He glared at his security chief. "They have taken my wife."

"I know. We'll get her back."

Reyhan felt himself consumed by the fires of rage. He wanted to destroy with his bare hands. He wanted, at his feet, the broken and bleeding body of the man who had dared to take Emma, and then he wanted the opportunity to kill him a second time.

Fear lurked inside him, as well. Fear for her and what she must be feeling. Fear that she wouldn't believe he would move the rotation of the earth itself to get her back. He'd been so cold, had rejected her so many times. His efforts to convince her he didn't care had been too successful by far. What if she thought he wouldn't be bothered?

He clenched his hands into fists and turned to Will. "Find out how much they want. This is all about money." Will nodded and left.

Reyhan glared at Fadl. "Your attempts to play at danger have cost me something precious. You will pay, as will your entire family. The cost will bleed down through a hundred generations of your people."

Fadl hung his head. "I'm sorry," he whispered through his tears.

Reyhan walked out of the room. He needed to move, to act, to do something. Instead he could only wait for information. In the main security center, a dozen men worked phones and computers. His security chief walked over to him.

"Reinforcements will be here within the hour," Will said. "Troops are coming in from El Bahar and the City of Thieves. I've got my best computer guy working on a special kind of Trojan horse. Basically it allows the ransom to show up in the offshore account, but it's only good for ninety minutes. Then poof, the money isn't there anymore."

"That doesn't give us much time to get Emma back," Reyhan said, knowing he would gladly pay any price for her safe return.

"We set up the exchange so that we're face-to-face when it happens. We see Emma, we send the money transfer. They get notification of the deposit and they release her. It should only take about five minutes. That gives us the rest of the time to get the hell away."

"Do it," he said.

Will nodded. "Just as soon as they tell us how much. We should—"

A young man in uniform came running up. "Sir, we've heard. Sixty million in euros. I have the account number."

Will looked at Reyhan who nodded. "Agree to it."

The young man swallowed. "There's something else, sir." He glanced from Will to Reyhan and back. "A storm. It didn't look like much an hour ago, but now…" His voice trailed off.

Reyhan's chest tightened. "Sandstorm?" The officer nodded. "It looks bad."

Reyhan stared at Will. "The helicopters won't be able to fly."

Which meant the reinforcements wouldn't arrive anytime soon and Reyhan couldn't fly Emma to safety.

"We could stall them," the young man said. "Explain that it takes time to raise that kind of money and—"

"No!" Reyhan's gaze narrowed. "My wife is not to stay with them one second more than necessary. Do you understand?"

"Yes, sir. Of course." He scurried away.

Will shook his head. "It's more risky without the backup but we can still make it happen."

"We have no choice. If necessary, I will fight them all myself."

The tattooed-snake guy who turned out to be called Billy pulled Emma out of the truck.

"Looks like this is your lucky day, too, sweetheart," he said as he helped her to the ground. "Your old man is going to pay up. Sixty million euros. Not bad for an afternoon's work."

She was stunned. Sixty million euros? That was close to sixty million dollars. An insane amount of money. She couldn't imagine there was that much wealth in the whole world. Reyhan couldn't pay that. Just the thought of it made her sick to her stomach.

"You look shocked," Billy said. "Don't be. These prince guys really have a thing about other men hanging around their women. Of course I thought he'd try to negotiate me down a little, but he didn't. I'm not going to complain. That's twenty million for each of us."

She glanced around the camp. The sky had darkened and the

air seemed thick, but she could still make out nearly two dozen men. She looked at Billy.

He nodded. "I know what you're thinking. There's more than three of us here. But see, these aren't my guys. They're those kids who hired us. The ones who chickened out. So I say screw 'em. Me and my boys will be long gone with the money while these stupid kids take the fall. Good plan, huh?" She nodded and wondered how she could get the information to Reyhan.

"Hold on," Billy said, and tugged at her gag. When it was removed, she sucked in a breath of air.

"Better?" he asked.

She nodded, her mouth too dry for her to speak.

He glanced at the sky. "There's a storm coming. Good for us, bad for them. They would have called in for help, but it ain't coming in the middle of a sandstorm. Come on, Princess. Your ride is this way."

Emma followed the man. As she walked, she tried to figure out how long she'd been held in the truck. She would guess two or three hours at most. With clouds rolling in and covering the sun, there was no way for her to judge time that way. The air was so thick with sand that it was difficult to breathe.

Should she try to escape? If Reyhan had made a deal, maybe it would be better to go along with the plan. But she wanted him to know that the young men they had captured had nothing to do with the trouble.

"Be prepared," Reyhan told Will. "If things go badly and we can't get away in time, there could be a fight."

"Agreed." Will patted the gun at his side. "My men are ready."

Reyhan was also armed and determined. He'd given firm instructions that no one was to do anything until Emma was back in his arms. Once she was safe, their side would walk away.

"Is your team in place?" he asked Will.

The other man nodded. "They'll get behind the trucks and

put on the tracking devices. Then when the storm lifts, we'll send in an armed contingent to take them." He grinned. "They won't know what hit them."

"Good."

Reyhan's first instinct was to punish the men immediately, but he had to think about Emma. Getting her to safety was his primary concern. The bastards who had taken her would be brought to justice. He would not rest until it was so.

He checked his watch, then stepped into the open Jeep. The vehicle offered little protection against the growing storm.

"It's time," he said against the wind.

Will started the engine and they drove into the desert.

Emma couldn't see anything. The sand was thick and hot and her face felt as if it were being scraped by sandpaper. She squinted against the windshield.

"How do you know where you're going?" she asked Billy.

He tapped the compass on the dashboard. "I'll find the rendezvous.

Don't you worry, Princess."

She wasn't worried. Not for herself. Did Billy and his men have any idea about the danger they were in? Reyhan wasn't simply going to pay them, and if Billy thought he was, the man was a fool.

His two companions were in the truck behind them and the young nomad-rebels farther back.

"When will you three head out?" she asked casually, wishing he would untie her wrists. Her shoulders ached and her skin was raw.

"Don't even think you can bat your eyes at me and get me to spill my plans, Princess. You're pretty, but I'm not going to fall for it."

She shrugged as if it didn't matter, then stared out of the windshield.

Visibility had dropped to a few hundred yards. The road

was covered with blowing sand and debris. She squinted as she thought she saw an outcrop of rocks in the distance.

"Here's the place," Billy said, stopping the truck. He took the keys and tucked them into his shirt pocket. "I'm going to leave you here, Princess. Tell me you're not stupid enough to try and escape into this mess."

"I'll stay here," she promised, knowing she would. Running now would be idiotic and suicidal.

Billy disappeared into the storm. Emma waited, trying to be patient, knowing Reyhan was close and wanting to run to him. But she couldn't be a distraction. He would have a plan and she didn't want to get in the way of that.

After what felt like a lifetime, but was probably only ten or fifteen minutes later, Billy opened the truck door.

"Show time," he said, and pulled out a knife.

He slit the ropes holding her wrists together. When she tried to move her arms, pain shot through her. She forced herself to ignore it and flex her arms until she could move them freely.

She saw Billy's two companions just behind him. They were equally scary with their close-cropped hair and multiple weapons.

"Climb on down," Billy said, motioning for her to step out of the truck.

When she stepped onto the ground she realized her escorts were the least of her problems. Sand attacked her like a giant angry beast. She couldn't see, couldn't breathe, could barely move. Grateful for the voluminous material covering her body, she pulled up her head covering and tugged the edges so she could protect her nose and mouth. Billy grabbed her arm and led her deeper into the storm. When they stopped, she looked up and saw Reyhan.

"I'm here," she called, trying to jerk free of Billy's hold.

The mercenary didn't let go. "Transfer the money," he yelled, then jerked his head toward his buddies. "Check the download."

The men pulled out small handheld devices. Emma strained

to break free, never taking her eyes from Reyhan. He wore protective glasses and a heavy cloak, but she would swear he was staring right at her. She could almost hear his voice, willing her to be strong.

"Here it comes," Billy's friend yelled.

"What have you done?"

The fierce question came from somewhere on the left. Billy turned toward the man racing toward them.

"Shut up, kid. Stay out of this."

"No! You have kidnapped the wife of Prince Reyhan and now you ransom her?"

"Welcome to the games the big boys play. You and your friends were too much like girls to go through with your plans, so I had to pick up a little expense money elsewhere." Suddenly Billy was holding a gun in his other hand. "Stay out of this kid, or die. It's your choice."

Emma was so stunned, she nearly stumbled. "Don't hurt him," she demanded, pulling at her arm and suddenly jerking free.

Billy spun toward her. "Don't screw this up, sweetheart. I'll take you out if I have to."

"Emma."

She heard Reyhan's voice over the storm, over her fear and over the rapid pounding of her heart.

"Let her go," the first man insisted. He charged Billy.

Emma read the mercenary's intent before he ever acted. Even as he raised the gun, she flung herself at his arm, shoving him down. The gun went off.

The sound of the gunshot cut through the roar of the storm. Suddenly men were everywhere and bullets filled the air. Emma didn't know where to run or hide, nor did it matter. All she could think was that she had to get to Reyhan. Then something large and heavy crashed into her and she was trapped on the ground.

Panic flared. She couldn't breathe. She struggled until a familiar voice spoke into her ear.

"Be still. You are safe."

Reyhan. Fierce gladness swept through her and she wanted to roll over so she could cling to him.

More bullets cut through the storm. There were cries of pain, curses and the howl of the wind. Suddenly Reyhan was off her and pulling her to her feet. They were running toward the truck.

"Billy has the keys," she yelled to Reyhan. "In his pocket."

Reyhan didn't answer. Instead he circled around to the passenger side and shoved her inside.

"Stay down," he ordered. "Under the dash." Then he was gone.

Emma huddled on the floorboards and prayed as she had never prayed in her life. That Reyhan would be safe. That no one else would be hurt. That they would all get out of this alive.

Time ticked by. Hours? Minutes? She wasn't sure. At last there was only the sound of the storm and she risked looking out the passenger window.

The three mercenaries were captured, sitting on the ground, their arms and legs bound. Several of the injured were being treated by men she thought must work for Reyhan. Relief coursed through her, making her weak and nauseated. They had survived.

After a time, Reyhan returned to the truck. "Are you all right?" he asked as he climbed in beside her and put a key in the ignition.

"I'm fine. Is there..." She glanced out the window. "Are there a lot of injuries? My bodyguards?"

"A few. One of the mercenaries took a bullet to the arm. A couple of the rebels were shot, as were three of Will's men."

She swallowed. "Was anyone killed?"

"One of the rebels. I knew him and his father. He was just seventeen." Reyhan looked weary and distressed.

Emma's stomach lurched. "Oh, God. It was my fault."

"No." He turned on her. "Not your fault. These boys who wanted to play at being dangerous men brought this upon themselves. No one took them seriously, not even me. I knew their game and thought they would outgrow it. We were all wrong."

He started the truck. "It's time to get you to safety."

She was still stunned by the news that there had been a death. "I'm a nurse. I could help."

"They'll be fine. Will's men are all trained in combat first aid. He's very thorough. That's why I hired him."

He started driving. She stared out the windshield and tried to come to terms with all that had happened in the past few hours.

"I'm sorry I was captured," she said. "I wasn't trying to make trouble."

"The fault is mine. I shouldn't have allowed you to come here. I should have ignored my father."

"Hard to do when he's the king."

Reyhan clutched the steering wheel more tightly. "He presumes too much and plays games with us all. This one could have cost you your life. I will never forgive him for that."

The force of his words stunned her. "Reyhan, he didn't know. None of us knew."

"Agreed. But it was a possibility."

He was acting as if he cared. This from the man who couldn't wait to divorce her. Thoughts swirled in her head. She felt exhausted.

He read her mind. "Close your eyes," he told her. "Rest."

"No. I want to stay awake and keep you company on the drive." The storm still swirled around them and made visibility nearly impossible.

"I know my way."

She supposed he would. This was his land, his desert. She leaned against the side of door and let her eyes drift closed. Maybe she would relax for a couple of minutes. What could it hurt?

Emma drifted off to sleep. She didn't know how long she'd been out, but she was awakened by a horrible crashing as the truck roared into what looked like the side of a mountain.

For a second, she was disoriented. Not sure where she was or why, she frantically glanced around. When she saw Reyhan slumped over the steering wheel, her memory returned and with it, panic.

Had they run off the road? Why had he driven into the rocks? She unfastened her seat belt and scrambled across the bench seat, then eased Reyhan into a sitting position.

His face was unscathed. She checked for bumps and bruises, but there weren't any. He hadn't hit his head.

"Reyhan," she called frantically. "Can you hear me?" He didn't answer.

Why was he unconscious? She began to check for other injuries. First his shoulders, then his arms. She slid her hand down his side and drew them back when she felt wetness. Blood covered her right hand.

"No!" she whispered, horrified and afraid. The thick stickiness told her he'd been bleeding for some time. Reality crashed in on her.

"You were shot," she breathed. "Oh, God. It can't be." Hadn't he known?

She glanced around frantically. She had to get him somewhere that she could examine him. Maybe the back of the truck. But without a first-aid kit, what could she do? She didn't even know where they were.

He stirred and groaned.

"Reyhan? Can you hear me? You've been shot." He opened his eyes. "It's nothing."

"You're bleeding and you passed out."

He blinked at her, then stared out the front of the truck. "We're at the caves," he said.

"At them? We're practically in them." She looked at the crumpled front of the truck. "I'm not sure it's going to still run. Are we close to the security camp?"

He shook his head, then groaned. "We're at the Desert Palace. My aunt's house. Through the caves. We need to go through the caves."

Emma wasn't sure if he was delirious or not. But if there was a house nearby, maybe she could get some help.

She stepped out onto the ground. The storm had lessened to the point where she could see the landscape around them. They were in some kind of small canyon with the front of the truck mashed up against a sheer rock wall. To the right was an opening to a cave.

She turned in a slow circle and saw nothing. Not a road, not a building, not a hint of life. They were truly alone.

The fear returned and with it a conviction that she wouldn't let Reyhan die. She couldn't. He might not care about her, but she loved him.

She crossed into the mouth of the cave. The opening was huge with the ceiling soaring up what looked like two stories. There was a small chest to the right of the opening and she crossed to it.

She opened it and inside she found flashlights, batteries, water, food and a first-aid kit. When she turned back to the truck, she screamed. Reyhan leaned against the entrance. He was pale, shaking and bleeding.

"What are you doing?" she demanded as she raced back to him. "Stay still. You can't lose any more blood."

"It's about two miles that way," he said, pointing into the cave. "You'll have to pull the truck into the cave, then help me walk the rest of the way."

"You're not walking two miles anytime soon," she told him. "We'll camp right here until help arrives."

"Not likely soon, and there aren't enough supplies," he said, and winced.

She glanced at the food and water provided and knew he was right. The trunk provided emergency rations, not enough to live on.

"One thing at a time," she told him. "I have to get you bandaged up.

Then we'll talk about moving you."

"We have to make the trip before dark," he said. "There's not much time."

Chapter Thirteen

Aware of the passage of time, Emma worked quickly. She pulled all the supplies out of the trunk and was relieved to find a blanket folded in the bottom. After gathering everything together, she helped Reyhan into a seated position.

His robes came off easily. Once she'd tossed them aside she could see the bloodstained shirt clinging to his torso. He barely hissed as she took off the drenched cotton, even when it pulled in places. When she was done, she examined the wound.

The bullet had gone through him. She had no way of knowing if anything vital had been damaged nor could she have fixed anything if it had.

Her emergency training came back to her and she worked quickly, grateful for her stint in the emergency room back home. Less than twenty minutes later she'd nearly stopped the bleeding, which meant she could finish bandaging the wound.

She was shaken, scared and ready for someone to rescue them, but she had a feeling they were on their own until she could figure out a way to call for help.

She crouched in front of Reyhan and smoothed back his sweat-soaked hair. "I'm done," she whispered. "It shouldn't hurt so badly now."

"I'm fine."

She doubted that, but while the first-aid kit had plenty of bandages and antiseptic, there hadn't been any painkillers.

"Is there a cell phone I can use?" she asked. "Can I call for help?"

"In the Desert Palace," he said between clenched teeth. He sucked in a breath and rolled to his knees, then started to stand.

She clutched his arm. "You can't. We'll stay here."

"No. We go now. There's little time."

She glanced outside and figured they had about two hours left of daylight. Depending on how fast they could move, they had a chance of getting to the palace by dark. But it wasn't a sure thing, and she didn't know whether any daylight would filter into the caves, in any case.

"We should wait and go in the morning."

He looked at her. "You don't want to face what roams the desert at night."

Good point.

She collected their supplies and put them in the blanket, then knotted the ends together so she could wear it like a sling. She had them each drink some water, then she got Reyhan to his feet and leaned him against the wall. Finally she went out to the truck.

Surprisingly it started. She maneuvered it into the cave where it sputtered and died before she had a chance to turn off the ignition. So much for the backup plan of trying to find the camp via the truck.

She took one of the flashlights and handed the other to Reyhan. Then standing on his injured side, she took as much of his weight as she could.

It was slow going. She didn't want to think how much his side must hurt him or how weak and out of it he must feel from the blood loss. But he didn't complain, didn't slow down. He moved steadily, at a pace that stunned her, turning left, then right, going deeper and deeper into the mountain, following directions only he could recognize.

There were hundreds of places to get lost, she thought nervously as they came to yet another fork in the path. Reyhan went to the left, passed three other trails, before picking the fourth.

Despite the distance they'd traveled, Emma knew they weren't going deeper underground because there were bits of light filtering through the rocks above. Although as time passed, the light seemed to get more and more dim.

"We're nearly there," he said, his voice low and raspy.

She stopped and urged him to lean against the wall. "Have some water," she said. "You're dehydrated."

He took the water and drank. His willingness to listen to her told her just how badly he'd been hurt.

They started walking again.

After about twenty minutes, Reyhan spoke. "There's a satellite phone in the office," he said. "Find it tonight and put it out in the courtyard tomorrow. There's a solar cell. It will take twelve hours to charge."

Twelve hours? That meant they couldn't call for help until tomorrow night. What if Reyhan was bleeding to death on the inside? What if the bullet had pierced his intestines or his spleen or...?

The path blurred and she realized she was crying. Blinking away the tears, she did her best to ignore the panic filling her and think about what was important. They'd survived this long. She could manage emergency first aid. Any crisis could be dealt with at the time. They would survive—she would make sure of it. She hadn't come this far and realized she loved him only to lose him now.

Nearly a half hour later, she realized the sun was definitely setting. Soon it would be completely dark except for the light from their flashlights. Her body ached from Reyhan leaning on her. She was tired, hungry and thirsty. If she felt this bad, he must feel a hundred times worse.

She was about to ask how much farther when he stopped and pointed. "There."

Emma peered into the murky darkness and saw what looked like a solid stone wall.

"It's a dead end," she said, fighting both panic and resignation. They weren't going to make it.

He glanced at her and raised his eyebrows.

"Do not believe everything you see. Go stand in front of the wall."

She made sure he was leaning against the rocks before shrugging off his arm and approaching the wall. She pressed her hand against the stones.

"Cold and solid."

"The bricks are a grid," he said. "Count across from left to right and down from top to bottom. Three over and five down. Push."

She blinked in the darkness, then did as he requested. The stone moved.

Her heart nearly leapt out of her chest. "It's working."

"Of course it is," he said, and gave her the next instruction.

So they went for a total of eight stones. On the last one, there was an audible click, then the stone wall swung in like a well-oiled door. The ground changed from uneven rock to polished stone and slowly sloped up.

"We are here," he said, and walked into the palace.

Emma followed him. Reyhan kept his balance by pressing one hand against the wall and holding his flashlight with the other. At the top of the ramp, they entered what appeared to be a basement or cellar. He turned a lever and the stone door swung shut.

"There is a short flight of stairs," he said. "On the main floor are several bedrooms, the kitchen and the office. You'll find the satellite phone in there."

He crossed the open area and headed for a flight of stairs at the far end. Emma was surprised that he barely limped. It was as if being in the Desert Palace gave him strength.

"Is there food and water?" she asked.

"Yes. No fresh food, but staples. And fresh water is always available.

There's an underground spring."

He climbed the stairs, slowing only slightly toward the top. She saw blood seeping through his bandage and winced. "You need to lie down," she told him.

"Soon."

At the top of the stairs was another door. This one had a knob. He turned it and they stepped into a beautifully tiled hallway. The air was cool but fresh and there were still hints of sunlight coming in through large windows.

"There are battery-operated lanterns," he said. "Several in each room."

He moved down the hallway, pausing only to point out the direction to the kitchen, the placement of the office and where the wing of bedrooms began.

He entered the first one, made his way to the bed, sat down and passed out before he could put his head on the pillow.

Fear returned but by now Emma was familiar with the knot in her stomach and the tightness in her chest. She ignored it and went to work.

After setting down the supplies she carried, she found the batterypowered lantern in the room and clicked it on. Then she made sure Reyhan was comfortable on the bed and checked his wound.

The seepage from before had stopped, which was a relief. So far there was no red, swollen flesh to indicate infection. Was it possible they'd gotten off relatively easily?

Confident he was all right for the moment, she took one of the flashlights and did a quick search of the main floor of the large house.

There were over a dozen rooms on this level and at least three staircases. The kitchen was huge and well stocked. Cold water gushed from the faucet. She found a propane-heated stove and oven, along with an empty refrigerator that probably needed a generator in order to run.

In the book-lined office, she found a case on the big desk that looked somewhat like a phone. She made a mental note to stick that outside sometime tonight so that it could start charging in the morning.

None of the four downstairs bathrooms offered a first-aid kit, so she returned to the kitchen and went into the pantry. Sure enough, on the bottom shelf was an assortment of medical supplies to supplement what had been in the first-aid kit in the case.

She collected what she needed and returned to Reyhan's room.

He hadn't moved. She checked his temperature, which was normal, then changed the bandage and decided to wait on everything else. If he regained consciousness, she would see if he could drink water and eat. If he didn't...she would face that problem later.

She returned to the kitchen where she dumped the old bandages and opened a can of soup. She ate it cold, too tired to bother with trying to heat it. After swallowing the contents and three full glasses of water, she made use of one of the luxury bathrooms, then returned to Reyhan's room.

He was still cool to the touch and there wasn't any more bleeding. She had no way to tell about internal injuries, but she was hopeful that he'd been very lucky and that the bullet had missed everything.

Weary behind words, she curled up next to him on the bed and closed her eyes. Just for a few minutes, she told herself. She still had to get the phone outside and figure out what she was going to feed him when he woke....

Someone stroked her hair. Emma felt the light touch even in her sleep and smiled. She was warm all over and rested and in

just a second she would open her eyes and see— Consciousness returned and with it the memories of what had happened
the previous day. She sat up and realized it was morning and
Reyhan was awake.

"Good morning," he said.

She stared at him, at his bare chest and the clarity in his eyes.
His color was good. Except for the white bandage at his waist,
she wouldn't have known he'd ever been injured.

"How are you feeling?" she asked.

"Good. A little sore, but otherwise fine. I am hungry and
thirsty."

"Positive signs." She touched his forehead. "No fever?"

"Not that I can feel."

Suddenly aware that she was pressed against him and that
they were on a bed, she shifted toward the edge then stood.

"Let me check your bandage. If there's no sign of infection,
we can all breathe a little easier."

She removed the dressing. The wound was clean, the surrounding skin pale.

"It's already healing," she told him. "Good. Then we can eat."

He swung his legs to the floor and stood. She hovered by his
side, but he seemed fine. Strong and capable. Once again the
prince and no longer the man who needed her.

"I would like a shower," he said.

"Me, too, but there's no hot water. At least there wasn't last
night."

"The water heater needs to be turned on. I'll take care of that
if you want to start on breakfast."

She nodded and followed him out of the room. He didn't
even sway as he walked, she thought, amazed by his powers of
recovery. As they passed the office, she remembered the telephone and collected it. Reyhan disappeared into a small room
behind the pantry while she took the phone out into the courtyard and opened the case so the rising sun would charge the
solar cell. Then she took a moment and looked around at the

lush, nondesertlike garden in the middle of a three-story sand-and-stone house.

Plants bloomed and trailed everywhere. She couldn't name the various pink, red and white flowers, but she could inhale their sweet fragrance. Water trickled through several fountains and circled the garden before flowing into a stone-lined pond.

No doubt the underground spring was responsible for the flow of water. Emma sighed as she caught sight of a bench in the corner and a small grassy patch. This was a dream house— somewhere she could happily stay forever.

She left the courtyard garden and returned to the kitchen. By the time she'd put together a meal, Reyhan had returned with word that there would soon be hot water. He'd also started the generator.

"We'll have immediate electricity," he said. "We have to use it sparingly until the solar panels start working. Hot water will take an hour or so."

"There's nothing like a day in the desert to make one grateful for the little things," she said, smiling as if being alone with him was no big deal. As if she didn't remember how scared she'd been when she'd found out he'd been shot, and how much he'd hurt her, before they'd left, with his agreement that it was time for her to go home.

As she sat across from him, she tried not to stare at his features. There was no need to memorize his face. Their time together had changed her forever and she would never forget what he looked like. Even now, without a shirt, in need of a shave and less than twenty-four hours after being shot, he still looked masculine, powerful and very princelike.

Silence descended. She searched for a topic to keep the moment from being too awkward.

"Whose house is this?" she asked as she sipped the coffee she'd prepared.

"Mine. It belonged to my aunt. She left it to me when she died."

"This is where you came to after we got married," she said as the pieces of the past clicked into place.

He nodded. "I needed to be here for her funeral service and then I had to settle her affairs." He stared past her, as if seeing into that long-ago time. "She and I were very close. My parents loved each other more than they loved their children. My brother Jefri didn't seem to mind, but I noticed." He shrugged. "When things were difficult, Sheza was there for me."

Simple words, she thought, reading the pain behind them. She could imagine a young, lonely prince, growing up in privilege, but without affection. The woman who took his parents' place would always hold a special place in his heart. No wonder he'd been devastated by her loss.

"I'm sorry," she said quietly. "I wish I'd known what you were going through."

He sipped his coffee. "It wouldn't have made a difference. I would never have let you comfort me."

"Why not?"

One corner of his mouth turned up. "I am Prince Reyhan of Bahania. I am not in need of comforting."

She leaned toward him. "I see. And who exactly buys into that line?"

"You would have."

"You're right. It's something a child would have believed. But I'm not that little girl anymore. Now I know better."

His dark gaze settled on her face. "You were very brave yesterday."

"Not really. At first I was furious at being taken hostage. I knew they'd try to get money from you. They didn't, did they?"

"No. We were able to cancel the transfer. My security chief had a plan to get the money back even if the transfer had gone through. But if necessary, I would have paid."

"Nice to know," she said, not surprised, but still pleased.

"You are my wife, Emma. I could not let you be harmed."

She didn't feel like his wife. She didn't feel like anything except excess baggage.

"Thank you for saving my life," he said. "Thank you for saving mine."

"So we are even, which is better than one of us being in debt to another." He smiled. "You did not expect danger to be a part of your visit to Bahania. This experience must make you eager to be back in Dallas."

So much less than he thought. "There are things I'll miss about being here," she told him. Mostly him.

His smile faded. "I'm sorry I hurt you when we were at the palace."

When he'd rejected her, she thought. When he'd turned his back on her offer to make love.

"Yes, well, it's not a big deal."

"I don't believe you," he said. "It was a big deal to both of us. There are things you don't understand."

"Then explain them to me."

He glanced out the window. "There is a legend that the spring that runs under this house is the result of heartache. That a young man got lost in the desert and wandered for days. He was nearly out of water when he found a single blooming plant. So impressed by the beauty of the flower, he poured his last drops of water onto the parched leaves to give it longer life. Grateful, the flower became a beautiful woman. They made love but in the morning, the young man died from dehydration. The woman wept and her tears became a river."

He turned back to her. "The garden in the courtyard pays homage to them both. Some of the plants date back nearly a hundred years."

"That's a very sad story."

"It is a lesson. We must pay attention to what matters. The young woman possessed magical powers. She could have restored the young man first. Instead she took what she wanted and as a result, lost him."

She shook her head. "I think the lesson is to seize whatever love we can find for as long as we have it."

"Perhaps you are right." He rose. "The hot water should be ready soon.

You may shower first."

As appealing as a shower sounded, she had other things on her mind. Maybe it was stupid to take another chance on him and lay her heart on the line. Maybe she didn't have a choice.

"You don't have to let me go, Reyhan."

He stiffened slightly and didn't look at her as he spoke. "Yes, I do."

"Why? Who is this other woman you plan to marry? What will she give you that I can't?"

"Peace of mind."

Chapter Fourteen

After her shower, Emma decided to explore the rest of the small palace. Reyhan had settled in the library and after the cryptic end to their breakfast conversation, she wasn't sure what was left to say between them.

She had a thousand questions, but what was new about that? She'd had questions from the beginning—such as why had he married her in the first place and why had he *stayed* married to her? Asking why he had to marry someone else for his peace of mind was way down there on the "questions to ask" priority list.

She climbed to the second story and explored the amazing rooms. There was a large open area that had to be a ballroom, some kind of living room and four incredibly luxurious bedrooms that would rival the elegance of the famous pink palace in the capital city.

Even without any knowledge about antiques, she recognized the beauty of the carved furniture and the glittering gold leaf edging the chairs. There were dressers and armoires and four-poster beds with stairs leading to high mattresses. Amazing murals covered the walls. In one bedroom, she found a pumpkin coach and six horses, all made of crystal. In another there was a carved set of toy soldiers.

On the third floor were more spartan rooms, except for a round room in a tower. Stained-glass windows cast a rainbow of light on the marble floor. The room was completely empty except for a desk with a chest in the middle.

Curious, she crossed to the desk and opened the chest. When she saw what was inside, her breath caught.

There were pictures. Dozens of pictures, all of a young woman. In some she was laughing, in others serious. Sometimes she faced the camera, sometimes she hid her face. One had been taken while she slept.

Emma felt her heart constrict as she recognized a much-younger version of herself. Reyhan had taken these pictures while they'd been dating and then after they'd married.

Below the pictures were mementos from their dates, all the notes she'd written—and several detective reports. She flipped through them and read his messages to the company he'd hired to check on her for the first few months they'd been separated. He'd obviously wanted to know that she was all right. A few pictures of her had been included with the reports and they were as well-worn as the pages of the report.

"I don't understand," she whispered into the silence. Why had he done this? Why had he kept everything?

Had he been any other man, she would have thought—hoped—that he cared about her. That she mattered. But he wasn't. He was Prince Reyhan of Bahania and he didn't let himself care.

Or did he? Emma sank onto the floor and studied the detective reports more closely. Reyhan was proud. He would not give his heart easily, nor would he want it toyed with. Had he cared about her and had she not understood the depth of his feelings? He wasn't the kind of man who would marry on a whim. He'd chosen her—only her. Now he didn't want a divorce because he loved someone else but so that he could make a marriage of convenience to produce heirs. He didn't want to fall in love again—was that because he still loved her, or because the first time things had ended so badly?

She thought about all that had happened so long ago. How she'd hidden away from him, like a child afraid of being punished. How she'd let her parents convince her he didn't care because it was easier than confessing her guilty secret.

She claimed to be someone different from that scared young woman, yet was she any more willing to fight for what she wanted? If she loved Reyhan, she needed to tell him. If she wanted a chance at making their marriage work, then she would have to fight for him.

She tossed down the report and scrambled to her feet. She wasn't going to wait another second. They belonged together and she was going to help him see that. No matter how long it took.

She raced down the stairs. Once she reached the main floor, she called out his name as she ran from room to room. She burst into the bedroom he'd been using just as he stepped out of the bathroom.

He wore nothing but a towel, and both it and the bandage were white against his skin. Her throat closed as she remembered the last time they'd been in this position—how he'd rejected her. Determined not to be swayed by fear of rejection and his pride, she squared her shoulders.

"We have to talk," she told him.

His dark eyes burned with a fire she recognized. Her insides quivered slightly and her thighs trembled.

"No."

The single word didn't frighten her. He wasn't going to get his waynot anymore. This was too important to let his pride win. Of course if he really didn't care about her at all, she was about to experience the most humiliating moment of her life, but she had to be willing to risk it all if she wanted to win it all.

"I know you want me," she said, crossing the room to stand directly in front of him.

"Desire means nothing," he told her, turning his back on her. "It is simply a reaction."

"To all women or just to me?" She walked up behind him and placed her hands on his bare shoulders. "What happens when I touch you, Reyhan? I know what happens to me. My insides melt while my whole body starts to ache with a hunger I can barely control." She stroked the length of his spine. "My breathing quickens. There is fire everywhere."

His skin was smooth, his muscles unyielding. When her fingers reached the edge of the towel, he shuddered.

"You're so sleek and strong," she murmured, then pressed a kiss to his back. "Straight to my curves, hard to my soft. Is it just me?" she asked. "Tell me."

He turned on her with a roar that could have been anger or passion or maybe both. He reached for her and hauled her against him, apparently unaware or unconcerned about his bullet wound.

She was more than willing to ignore it, too, as he kissed her with a need that was even stronger than her own. There were no preliminarily kisses, no soft queries. Instead he took her mouth and claimed her. His lips pressed against hers with a pressure that had her arching against him.

More, she thought frantically as she clung to him and kissed him back.

She wanted it all.

His tongue swept over and around hers even as he pushed and tugged at her clothing. She wore only a T-shirt and jeans, but they were too much of a barrier when all she had to do was tug at his towel to undress *him*.

And then he was naked and she didn't worry about her own clothing.

Not when she could reach her hand between them and touch his arousal.

As her fingers closed over him, he groaned, then swore and

tore his mouth away. "Get these damn clothes off!" he demanded.

She looked into his eyes and laughed softly. "Impatient, are we?"

"I'll die if I don't have you now."

"Good. Because that's exactly how I feel."

She pulled off her T-shirt and kicked off her sandals while he worked on her jeans. Her bra went next, then she pulled down her panties.

The next second she was falling onto the bed and Reyhan was on top of her.

"I want you," he breathed. "Emma, I need you."

Uncontrollable desire tightened his features. She felt his need, because it was her own. She understood his dilemma even as she reached between them and guided him inside of her.

"You're not ready," he protested, trying to hold back. She knew she was hot, wet and slick. "Yes, I am."

He plunged into her and they both cried out. Within seconds they were lost in a frenzy of sensation and wanting. She pulled him closer, wanting him deeper. He kissed her eyes, her cheeks, before claiming her mouth. She wrapped her legs around him and as her orgasm approached had to break the kiss to gasp for air.

"Reyhan," she breathed as her body stiffened before convulsing into release.

He continued to fill her over and over until the shudders faded. It was only then that he groaned out her name and was still.

She closed her eyes and let herself relax into his embrace. Her need for him hadn't faded, only shifted. Now she wanted to be as emotionally connected as they had been physically.

Reyhan withdrew and rolled onto his back, pulling her with him so that she draped across his chest.

"We should not have done that," he said as he stroked her hair.

"Because you're worried about me getting pregnant," she said.

"That is one consideration. Eventually the odds will catch up with us."

They already had. Emma felt time shift and bend and suddenly she was eighteen, alone in her room and crying. Pain filled her body, but not from a physical source. Instead she felt the ache of being alone and so lost, she would never find her way back.

"What?" he asked, continuing to touch her hair. "Where have you gone?

I see such sadness in your eyes."

She hadn't been sure she was going to tell him. What was the point? But now, suddenly she wanted him to know. Not to make him feel badly but so that he would understand more.

"I was pregnant before," she whispered. "From our honeymoon."

She braced herself for his violent reaction. She didn't expect him to get angry, but she knew there would be energy and demands for information. Perhaps even accusations. But instead he stayed on the bed, his fingers brushing against her scalp, his other hand tucked behind his head.

"What happened?"

A simple question, yet it was as if he'd unlocked a hidden door. She felt her heart shudder as the memories escaped and raced to the light of day for the first time in six years.

"The doctor said it wasn't uncommon to lose a baby in the first few weeks of pregnancy, especially for a young woman. He said there was probably something wrong with it and that was nature's way of making things right." She blinked to hold back tears, but still they spilled over onto her cheeks. "I was so upset when you left that I locked myself in my room at my parents' house and cried for nearly two weeks. I've always wondered if our child couldn't stand the thought of a mother who was so sad all the time."

"So you take responsibility for what happened?" She nodded.

"I see." He cupped her cheek. "Perhaps our child didn't want a father who disappeared without word."

"You had nothing to do with me losing the baby."

"Neither did you." His dark gaze locked on her face. "So that is why you refused to see me. You were too upset."

She nodded. "That's a part of it. I was ashamed, too. And scared. I thought you'd be so angry with me."

He wrapped his arms around her and drew her closer until she rested on top of him and they could kiss. He brushed his mouth against hers. "Never.

With the wisdom of hindsight I know that I shouldn't have left you behind when my aunt died. I should have brought you with me."

"I'm not sure that would have helped. I couldn't have handled the situation, or you. Not then."

One corner of his mouth turned up. "You think you can handle me now?"

"Yes."

"What makes you so sure?"

This was, as her father would say, where the rubber met the road. How willing was she to risk everything and lay it on the line?

"Because before I didn't know why you'd married me. I was young and scared and too inexperienced to know how to please a man. Everything is different now."

The humor disappeared as if it had never been. He started to sit up.

Emma pushed on his shoulders, trying desperately to hold him in place. "Reyhan, don't. We have to talk about it."

"There is nothing to say."

"I think we could talk for a lifetime and never say all the things we missed by being apart. Reyhan, why didn't you ever tell me you loved me?"

He grasped her by the waist and slid her aside, then sat up. That simple action warned her he was already slipping away.

"Why is it such a horrible thing to admit?" she asked desperately. "Is it because I was so immature? I know I couldn't be a partner for you then, but things are different now. We're *both* different. You loved me then. Couldn't you care a little for me now?"

He didn't speak, didn't move. She wasn't sure he was even breathing.

Frightened, and not sure how to convince him, mostly because she didn't understand what she was fighting against, she tried to speak from the heart.

"I don't know what I felt back then. I was a kid. I keep saying that but it's true. I had a fantasy about love and marriage and what my husband would be like. You rescued me that very first day and I'm not sure I saw you as a real person. You were more like a superhero or something. But now I can see the man and he's a good and honorable person."

She leaned against Reyhan's back and wrapped her arms around his shoulders.

"You're proud and sometimes that's annoying, but I can live with it," she continued. "I want to stay here with you. I want us to stay married, to love each other and have babies together." She swallowed before confessing her most intimate secret. "I'm in love with you."

Reyhan felt each word. They cut him like knives. When he'd been shot the day before, he'd barely felt the pain, but now, with Emma, he was ripped apart.

Love. She spoke the words he would have sold his soul to hear. Words that would drive him to his knees with gratitude. But then what? Who would he be if he gave in to his love and desire for this woman? How could he be strong? How could he be a man if he was controlled by a woman?

"No!" he roared, and sprang to his feet. "Do not love me. I will not love you in return. Not again. I will not be crushed by the needing and wanting. I will not have you fill my head and consume the very breath from my body. I will not be made weak by all that I feel for you."

He glared at her, but she didn't flinch. Instead she met his angry gaze with a look so filled with love that he could have captured the emotion in his hand and trapped it in a box.

"It doesn't have to be like that," she said as she stood naked in front of him. Her long hair spread across her shoulders and teased the tops of her breasts. "We can support each other, gaining strength from what the other gives. A team is better than a single man. I want to make you happy, Reyhan. I want to be the one person in the world you can trust with everything and I want to trust you the same way."

He knew what she asked, what she wanted. He knew the truth—it was better to be safe and alone. Better to walk away.

He started to do just that, but before he did so, he allowed himself one last look at her. He took in her beautiful face, the slight tilt of her eyes and the fullness of her mouth. He memorized the sound of her laugh and how she scowled when she was angry. He pictured her hair up, as she'd worn it to the formal reception at the palace.

His gaze dropped lower to her full breasts, the tight nipples that called to him like a siren. Wanting stirred, but he ignored it. Next he studied her narrow waist and the fullness of her hips. He felt badly about the child they'd lost, about the pain she'd suffered alone. Had she been recovering when he'd first tried to see her? Her father had said she was ill. Reyhan had assumed the old man was lying, but perhaps not.

They hadn't used birth control. Why hadn't he considered the possibility of her having his child?

A son, he thought with regret. Or a pretty little girl of five who ran through the halls of the palace and wrapped him around her finger as much as he would wrap her around his heart.

Standing there naked, with sunlight filling the room, Reyhan felt the weight of all he'd lost when he'd abandoned Emma, and the weight of it made it impossible for him to stand. He sank to his knees.

She was at his side in an instant.

"Don't let me go," she pleaded. "We've been given a second chance.

Can't you see how rare and precious that is?"

He clung to her because she was as she had always been—his lifeline. He had tried to live without her. He had convinced himself a cold gray world was a safe place to be, but it was not living. It was an existence that offended those brave enough to reach for what they wanted.

"I am a man humbled by a woman," he said, taking her face in his hands and kissing her.

"I am the one who is humbled," she breathed as she kissed him over and over again. "I love you, Reyhan. For always."

"And I love you. From the first moment I saw you."

He drew her into his arms then carried her to the bed where he settled both of them on the tangled sheets.

"Stay with me," he pleaded. "Love me. Have my children, work at my side, fill my nights and my heart."

Tears spilled out of the corners of her eyes. "Yes. For always."

He wrapped his arms around her. Emma could feel the steady beating of his heart. His skin was warm against her own, both comforting and arousing.

There was much to discuss, she thought as she snuggled closer still. Where they would make their home—either here or the pink palace. How often she would be visiting her parents in Texas. What Reyhan was going to say when she told him she loved her work too much to give it up. While being a delivery room nurse would be difficult, she would have to find another way to use her skills.

Last, and perhaps most important, she wondered when she would tell him about the tiny life growing inside of her. She knew with the certainty that had served women well since the dawn of time that they had made a baby that morning. A child who would be the first of many. The new life was their promise to each other—that they would love with all their hearts. Having nearly lost everything, they would hold on to each other while nurturing a love as constant and endless as the desert itself.

* * * * *

The Bride Who Said No

Chapter One

"I know marrying the crown prince and eventually being queen *sounds* terrific," Daphne Snowden said in what she hoped was a calm I'm-your-aunt-who-loves-you-and-I-know-better voice instead of a shrill, panicked tone. "But the truth of the matter is very different. You've never met Prince Murat. He's a difficult and stubborn man."

Daphne knew this from personal experience. "He's also nearly twice your age."

Brittany looked up from the fashion magazine she'd been scanning. "You worry too much," she said. "Relax, Aunt Daphne. I'll be fine."

Fine? Fine? Daphne sank back into the comfortable leather seat of the luxury private jet and tried not to scream. This could not be happening. It was a dream. It had to be. She refused to believe that her favorite—and only—niece had agreed to marry a man she'd never met. Prince or no prince, this could be a disaster. Despite the fact that she and Brittany had been having the same series of conversations for nearly three weeks now, she felt compelled to make all her points again.

"I want you to be happy," Daphne said. "I love you."

Brittany, a tall willowy blonde with delicately pretty features in the tradition of the Snowden women, smiled. "I love you, too, and you're worrying about nothing. I know Murat is, like, really old."

Daphne pressed her lips together and tried not to wince. She knew that to an eighteen-year-old, thirty-five was practically geriatric, but it was only five years beyond her own thirty years.

"But he's pretty cute," her niece added. "And rich. I'll get to travel and live in a palace." She put down the magazine and stuck out her feet. "Do you think I should have gone with the other sandals instead of these?"

Daphne held in a shriek. "I don't care about your shoes. I'm talking about your *life* here. Being married to the crown prince means you won't get to spend your day shopping. You'll have responsibilities for the welfare of the people of Bahania. You'll have to entertain visiting dignitaries and support charities. You'll be expected to produce children."

Brittany nodded. "I figured that part out. The parties will be great. I can invite all my friends, and we'll talk about, like, what the guy who runs France is wearing."

"And the baby part?"

Brittany shrugged. "If he's old, he probably knows what he's doing. My friend Deanna had sex with her college boyfriend and she said it was totally better than with her boyfriend in high school. Experience counts."

Daphne wanted to shake Brittany. She knew from dozens of after-midnight conversations, when her niece had spent the night, that Brittany had never been intimate with any of her boyfriends. Brittany had been very careful not to let things go too far. So what had changed? Daphne couldn't believe that the child she'd loved from birth and had practically raised, could have turned into this shallow, unfeeling young woman.

She glanced at her watch and knew that time was running short. Once they landed and reached the palace, there would be no turning back. One Snowden bride-to-be had already left

Murat practically at the altar. She had a feeling that Brittany wouldn't be given the opportunity to bolt.

"What was your mother thinking?" she asked, more to herself than Brittany. "Why did she agree?"

"Mom thought it would be completely cool," Brittany said easily. "I think she's hoping there will be some amazing jewelry for the mother of the bride. Plus me marrying a prince beats out Aunt Grace's piggy Justin getting into Harvard any day, right?"

Daphne nodded without speaking. Some families were competitive about sports while others kept score using social status and money. In her family it was all about power—political or otherwise. One of her sisters had married a senator who planned to run for president, the other married a captain of industry. She had been the only sibling to pick another path.

She scooted to the edge of her seat and took Brittany's perfectly manicured hands into her own.

"You have to listen," she said earnestly. "I love you more than I've ever loved another human being in my life. You're practically my daughter."

Brittany's expression softened. "I love you, too. You know you've been there for me way more than my own mother."

"Then, please, please, think this through. You're young and smart and you can have anything you want in the world. Why would you be willing to tie yourself to a man you've never met in a country you've never visited? What if you hate Bahania?"

Daphne didn't think that was possible—personally she loved the desert country—but at this point she was done playing fair.

"Travel isn't going to be what you think," Daphne continued before Brittany could interrupt. "Any visits will be state events. They'll be planned and photographed. Once you agree to marry the prince you'll never be able to just run over and see a girlfriend or head to the mall or the movies."

Brittany stared at her. "What do you mean I can't go to the mall?"

Daphne blinked. Was this progress at last? "You'll be the future queen. You won't be able to rush off and buy a last-minute cashmere sweater just because it's on sale."

"Why not?"

Daphne sighed. "I've been trying to explain this to you. You won't get to be your own person anymore. You'll be living a life in a foreign country with unfamiliar rules and expectations. You will have to adhere to them."

None of which sounded all that tough to her, but she wasn't the one signing up for a lifetime of queenhood.

"I never thought about having to stay in the palace a lot," Brittany said slowly. "I just sort of figured I could fly back home whenever I wanted and hang with my friends."

"Bahania will be your home now."

Brittany's eyes darkened. "I wouldn't miss Mom and Dad so much, but Deanna and you." She bit her lower lip. "I guess if I love the prince…"

"Do you?" Daphne asked. "You've never met him. You're risking a whole lot on the off chance you two will get along." She squeezed her niece's fingers. "You've only had a couple of boyfriends, none of them serious. Do you really want to give all that up? Dating? College?"

Brittany frowned. "I can't go to college?"

"Do you think any professor is going to want the future queen in his class? How could he or she give you a real grade? Even if you did get that worked out, you'd just be attending classes part-time. You couldn't live on campus."

"That's right. Because I'd be in the palace."

"Possibly pregnant," Daphne added for good measure.

"No way. I'm not ready to have a baby *now.*"

"And if Prince Murat is?"

Her niece glared at her. "You're trying to scare me."

"You bet. I'm willing to do just about anything to keep you from throwing away your life. If you'd met someone and had fallen in love, then I wouldn't care if he was a prince or an alien from planet Xeon. But you didn't. I would have gotten involved with this sooner, but your mother did her best to keep the truth from me."

Brittany sighed. "She's pretty determined to have her way."

"I'm not going to let that happen. Tell me honestly. Tell me you're completely committed to this and I'll back off. But if you have even one hint of a doubt, you need to give yourself time to think."

Brittany swallowed. "I'm not sure," she admitted in a tiny voice. "I want things to go great with the prince, but what if they don't?" Tears filled her eyes. "I've been trying to do what my parents want me to do and I'm scared." She glanced around the luxury plane. "The pilot said we were landing in twenty minutes. That's about up. I can't meet the prince and tell him I'm not sure."

Daphne vowed that when she returned to the States she was going to kill her oldest sister, Laurel. How dare she try to guilt her only daughter into something like this? Outrage mingled with relief. She held open her arms, and Brittany fell into her embrace.

"Is it too late?" the teenager asked.

"Of course not. You're going to be fine." She hugged her tight. "You had me worried for a while. I thought you were really going through with this."

Brittany sniffed. "Some parts of it sounded pretty fun. Having all that money and crowns and stuff, but I tried not to think about actually being married to someone that old."

"I don't blame you." The age difference was impossible, Daphne thought. What on earth could Murat be thinking, considering an engagement to a teenager?

"I'll take care of everything," she promised. "You'll stay on the plane and go directly home while I handle things at the palace."

Brittany straightened. "Really? I don't even have to meet him?"

"Nope. You go back and pretend this never happened."

"What about Mom?"

Daphne's eyes narrowed. "You can leave her to me, as well."

Just over an hour later Daphne found herself in the back of a limo, heading to the fabled Pink Palace of Bahania. Because of the long plane trip, she expected to find the city in darkness, but with the time difference, it was late afternoon. She sat right by the window so she could take in everything—the ancient buildings that butted up against the new financial district. The amazing blue of the Arabian Sea just south of the city. The views were breathtaking and familiar. She'd grown to love this country when she'd visited ten years ago.

"Don't go there," she told herself. There was no time for a trip down memory lane. Instead she needed to focus and figure out what she was going to say to Murat.

She glanced at her watch. With every second that ticked by, finding the perfect words became less and less important. Once Brittany landed back in the States, she would be safe from Murat's clutches. Still, she couldn't help feeling a little nervous as the long, black car turned left and drove past elegant wrought-iron gates.

The car pulled to a stop in front of the main entrance. Daphne drew in a deep breath to calm herself as she waited for one of the guards to open the door. She stepped out into the warm afternoon and glanced around.

The gardens were as beautiful as she remembered. Sweet, lush scents competed for her attention. To the left was the gate that led to the private English-style garden she'd always loved. To the right was a path that led to the most perfect view of the sea. And in front of her...well, that was the way into the lion's den.

She tried to tell herself she had no reason to be afraid, that she'd done nothing wrong. Murat was the one interested in marrying a teenager nearly half his age. If anyone should be feeling foolish and ashamed, it was him.

But despite being in the right, and determined to stand strong against any and all who might try to get in her way, she couldn't help a tiny shiver of apprehension. After all, ten years ago she'd been a guest in this very palace. She'd been young and in love and engaged to be married.

To Murat.

Then three weeks before the wedding, she'd bolted, leaving him without even a whisper of an explanation.

Chapter Two

"**M**s. Snowden?"

Daphne saw a well-dressed young man walking toward her. "Yes?"

"The prince is waiting. If you will follow me?"

As Daphne trailed after the man, she wondered if he had any idea she wasn't Brittany. She doubted Murat had bothered to brief his staff on the arrival of a potential bride. He'd rarely concerned himself with details like that. So she would guess that his staff member had simply been told to escort the woman who arrived to an appropriate meeting area.

"Someone is in for a surprise," she murmured under her breath as she walked down a wide corridor lined with stunning mosaics and elegant antiques.

Just being back in the palace made her feel better. She wanted to ask her guide to wait a few minutes while she stopped to enjoy an especially beautiful view from a window or a spectacular piece of artwork. Instead she trailed along dutifully, concentrating on tapestries and carvings instead of what she was going to say when she saw Murat.

They turned a corner. Up ahead Daphne saw a large tabby cat sitting in a patch of sun and washing her face. She smiled as she recalled the dozens and dozens of cats the king kept in the palace.

"In here, Ms. Snowden," the man said as he paused in front of an open door. "The prince will be with you shortly."

She nodded, then walked past him into a small sitting room. The furniture was Western, complete with a sofa, three chairs, a coffee table and a buffet along the far wall. A carafe of ice water and several glasses sat next to a phone on the buffet. She walked over and helped herself to the refreshment.

As she drank she looked around the room and shook her head. How like Murat to have a stranger bring his prospective bride to a room and then drop her off. If Brittany had been here, the teenager would have been terrified by now. The least he could have done was to have sent a woman and then have her keep Brittany company.

But she wasn't Brittany, Daphne reminded herself. Nor was she afraid. Ten years had given her a lot of experience and perspective. Murat might be expecting a young, malleable bride who would bow to his every wish and quiver with fear at the thought of displeasing him, but what he was getting instead was a very different matter.

Footsteps sounded in the hallway. She set down the glass and squared her shoulders. Seconds later the prince from her past strolled into the room.

He still moved with an easy grace of one 'to the manor born," she thought as she took in his powerful body and elegant suit. And he was still a formidable opponent, she reminded herself as he stopped and stared at her.

Not by a flicker of a lash did he indicate he was the least bit surprised.

"Daphne," the crown prince said with a slight smile. "You have returned at last."

"I know you weren't expecting me," she said. "But Brittany couldn't make it."

He raised one dark eyebrow. "Has she been taken ill?"

"No. She simply came to her senses. Even as we speak, she's on a plane back to the United States. There isn't going to be a wedding." She thought maybe she'd been a bit abrupt, so she added a somewhat insincere, "I'm sorry."

"Yes, I can feel your compassion from here," Murat said as he crossed to the buffet and picked up the phone. He dialed four numbers, then spoke. "The airport. Flight control."

He waited a few seconds, then spoke again. "My plane?"

She watched while he listened. It was possible a muscle tightened in his jaw, but she couldn't be sure. He had to be feeling something, she told herself. Or maybe not. Ten years ago he'd let her go without a word. Why should this runaway bride matter?

He hung up the phone and turned back to her. "I assume you had something to do with Brittany's decision."

He wasn't asking a question, but she answered it all the same. "Of course. It was madness. I can't imagine what you were thinking. She's barely eighteen, Murat. Still a child. If you're so desperate for a bride, at least pick someone who is close to being an equal."

For the first time since he walked into the room, he showed emotion, and it wasn't a happy one. Temper drew his eyebrows together.

"You insult me with both your familiarity and your assumption."

She winced silently. Of course. She'd called him by his first name. "I apologize for not using the proper title."

"And the other?"

"I'll do whatever is necessary to keep Brittany safe from you."

"Just because you were not interested in being my wife doesn't mean that others feel the same way."

"I agree completely. There is a world filled with willing young women. Have them all—I don't care. But you're not marrying my niece."

Instead of answering her, he pulled a small device out of

his pocket. It was about the size of a key fob. Seconds later a half dozen armed guards burst into the room and surrounded Daphne. Two of them grabbed her by the arms.

She was too stunned to protest.

"What are you doing?" she demanded.

"Myself? Nothing." Murat returned what she assumed was a security device to his jacket pocket, then adjusted his cuffs. "The guards are another story."

Daphne glared at him. "What? You're arresting me because I wouldn't let you marry my niece?"

"I'm holding you in protective custody for interfering with the private business of the Crown Prince of Bahania."

She narrowed her gaze. "This is crazy. You can't do this to me."

"All evidence to the contrary."

"Bastard."

She tried to squirm away from the guards, but they didn't let her go.

"You'd better not try to turn that plane around," she said, her fury growing. "I won't let you touch her. Not for a second."

Murat crossed toward the door, then paused and glanced at her. "Make no mistake, Daphne. One way or another, there will be a wedding in four months, and the bride will be a Snowden. There is nothing you can do to stop me."

"Want to bet?" she asked, knowing the words were as futile as her attempt to twist free of the guards.

"Of course. I have no fear of wagering with you." He smiled again. "What will you give me when I win?"

She lunged for him and only got a sharp pain in her arm for her reward. Murat chuckled as he walked away.

"When I get my hands on him," she said. "I swear I'll…" She pressed her lips together. On second thought, threatening the prince while still in the presence of several burly guards wasn't exactly smart.

"Where are you taking me?" she asked when the guards continued to just stand here, holding her in place.

The one by the door touched an earpiece, then nodded.

"What? Getting instructions from the crown prince himself?" she asked. "Couldn't he have told you while he was still in the room?"

Apparently not, she realized as the guards started moving. The two holding on to her kept their grips firm enough that she didn't want to risk pulling away. She had a feeling she was already going to be plenty bruised by her experience.

The group of guards, with her in the center, walked down the main corridor, then stopped at a bank of elevators. The one in communication with Murat pushed the down button. When the car arrived, it was a tight fit, but they all made it inside. Daphne noticed how none of the men stood too close to her. In fact, except for the hold on her arms, they were pretty much ignoring her.

She tried to remember the layout of the palace so she could figure out where they were going. *Down* wasn't her idea of a happy thought. Were there still dungeons in the palace? She wouldn't put it past Murat to lock her up.

But when they stepped out of the elevator and headed along a more narrow corridor, Daphne suddenly realized their destination. It was much worse than any dungeon.

"You're not taking me there," she said, wiggling and twisting to escape.

The guard on her left tightened his grip on her arm. "Ma'am, we don't want to hurt you."

The implication being they would if necessary.

I'll get him for this, she thought as she stopped fighting. One way or another, Murat would pay.

They turned a corner, and Daphne saw the famous gold double doors. They stood nearly ten feet tall and were heavily embossed with a scene of several young women frolicking at an oasis.

One of the guards stepped forward and opened the door on the left. The rest marched her inside.

When the men released her, she thought briefly about making a dash for freedom but knew she would be caught and returned here. So she accepted her fate with dignity and a vow that she would find her way out as soon as she could.

The guards left. She heard the heavy clang as the doors closed behind them and the thunk of the gold cross bar being locked into place. Low conversation from the hallway told her that someone would be left on duty to watch over her.

"This is just like you, Murat," she said as she placed her hands on her hips. "You might be an imperial, piggish prince, but I can stand it. I can stand anything to keep you from marrying Brittany."

Daphne looked for something to throw, but the thick, cream-colored walls were completely bare. The only decoration was the brightly colored tile floor.

She moved through the arched entryway, into the large open living area. Dozens of chairs and sofas filled the vast space. The doorway to the left led to the baths, the one on the right led to the sleeping rooms. She recognized this part of the palace from her explorations ten years before. Recognized and fumed because of it.

Dammit all, if Murat hadn't locked her in the harem.

Murat stalked toward the business wing of the palace. Fury quickened his steps. After all this time Daphne Snowden had dared to return to Bahania, only to once again disrupt his world.

Had she come modestly, begging his apology for her unforgivable acts? Of course not. He swore silently. The woman had stared him in the eye, speaking as if they were equals. She had *defied* him.

Murat swept past the guards outside his father's business suite and stepped into the inner office.

"She is here," he announced as he came to a stop in front of the large, carved desk.

The king raised his eyebrows. "You do not sound happy. Has your fiancée displeased you already?"

"She is not my fiancée."

His father sighed, then stood and walked around the desk. "Murat, I know you have reservations about this engagement. You complain that the girl is too young and inexperienced, that she can never be happy here, but once again I ask you to give her a chance."

Murat stared at his father. Anger bubbled inside of him, although he was careful to keep it from showing. He'd spent a lifetime not reacting to anything, and that practice served him well now.

"You misunderstand me, Father," he said in a low voice. "Brittany Snowden is not here in the palace. She is flying back to America even as we speak."

The king frowned. "Then who is here?"

"Daphne."

"Your former—"

Murat cut him off with a quick, "Yes."

One of the many advantages of being the crown prince was the ability to assert his will on others. Ten years ago, when his former fiancée had left without so much as a note, he'd forbidden any to speak her name. All had obeyed except his father, who did not need to pay attention to the will of the crown prince.

"She attempts to defy me," Murat said as he walked to the window and leaned against the sill. "She stood there and told me she would not permit me to marry her niece." He laughed harshly. "As if her desires matter at all to me. I am Crown Prince Murat of Bahania. I determine my fate. No one, especially not a mere woman, dares to instruct me."

His father nodded. "I see. So you complain that Daphne wants to prevent you from marrying someone whom you did not want to marry in the first place."

"That is not the point," Murat told him as he folded his arms across his chest. "There is a principle at stake. The woman did not respect my position ten years ago and nothing has changed."

"I can see how that would be difficult," the king said. "Where is she now?"

Murat glanced down as one of his father's cats stood on the sofa, stretched, then curled back up and closed its eyes.

"I have offered her a place to stay while this is sorted out," he said.

"I'm surprised Daphne would want to remain in the palace. She has delivered her message."

Murat stared at his father. "I did not give her a choice. I had the guards deliver her to the harem."

Very little startled the king, so Murat enjoyed seeing his father's mouth drop open with surprise.

"The harem?" the older man repeated.

Murat shrugged. "I had to detain her. Although she has defied me and spoken with disrespect, I was not willing to lock her in the dungeons. The harem is pleasant enough and will hold her until I decide I wish to let her go."

Although that section of the palace hadn't been used for its intended purpose for more than sixty years, the rooms themselves were maintained in their original splendor. Daphne would be surrounded by every luxury, except that of her freedom.

"It is her own fault," he added. "She had no right to interfere and keep her niece from me. Even though I was never interested in Brittany and only agreed to meet with her to please you, Daphne was wrong to try to foil me."

"I understand completely," his father said. "What do you intend to do with her now?"

Murat hadn't done anything but react. He had no plan where she was concerned.

"I do not know," he admitted.

"Will you order the plane to return Brittany to Bahania?"

"No. I know you wanted me to consider her, but in truth,

Father, I could not be less interested." While Murat accepted that he had to marry and produce heirs, he could not imagine spending the rest of his life with a foolish young wife.

"Perhaps I will keep Daphne for a few days," Murat said. "To teach her a lesson."

"In the harem?" his father asked.

"Yes." He smiled. "She will be most displeased."

She would argue and fume and call him names. She would continue to defy him. Despite all that had gone on before—what she had done and what he had yet to forgive—he found himself looking forward to the encounter.

Daphne discovered her luggage in one of the largest bedrooms in the harem. The sleeping quarters consisted of several private rooms, reserved for those in favor with the king, and large dormitory-like rooms with ten or twelve beautiful beds lined up against the thick walls.

She doubted there was any furniture newer than a hundred years old. Handmade rugs covered the tiled floors in the sleeping rooms, while carved and gilded pieces of furniture added to the decor.

She ignored the suitcases and instead walked close to the walls. No one could have come in through the main door to deliver her luggage—she would have seen. Which meant there was a secret passage and door. The getting in didn't interest her as much as the getting out.

When a careful exploration of the rough walls didn't reveal any hidden doorway, she moved to the hall. It had to be somewhere. She felt around furniture and baseboards, paying particular attention to the inner walls. Still she found nothing.

"I'm sure I'll have plenty of time to keeping checking," she said aloud as she paused in front of a French door that led to a massive walled garden.

Daphne stepped out into the late-afternoon sun and breathed in the scent of the lush plant life. There were trees and shrubs, tiny flowers and huge birds of paradise. A narrow path led through the garden, while stone benches offered a place to sit and reflect. Fluttering movement caught her attention, and she glanced up in time to see two parrots fly across the open area.

"Their loud cries cover the sound of women's voices."

Daphne spun toward the speaker and saw Murat standing behind her. He still wore his suit and his imperious expression. She hated that he was the most handsome man she'd ever met and that, instead of being furious, she actually felt a little tingle of pleasure at seeing him.

Betrayed by her hormones, she thought in disgust. While leaving him ten years ago had been completely sensible, it had taken her far too long to stop loving him. Even the pain of knowing he hadn't cared enough to come after her hadn't made the recovery any shorter.

"Many of the parrots here are quite old," he continued. "But there is a single breeding pair that has given us a new generation."

"You no longer have women in the harem. Why do you keep the parrots?"

He shrugged. "Sometimes there is difficulty in letting go of the old ways. But you are not interested in our traditions. You wish to berate me and tell me what I can and cannot do." He nodded. "You may begin now if you wish."

Suspicious of his motives, she studied him. But his dark eyes and chiseled features gave nothing away. Still, that didn't stop her from wanting to know what was going to happen.

"What are you going to do about Brittany?" she asked.

"Nothing."

Like she believed that. "Are you ordering the jet to turn around?"

"No. Despite what you think of me, I will not force my bride to present herself. She will be here in time."

Daphne glared at him. "No, she won't. Brittany isn't going to marry you."

The Bride Who Said No

He dismissed her with a flick of his hand. "The gardens have grown since you were last here. Do you remember? You were quite enchanted with the idea of the harem and disappointed that we no longer used it for its original purpose."

"I was not," she protested. "I think it's terrible that women were kept locked up for the sole purpose of offering sexual pleasure for the king."

He smiled. "So you say now. But I distinctly recall how you found the idea exciting. You asked endless questions."

Daphne felt heat on her cheeks. Okay, maybe she *had* been a little interested in the workings of the harem. Ten years ago she'd been all of twenty and a virtual innocent in the ways of the world. Everything about the palace had intrigued her. Especially Murat.

"I'm over it now," she said. "How long do you intend to keep me here?"

"I have not yet decided."

"My family will come to my rescue. You must know they have substantial political power."

He didn't seem the least bit intimidated by the threat.

"What I know," he said, "is that their ambitions have not changed. They still wish for a Snowden female to marry royalty."

She couldn't argue that. First her parents had pushed her at Murat, and now her own sister pushed Brittany.

"I'm not like them," she said.

"How true." He glanced at his watch. "Dinner is at seven. Please dress appropriately."

She laughed. "And if I don't want to have dinner with you?"

He raised one eyebrow. "The choice has never been yours, Daphne. When will you finally learn that? Besides, you *do* want to dine with me. You have many questions. I see them in your eyes."

With that he turned and left.

"Annoying man," she muttered when she was alone again.

Worse, he was right. She had questions—lots of them. And a burning desire to deal with the unfinished business between them.

As for the man himself...time had changed him, but it had not erased *her* interest in the only man she had ever loved.

Chapter Three

Daphne stood in front of her open suitcase and stared down at the contents. While a part of her wanted to ignore Murat's demand that she 'dress appropriately' for their dinner, another part of her liked the idea of looking so fabulous that she would leave him speechless. It was a battle between principles and beauty and she already knew which would win.

After sorting through the contents of her luggage, she withdrew a simple sleeveless dress and carried it into the bathroom. She would let it hang in the steam while she showered. She plugged in the electric curlers she'd already unpacked, then pinned up her hair and stepped into the shower.

Fifteen minutes later she emerged all cleaned and buffed and smoothed. The bath towels provided were big enough to carpet an entire room. An array of cosmetics and skin-care products filled the cabinets by the huge mirror and vanity.

Everywhere she looked she saw marble, gold, carved wood or beveled glass. How many women had stood in front of this mirror and prepared to meet a member of the royal family? What kind of stories had these walls witnessed? How much laughter? How many tears? Under other circumstances she could enjoy her stay in this historical part of the palace.

"Who am I kidding?" she murmured as she unpinned her hair and brushed it out. "I'm enjoying it now."

She'd always loved Bahania and the palace. Murat had been the problem.

He hadn't been that way in the beginning. He'd been charming and intriguing and exactly the kind of man she'd always wanted to meet. As she reached for the first hot curler, she remembered that party she'd attended in Spain where they had first met.

Traveling through Europe the summer between her sophomore and junior year of college had meant doing her best to avoid all her parents' upper-class and political friends. But in Barcelona, Daphne had finally caved to her mother's insistence that she accept an invitation to a cocktail party for some ambassador or prime minister or something. She'd been bored and ready to leave after ten minutes. But then, on a stone balcony with a perfect view of the sunset, she'd met a man.

He'd been tall, handsome and he'd made her laugh when he'd confessed that he needed her help—that he was hiding from the far-too-amorous youngest daughter of their host.

"When she comes upstairs looking for me, I'll hide under the table and you will send her away," he said. "Will you do that for me?"

He stared at her with eyes as dark as midnight. At that second her stomach had flipped over, her cheeks had flushed and she would have followed him to the ends of the earth.

He'd spent the entire evening with her, escorting her to dinner and then dancing with her under the stars. They'd talked of books and movies, of childhood fantasies and grown-up dreams. And when he'd walked her back to her hotel and kissed her, she'd known that she was in danger of falling for him.

He hadn't told her who he was until their third date. At first she'd been nervous—after all, even she had never met a prince—but then she realized that for once being a Snowden was a good thing. She'd been raised to be the wife of a president, or even a prince.

"Come back with me," he'd pleaded when he had to return to Bahania. "Come see my country, meet my people. Let them discover how delightful you are, as I have."

It wasn't a declaration of love—she saw that now. But at twenty, it had been enough. She'd abandoned the rest of her tour and had flown with him to Bahania, where she'd stayed at the fabled Pink Palace and had fallen deeply in love with both Murat and every part of his world.

Daphne finished applying her makeup, then unwrapped the towel and stepped into her lingerie. Next she took out the curlers and carefully finger-combed her hair before bending over and spraying the underside. She flipped her hair back and applied more hairspray before finally stepping into her dress.

The silk skimmed over her body to fall just above her knees. She stepped into high-heeled sandals, then stared at her reflection.

Daphne knew she looked tired. No doubt her mother could find several items to criticize. But what would Murat think? How was the woman different from the girl? Ten years ago she'd loved him with a devotion that had bordered on mindlessness. The only thing that could have forced her to leave was the one thing that had—the realization that he didn't love her back.

"Don't go there," she told herself as she turned away from the mirror and made her way out of the bathroom.

Maybe if she arrived at the main rooms early, she could see where the secret door was as the staff arrived with dinner. She had a feeling that Murat would not be letting her out of the harem anytime soon—certainly not for meals. Which meant meals would have to come to her.

But as she stepped into the large salon overlooking the gardens, she saw she was too late. A small cart with drinks stood in the center of the room, but even more interesting than that was the man waiting by the French doors.

She'd been thinking about him while getting ready, so seeing him now made her feel as if she'd stepped into an alternative universe—one where she could summon handsome princes at will.

He turned toward her and smiled.

"You are early," he said.

"I'd hoped to catch the staff delivering dinner."

One dark eyebrow rose. "I fail to see the excitement of watching them come in and out of the door."

"You're right. If they're using the door, it's not exciting at all. But if they were to use the secret passage…"

His smile widened. "Ah. You seek to escape. But it will not be so easy. You forget we have a tradition of holding beautiful women captive. If they were able to find their way from the palace, we would be thought of as fools."

"Is that your way of saying you'll make sure I don't find the secret passage?"

He walked toward the drinks cart. "No. It is my way of saying that it is impossible to open the door from this side. Only someone outside the harem can work the latch."

He held up a bottle of champagne and she nodded.

"I suppose that information shouldn't surprise me," she told him. "So there really is no escape?"

"Why would you want there to be?"

He popped the bottle expertly, then poured two glasses.

"I don't take well to being someone's prisoner," she said as she took the glass he offered.

"But this is paradise."

"Want to trade?"

Amusement brightened his eyes. "I see you have not changed. Ten years ago you spoke your mind and you still do today."

"You mean I haven't learned my place?"

"Exactly."

"I like to think my place is wherever I want it to be."

"How like a woman." He held up his glass. "A toast to our mutual past, and what the future will bring."

She thought about Brittany, who would be landing in New York shortly. "How about to our separate lives?"

"Not so very separate. We could be family soon."

"I don't think so. You're not marrying—"

"To the beauty of the Snowden women," he said, cutting her off. "Come, Daphne. Drink with me. We will leave our discussion of less pleasant matters to another day."

"Fine." The longer they talked about other things, the more time her niece had to get safely home. "To Bahania."

"At last something we can agree upon."

They touched glasses, then sipped their champagne. Murat motioned to one of the large sofas and waited until she was seated before joining her on the overstuffed furniture.

"You are comfortable here?" he asked.

"Aside from the whole idea of being kept against my will, pretty much." She set down the glass and sighed. "Okay. Honestly, the harem is beautiful. I plan to do some serious exploring while I'm here."

"My sister Sabrina is an expert on antiquities and our history. Would you like me to have her visit?"

Daphne laughed. "My own private lecture circuit? I'm sure your sister has better things to do with her life."

"Than serve me?"

He spoke teasingly, but she knew there was truth behind the humor. Murat had been raised to believe he was the center of the universe. She supposed that came with being the future king.

He sat angled toward her, his hand-tailored suit emphasizing the strength in his powerful body. Ten years ago he'd been the most handsome man she'd ever met. And now... She sighed. Not that much had changed.

"Did you get a chance to see much of the city as you drove in?" he asked.

"Just the view from the highway. I was pretty intent on getting to the palace."

"Ah, yes. So you could defy me at every turn. There are many new buildings in our financial district."

"I noticed those. The city is growing."

He nodded. "We seek success in the future without losing what is precious to us from our past. It is an act of balance."

She picked up her glass of champagne and took a sip. The cool, bubbly liquid tickled her tongue. "There have been other changes since I was last here," she said. "Your brothers have married."

"That is true. All to American women. There have been many editorials in the papers about why that is, although the consensus among the people is new blood will improve the lineage of the royal family."

"That must make the women in question feel really special."

He leaned back against the sofa. "Why would they not be pleased to improve the gene pool of such a noble family?"

"Few women fantasize about being a good brood mare."

He shook his head. "Why do you always want to twist things around to make me look bad? All my sisters-in-law are delightful women who are blissfully happy with their chosen mates. Cleo and Emma have given birth in the past year. Billie is newly pregnant. They are catered to by devoted husbands and do not want for anything."

He painted a picture that made her feel funny inside. Not sad, exactly. Just…envious. She'd always wanted a guy who would love her with his whole heart, but somehow she'd never seemed to find him.

"You're right," she said. "Everyone seems perfectly happy. You remain the last single prince."

He grimaced. "A point pressed home to me on a daily basis."

"Getting a little pressure to marry and produce heirs?"

"You have no idea."

"Then we should talk about Brittany and why that would never work."

His gaze lingered on her face. "You are a difficult and stubborn woman."

"So you keep saying."

"We will discuss your niece when I decide it is time."

"You don't get to choose," she told him.

"Of course I do. And you do not wish to speak of her right now. You wish to tell me all about yourself. What you have been doing since we last met. You want to impress me."

"I do not."

He raised one eyebrow and waited. She shifted in her seat. Okay, yes, maybe she wouldn't mind knocking his socks off with her accomplishments, but she didn't like that he'd guessed.

"Come, Daphne," he said, moving closer and focusing all of his considerable attention on her. "Tell me everything. Did you finish college? What have you been doing?" He picked up her left hand and examined the bare fingers. "I see you have not given your heart to anyone."

She didn't like the assessment, nor did she appreciate the tingles that rippled up from her hand to her arm. He'd always been able to do that—reduce her to pudding with a single touch. Why couldn't that have changed? Why couldn't time away have made her immune?

"I'm not engaged, if that's what you mean," she said. "I'm not willing to discuss the state of my heart with you. It's none of your business."

"As you wish. Tell me about college."

She clutched her champagne in her right hand and thought about swallowing the whole thing in one big gulp. It might provide her with a false sense of courage, which was better than no courage at all.

"I completed my degree as planned, then went on to become a veterinarian."

He looked two parts delighted, one part surprised. "Good for you. You enjoy the work?"

"Very much. Until recently I've been with a large practice in Chicago. My first two years with them I spent summers in Indiana, working on a dairy farm."

She couldn't remember ever really shocking Murat before, so now she allowed herself to enjoy his expression of astonishment. "Delivering calves?"

"Pretty much."

"It is not seemly."

She laughed. "It was my job. I loved it. But lately I've been working with small animals. Dogs, cats, birds. The usual." She took another sip and smiled. "If your father needs any help with the cats he should let me know."

"I will be sure to pass along your offer. Chicago is very different from Bahania."

"I agree. For one thing, there aren't any words to describe how cold that wind can be in the winter."

"We have no such discomfort here."

That was true. The weather in paradise was pretty darned good.

"You're not very close to your family," he said.

Daphne nearly spilled her champagne. Okay, so it didn't take a rocket scientist to figure out that she didn't fit in with the 'real' Snowdens, but she was surprised Murat would say something like that so blatantly. After all...

The light went on in her head. "You mean I live far away," she said.

"Yes. They are all on the East Coast. Is that the reason you chose to settle in Chicago?"

"Part of it," she admitted. "I handle the constant disapproval better from a distance."

"Aren't your parents proud of what you have accomplished?"

"Not really. They keep waiting for me to wake up and get engaged to a senator. I'm resisting the impulse."

She spoke with a casualness, as if her family's expectations didn't matter, but Murat saw the truth in her blue eyes.

Pain, he thought. Pain from disappointing them, pain from not being accepted for who and what she was. Daphne had always been stubborn and determined and proud. From what he could see, little had changed about that.

Her appearance had been altered, though. Her face was thinner, her features more defined. Whereas at twenty she had held the promise of great beauty, now she fulfilled it. There was an air of confidence about her he liked.

She leaned forward. "I've spent the past couple of years studying pet psychology."

"I have not heard of that."

She smiled again, her full lips curving upward as if she were about to share a delicious private joke. "You'd appreciate it. The field is growing rapidly. We're interested in why animals act the way they do. What set of circumstances combine with their personality to make them act aggressively or chew furniture or not accept a new baby. That sort of thing."

He couldn't believe such information existed. "This is what you are doing now?"

"I'm getting into it. I've learned some interesting things about dealing with alpha males." She tilted her head. "Maybe I could use the techniques to tame you."

"Neither of us is interested in me being tame."

"Oh, I don't know."

"I do."

"You're certainly sure of yourself."

"The privilege of being the alpha male."

She continued to study him. Awareness crackled between them. He could smell the faint scent of the soap she'd used and some other subtle fragrance he associated only with her.

Wanting coiled low in his gut, surprising him with both its presence and its intensity. After all this time? He'd always wondered what he would feel if he saw her again, but somehow he'd never expected to have a strong need to touch her, explore her, take her.

He wanted to lead her into one of the many harem bedrooms and make her shudder beneath him. Funny how so much time had passed and the desire hadn't gone away.

"You're looking very predatory," she said. "What are you thinking?"

"I was wondering about your art. Do you still make time to do your sculptures?"

She hesitated, as if she didn't quite believe that was what he'd been thinking, then she answered.

"I still love it, but time is always an issue."

"Perhaps I should provide you with clay while you are here. You can indulge your passion."

"How long do you intend to keep me in the harem?"

"I have not yet decided."

"So we really do need to talk about Brittany."

Just then the large golden doors opened and several servants walked in pushing carts.

"Dinner," he said, rising to his feet.

"If I didn't know better, I would say you did that on purpose."

He smiled. "Even I can't command my staff with just a thought."

"Why do I know you're working on it?"

"I have no idea."

Murat had left the menu up to his head chef, and he was not disappointed with the meal. Neither was Daphne, he thought as she ran her fork across the remaining crumbs of chocolate from the torte served for dessert.

"Amazing," she breathed. "I could blow up like a beached whale if I lived here for too long."

"Not every meal is so very formal," he said, enjoying her pleasure in the food.

"Good thing. I'll have to do about fifty laps in the garden tomorrow." She picked up her wine and eyed him over the glass. "Unless you plan on cutting me loose sometime soon."

"Are we back to that?"

"We are. Murat, I'm serious. You can't keep me here forever."

"Perhaps I wish to resume the traditional use of these rooms."

He held in a smile as her eyes widened. "You are *so* kidding," she said, although she didn't sound quite sure of herself. "I'm not going to volunteer."

"Few women did at first, even though it was a great honor. But in time they came to enjoy their lives. Luxury, pleasure. What more could you want?"

"How about freedom and autonomy?"

"There is power in being desired. The smart women learned that and used it to their advantage. They ruled the ruler."

"I've never been good at subterfuge," she told him. "Besides, I'm not interested in working behind the scenes. I want to be up front and in the thick of things. I want to be an equal."

"That will never be. I am to be king of Bahania, with all the advantages and disadvantages that go with the position."

Daphne sipped her dessert wine. Disadvantages? She hadn't thought there could be any. Even if there weren't, it was a much safer topic than what life would be like in the harem.

"What's so bad about being the king?" she asked.

"Nothing bad, as you say. Just restrictions. Rules. Responsibilities."

"Always being in the spotlight," she said. "Always having to do the right thing."

"Exactly."

"Marrying a teenager you've never met can't be right, Murat, can it?"

His gaze narrowed. "You are persistent."

"And determined. I love her. I would do anything for her."

"Even displease me?"

"Apparently," she said with a shrug. "Are you going to behead me for it?"

"Your casual question tells me you are not in the least bit worried. I will have to do something to convince you of my power."

"I'm very clear on your power. I just want you to use it for good." She set down her glass and leaned toward him. "Come on. It's just the two of us, and I promise never to tell. You can't have been serious about her. A young girl you've never met?"

"Perhaps I wanted a brainless young woman to do my bidding."

Daphne stiffened. "She's not brainless. And she wouldn't have done your bidding. You're trying to annoy me on purpose, aren't you?"

"Is it working?"

"Pretty much." She sagged back in her chair. "I don't want you to be like that. I don't want you to be the kind of man who would marry Brittany."

"Do you think I am?"

"I hope not. But even if you are, I won't let you."

"You can't stop me."

"I'll do whatever is necessary to stop you."

His dark eyes twinkled with amusement. "I am Crown Prince Murat of Bahania. Who are you to threaten me?"

Good question. Maybe it was the night and the man, or just the alcohol, but her head was a little fuzzy. There had been a different wine with each course. She'd only taken a sip of each, but those sips added up and muddled her thinking. It was the only explanation for what she said next.

"You're just some alpha-male dog peeing on every tree to mark his territory. That's all Brittany is to you. A tree or a bush."

As soon as the words were out, she wanted to call them back. Murat stunned her by tossing back his head and roaring with laughter.

Still chuckling, he stood. "Come, we will go for a walk to clear your head. You can tell me all your theories about domesticating men such as me."

He walked around the table and pulled back her chair. She rose and faced him.

"It's not a joke. You're acting like a territorial German shepherd. You could use a little obedience training to keep you in line."

"I am not the one who needs to stay in line."

"Are you threatening me?"

As she spoke, she took a step toward him. Unfortunately her feet weren't getting the right signals from her brain, and she stumbled. He caught her and pulled her against him.

"You speak of domestication, but is that what you want?" he asked. "A trained man would not do this."

The 'this' turned out to be nothing more than his mouth pressing against hers. A kiss. No biggie.

Except the second his lips brushed against hers, every part of her body seemed to go up in flames. Desperate hot need pulsed through her, forcing her to cling to him or collapse at his feet.

They'd kissed before, she remembered hazily. A lifetime ago. He'd held her tenderly and delighted her with gentle embraces.

But not this time. Now he claimed her with a passion that left her breathless and hungry for more. He wrapped his arms around her, drawing her up against his hard body.

She melted into him, savoring the heat and the strength. When he tilted his head, she did the same and parted her lips before he even asked. He plunged inside, stroking, circling, teasing, making her breath catch and her body weep with desire.

More, she thought as she kissed him back. There had to be more.

But there wasn't. He straightened, forcing her to consider standing on her own. She pushed back and found her balance, then struggled to catch her breath.

"Brittany will be in New York by now," he said.

The sudden change in topic caught her off guard. Weren't they going to discuss the kiss? Weren't they going to do it again?

Apparently not. She ordered herself to focus on Brittany. Murat. The wedding that could never be.

"I meant what I said," he told her. "There *will* be a Snowden bride."

"You'll need to rethink your plan," she said. "Brittany isn't going to marry you."

He stared at her, his dark eyes unreadable. "Are you sure?"

"Absolutely."

She braced herself for an argument or at least a pronouncement that he was the crown prince, blah, blah, blah. Instead he simply nodded.

"As you wish," he said. And then he left.

Daphne didn't fall asleep until sometime after two in the morning. She'd felt too out of sorts to relax. While she told herself she should be happy that Murat was finally seeing reason about Brittany, she didn't trust the man. Certainly not his last cryptic agreement. As she wished what? Was he really giving up on Brittany so easily? Somehow that didn't seem right.

So when she woke early the next morning, she felt more tired than when she'd gone to bed.

After slipping into her robe, she hurried toward the smell of fresh coffee wafting through the harem. A cart stood by the sofa.

Daphne ignored the fresh fruit and croissants and dove for the coffee. The steaming liquid perked her up with the first sip.

"Better," she said, when she'd swallowed half a cup.

She sat down in front of the cart and picked up the folded newspapers. The first was a copy of *USA TODAY.* Underneath was the local Bahanian paper. She flipped it open, then screamed.

On the front page was a color picture of her under a headline announcing her engagement to Murat.

Chapter Four

"I'll kill him!" Daphne yelled.

She set down her coffee before she dropped it and shrieked her fury.

"How dare he? Who does he think he is? Crown prince or not, I'll have his head for this!"

She couldn't believe it. Last night he'd been friendly and fun and sexy with his talking and touching, when the whole time he'd been planning an ambush.

She stomped her foot. He'd *kissed* her. He'd taken her in his arms and kissed her. She'd gotten all gooey and nostalgic while he'd known what he was going to do.

"Bastard. No. Wait. He's lower than that. He's a...a camel-dung sweeper. He's slime."

She tossed the paper down, then immediately bent over to pick it up. There, in perfect English, was the announcement for the upcoming wedding along with what looked like a very long story on her previous engagement to Murat.

"Just great," she muttered. "Now we're going to have to re-hash that again."

She threw the paper in the air and stalked around the room. "Are you listening, Murat?" she yelled. "Because if you are, know that you've gone too far. You can't do this to me. I won't let you."

There was no answer. Typical, she thought. He's done it and now he was hiding out.

Just then the phone rang.

"Ha! Afraid to face me in person?"

She crossed to the phone on the end table and snatched it up. "Yes?"

"How could you do this?" a familiar female voice demanded. "Laurel?"

A choke shook her sister's voice. "Who else? Dammit, Daphne, you always have to ruin everything. You did this on purpose, didn't you? You wanted him for yourself."

It took Daphne a second to figure out what her sister was talking about. "You know about the engagement?" she asked.

"Of course. What did you think? That it would happen in secret?"

"Of course not. I mean there's no engagement."

How on earth had her sister found out? There was a major time difference between Bahania and the American East Coast. "Shouldn't you be in bed?"

"Oh, sure. Because I'm going to sleep after this." Her sister drew in a ragged breath. "What I don't understand is how you could do this to Brittany. I thought you really cared about her."

"I do. I love her." Probably more than her sister ever had, Daphne thought grimly. "That's why I didn't want her marrying Murat. She's never even met the man."

"You took care of things, didn't you? Now you have him all for yourself. I can't believe I was stabbed in the back by my own sister."

Daphne clutched the phone. "This is crazy. Laurel, think about it. Why on earth would I want to marry Murat? Didn't I already dump him once?"

"You've probably regretted it ever since. You've just been waiting for the right opportunity to pounce."

"It's been ten years. Couldn't I have pounced before now?"

"You thought you'd find someone else. But you didn't. Who could measure up to the man who's going to be king? I understand that kind of ambition. I can even respect it. But to steal your only niece's fiancé is horrible. Brittany will be crushed."

"I doubt that."

"I never should have trusted you," Laurel said. "Why didn't I see what you had planned?"

"There wasn't a plan." Except making sure Brittany didn't throw her life away, but Laurel didn't have to know about that. "I told you, I'm not engaged to Murat. I don't know what the papers are talking about, but it's a huge mistake."

"Oh, sure. Like I believe that."

"Believe what you want. There's not going to be a wedding."

"Tell that to my heartsick daughter. You've always thought of yourself instead of your family. Just know I'll never forgive you. No matter what."

With that, Laurel hung up.

Daphne listened to the silence for a second, then put down the phone and covered her face with her hands. Nothing made sense. How could this be happening?

She had a lot of questions, but no answers, and she knew only one way to get them.

She stood and crossed to the heavy gold doors.

"Hey," she yelled. "Are you guards still out there?"

"Yes, ma'am. Is there a problem?"

"You bet there is. Tell Murat I want to see him right now."

She heard low conversation but not the individual words as the guards spoke to each other.

"We'll pass your message along to the crown prince," one of the men said at last.

"Not good enough. I want his royal fanny down here this second. And you can tell him I said that."

She pounded on the door a couple of times for good measure, then stalked back into her bedroom. Suddenly the phrase 'dressed to kill' took on a whole new meaning.

Murat finished his second cup of coffee as he read over the financial section of the *London Times*. Then the door to his suite opened, and his father stepped in.

The king was perfectly dressed, even with the Persian cat he carried in his arms. He nodded at the guard on duty, then walked into the dining room.

"Good morning," he said.

Murat rose and motioned to a chair. The king shook his head.

"I won't be staying long. I only came by to discuss the most fascinating item I saw in the paper this morning."

"That the value of the Euro is expected to rise?" Murat asked calmly, knowing it wasn't that.

"No." The king flipped through the pages until he found the local edition—the one with the large picture of Daphne on the front page. "Interesting solution."

Murat shrugged. "I said I would have a Snowden bride, and so I shall."

"I'm surprised she agreed."

Murat thought of the message he'd received from the guards outside the harem. Even though he suspected they'd edited the content, Daphne's demands made him smile.

"She has not," he admitted. "But she will. After all, the choice of fiancées was hers alone."

"Oh?"

"I told her there would be a wedding, and she said Brittany would not be the bride. That left Daphne to fill the position."

"I see." His father didn't react at all. "Do you have a time line in place for this wedding?"

"Four months."

"Not long to prepare for such an important occasion."

"I think we will manage."

"Perhaps I should go to her and offer my congratulations."

Murat raised his eyebrows. "I'm sure Daphne will welcome your visit, but may I suggest you wait a few days. Until she has had time to settle in to the idea of being my wife."

"Perhaps you are right." The king stroked the cat in his arms. "You have chosen wisely."

"Thank you. I'm sure Daphne and I will be very happy together." After she got over wanting him dead.

By ten that morning Daphne was convinced she'd worn a track in the marble tile floors. She'd showered, dressed and paced. So far she'd been unable to make any phone calls because of the stupid time difference. But she would eventually get through to someone and then Murat would taste her fury. She might not be the favorite Snowden, but she was still a member of the family and her name meant something. She would call in every favor possible and make him pay for this.

"Of all the arrogant, insensitive, chauvinistic, ridiculous ideas," she muttered as she walked to the French doors.

"So much energy."

She spun and saw him moving toward her. "I hate that you do that," she said. "Appear and disappear. I swear, when I find that secret door, I'm putting something in front of it so you can't use it anymore."

He seemed completely unruffled by her anger. "As you wish."

"Oh, sure. You say that now. Where were my wishes last night when you were sending your lies to the newspaper?" She stalked over to the dining room table and picked up the pages in question.

"How could you do this?" she asked as she shook them at him. "How dare you? Who gave you the right?"

"You did."

"What?" She hated that she practically shrieked, but the man was making her insane. "I most certainly did not."

"I told you there would be a Snowden bride and you declared it would not be your niece."

"What?" she repeated. "That's not making a choice. I never agreed with your original premise. Where do you get off saying you'll have a Snowden bride? We're not ice cream flavors to be ordered interchangeably. We're people."

"Yes, I know. Women. I have agreed not to marry Brittany. You should be pleased."

Pleased? "Are you crazy?" She dropped the papers and clutched at the back of the chair. "I'm furious. You've trapped me here and told lies about me to the press. I've already heard from my sister. Do you know how this is going to mess up my life? Both of our lives?"

"I agree that marriage will change things, but I'm hoping for the better."

"We're not getting married!" she yelled.

Instead of answering, he simply stared at her. Calm certainty radiated from him in nearly palpable waves. It made her want to choke him.

She drew in a deep breath and tried to relax. When that didn't work, she attempted to loosen her grip on the chair.

"Okay," she said. "Let's start from the beginning. You're not marrying Brittany, which is a good thing."

He had the gall to smile at her. "Did you really think I would be interested in a teenager for my wife? Bringing Brittany here was entirely my father's idea. I agreed to meet with her only to make him happy."

Spots appeared before her eyes. "You what?" No way. That couldn't be true. "Tell me that again."

"I never intended to marry Brittany."

"But you…" She couldn't breathe. Her chest felt hot and tight and she couldn't think. "But you said…"

"I wanted to annoy you for assuming the worst about me. Then when you offered yourself in Brittany's place, I decided to consider the possibility."

Offer? "I never offered."

"Oh, but you did. And I accepted."

"No. You can't." She pulled out the chair and sank onto the seat. "I know you're used to getting your way, but this time it isn't going to happen. I need to be very clear about that. There isn't going to be a wedding. You can't make me, and if you try, you'll be forced to tie me up and gag me as you drag me down the aisle. Won't that play well in the press."

"I do not care about the press."

She grabbed the paper again. "Then why did you bother telling them this?"

He sat down across from her. "Make no mistake. My mind is made up. We *will* be married. This announcement has forced you to see the truth. Now you will have time to accept it."

"What I accept is that you've slipped into madness. This isn't the fifteenth century. You can't force me to do what you want. This is a free country." She remembered she wasn't in America anymore. "Sort of."

"I am Crown Prince Murat of Bahania. Few would tell me no."

"Count me among them."

He leaned back in his chair. "You never disappoint me," he said. "How I enjoy the explosion. You're like fireworks."

She glared at him. "You haven't seen anything yet. I'll take this all the way to the White House if I have to."

"Good. The president will be invited to the wedding. He and I have been friends for many years now."

At that moment Daphne desperately wished for superpowers so she could overturn the heavy table and toss Murat out the window.

"I'm going to speak slowly," she said. "So you can understand me. I...won't...marry...you. I have a life. Friends. My work."

"Ah, yes. About your work. I made some phone calls last night and found it most interesting to learn that you have left your veterinary practice in Chicago."

"That was about making career choices, not marrying you."

"And you have been very determined to keep me from your niece. Are you sure you do not secretly want me for yourself?"

She rolled her eyes. "How amazing that you and your ego fit inside the room at the same time." Although her sister had made the same accusation.

It wasn't true, Daphne reminded herself. Murat was her past, and she was more than content to keep him there. She hadn't spent the last ten years pining. She'd dated, been happy. He was a non-event.

"I haven't thought about you in ages," she said honestly. "I'm even willing to take an oath. Just bring in the Bible. I wouldn't be here now if you hadn't acted all caveman over my niece. This is your fault."

He nodded. "There is a ring."

She blinked at him. "What? You want to try to buy me off with jewelry? Thank you very much but I'm not that kind of woman."

He smiled again. "I know."

Her rage returned, but before she could decide how to channel it, the phone rang again.

She hesitated before crossing the room to answer it. Was Laurel calling back to yell some more? Daphne had a feeling she was at the end of her rope and not up to taking that particular call. But what if it was Brittany, and her niece really was upset?

"Not possible," she said as she crossed to the phone and picked it up. "This is Daphne."

"Darling, we just heard. We're delighted."

Her mother's voice came over the line as clearly as if she'd been in the same room.

Daphne clutched the receiver. "Laurel called?"

"Yes. Oh, darling, how clever you are to have finally snagged Murat. The man who will be king." Her mother sighed. "I always knew you'd do us proud."

Daphne didn't know what to think. She wanted to tell her

mother the truth—that there wasn't going to be a wedding, that this was all a mistake, but she couldn't seem to speak.

"Your father is simply thrilled," her mother said. "We're looking forward to a lovely wedding. Do you have any idea when?"

"I—"

Her mother laughed. "Of course you don't. You've only just become engaged. Well, let me know as soon as the date is finalized. We'll need to rearrange some travel, but it will be worth it. Your father can't wait to walk you down the aisle."

Daphne turned her back so Murat couldn't see her expression. She didn't want him to know how much this conversation hurt.

"Laurel was pretty upset," she said, not knowing what else to say.

"I know. She got it in her head that Brittany would be the one for Murat. Honestly, the girl is lovely and will make a fine marriage in time, but she's just too young. There are responsibilities that come with being queen, and she simply wasn't ready." Her mother laughed. "Queen. I like the sound of that. My daughter, the queen. My sweet baby girl. All right, I'm going to run, but I'll call soon. You must be so very happy. This is wonderful, Daphne. Truly wonderful."

With that her mother hung up. Daphne replaced the receiver and did her best not to react in any way. Sure, her eyes burned and her body felt tense and sore, but she would get over it. She always did.

"Your parents?" Murat asked from his place at the table behind her.

She nodded. "My mother. My sister called and spoke with her. She's d-delighted."

The crack in her voice made her stiffen. No way was she going to give in to the emotion pulsing through her.

"She wants details about the wedding as soon as possible. So she can rearrange their travel schedule."

"You did not tell her there wouldn't be a wedding."

"No."

Because it had been too hard to speak. Because if she tried, she would give in to the pain and once that dam broke, there was no putting it together.

"Don't think that means I've accepted the engagement," she whispered.

"Not for a second."

She heard footsteps, then Murat's hands clasped her arms and he turned her toward him. Understanding darkened his eyes.

She was so unused to seeing any readable emotion in his gaze that she couldn't seem to react. Which meant she didn't protest when he pulled her close and wrapped his arms around her. Suddenly she was pressing against him, her head on his shoulder and the protective warmth of his body surrounding her.

"You can't do this," she said, her voice muffled against his suit jacket. "I hate you."

"I know you do, but right now there isn't anyone else." He stroked her hair. "Come now. Tell me what troubles you."

She shook her head. To speak of it would hurt too much.

"It's your mother," he murmured. "She said she was happy about the engagement. Your family has always been ambitious. In some ways a king for a son-in-law is even better than a president."

"I know." She wrapped her arms around his waist and hung on as hard as she could. "It's horrible. *She's* horrible. She said she was proud of me. That's the first time she's ever said that. Because I've always been a disappointment."

The hurt of a decade of indifference from her family swept through her. "Nobody came to my college graduation. Did you know that? They were all still angry because I'd refused to marry you. And they hated that I became a vet. No one even acknowledged my finishing school and going to work. My mother didn't say a word in the Christmas newsletter. She didn't mention me at all. It's as if by not marrying well, I'd ceased to exist."

She felt the light brush of his lips on her head. "I am sorry."

She sniffed. "I'm only their child when I do what they want.

I was afraid it would be the same for Brittany. I wanted her to be happy and strong so I tried to let her know that I loved her no matter what. That my love wasn't conditional on her marrying the right man."

"I'm sure she knows how much you care."

"I hope so. Laurel said she would be heartbroken."

Murat chuckled. "Not to marry a man twice her age whom she has never met? I suspect you raised her better than that."

"What?" She lifted her head and stared at him. They were far closer than she'd realized, which was really stupid—what with her being in his arms and all.

"I didn't raise her," she said. "She's not my daughter."

"Isn't she?"

It was what she'd always believed in her heart but never spoken of. Not to anyone. How could Murat grasp that personal truth so easily?

"I know all about expectations," he said, lightly tracing the curve of her cheek. "There was not a single day I was allowed to forget my responsibilities."

Which made sense. "I guess when you're going to grow up and be king, you aren't supposed to make as many mistakes as the rest of us."

"Exactly. So I understand about having to do what others want, even when that means not doing what is in your heart."

"Except I wasn't willing to do that," she reminded him. "I did what I wanted and they punished me. Not just my parents, but my sisters, too. I ceased to exist."

His dark gaze held her captive. She liked being held by him, which was crazy, because he was the enemy. Only, right this second, he didn't seem so bad.

"You exist to me," he said.

If only that were true. Reluctantly she pushed away and stood on her own.

"I don't," she said. "I have no idea what your engagement game is about, but I know it's not about me."

"How can you say that? You're the one I've chosen."

"Why?" she asked. "I think you're being stubborn and difficult. You don't care about me. You never did."

He frowned. "How can you say that? Ten years ago I asked you to marry me."

"What does that have to do with anything? If you'd really loved me, you wouldn't have let me go. But you didn't care when I left. I walked away and you never once came after me to find out why."

Chapter Five

Murat left Daphne and returned to his office. But despite the meeting he was supposed to attend, he told his assistant not to bother him and closed his door.

The space was large and open, as befitted the crown prince of such a wealthy nation. The conversation area of three sofas sat by several tall windows and the conference table easily seated sixteen.

Murat ignored it all as he crossed to the balcony overlooking a private garden and stepped outside. The spring air hinted at the heat to come. He ignored it and the call of the birds. Instead he stared into the distance as he wrestled with the past.

How like a woman, he thought. She questioned why he had not gone after her when she had been the one to leave him. Why would he want to follow such a woman? Besides, even if the thought had occurred to him—which it had not—it wasn't his place. If she wished them to be in contact, then she should come crawling back, begging forgiveness for having left in the first place.

She should know all of this. She came from a family famil-iar with power and how the world worked. He had known that they favored the match, and he was willing to admit he had been surprised she would stand against them.

Murat turned his back on the view but did not enter his office. The past flashed before him—a tableau of what had been. His father had told him she left. The king had come to him full of plans of how they would go after her and bring her back, but Murat had refused. He would not chase her around the world. If Daphne wanted to be gone, then let her. She had been a mere woman. Easy to replace.

Now, with the wisdom of hindsight, he admitted to himself that she had been different from anyone he had ever known. As for replacing her...that had never occurred. He had met other women, bedded them, been interested and intrigued. But he had never been willing to marry any of them.

He knew he should wonder why. What was it about her that had made her stand out? Not her great beauty. She was attractive and sensual, but he had known women who seemed more goddess than human. Not her intelligence. While hers was better than average, he had dated women whose comprehension of technical and scientific matters had left him speechless.

She was funny and charming, but he had known those with more of those qualities. So what combination of traits had made him willing to marry her and not another?

As he walked back into his office, he remembered what it had been like after she had left. He hadn't allowed himself to mourn her. No one had been permitted to speak her name. For him, it was as if she had never been.

And now she had returned and they would marry. In time she would see that was right. She might always argue with him, but she knew who was in charge.

He moved to his desk and took a seat. In a locked drawer sat a red leather box that contained the official seal of his office. He opened that box and removed the seal, then moved aside the silk lining. Tucked in the bottom, in between folds of protective padding, lay a diamond ring.

The stone had been given by a Bahanian king to his favorite mistress in 1685. He had been loyal to her for nearly thirty years and when his queen died, he married his mistress. Many told the story of how the ring had saved the mistress's life more than once, as other jealous women in the harem sought to do her harm. The stone was said to possess magical powers to heal and evoke love.

Of all the diamonds in the royal family's possession, this had been the one Murat had chosen for Daphne and the one she had left behind when she'd gone. He picked it up now and studied the carefully cut stone.

Such a small thing, he thought. Barely three carats. He'd been a fool to think it contained any magic at all.

He returned the ring to its hiding place, replaced the seal, then put the box back in the drawer and locked it. Later that afternoon the royal jeweler would offer a selection of rings for Murat's consideration. He would choose another one for Daphne. A stone without history or meaning. Or magic.

Daphne spent the morning considering her options. Murat had left in a huff without saying much to make her feel any better. He refused to admit there wasn't going to be a wedding, nor had he told her how her sister and the newspaper had found out so quickly. Obviously, he was to blame, but why wouldn't he just say so?

As she walked through the garden she told herself that an unexpected engagement certainly put things in perspective. Twenty-four hours ago her biggest concern had been how long he would keep her trapped in the harem. She'd been sure he would want to make his point—that she'd defied him and had to be punished in some way—but she'd looked at it as an unexpected vacation in a place not of her choosing. Now everything was different.

She wanted to tell herself that he couldn't possibly marry her without her permission, only she didn't know if that was true.

Murat was determined and obviously sneaky. Should anyone be able to pull that off—he was the guy. She was going to have to stay on her toes and prevent the wedding from happening. Finding herself married to him would be a disaster of monumental proportions. Getting out of this engagement was going to be difficult enough.

She needed a plan. Which meant she needed more information. But how to get it?

"Hello? Anybody home?"

Daphne turned toward the sound of the female voice. None of the servants would address her that way. Not after they knew about the engagement. To be honest, none of the servants had addressed her at all—it was as if they'd been told to avoid conversation.

She hurried back into the harem.

"Hello," she said as she stepped into the large, cool main room.

Three women stood together. They were beautiful, elegantly dressed and smiling.

Two blondes and a redhead. One of the blondes—a petite woman with short, spiky hair and a curvy body to die for—stepped forward.

"We're your basic princess contingent sneaking in to speak with the prisoner." She grinned. "Not that you're really a prisoner. There were rumors, of course. But now you're engaged to Murat, which makes you family. I'm Cleo. Married to Sadik." She rolled her big, blue eyes. "How totally *Lawrence of Arabia* to introduce myself in terms of who my husband is."

"You're a disgrace to us all, Cleo," the other blonde said fondly. She was a little taller, even more curvy, with big hair and sandals that looked high enough to be a walking hazard, especially considering her obvious pregnancy.

"Daphne Snowden."

"Hi." The redhead waved. "I'm Emma. Reyhan's wife." She motioned to the pregnant woman. "That's Billie."

Billie frowned. "Didn't I give her my name?"

"No," Cleo and Emma said together. Cleo sighed. "Billie thinks she's all that because she can fly jets. Like that's a big deal."

"It *is* a big deal," Emma whispered. "We talked about it."

"I know, but we don't want her to get a big head or anything."

"It'll match my big stomach," Billie said with a grin.

Daphne didn't know what to say. Just then she heard a rapid clicking sound. She glanced around and saw a small Yorkshire terrier exploring the main salon of the harem.

"That's Muffin," Billie said. "My other baby."

"I didn't know there were any dogs at the palace," Daphne said. "Doesn't the king only keep cats?"

"He's taken a liking to Muffin," Billie said. "Which is great because she gets into all kinds of trouble." She rubbed the small of her back. "Mind if I take a load off?"

"What? Oh, sorry. Please." Daphne motioned to the closest grouping of sofas. "Make yourselves comfortable."

The women sat down. Daphne stared from one to the other, not sure what to make of them. The last time she'd been in Bahania, all of Murat's brothers had been happy bachelors.

"I read about your weddings, of course," she said, then glanced at Emma. "Well, not yours."

"I know," she said as she flipped her red hair over her shoulder. "We were a scandal. But I thought the ceremony to renew our vows was very lovely."

"The pictures were great." Daphne turned to Billie. "You're married to Jefri?"

The pregnant woman nodded. "I'm embarrassed to say he swept me off my feet, and in the shoes I wear, that's a trick."

The women laughed. Daphne sensed their closeness and felt a twinge of envy. She'd never had that kind of relationship with her own sisters.

Cleo scooted forward on the sofa. "There are five of us altogether. I know it sounds confusing, but it's really simple. The king has four sons and two daughters. Of the girls, Sabrina is married to Kardal and they live, ah, out of the country. Zara, his other daughter, is married to Rafe. Zara didn't know the king was her father until a few years ago."

"I remember reading about that. Very romantic."

"I thought so," Cleo said.

Billie groaned. "You think everything is romantic."

Emma sighed. "These two argue a lot. I think they're too much alike. The fighting doesn't mean anything, but sometimes it gets a little old."

"I'm ignoring you," Cleo said to Emma.

"Me, too," Billie added.

Daphne couldn't help grinning. "Do you three live in the palace?" They could certainly make her brief stay more fun.

"*They* do," Emma said, pointing to the other two women. "As I said, I'm married to Reyhan, and we spend much of our time out in the desert. Reyhan inherited a house there from his aunt. Billie and Jefri and Cleo and Sadik make their home in the palace. Billie and Jefri are involved with the new air force. Billie's a flight instructor. She flies jets."

Daphne couldn't imagine the big-haired sex kitten flying anything more complicated than a paper airplane. "You're kidding?"

Billie grinned. "Never underestimate the power of a woman."

"I guess not."

Emma continued. "I'm in town for a few days while Reyhan has some meetings. We brought the baby." Her face softened as she smiled. "We have a daughter."

"That's four for four," Billie said. "I have a daughter, too, and so do Zara and Sabrina. Wouldn't it be funny if there weren't any male heirs?"

"Not to the men in the family," Daphne said.

"Good point," Billie said. "So Zara and Sabrina will be out in a few weeks to meet you. They said to say hi for them in the meantime."

Talk about overwhelming, Daphne thought. "You're very sweet to visit me."

"Not a problem," Cleo said. She fluffed her short, blond hair. "Besides, we want all the details. This engagement has come about very quickly."

"That's subtle," Billie said.

"Well, it has," Cleo insisted.

Emma cleared her throat. "I think what she means is how wonderful that you and Murat have found each other."

Daphne hated to burst their bubble, but she wouldn't pretend to be something she wasn't. "Murat and I haven't found anything. I don't know why he announced we're engaged, because we're not. And there isn't going to be a wedding."

The three women looked at each other, then at her.

"That changes things," Cleo said brightly.

Daphne smoothed the hem of her skirt. "I know it sounds terrible."

"Not at all," Emma said.

"Sort of," Billie said.

Daphne couldn't help smiling. "You guys are great."

"Thanks," Cleo said, preening a little. "I like to think we're pretty special."

Daphne chuckled for a second, then sobered as she thought about her impossible situation. "My family is big into politics and power," she said. "Years ago I was traveling through Europe during a summer break from college and I met Murat. I didn't know who he was and we hit it off. When he invited me back here, I was stunned to find out I'd been dating the crown prince."

"I know that feeling," Emma said. "Reyhan isn't going to be king, but he's still royal. I had no idea."

Billie put her arm around Emma. "She's our innocent."

Daphne sighed. "Then you can imagine my shock. Before I knew what had happened, we were engaged and everything was moving so quickly."

Billie frowned. "*Were* engaged. Obviously you didn't get married."

"I think I remember reading about that," Billie said. "Ten years ago I was a serious tabloid junkie."

"You still read the tabloids," Cleo said.

"Yeah, and then you steal them from me."

"Ladies," Emma said, holding up her hand to stop their bickering. "I believe Daphne was talking."

Cleo smiled at her. "Go on, Daphne."

"There's not much else to say. Things didn't work out and I left. My family was furious and didn't speak to me for ages. Eventually we patched things up." Sort of. Her mother had never really forgiven her for not marrying a future king. "Then a few weeks ago my niece, who is barely eighteen, told me that she was flying over to meet Murat and get engaged."

Billie raised her eyebrows. "What? That doesn't sound right."

"I agree," Cleo said. "Murat can be all formal with his 'I'm the crown prince' but he's never been into silly young women." She winced. "Sorry. Not that your niece is silly or anything."

"I know what you mean," Daphne said. "She's still a kid in so many ways. She's only had a couple of boyfriends and none of them were serious. Murat is nearly twice her age. I was determined to talk her out of it, which I did, just in the nick of time. We were flying here when she suddenly realized she was making a huge mistake. So she went back to the States, and I stayed to tell Murat there wasn't going to be an engagement. The next thing I knew I was locked in the harem and he was announcing *our* engagement in the papers."

Emma sighed. "That's so romantic."

Cleo and Billie looked at her. "That's kidnapping," Cleo said.

"Well, maybe technically, but he must really love her."

Daphne shook her head. "I hate to burst your bubble, but Murat doesn't love me. It's been ten years. He doesn't even *know* me anymore."

"So why the sudden engagement?" Billie asked.

"I have no idea," Daphne told her.

"He has to have a reason," Cleo said. "Men always do things for a reason. Has he been pining for you all these years?"

"Gee, let's count the number of women he's been out with in that time," Daphne said humorously. "I'm going to guess it's around a hundred or so."

"But he wasn't serious about any of them."

Emma scooted forward in her seat. "If it's not too personal, why did you leave last time?"

Good question. "There were a lot of reasons. Things moved so quickly—I didn't get a chance to figure out if this was the life I wanted before I found myself engaged. When reality set in, I panicked."

"But you loved him," Billie said. "Didn't you?"

"As much as I could at the time." Daphne thought back to how brightly her feelings had burned. "I was pretty innocent, and Murat was the first guy I'd been serious about. I'm not sure I knew what love was. We were so different."

Although getting over him had taken what felt like a lifetime. She still had scars.

Cleo smiled at her. "Ah, to be that young again. Wouldn't you like to go back in time and talk to that Daphne?"

"I don't know what I would say to her."

"Would you tell her to stay?" Cleo asked.

"No."

"Why not?" Emma asked. "Are we getting too personal? Does this feel like an interrogation?"

"I'm okay," Daphne told her. "And I wouldn't have told her to stay because I know what happened after. Murat didn't love her…me. He didn't bother to come after me. Not a phone call or a letter. He never cared enough to find out why I'd left."

She expected the three princesses to look shocked. Instead Cleo sighed, Billie shook her head and Emma's expression turned sad.

"It's pride," Emma said. "They have too much of it. It's a sheik thing. Or maybe a royal thing."

"I'm not sure what pride has to do with it."

Cleo shrugged. "You have to look at it from his point of view. He offered you everything, and you walked away. That had to have tweaked his tail just a little. Tweaked princes don't go running after women."

"Mere women," Billie said in a stern voice. "You are a mere woman."

Emma grinned. "The princes are so cute when they're all imperious."

Daphne felt as if she'd just sat down with the crazy family. "What are you talking about?"

"That you can't judge Murat's feelings for you solely on whether or not he came running after you when you left," Cleo said. "He's the crown prince and has that ego thing going on even more than his brothers. It's possible that in that twisted 'I'm the man' brain of his, he thought it would show too much weakness."

"But if he'd cared…"

"It's not about caring," Emma said. "You're looking at the situation logically, and like a woman. Reyhan loved me and yet he ignored me for years. His pride wouldn't let him talk to someone he thought had rejected him, let alone admit his feelings. Murat could be the same way."

Daphne thought about all the women he'd seen over the past decade. "I don't think he's actually been doing a lot of suffering."

"Maybe not," Cleo said. "But it's something to think about. If he matters at all."

Just then the gold doors opened and several servants entered with carts.

Billie smiled. "Did we mention we'd brought lunch?"

The women gathered around the dining room table and enjoyed the delicious food. Conversation shifted from Daphne and her situation to how each of them had met their husbands, then to shopping and the best place to get really gorgeous, if uncomfortable, shoes. They left a little after three.

Daphne closed the door behind them, then retreated to the sofa in front of the garden window. Despite everything, she'd had a nice day. Had her engagement to Murat been real, she would have been delighted to know that these women would be a part of her life.

But it wasn't real, and their theory that Murat's pride had kept him from holding on to her was nice to think about but was not in any way true.

"Not that it matters now," she whispered. Somehow she'd managed to get over him. At least she didn't have to worry about that now. Her feelings weren't engaged and her heart was firmly out of reach. She was going to make sure things stayed that way.

Daphne planned a quiet remainder of the day. She assumed Murat wouldn't come back to torment her until the morning, and she was partially right. Around four the gold doors opened again, but instead of the crown prince, she saw the king.

"Your Majesty," she said, coming to her feet before dropping into a low curtsy.

"Daphne."

Murat's father walked toward her and held out both his hands. He captured hers and kissed her knuckles. "How lovely to have you back in Bahania." The handsome older man chuckled. "Most young women today don't know the first thing about a good curtsy, but you've always had style."

"I had several years of training in etiquette. Some of it had to rub off," she said with a smile. While she might not be excited about what Murat was up to, she couldn't help being pleased at seeing the king. He had always been very kind to her, especially when she'd been young, in love and terrified.

"Come," King Hassan said as he led her to the cluster of sofas. "Tell me everything. You and your family are well?"

"Everyone is great." Except for Laurel who was furious about Brittany not marrying Murat. "They send their best." Or they would have if they'd known she would be speaking with the king.

"I'm sure they're very excited about what has happened."

Her good mood slipped. "Yes. My parents are delighted."

King Hassan had to be over sixty, but he looked much younger. There was an air of strength about him. Authority and determination. No doubt that came from a royal lineage that stretched back over a thousand years. He was considered one of the most forward-thinking leaders in the world. A king who earned his people's respect through his actions and loyalty to his country.

Murat would be equally as excellent a leader, Daphne thought. He'd been born to the position and had never once stumbled. Which made him admirable, but not someone she wanted to marry.

"My son sends you a surprise," the king said as the gold doors opened again.

Servants appeared with the carts they seemed to favor. But this time instead of food they brought clay and sculpting tools.

Her fingers instantly itched for the feel of clay, while the cynical part of her brain wondered if he thought he could bribe her with her hobby.

"You must thank him for me," she said as the servants bowed and left.

"You can thank him yourself. He'll be by later."

Oh, joy, she thought as she smiled politely.

"You are aware of the date," King Hassan said.

Daphne blinked at him. "Today's date?"

"No. That the wedding date has been set. It is in four months. The challenge will be to get everything done in such a short period of time, but I am sure that with the right staff, we will be successful."

She stiffened her spine and drew in a breath. "Your Majesty,

I mean no disrespect, but the problem isn't finding the right staff. The problem is I am not going to marry Murat, and there is nothing anyone can say to convince me otherwise."

She'd thought the monarch might be surprised, but he only chuckled. "Ah, two stubborn people. So who will win this battle?"

"I will. It is the old story of the rabbit and the hound. The rabbit gets away because while the hound runs for its supper, the rabbit runs for its life."

"An interesting point." The king took her hand again and lightly squeezed her fingers. "I have often wondered how things would have been different if you had stayed and married Murat. Have you?"

"No." Well, maybe a little, but she wasn't interested in admitting it. "I wasn't ready to be married. I was too young, as was your son. The position of his wife requires much, and I'm not sure I would have been up to the task."

"Perhaps. There are many responsibilities in being queen, although your questions and self-doubts make me think you would have done well in the position. He never married."

Daphne drew her hand from his and laced her fingers together on her lap. "Murat? I'm aware of that. Had he married I would not currently be a prisoner in the harem."

"You know that is not my point," Hassan said humorously. "You never married, either."

"I've been busy with my studies and establishing my career."

"It is not much of an excuse. Perhaps each of you were waiting for the other to make the first move."

Daphne nearly sprang to her feet. At the last second she remembered that action would be a fairly serious breach of protocol. "I assure you that is not even close to true. Murat has enjoyed the company of so many beautiful women, I doubt he remembers them all, let alone a young woman from a decade ago."

"And now?" the king asked.

"We barely know each other."

"An excellent point. Perhaps this is a good time to change that." The king rose. "Murat wants this wedding, Daphne, as do your parents. As do I. Are you willing to take on the world?"

She stood and tried not to give in to the sudden rush of fear. "If I have to."

"Perhaps it would be easier to give in graciously. Would marriage to Murat be so horrible?"

"Yes. I think it would be." She bit her lower lip. "Your Majesty, would you really force me to marry your son against my will?"

His dark eyes never wavered as he spoke. "If I have to."

Murat found Daphne in the garden. The sun had nearly slipped below the horizon, and the first whispers of the cool evening air brushed against his face.

She sat on a stone bench, her shoulders slumped, her chin nearly touching her chest. The only word that came to his mind at that moment was...*broken*.

He hurried forward and pulled her to her feet. She gasped in surprise, but didn't resist until he tried to draw her close.

"What do you think you're doing?" she demanded, twisting free of his embrace.

"Comforting you."

She glared at him. "You're the source of my troubles, not the relief from them."

"I'm all you have."

She took a step back. "What a sorry state of affairs. What on earth does that sentence say about my life?"

"That at least there is one person on your side."

Little light spilled into the garden, but there was enough for him to see her beautiful features. Her wide eyes had darkened with pain and confusion. Her full lips trembled. It was as if the weight of the world pressed down upon her, and he ached for her.

"Come," he said, holding out his arms. "You'll feel better."

"Maybe I don't want to," she said stubbornly, even as she moved forward and leaned against him.

He wrapped his arms around her. She was slight, so delicate and yet so strong. She smelled of flowers and soap and of herself. That arousing fragrance he had never been able to forget.

Wanting filled him, but something else, as well. Something that made this moment feel right.

He felt her hands on his back, and she rested her forehead against his shoulder.

"No one will help me," she said. "I've been making phone calls for nearly two hours. Not my family—which isn't a big surprise—nor any of my friends. I even called my congressman. Everyone thinks us getting married is a fine idea. They refused to believe that I'm being held against my will, and they all hinted for an invitation to the wedding."

"Then you may add them to the list."

She raised her head. Tears glittered in her eyes. "That's not what I wanted to hear."

He knew what she wanted him to say, but he would not speak the words. To set her free…it would not happen.

"You will enjoy being queen," he said. "There is much power in the position."

"I've never been that interested in power."

"You've never had it before."

"Murat, you know this is wrong."

"Why? You are to marry me, Crown Prince Murat. It is not as if you're being asked to wed a used-camel dealer."

She gave a half laugh, half sob and pushed away from him. The tears had trickled down her face. He wiped them away with his fingers.

"Do not cry," he murmured. "I offer you the world."

"I only want my freedom."

"To do what? To give shots to overweight dogs and cats? Here you can make a difference. Here you will be a part of history. Your children and grandchildren will rule this land."

"It's not enough."

He growled low in his throat. Had she always been this stubborn? Was she trying to punish him for what had happened before? All right. Perhaps he could give a little on that point.

"Why did you leave me?" he asked. "Before. Ten years ago. Why did you go?"

Her shoulders slumped again, and the pain returned to her eyes. "It doesn't matter."

"Yes, it does. I wish to know."

"You wouldn't understand."

"Then explain it to me. I am very intelligent."

"Not about me." She swallowed. "Murat, you have to let me go."

Instead of answering her statement, he stepped forward and kissed her. He caught her by surprise—he could tell by the sudden intake of air and the way she hesitated before responding. But instead of retreating, he settled his hand on her hip and the back of her neck and brushed his tongue against her lower lip.

She parted instantly. As he swept inside he felt the heat flaring between them. Wanting poured through him, making it difficult to hold back when he wanted to rip off her clothing and claim her right there on the bench.

Instead he continued to kiss her, moving slowly, retreating, pulling back until she was the one to grab him and deepen the embrace. When he finally straightened, she looked as aroused as he felt.

"You see," he said, "there is much between us. We will take the time to get to know each other better. That will make you comfortable with the thought of our marriage."

"Don't bet on it," she said, but her swollen mouth and passion-filled eyes betrayed her.

Murat brushed her cheek with his fingers, then walked out of the harem. Victory was at hand. He would wear away Daphne's defenses until she understood that their marriage was inevitable.

Then she would acquiesce and they would be wed. She would love him and be happy and he…

He stepped through the gold doors and into the hallway. He would return to his regular life, content, but untouched by the experience.

Chapter Six

Daphne rolled the cool clay in her hands until the combination of heat from her skin and the friction of the action caused the thick rope to yield to her will. She tore off a piece of clay and pressed it flat, then added it to the sculpture in progress.

The half-finished project had finally begun to take shape. There was a sense of movement in the way the man leaned too far to the right. His body was still a squarish lump, but she knew how she would slice away the excess clay and mold what was left. The head would follow, with the arms and the tray of dishes to come last. The tray that would be on the verge of tumbling to the ground.

Around her, the garden vibrated with life. She heard the chatter of the parrots and the rustle of small creatures hiding in the thick foliage. Several of the king's cats stretched out in the sun, the slow rise and fall of their chests the only sign of life.

As far as prisons went, this wasn't a bad one, Daphne told herself, as she picked up another clump of clay. Not that she had a whole lot of experience with which to compare. She'd never been held against her will before. Still, if one had to be, the Bahania harem was the place.

She couldn't complain about the service, either. Delicious

meals appeared whenever she requested them. Her large bed was plenty comfortable, and the bathroom was so luxurious that it bordered on sinful. Still, none of these pleasures made up for the fact that she had been confined against her will with the threat of marriage to Murat hanging over her head.

He had spoken of getting to know each other, but she wasn't so sure that was a good idea. Men like him didn't make a habit of letting just anyone see the inner person, and she doubted their engagement gave her extra privileges in that area. Which left her with the distinct impression that his request had been a lot more about giving himself time to convince her that this was a good idea than any desire he had to share his feelings.

Even more annoying was the fact that a part of her *was* interested in learning more about the man. Life was never easy when the one who got away was a future king.

She picked up a sharp piece of wood that was part knife, part chisel and went to work on the torso of the sculpture. When the rough shape was correct, she added features to the head, creating a face that was a fair representation of the man in question. A smile pulled at her mouth. She only had to complete the arms and the tray.

"Men have died for less."

Daphne heard the voice about the same time the sound of footsteps entered her consciousness. She'd been so focused on her work that she hadn't been paying attention. Now she pressed clay into the shape of a tray and did her best not to react to Murat's nearness.

"I thought there was artistic freedom here in Bahania," she said, not looking up from her clay.

"Most artists are too intelligent to mock me."

Daphne spared him a glance. As always he wore a suit, although this time he'd left the jacket behind. The crisp white shirt he wore contrasted with his dark skin. He'd rolled the sleeves up to the elbow, and she found the sight of his bare forearms oddly erotic.

Sheesh. She really had to get out more.

"My intelligence has never been an issue," she said. "Do you doubt it now?"

He glanced at the tray taking shape in her hands. "You sculpt me carrying dishes?"

She grinned. "Actually I sculpt you about to drop the dishes you're carrying. There's a difference."

He made a noise low in his throat, which she knew she should take for displeasure, but there was something about it that made her stomach clench. Perhaps the noise was too close to desire.

Stop that! She grabbed hold of any wayward emotions and reminded herself she needed to keep things firmly in check. Wanting Murat wasn't in the rules. It would only make things difficult and awkward. Hadn't she already had to deal with a broken heart once where he was concerned? Was she really willing to forget that the man held her prisoner and threatened a wedding, regardless of her wishes?

"Why are you here?" she asked as she felt her temper grow and with it her strength to resist him.

"Am I not allowed to come and visit with my bride?"

She rolled her eyes and set down the small tray. Next up she began to form tiny glasses and plates.

"I will take your silence as agreement," he said.

"You may take it any way you'd like, but you'd be wrong."

He sighed. "You are most difficult."

"Tell me about it. Of course you've made 'difficult' an art form. I'm still little more than a student."

He ignored that, saying nothing as he walked around her and the sculpture. "You have an energy I haven't seen before," he said. "Perhaps you needed this time to relax."

Perhaps, but she wasn't about to admit that to him. "Is there a point to your visit or are you simply here to annoy me?"

"You will be visited by someone later."

"The first of three ghosts?"

He frowned slightly, then his expression cleared. "Are you

in need of a visit by the ghosts of Christmas past, present and future?"

"No. I've always kept the spirit of Christmas in my heart."

"I am pleased to hear it is so. That will bode well for our children. They will have a festive season to look forward to."

Her jaw clenched. "Is this where I point out, yet again, that I haven't agreed to marry you, nor am I likely to?"

"You may if it makes you happy. However, I will not listen. Instead I will inform you that Mr. Peterson is an old and valued member of our staff here. He specializes in coordinating formal state events."

She got it right away. "Like weddings."

"Exactly. I would appreciate it if you were polite and cooperative."

She formed a tiny clay bowl and set it on the tray. "I would appreciate being set free. It seems we are both destined for disappointment."

Murat moved closer. "Why do you attempt to thwart me?"

"Because I can't seem to get through to you any other way." She wiped her hands on the damp towel on her workbench, then turned to face him. "I don't get it, Murat. What's in this for you?" She held up her hand. "Spare me the party line about marriage and destiny or whatever. Why on earth are you insisting on marrying a woman who doesn't want you?"

Her gaze met Murat's with a familiarity that should have annoyed him, but this was Daphne, and he found himself enjoying most everything she did. Even her challenges.

He smiled as he moved close, crowding her. Daphne, being stubborn and difficult *and* predictable, didn't move back. She made it so easy, he thought with pleasure. He liked that about her.

"You claim not to want me," he murmured as he cupped her head in one hand and bent low to kiss her. "Your body tells me otherwise."

Then, before she could speak whatever nonsense she had in mind, he brushed his mouth against hers.

She squirmed, but he wove his fingers through her hair to hold her in place. When she pressed her lips together to resist his claim on her, he chuckled, then raised his free hand to her breast.

Instantly she gasped. He took advantage of her parted lips and swept inside. At the same time, he brushed his thumb against her hard nipple.

She held out against him for the space of a heartbeat before she wrapped her arms around his neck and surrendered. Her mouth softened against him, her tongue greeted him with an erotic dance, and her entire body melted into his.

Heat exploded between them, and Murat found himself fighting his own desire. He had touched her in an effort to teach her a lesson, but now he was the one being schooled on the power of unfulfilled need.

Her hands clutched at him, pulling him closer. She tilted her head and deepened the kiss, even as she pressed into his hand. He explored her breast and found himself hungering to know the taste of her hot skin.

But that was not for now, he reminded himself as he gathered the strength to step back. He would know her soon enough—once she understood that their marriage was as inevitable as the tide.

"You see," he said with a calmness he did not feel. "You *do* want me."

She shook her head as if to clear her thoughts. Her eyes were large and unfocused, her face flushed.

"There's a difference between wanting a man in my bed for a couple of weeks and wanting him in my life permanently," she said, her voice low and angry. "If you were trying to prove a point, I'm not impressed."

"Your body says otherwise."

"Fortunately I make my decisions with my brain."

"Your brain wants me, as well," he told her. "You resist only to be stubborn. I am pleased the sexual spark has lasted so long between us. It bodes well for our marriage. You will be a good wife and provide me with many strong, healthy, intelligent children, including an heir to carry on the monarchy."

"And my reward in all this is your pleasure. Gee, how thrilling."

He refused to be provoked by her. "Your reward is in the honor I bestow upon you. I believe you already understand that, and in time you will grow more comfortable showing me your pleasure in your situation."

She opened her mouth, then closed it. He could almost see the steam building up inside of her.

"Of all the arrogant, egotistical, annoying things you've ever said to me," she began.

He cut her off with a wave of his hand. "Say what you like, but I know the truth. You're already begging to love me. In a matter of weeks you will want nothing but the pleasure of being near me."

"When pigs fly."

Daphne thought Murat was assuming an awful lot, especially that she was interested in him sexually. Whatever warm and yummy feelings he'd generated a couple of minutes ago with his hot kisses and knowing hands, he'd destroyed with a few badly chosen words.

"I wouldn't marry you if you were the last man alive. I said no before, I'm saying no again. No. No!"

The infuriating man simply smiled. "Mr. Peterson will be here shortly. I trust you will act appropriately."

Anger filled her. She reached for something to throw, but there was only her clay statue, and she loved it too much to smash it.

"Get out!" she yelled.

"As you wish, my bride."

She screamed and grabbed the remaining block of clay. When she turned back, Murat had already walked toward the harem itself. Even though she knew she couldn't throw that far, she pitched the clay at him and had the satisfaction of hearing it splat on the stone path.

"I'll get you for this," she vowed. Somehow, some way, she would come up with a plan, and he would be sorry he'd ever tried to mess with her.

Mr. Peterson might be old and valued but he was also the prissiest man Daphne had ever met.

He was small—maybe five-four—so she towered over him even in low-heeled sandals. He had the delicate bone structure of a bird, with tiny hands and feet. Next to him she felt like an awkward and ill-mannered Amazon giant.

"Ms. Snowden," he said as he entered the harem and bowed. "It is more than a great pleasure to meet you."

She wasn't sure how it could be *more* than a great pleasure, but she wasn't the fancy-party expert.

"The pleasure is mine," she said as she led the way to the sitting area and motioned to the collection of sofas there.

Mr. Peterson looked them over closely, then chose the one that was lowest to the floor. No doubt he hated when his feet dangled.

She sat across from him and wondered how badly this was going to go. Mr. Peterson wanted to plan a wedding and she didn't. That was bound to create some friction.

"We're working on a very tight schedule," he began as he set his briefcase on the table in front of him and opened the locks with a click.

She noticed that the silk hankie in his jacket breast pocket perfectly matched his tie. He sounded as if he'd been born in Britain but hadn't lived there in a number of years. Perhaps he'd moved here with his parents back in the eighteenth century.

"Prince Murat informed me that the wedding will be in four months," he said. "I'll be providing you with historical information on previous weddings, along with my list of suggestions on flower choices and the like. Some of my ideas may seem silly to a modern young woman such as yourself, but we have a history here in Bahania. A long and honorable history that needs to be respected."

He drew in his breath for what she assumed would be another long speech specifically designed to make her feel like a twelve-year-old who had just spilled fruit punch on a very important houseguest.

She decided it was time to change the direction of the conversation.

"There isn't going to be a wedding," she said, and had the satisfaction of watching Mr. Peterson freeze in place.

It was amazing. The man didn't breathe or move or do anything but sit there, one hand grasping a sheath of papers, another reaching for a pen. At last he blinked.

"Excuse me?"

"No wedding," she said, speaking slowly. "I'm not marrying Murat."

"Prince Murat," he said.

He was correcting her address of the man who wanted to marry her?

"Prince or not, there's no engagement."

"I see."

She doubted that. "So there's no point in us having this conversation. I do appreciate that you were willing to stop by though. It was very kind of you."

She offered a bright smile in the hopes that the little man would simply stand and leave. But of course her luck wasn't that good.

"Prince Murat assures me that—"

"I know what he told you and what he's thinking, but he's wrong. No wedding. *N-O* on the wedding front. Am I making myself clear?"

Mr. Peterson obviously hadn't been expecting a reluctant bride. He fussed with his papers for a few seconds, then picked up his pen. "About the guest list. I was told you come from a large and distinguished family. Do you have any idea how many of them will be attending?"

Daphne sighed. So Mr. Peterson had decided to simply ignore her claims and move forward.

"Ms. Snowden?" he prodded. "How many family members."

"Not a clue," she told him cheerfully.

"Will you be providing me with a guest list of any kind?"

"Nope."

The little man shook his head. "If necessary I can contact your mother."

"I'm sure you can." And her mother would be delighted by the question and the chance to influence the wedding.

Wasn't it enough that Murat insisted on this charade? How far was he willing to take it?

"Excuse me," she said as she rose to her feet. "I need to put a stop to this right now."

She walked toward the door and once she got there, she simply pushed it open.

The cross bar wasn't in place, no doubt so Mr. Peterson could leave when he was finished. There were only two guards on duty and neither of them looked as if they'd expected her to come strolling out of the harem. When they saw her, they glanced at each other, as if uncertain about what to do.

Daphne took advantage of their confusion and started running. She made it halfway down the long hall before she heard footsteps racing after her. Up ahead the elevator beckoned like a beacon of freedom.

"Be there, be there," she chanted as she ran. She skidded to a stop in front of the doors and pushed the up button. Thankfully, the doors immediately slid open.

She stepped inside and pressed the button for the second floor and watched as the doors closed in the faces of the guards.

Ha! She'd escaped. Probably not for long, but the feeling of freedom was heady.

She exited on the second floor and hurried toward the business wing of the palace. She had a vague recollection of the way from her detailed explorations ten years ago. At a T intersection, she hesitated, not sure which way to go, then followed a young man in a tailored suit as he turned left.

Seconds later she entered a large, round foyer. A middle-aged man sat at the desk and raised his eyebrows inquiringly.

"Crown Prince Murat," she said.

"Is he expecting you?"

In the distance she heard running feet. The guards, no doubt. She suspected reinforcements had been called.

"I'm his fiancée," she said briskly.

The man straightened in his seat. "Yes. Of course, Ms. Snowden. Down that hallway, to your left. There are guards at the door. You can't miss it. If you'll give me a moment, I'll escort you there myself."

"No need," she said, taking off in the direction he'd indicated. She saw massive, carved, dark wood double doors and two guards standing on duty. One of them had his fingers pressed to his ear as if he were listening to something. When he saw her, he spoke quickly.

"I'm going in there," she said as she hurried toward the doors. "And you can't stop me."

The guards stepped forward and actually drew their weapons. A cold blade of fear sliced through her midsection.

"Murat isn't going to be very happy if you shoot me," she said, hoping it was true.

The guards moved toward her.

More footsteps thundered from behind, and she was seconds from being trapped.

"Murat!" she screamed as one of the men reached for her.

The huge door on the right opened and Murat stalked out.

"What is going on here?" he demanded. He glanced at the guards, then settled his stern gaze on her. "Release her at once."

The man did so, and Daphne quickly stepped behind Murat. "I escaped," she murmured in his ear. "That made them cranky."

He looked at her and raised one eyebrow. "I see. And Mr. Peterson?"

"We didn't much get along. All he wanted to talk about was the wedding, and I kept saying there wasn't going to be one. It wasn't very pleasant for either of us."

Murat didn't respond verbally. Instead he took her by the hand and led her into his office.

"Stay here," he said as he placed her in the center of an exceptionally beautiful rug. "I will return shortly."

With that he turned and left. She heard him speaking with the guards.

Daphne glanced around at the large office, noting the beautifully carved desk and the view of the gardens. None of the royal family had offices that faced the front of the palace. Years ago Murat had told her it was for security reasons. She'd been afraid for him at the time, but he had smiled and pulled her close and told her not to worry.

She shook off the memory. Murat returned and closed the door behind him.

"You are safe for now," he said. "I'll be having an interesting talk with my security team later. They should not have let you escape."

"Points for me," she said.

"Interesting that in your moment of freedom, you chose to run here. To me."

"Don't read too much into it. I didn't come here for a good reason."

"No? Then why?"

"Because I want to talk about the wedding, or lack thereof. You can't make me do it, Murat."

He moved close and touched her cheek. She hated how her body instantly went up in flames.

"You enjoy challenging me," he said. "However, I think the

real problem lies elsewhere. You have been cooped up for too long. Go change your clothes, and we'll take a ride into the desert."

"And if I don't want to go?" she asked.

He looked at her. "Do you?"

She remembered those long-ago desert rides. The scent of the fresh air, the movement of the horse, and the beauty all around her.

"I do, but I hate that you assume you know best."

"I *do* know best. Now return to the harem and change your clothes. I'll meet you downstairs in thirty minutes."

"Does this mean I'm allowed to roam freely about the palace?"

He grinned. "Not even on a bet."

Chapter Seven

Daphne settled into the saddle and breathed in the fresh air. She'd been spending plenty of time outdoors in the harem garden but for some reason, everything seemed better, brighter now that she was sitting on a horse about to ride into the desert on a great adventure. Or to the nearest oasis, whichever came first.

There were a thousand reasons to still be angry with Murat—not the least was the man continued to hold her prisoner and insist they were to be married. Somehow none of that mattered anymore. At least not right now. She wanted to ride fast and feel the wind in her hair. She wanted to spin in circles on the sand, her arms outstretched, until she was too dizzy to stand. She wanted to drink cool, clear water from an underground spring and taste life. Then she would be mad at him again.

"Ready?" he asked.

She nodded as she pulled her hat lower over her forehead. All the sunscreen in the world couldn't completely protect her fair skin. So to keep herself from reaching the crone years too early, she'd worn a loose fitting, long-sleeved white shirt and a hat. Beside her, Murat looked handsome and timeless in his black riding pants and tailored white shirt. His black stallion was so large and difficult to manage as to be a cliché. Her own mount, a gray gelding of particularly fine build, also danced impatiently but with a little more restraint.

"When did you last ride?" Murat asked, as he urged his horse forward. The stallion leaped ahead several feet before agreeing to a more sedate walk.

"A couple of months ago. I usually go regularly, but I've been caught up with work."

"Then we will take things easily. This is unfamiliar country."

She glanced at him from under her lashes. "I don't mind if we go fast."

He grinned. "Of course you don't. But we will wait until you find your seat again."

She wanted to point out that she hadn't lost it in the first place—it was where it had always been. But she knew what he meant. That she had to get comfortable on her horse. So she contented herself with enjoying the scenery.

The royal stable sat on the edge of the desert, about a forty-minute drive from the Pink Palace. Daphne knew she could happily spend her life there, studying bloodlines and planning future generations of amazing Arabian horses. Not that she wanted Murat to know. He had too much power already—he didn't need to discover more of her weaknesses.

She glanced around as the last bits of civilization gave way to the wildness of the desert. When their horses stepped onto sand, she couldn't help laughing out loud.

"Whatever you thought about me," Murat said. "You always loved Bahania."

"I agree."

"You should have returned for a visit."

"Somehow that didn't seem exactly wise."

"Did you think I would make things difficult?"

She wasn't sure how to answer that. If she said yes, it implied that he had cared for her after she left and she didn't think that was true. If she said no, she risked going in the opposite direction and she didn't think Murat would like that. As a rule, she didn't much care about what he liked, but this afternoon was different. For once, she didn't want to fight.

"I thought it might make things awkward," she admitted.

"That is a possibility," he said, surprising her. "But it is sad that you could not see this for so long."

She glanced around at the beauty of the desert and had to agree. She loved the rolling hills that gave way to vast stretches of emptiness. She loved the tiny creatures who managed to thrive in such harsh surroundings. Most of all she loved coming upon an oasis—a gift from God plopped down in the middle of nothing.

"You can taste the history out here," she said, thinking of all the generations who had walked this exact path and seen these same sights.

"We are closer to the past in the desert. I can feel my heritage all around me."

She grinned. "You come from a long line of men compelled to steal or kidnap their brides. Why is that? Are you all genetically unable to woo women in a normal way?"

He made a noise low in his throat. Daphne grinned.

"I'm serious," she said.

"No, you are tweaking the tiger's tail. Take care that he doesn't turn on you and gobble you up."

As Murat wasn't an actual tiger, she didn't have to worry about being eaten. Instead his words painted a picture of a different kind of devouring…one that involved bodies and touching and exquisite feelings of passion and surrender.

A dull ache settled in her stomach, making her shift on the saddle. Probably best not to think about that sort of thing, she told herself. Under the circumstances, sleeping with Murat would be a disaster. He would take her sexual surrender as a resounding 'yes' on the marriage front.

But she couldn't help wondering what he would be like in bed. So far his kisses had reduced her to a quivering mass. Ten years ago she'd been too innocent and out of her element to be much more than intimidated by the obvious sexual experience of the man. Now she found herself wanting to sign up for a weekend seminar on the subject.

Next time, she promised herself. When her future and her freedom weren't on the line.

"Those marriages you mentioned may have started in violence, but they all ended happily."

She glanced at him. "You know this how?"

"There are letters and diaries."

"I'd like to read them sometime," she said. "Not that I don't trust you to tell me the truth..." She smiled. "Well, I don't, actually."

"You think I would lie?"

"I think you would stretch the truth if it suited your purpose."

He muttered something she couldn't hear. "How do you explain a relationship that lasts thirty or forty years and produces so many children?"

"Women don't have to be happy to get pregnant."

"I will give you the diaries," he said. "You will see for yourself that you misjudge my ancestors as much as you misjudge me. Are you ready to go faster?"

The quick change in subject caught her unaware, but she immediately nodded her agreement.

"I'm fine," she said. "Lead the way."

He nodded then urged his horse forward. The powerful stallion leaped from walking to a gallop. Her horse followed.

Daphne leaned forward into the powerful gait. The ground seemed to blur as they raced across the open area. She wanted to laugh from the pleasure of the moment.

Pure freedom, she thought, wishing there was more of this in her regular life. But her rides were sedate, on trails in well-known areas. There was little left to discover outside of Chicago.

Unlike here, where the desert kept secrets for thousands of years. While she could trace her family history back to the early 1700s, Murat could trace his for a millennium.

His name would be carved in the walls of the palace. His likeness stored, his life remembered. He had offered all that to her, as well. The privilege of being a part of Bahanian history. Her body could have been the safe haven of future kings yet to be born.

They sped across the desert for several miles. At last Murat slowed his mount and hers followed suit.

"We will walk them now," he said. "Allow them to cool down. We are close to the oasis."

She nodded, still caught up in her thoughts. What would it be like to be a part of something this amazing? Ten years ago she'd never considered all that he offered. Lately it seemed she could think of nothing else.

"The light is gone from your eyes," he said. "What troubles you?"

"I'm not troubled, just thoughtful."

"Tell me what you have on your mind."

She looked at him, at his handsome, chiseled face, at the power in his body and the authority he wore like a second skin.

"You are Crown Prince Murat of Bahania," she said. "You will one day rule all that we see and miles beyond. You come from a history that stretches back through the ages to a time when my ancestors lived in huts and shivered through the winter. Why on earth would you choose me to share all this? Why me? Why not someone else?"

Murat didn't look at her. Instead he stared straight ahead. There was no way to tell what he was thinking.

"The oasis is just up there," he said, pointing to the right. "Over that dune."

"You're not going to answer my question?"

"No."

She wanted to push him for the truth, but at the same time, felt a reluctance to do so. There were many things she didn't want to discuss, including the fact—which he'd already pointed out—that when she'd burst free of the harem, instead of heading out of the palace, she'd run directly to the man holding her prisoner. Talk about a mixed message.

They rode in silence until they reached the oasis. Daphne stared at the small refuge in the desert, taking in the cluster of palm and date trees, the clear blue water gently lapping against the grass-covered shore and the bushes that seemed to provide a screen of privacy.

"Lovely," she said as she dismounted and pulled off her hat.

"I am glad you are pleased."

"Oh, yeah, because my pleasure makes your day."

She meant the comment as flip and teasing, but Murat didn't smile.

"Perhaps it does," he said. "Perhaps that is what you don't understand."

Before she could absorb what he'd just said, let alone think up a response, he led his horse over to a patch of shade. "We will rest here before heading back."

She followed. When he stopped, she turned to her horse and began stroking the animal's neck.

"Good, strong boy," she murmured as she examined the shoulder muscles, then bent down to run her hands along the well-formed front legs.

"I assure you I have a most capable staff in my stable," Murat said.

She straightened. "Oh. Sorry. Occupational hazard. I can't help checking." She patted the horse's side. "He's in great shape. Just like the cats back at the palace."

"I will be sure to pass along your compliments," Murat said dryly.

She loosely tied the horse to a tree, then joined Murat as he walked toward the water.

"It's quiet," she said.

"Yes. That is why I enjoy coming here."

She glanced around. "No guards?"

"This area is patrolled regularly, but at the moment we are

alone." He glanced at her. "If you wish to kill me, now is the time."

"Good to know, but I'm not that annoyed. Yet."

He smiled. "How you continue to challenge me, but we both know who will be victorious in the end."

"Not you."

"Exactly me." He moved close and stared down at her. "Your surrender is at hand. Do you not feel it?"

What she felt was a trickle of something that could very well have been anticipation slipping down her spine. Her skin got all hot and prickly and she had the incredibly irrational urge to throw herself into his arms and beg for a surrender of another kind. Or maybe that was the surrender he meant. In which case she was more than willing to be the one giving in.

"I'm not going to marry you," she said.

He rested his hands on her shoulders. "You say the same thing over and over. It grows most tiresome."

"That's because you're not listening. If you were, I'd stop having to say it."

"How like a woman to make it the man's fault."

"How like a man to be stubborn and unreasonable."

"I am very reasonable. Right now you want me, and I intend to let you have me."

Before she could even gasp in outrage, he claimed her mouth with his. His firm, warm lips caressed her own until she felt compelled to wrap her arms around his neck and never let go. The outrage melted away.

He kissed her gently, teasing her with light brushes that made her nerve endings tingle. He stroked her lower lip with his tongue, but when she parted for him he nipped her instead of entering. He dropped his hands to her hips and drew her against him so that her belly pressed flat against his arousal.

The hardness there made her gasp, but again he chose not to take advantage of her invitation. Instead he kissed along her jaw and nibbled the sensitive skin under her ear. He made her squirm and gasp as need swept through her with the driving force of a sandstorm. He licked her earlobe, then traced a path down the side of her neck to the V of her shirt where he sucked gently on her skin.

She felt hot and uncomfortable, as if she'd been wound too tight. Her breasts ached, her thighs trembled, and she really wanted the man to kiss her.

Unable to control herself any longer, she dropped her hands to his face and drew his head up.

"Now," she said, her voice low and impatient.

"As you wish," he murmured right before he claimed her mouth.

This time he did as she wanted. He swept inside with the purposeful intent of a man set on pleasing a woman. He circled her tongue with his own. He explored and danced and surged until she was breathless with wanting.

His hands moved from her hips to her back. One slipped around to her waist and she caught her breath in anticipation as he moved higher and higher. Closer until he at last cupped her breast in his long, lean fingers.

The pressure was unbearably perfect, she thought through a haze of desire. As his fingers brushed against her tight nipples, she withdrew from the kiss so she could focus completely on his touch. Her breathing increased. She looped her arms around his neck and held on as her knees began to give way.

He brought up his other hand so he could cup both breasts. The delicious torture made her shiver. He raised his head and looked into her eyes.

"You are more beautiful than the dawn," he whispered. "I feel you respond to me. Can you deny what you want?"

She shook her head.

At that moment she had the sense she could disappear into his dark eyes and that it wouldn't be such a bad fate. Not if there were nights filled with this kind of attention. Not if he kept touching her.

She felt her body swelling in anticipation. Her panties dampened as flesh begged and wept for release.

He moved to the buttons on her shirt and quickly unfastened them. But he only went down to the waistband of her jeans and didn't bother pulling the shirt free. Which meant when he tugged the garment down her shoulders, he pinned her arms at her side.

She knew she could free herself with a quick jerk against the fabric, but for the moment, she felt oddly trapped. As if she were at his mercy. As if he could take her against her will. Crazy, she told herself. Yet…oddly erotic.

He moved to the hook between her breasts and unfastened it. She watched as he slipped the bra away, exposing her skin to sun and air…and to his heated gaze.

He stared at her like a hungry man facing a last meal. Slowly he traced her curves, touching so lightly he almost tickled her. When he touched the tip of his finger against the very tip of her nipple, she felt the jolt clear down to her thighs.

She groaned. His breathing increased, then he bent low and drew her nipple into his mouth.

The combination of damp heat and gentle sucking nearly sent her to her knees. She struggled to free herself from her shirt so she could cling to him. The wanting grew. She didn't remember ever being this aroused before. She wasn't sure it was possible to need so much and stay conscious.

At last she was able to pull her shirt free of her jeans. She shrugged out of it and her bra, then clutched his head, holding him in place against her breasts.

"More," she breathed as he circled with his tongue.

Tension filled her body. She felt herself getting closer and closer to her release. Passion spiraled out of control.

With her free hand, she tugged at his shirt. He straightened and pulled it off in one easy, graceful movement. Then he stood before her, bare-chested, his arousal clearly outlined in his dark slacks.

"Tell me you want me," he demanded.

"How can you doubt it?"

"Say the words."

She stared into his dark eyes and knew that there was no going back. She had to know what it felt like to make love with Murat. She had to have that memory to take with her when she left.

"I want you."

For a heartbeat he did nothing. Then he gathered her up in his arms and lowered her to the ground.

"We must be practical," he said as he sat next to her. "Riding boots are not romantic."

She grinned as he pulled his off, then went to work on her. When their feet were bare, she stretched out on his shirt and held open her arms.

"Make love with me, Murat."

He claimed her with a soul-touching kiss and a growl. His clever fingers returned to her breasts where he teased her into a frenzy. She squirmed and writhed, wanting more, needing more to find her release.

At last he moved lower, to the button of her jeans. He unfastened it and lowered the zipper. She pushed down with him, helping him remove the heavy fabric, along with her panties.

And then she was naked before him. Rather than feel embarrassed, Daphne let her legs fall open in a brazen invitation for what she really wanted. He did not disappoint. Even as he lowered his head and began to kiss her breasts, he slipped his fingers between her thighs and into her waiting dampness.

He found that one perfect spot on the first try. Just the slight brush of skin against the swollen knot of nerves made her jump. He shifted slightly so that he could rub that spot with his thumb while slipping his fingers deep inside her.

This was too much, she thought as she found herself caught up in a sensual vortex. His mouth on her breasts, his thumb rubbing, his fingers moving around and around. She was slick and more than ready, and it was just a matter of seconds until the tension filled her.

She tried to hold back, to breathe, to do anything to keep herself from falling so quickly. But it felt too good. She clutched at him and gave up the battle.

"Now!" she gasped as her release washed over her. Wave after wave of pleasure surrounded her, filled her, caught her and then let her fall. She pulsed her hips in time with his movements, slowing as she neared the end. He slowed, as well.

When she'd finished, she sank back onto his shirt and draped one forearm across her eyes. It was one thing to impulsively give in to sex with a man. It was another when he was as imperious as Murat. What would happen now?

She braced herself for some comment about his prowess with women or how easily she'd surrendered, and tried to tell herself it didn't matter.

But he said nothing.

The silence grew until Daphne finally dropped her arm and opened her eyes. Murat leaned over her, but he didn't look overly pleased with himself. Instead he seemed…humbled.

No way, she thought, even as he brushed his mouth against hers.

"Thank you," he said quietly.

She blinked. "Excuse me?"

"Thank you for letting me pleasure you. I know that you could have held back and kept me from taking you to paradise, and you did not."

The man was crazy. She could no more have held back than she could have flown to the moon. But he didn't have to know that.

"I liked what you were doing," she said.

"Perhaps you would like something else, as well."

She thought about how hard he'd been, how long and thick. Then she thought about him inside of her.

"I think I would," she told him with a smile.

He didn't have to be asked twice. Seconds later he was naked and kneeling between her knees. He braced himself on his hands and slowly entered her.

He felt exactly right, she thought as she reached up to caress his back. When he filled her, nerve endings cheered and began to do a little dance. Despite her first release, she felt the tension building again and knew it was going to be even better the second time around.

He moved slowly, giving them both time to adjust and anticipate. About the third time he stroked all the way in, she gave up acting like a lady and pulled him down against her. He wrapped his arms around her and kissed her. As their tongues mated, she shifted so she could hug his hips with her legs. That caused him to push in even deeper and she was instantly lost.

Murat felt the first pulsing ripples of Daphne's release. His plans to dazzle her with his stamina quickly faded as each contraction pushed him closer to the edge. She gasped and moaned and clung to him, begging him to continue. He forced himself to hold back until she had stilled and only then did he allow himself to give in to the building explosion of desire.

Daphne knew that it was best to act as casual as possible, but she wasn't sure how to accomplish the task, given what had just happened. She felt as if Murat had somehow touched every cell in her body and made it scream with pleasure. Still, as he rolled onto his back and drew her close so she could rest her head on his shoulder, she was determined not to gush. He hardly needed the increase in his already impressive ego.

"You are amazing," he said as he stroked her bare back.

"Thank you. I could say the same thing about you."

"As you should."

She laughed. "How like a crown prince to insist on defining the compliments."

"You are made for pleasure."

"I don't know about that, but I don't mind giving in to it

from time to time." Especially to a man as skilled as him. He sure knew his way around the female anatomy. Did princes get classes in that sort of thing so they didn't embarrass themselves? Were there—

"You are not a virgin."

The unexpected statement nearly didn't register. Daphne pushed herself up on one elbow and stared at him.

"Excuse me?"

"You are not a virgin."

She laughed. "Murat, I'm thirty. What did you think?"

"That you would not give yourself away so easily."

Her warm, fuzzy feelings began to fade. "You're judging me?"

He put his free hand behind his head and regarded her thoughtfully. "Even though we were engaged ten years ago, I never touched you. You left here as innocent as you arrived."

"So?"

"So tell me the name of the man who has defiled you, and I will have him tortured and beheaded."

She started to laugh, then realized he wasn't kidding. There was some definite rage bubbling under the surface.

She sat up and stared at him. "Wait a minute. You're serious."

"Deadly so."

"That's crazy. You can't kill every man I've slept with."

He frowned. "How many have there been?"

"How many women have you slept with in the past ten years?"

"That is not your concern."

"My answer exactly."

"Your situation is completely different. You are a woman. Men took advantage of you. Tell me who they are."

"You belong in the Dark Ages," she said as she scrambled to her feet and grabbed for her panties. She pulled them on, then found her bra and put that on, as well.

"You're also making me crazy," she continued as she glared

down at him. "I am a modern woman and have lived a relatively quiet life. Yes, there have been a few men, but I was careful about whom I chose, and no one ever took advantage of me." She threw up her hands. "Why am I explaining myself to you?"

"Because you feel bad about what happened."

"I didn't before, but I'm starting to now."

"I don't mean here," he said as he sat up. "Those other men..."

"Are none of your business." She stepped into her jeans. "You're acting like an idiot. Worse, you're acting like a sexist pig and that's even more unforgivable."

"I care about you. I want to look after you."

She picked up her shirt and slipped into it. "I don't need looking after. I've been fine for years. As for the men I slept with, I will never tell you their names. I don't want or need your protection."

Murat stood. She hated how good he looked naked and the way her body responded. Get a grip, she told herself. He was nothing but trouble. Stupid, sexist trouble. To think she'd actually been attracted to him!

While he collected his clothes, she pulled on her socks and boots.

"You're even worse than I thought," she said when she'd finished. "I don't care how good the sex is, I wouldn't marry you if the entire fate of the human race depended on it. There is nothing you can ever say or do to get me to change my mind."

He paused in the act of shrugging into his shirt. "I am Crown Prince Murat of—"

"You know what? I've heard the speech dozens of times and I'm not impressed. Not by it or you." She glared at him. "You want to know why I left you ten years ago? It's because you couldn't see past who you were enough to notice me. You didn't love me. You barely cared about me. I was just one more item on your royal to-do list. "Get married and produce heirs." Here's a news flash, Your Highness. A woman needs to matter to the man she marries. She needs to be with someone who needs her. I wasn't interested in marrying a man who thought of me as a mere woman."

She spied her hat and quickly scooped it up. "I left because you're just not good enough for me."

Murat could not believe what Daphne had just said. How dare she say such things to him? But before he could voice his outrage, she walked away toward the horses, collected her mount and quickly swung into the saddle. When he realized she intended to ride off without him, he grabbed his boots.

"Stop. You don't know the way."

She didn't bother answering or even looking back. Instead she gave the animal its head and took off at a canter.

"Damn her stubbornness," he muttered as he quickly pulled on his boots.

Still buttoning his shirt, he hurried to his horse and went after her.

But her head start and her mount's speed meant it would be several minutes before Murat could catch up with her. By then she had already turned toward the east and the rocky part of the desert.

"Do not go there," Murat yelled into the wind. "Stay on the path."

But Daphne either could not hear or chose not to listen. Instead of staying on the marked dirt road cut into the desert, she headed directly toward the stables in what she most likely thought would be a quicker route back.

His heart rate increased, and it had nothing to do with the speed of his horse. Instead he watched and worried until fear turned to horror as Daphne's horse came to a sudden stop and she went flying over its head and landed heavily on the hard, stony ground.

Chapter Eight

Murat lived an eternity in hell, with time crawling as he raced toward Daphne. He fumbled for his security beacon and pressed it in rapid, frantic movements, signaling an emergency. It seemed that days passed, weeks, until he could vault off his horse and crouch down beside her.

Daphne lay on the rocky ground, her legs bent beneath her, her arm thrown over her face.

He lowered it gently, then sucked in a breath as he saw her still, pale face and the pool of blood on the ground.

"No," he said to whomever would listen. "You will be fine. You must be fine."

But she did not respond, and when he touched her cheek, her skin felt cold.

Pain filled him, and fury. That such a simple mistake could cause so much damage. Then he shook off all emotion and quickly went to work examining her.

The only external bleeding came from her head and it had already begun to slow. He could not assess internal injuries but her pulse was steady and strong. If only she would awaken and start yelling at him again. If only...

The distant sound of a helicopter cut through the silence of the desert. Murat rose and waved it in, shielding her with his body when the blades kicked up dust and sand.

"She is injured," he yelled to his men. "I cannot tell how badly. We'll have to be careful of her neck and spine."

He waited until the men brought out the emergency equipment and went to work securing her before calling the stable and telling them about his horse and hers. His stallion was trained not to wander far, but her mount could be halfway to El Bahar by now.

When she had been carried into the helicopter, he joined her and took her hand in his.

"I command you to be healed," he murmured, his face close to hers, his breath stirring her hair. "I am Crown Prince Murat, and I command that you open your eyes and speak to me right now."

Nothing happened. Murat swallowed hard, then pressed his lips to her cheek. "Daphne, *please*."

Murat paced the length of the main room in the harem. In the bedroom his personal physician reconfirmed what the doctors at the emergency room had told him. Murat tried to find a measure of peace in the knowledge that there were no internal injuries, no broken bones.

"She was very lucky," his father said from his place on the sofa. "I never thought of Daphne as a foolish young woman. To go riding off like that. You must have annoyed her."

Murat continued to watch the bedroom door. "I do so on a regular basis. It is one of my great talents." Only this time it had had too great a price.

Never again, he thought. He would not permit her to act so hastily. Left on her own, she could seriously hurt herself.

"I will stay while the doctor examines her if you wish to shower and change," the king said.

"No," Murat said immediately, then drew in a breath. "Thank you, Father, but I will stay. She is my fiancée, my responsibility."

"I see."

He doubted the king saw much, and nothing of consequence. This was Daphne. She could not be permitted to die.

At last his doctor appeared. The older man smiled.

"Good news," he said as he crossed to Murat. "It is as the other doctors told you. She has a mild concussion and some slight trauma to the brain. She will stay unconscious for a few hours, maybe a day. Then she should awaken and begin the recovery process. Within a week she will be as good as new."

"Is she in pain?" he asked.

"Not now, but when she wakes she will have a bad headache. I've left some medication to help with that. Once she's awake, keep her in bed for a couple of days, then she should take it easy for the rest of the week. I, of course, will be back in the morning and each day until she is fit again."

Murat nodded. "Thank you."

The doctor touched his arm. "Your fiancée will live to give you many healthy children, Your Highness. Fear not."

Murat heard the words, but he could not let the fear go. Not until she opened her eyes and started calling him names again.

He concluded his business with the doctor, wrote down the rest of the instructions, then hurried into the bedroom. Daphne lay in the center of the bed, hooked up to several monitors. A nurse sat in the corner. The king followed.

When Murat nodded at the nurse, she stood and quickly retreated to the living room.

"Daphne will be fine," his father said. "You heard the doctor. A nurse will be here twenty-four hours a day until she wakes up."

"No." Murat moved closer to the bed and reached for Daphne's hand. "I will be here. The nurse can wait in the living room in case there is an emergency. But until she wakes, I will tend to her."

"Murat."

He glared at his father. "No one but me."

The king nodded slowly. "As you wish."

There was only one wish, Murat thought grimly. That Daphne open her eyes.

Now, he willed her. *Look at me now.* But she slept on, unaware of his command. Even in illness she defied him. Pray God she lived to defy him another day.

Daphne felt as if someone was banging on her head with a frying pan. She remembered a frat party she'd gone to years ago while she'd been in college. She generally avoided loud parties with alcohol, but fresh from her broken engagement, she felt the need to participate in something fun and mind numbing.

So she'd gone with a couple of girlfriends and had stayed up way too late and had had too much spiked punch. In the morning she'd found herself with the mother of all hangovers and had basically wanted to die.

This was worse.

She struggled through what felt like miles of thick, sticky water, before finally surfacing. She felt bruised and sore everywhere, but it was her head that got her attention the most. Even her eyebrows hurt.

She was also, she realized, starving and in bed. The thing was, she didn't remember going to bed. She didn't remember much of anything except...

The horses. She'd been riding. She'd been angry at Murat and she'd gone on ahead, determined not to speak to him again, and then she'd been flying through the air and falling and falling and...

She opened her eyes to find herself back in the bedroom she'd been using in the harem. The walls were familiar, as was the furniture. Lamps illuminated the large space.

She glanced around, relaxing as the rest of her memory returned, only to stiffen when she saw a strange man dozing in a chair next to her bed.

He was big—tall and powerful—she could tell that even

while he slept. But his hair was mussed and dark stubble darkened his jaw.

A quick glance at the clock told her the time was two. The lamplight made her think it was probably two in the morning, and turning her head increased the pounding to the point of being unbearable.

She sagged back against the pillow and studied the man. In a matter of seconds she recognized the shape of his firm jaw and mouth, the breadth of his shoulders.

"Murat?" she whispered.

Was it possible? In all the time she'd known him, both ten years ago and present day, she had never seen him anything but perfectly groomed. Why did he look so mussed, and why did he sleep in a chair beside her bed?

One of his hands lay on the blanket. She reached out and rested her fingers against his palm.

He woke instantly and glanced at her. His eyes widened.

"Daphne?"

"Hey."

He leaned forward and studied her anxiously. "How do you feel? Your head will hurt—the doctor warned me about that. I have medication for you. And if you're hungry, you can eat, but only lightly for the first day or so. You are not to get up, either. I know you can be stubborn, but I insist you follow the doctor's orders. Rest for two days, then you may begin to resume your normal activities through the end of the week. I will not accept any arguments on this matter."

Despite her aching head, she couldn't help smiling. "Of course you won't. Because this is all about you, right?"

He took her hand in both of his and kissed her fingers. "No. It is about you getting well."

His tenderness made her want to cry, which only went to show that her head injury had affected her brain.

She squeezed his hand. "How long have I been out?"

"Thirty-five hours and—" he glanced at the clock "—eight minutes."

"Wow. What happened?"

"You were thrown from your horse."

"I remember that." She reached up with her free hand and gingerly touched the raised bump on her scalp. "I guess I fell headfirst."

"You did. I was concerned you had hurt yourself elsewhere, but you are fine. No broken bones, no internal injuries."

She returned her attention to him, then pulled her hand free and rubbed his cheek. The thick whiskers there grated against her skin.

"You look terrible."

He smiled. "For a good cause."

She studied his shirt and pants. "You were wearing those clothes when we went riding."

"Yes."

"You haven't showered or shaved since?"

"I wanted to be with you."

She blinked. "I don't understand."

"I have been here, with you, since we returned from the hospital."

Her head felt as if it might explode, yet she didn't feel disconnected from the conversation. Which meant she should understand what Murat was saying.

"In that chair?" she asked, trying not to sound incredulous.

"Yes."

"Beside me."

"Yes."

"Because you were…"

"Worried."

He kissed her fingers again.

Something warm and bright blossomed in her chest. Murat didn't have to stay here to watch over her. She was in his palace and completely safe. He could have an entire hospital medical team at his disposal and yet he'd stayed with her himself.

"I don't know what to say," she admitted.

"Then do not speak. There is a nurse in the other room. Let me call her to bring you the medication for your headache."

Her stomach growled.

He smiled again. "And perhaps some soup."

He rose and crossed to the doorway. As she watched him go, Daphne had to admit that she might have been a little hasty in her judgment of Murat. Sure he acted all in charge and 'my way or the highway' but his actions told her something far different and far more important.

He *cared* about her. When he thought she might be in danger, he stayed by her side. What about his meetings? His princely duties? Had he neglected them all while she'd been out of it?

She relaxed back against the pillow and sighed. She'd been so busy resisting his demands that she'd never taken the time to get to know the man inside. Maybe it was time to change that. Maybe—

The nurse appeared in the doorway. She listened while Murat spoke, nodded and left. Seconds later she reappeared with a small plastic container in her hands.

"Take two," she said. "I will order the soup."

Murat carried the medicine over to the bed, then helped Daphne into a sitting position. She felt her head swim, but forced herself to stay upright long enough to swallow the pills. He eased her back onto the bed.

"You will feel better soon," he told her.

"Thank you."

He resumed his seat and took her hand again. "My father was here for a time. He, too, was worried."

"That was very nice of him."

The nurse walked back into the room. "I have ordered a light meal," she said. "It will be here in about ten minutes."

Daphne winced. "I just realized the time. You had to wake someone, didn't you?"

The nurse, an attractive woman in her late forties, only smiled. "The staff was delighted to hear you are awake, Your Highness. No one minded the late hour."

"You're very kind, but—" Daphne froze as her mind replayed the woman's words. "I'm sorry. What did you call me?"

The nurse frowned slightly. "Your Highness." She glanced at Murat. "I was sure that was the right address. Am I incorrect, sir?"

He shook his head. "You did well. Now if you would please go wait for the meal?"

"Of course."

The woman left.

Daphne stared after her. A thousand thoughts bombarded her bruised brain and made it impossible for her to think clearly.

Something was wrong. Very wrong.

"Murat," she began.

"Do not trouble yourself," he told her. "All will be well."

She wasn't about to be put off. Not now. "She called me Your Highness, and you said that was correct."

"It is."

Panic flooded her. She struggled to sit up, but he pressed down on her shoulders.

"You must rest," he said.

"I must know the truth." She glared at him, willing herself to be wrong. Completely and totally wrong. "Why did she call me that?"

He picked up her left hand and fingered the diamond band on her ring finger. A diamond ring she'd never seen before in her life.

"Because you are now my wife."

Chapter Nine

Daphne wanted to shriek loudly enough to cause the ancient stone walls to crack. She wanted oceans to rise up, and thunder to shake the heavens. But she knew if she opened her mouth and really let loose, all she would have to show for it was a worsening of her already pounding headache.

Murat was speaking a foreign language, she told herself in an effort to stay calm, or he was the one with the head injury. Except, she knew neither was true and that this was all real, yet how was it possible?

"You married me while I was unconscious?" she demanded in a voice that was perilously close to shrieky.

"You need to stay calm."

"I need to have you killed," she said, narrowing her eyes, then wishing she hadn't when the pain increased. "What is wrong with you? You can't do that sort of thing. It's horrible and it's illegal."

"Not technically."

Murat continued to rub her fingers. When she realized that, she pulled them free.

"In a Bahanian royal marriage, the bride does not have to agree," he continued. "She merely has to not disagree."

"Silence as consent?" she asked, unable to believe this.

"Yes."

"Did anyone notice that I wasn't in a position to agree *or* disagree? I was *unconscious* with a head injury?"

He shrugged. "It was a matter of discussion."

"That's it? No one protested?"

"No."

Of course not. Because who would? Certainly not Murat and—"Who else was there?"

"The man who officiated and the king."

"That's it? No other witnesses?"

He smiled. "The king is enough of a witness."

She couldn't believe Murat's father had been in on this. Her head continued to throb, and now she felt tears burning in her eyes.

Don't cry, she told herself. Crying would only make her weak, and she had to stay strong, but it was hard. All she wanted to do was curl up in a ball and sob her heart out.

"You can't do this," she said.

"It is already done."

"Then I'll undo it. I'll get an annulment or a divorce. I don't care about the scandal."

"The king must give his permission for the union of a crown prince to be dissolved."

Which meant when pigs fly, what with the monarch being in on the sleazy ceremony.

"You're a lying weasel bastard with the morals of a pack of wild dogs," she said angrily. "I'll never forgive you for this. Mark my words. I *will* find a way out of this."

He had the nerve to brush her hair off her face. "Rest now, Daphne. You can deal with our marriage in a few days."

She smacked his hand away. "Don't touch me. Not ever again. I hate you."

That got his attention. Murat straightened, then stood and walked to the foot of the bed where he loomed over her.

"You forget yourself."

"Not even for a second. If I'm your *wife*—" the word tasted bitter on her tongue "—then I can do as I please."

"You will still remember your place."

"Oh, right. That would be as your slave here in the harem. Gee, how exciting. I'm delighted to be the unimportant plaything of a dictatorial, arrogant, selfish prince."

He glowered at her.

She didn't care about anything he might be thinking. And the pill must be kicking in because the pain started to fade.

She pushed herself into a sitting position and glared back at him with all her considerable fury.

"You are a most frustrating woman," he said.

"Let me tell you how much I don't care about your opinion."

He drew his eyebrows together. "You complain now, but I did this for you."

"Oh, right. Because I've been begging for us to be married."

"No, because of what happened. You hurt yourself. Someone has to watch over you."

"You married me to protect me from myself?" She didn't dare shake her head in disbelief, although she wanted to. "I guess you're reduced to telling yourself lies so you can sleep at night."

To think that she'd gotten all soft and gooey inside thinking he actually cared about her, that he'd worried while she'd been out of it. Instead he'd simply been protecting his new toy.

"There is also the fact that we made love," he said, as if explaining things to a small and slow child. "You were not a virgin."

What on earth did that have to do with anything? "So?"

"You should have been."

"You married me to punish me?"

"Of course not." The glower returned. "You are being most difficult."

"Gee, I wonder why. So you're saying you married me because I wasn't a virgin, but if I had been we would have been flirting with defiling territory, so that wouldn't have been much better."

"You are correct. I would have married you if you had been a virgin."

Talk about being between a rock and a hard place.

The sensation of being trapped sucked the last of her energy. Daphne slid down onto the mattress and closed her eyes.

"You are feeling unwell?" he asked.

"Go away."

She heard him walk closer, then he touched her forehead. "I wish to help."

She forced herself to open her eyes and stare at him. "Do you think I will ever care about what you want? Get out now. I never want to see you again. Get out. Get out!"

She screamed as loudly as she could. When Murat still hesitated, she reached for the empty glass on her nightstand and picked it up to use as a weapon.

"Get out!"

"I will check on you in the morning."

"Get out!"

He turned and left.

She put down the glass, then curled up in the big bed and closed her eyes. The pain was still with her, but this one had nothing to do with her head injury and everything to do with the loss of her freedom.

She didn't doubt that Murat had married her and that she was well and truly caught in circumstances that would be difficult to undo. The sense of betrayal hurt more than anything. Her eyes began to burn again, but this time she didn't fight the tears. She gave in to them, even though she knew they wouldn't help in the least.

With the aid of the painkillers, Daphne managed to sleep through the night. She saw the doctor the next morning, who told her to stay in bed at least twenty-four more hours and not to return to her normal routine for a few days.

For reasons she didn't understand but was grateful for, Murat didn't return to visit her, which meant she was left in solitude, except for the quiet presence of the nurse who brought her meals and stayed out of her way.

On day three, Daphne sent the poor woman away. "I'm fine," she said after she'd showered and dressed and found that walking wasn't all that difficult. "You should return to someone who actually needs your help."

"You're very kind, Your Highness," the woman said. "I wish you and the crown prince a long and happy marriage."

Daphne didn't know what to say, so she smiled and thanked her again. Obviously, she'd been out of the room when Daphne'd had her screaming fit. No one witnessing that could ever imagine a successful relationship as the outcome.

She still had bouts of weariness and despair, but when they hit, she used her anger to fuel herself. Murat wasn't going to get away with this. She wasn't sure what she was going to have to do to get away, but she would find out and make it happen.

After finishing her breakfast, she walked to the gold doors and pulled them open. No guards. No doubt Murat had released them from their duties after the wedding. He no longer had to worry about her escaping. As the queen, she couldn't go out unaccompanied. No driver would take her. No pilot would leave the country without express permission. She might have the freedom of the palace now, but that simply meant she'd graduated to a larger prison.

She walked through the quiet halls of the palace. As always the beauty of the structure pleased her. She paused to admire a particularly lovely and detailed tapestry of several children in a garden. She recognized the stone wall and the placement of several trees. The scene might be from four hundred years ago, but the garden itself still existed just outside.

The history of Bahania called to her, but she ignored the

whispers. There was nothing anyone could say or do to convince her she had to make her peace with what had happened.

She saw several people hurrying from place to place. When she recognized one of the senior staff, she stopped the man and asked after the king. The man led her outside, and Daphne stepped into bright sunshine.

For a second the light hurt her eyes and made her head throb, but she adjusted, then made her way along the stone path. She heard voices before she saw the people, and when she turned the corner, she recognized Cleo, Sadik's wife, with the king.

They sat across from each other. A pretty baby stood between them.

"You are so very clever," the king said with obvious delight. "Come to Grandpa. You can do it."

The baby, dressed in pink from the bows in her fine hair down to the hearts on her tiny laces, laughed and toddled toward the king. He caught her and swept her up in the air.

"Ah, Calah, I had not thought to find love at this stage in my life, but you have truly stolen my heart." He kissed her cheek.

Cleo grinned. "I'll bet you say that to all the grandkids."

"Of course. Because it is true."

Daphne didn't know what to do. While she had business with the king, she didn't want to interrupt such a private family moment. She felt a twinge of longing for the connection the king had with his daughter-in-law. Cleo might have come from ordinary circumstances, but no one held that against her. Funny how a girl who grew up in foster care and worked in a copy shop could go on to marry a prince and be accepted by all involved, while Daphne had never been as welcome in her own family.

King Hassan looked up and saw her. "Daphne. You are looking well. Come." He patted the bench. "Join us."

She moved forward and greeted Cleo and her daughter. "She's walking," she said, touching Calah's plump cheek and smiling.

The baby gurgled back.

"Barely," Cleo said. "Which is okay with me. She's a complete terror when she crawls. I can only imagine what will happen when she starts running everywhere. I'm going to have to get one of those herding dogs to keep her out of trouble."

The king shook his head. "You will dote on her as you always do. As will Sadik."

"Probably." Cleo bent down and collected Calah. "But right now we have to deal with a dirty diaper. See you later."

Her exit was so quick and graceful, Daphne wondered if it had been planned in advance. Not that anyone would tell her. She seemed to be the last to know about almost everything.

"How are you?" the king asked as he turned toward Daphne and took one of her hands in his.

The right one, she noticed. Not the left one, now bare of the ring Murat had given her. She'd left that in her rooms.

"I'm feeling better physically," she said. "Emotionally I'm still in a turmoil." She stared directly at the king. "Is he telling the truth? Did Murat really marry me while I was unconscious?"

"Yes, he did."

It was as if all the air rushed out of her lungs. For a second she thought she might pass out.

"Are you all right?" King Hassan asked.

"Yes. I just…" Her last hope died. "I don't understand why you allowed this to happen. What Murat did was wrong."

"The crown prince cannot *be* wrong."

Ah, so they were going to close ranks around her. "I don't believe that, and I don't think you believe it, either. He had no right to trap me into a marriage I don't want. Neither of us will ever be happy. Surely you want more for your son."

"I am confident you can work things out."

She stared in the king's handsome face. He was so much like his son—stubborn, determined to get his own way, and he held all the cards.

"I want an annulment," she said quietly.

He patted the back of her hand. "Let us not speak of that. Instead, we will talk of the beauty of Bahania. If I remember correctly you enjoyed your time here. Now you will be able to explore the wonders of our country. You can meet the people. I understand you have become a veterinarian. Practicing your chosen profession outside of the palace could present a problem, but we can work on that. Perhaps you could do some teaching. Also, I have enough cats to keep you busy."

She felt as if she were sitting next to a wall. Nothing was getting through.

"Your Majesty, please. You have to help me."

He smiled. "Daphne, I believe there is a reason you never married. It has been ten years since you left Bahania. Why, in all that time, did no other man claim your heart?"

"I never met the right man. I've been busy with my career and—" She stared at him. "It's not because I've been pining for Murat."

"So you say. He tells me much the same. But he never found anyone, either. Now you are together, as it was always meant to be."

This wasn't happening. "He trapped me. Tricked me. How can you approve of that?"

"Give it time. Get to know him. I think you'll be happy with what you find."

The hopelessness of the situation propelled her to her feet. "If you'll excuse me," she mumbled before turning and hurrying back toward the side door into the palace.

She felt broken from the inside out. No one would listen; no one would help. The tangled web of her circumstances would tug at her until she gave in and surrendered.

"Never," she breathed. "I'll be strong."

She turned a corner and nearly ran into a young woman in a maid's uniform.

"Oh, Your Highness. I was sent to look for you." The woman smiled. "Your parents have called and wish to speak with you. If you will please follow me."

No doubt her parents had learned about the marriage. They wouldn't care about the circumstances, she thought glumly.

Sure enough, when she picked up the phone, her mother couldn't stop gushing.

"It's wonderful," she said. "We're thrilled."

Her father had picked up the extension. "You did good, baby girl."

Tears burned in Daphne's eyes. Funny how until this moment, she'd never heard those words from her father before. Apparently she'd never 'done good' until she'd been trapped in marriage to a man she didn't love.

Her mother sniffed. "We would have liked a big wedding, but this is fine, too. I read that there will be a huge reception in a few months, so as soon as you have the dates, let us know. We'll need to make arrangements to fly over. Oh, darling, I'm so happy for you. Are you happy? Isn't this fabulous? And just think—in a year or so, we'll hear the pitter patter of a little prince or princess. Oh, Daphne. You've made us so proud."

Her mother kept on talking while her father added his few comments, but Daphne wasn't listening anymore. Instead she stared blankly out a window as a horrible, stomach-dropping thought occurred to her.

She and Murat had made love without protection. Right there in the oasis, she'd let him take her to paradise and back, never once considering the consequences. She could be pregnant.

"I have to go," she said, and listened as they told her of course they understood. A woman in her position had responsibilities and they would talk soon.

She hung up and tried to shake off her daze.

Pregnant. Oh, God. If that was true… She knew enough about Bahanian law to know that no royal child was ever allowed to leave the country in the case of a divorce. Which meant if she had a baby, she would be forced to stay here forever. Abandoning her child wasn't an option.

"It was just one time," she told herself as she hurried back to the harem. She couldn't get pregnant that easily, could she?

As she stepped off the elevator, she saw another young woman in a maid's uniform sitting in a straight-back chair by the gold harem doors. When the woman saw her, she rose.

"Your Highness, I was asked to wait until you returned. It is my honor to show you to your new quarters."

Daphne's headache had returned. "New quarters?" Oh. "With the crown prince."

The young woman beamed. "Yes. If you will follow me."

She didn't want to. She wanted to sit down right there and never move again.

"My things?" she asked.

"Have been sent ahead."

Of course. Murat would want the details taken care of so she couldn't put up a fuss.

"Very well," she said, wanting only to find a quiet place and close her eyes until the pain went away. Not just the pain from her head, either, but the aching in her heart.

She allowed the woman to lead her to the elevator, then through a maze of hallways, with them finally stopping in front of a large, carved wooden door. The maid opened it and Daphne stepped inside.

Her first impression was of openness and light. Massive windows and French doors led onto a private balcony with what seemed to be a view of the world. It was only after she'd stared at the vastness of the city and the water did she realize they were at the very top of the palace, on the corner.

To the left was the Arabian Sea, twinkling blue and teal and green in the sunlight. To the right was the skyline of the city. And beyond it all, the desert stretched for miles, compelling in its starkness.

When she returned her attention from the view to the room, she saw comfortable furniture, an impressive collection of artwork and a space big enough to Rollerblade in. Doors led to other rooms. Most likely a dining area, a bedroom and an office, in case the crown prince wanted to work from 'home." Because she had no doubt she had been brought to Murat's suite of rooms. Where else would his wife live?

Her heart ached, her legs felt as if they would give way at any moment and her head throbbed. She thanked the maid and made her way to what she hoped was the bedroom. Unfortunately, when she stepped inside, she found she was not alone.

Murat sat in a chair in the corner. Waiting? She wasn't sure. She ignored him as she made her way to the huge bed and crawled onto the mattress.

"You are ill," he said as he jumped to his feet. "I will call the doctor."

"I'm fine," she told him. "Just tired. Please, leave me alone."

"I cannot."

She turned away, curling up on the embroidered bedspread and doing her best not to give in to the tears. Not again. There had been too many over the past few days.

But the strain was too much and the first tear leaked out of the corner of her eye. She did her best to hide it, but somehow Murat knew. He sat on the bed and gathered her in his arms.

"It is all right," he said quietly.

"No. It's not and you're the reason."

He stroked her hair and her back and rocked her. She wanted to protest that she wasn't a child, that he couldn't make things better with a kiss and a hug, but speaking was too difficult. Right now it was all she could do to breathe.

She wasn't sure how long he held her, but eventually the pain eased. The tears dried up, and when he offered her his handkerchief, she took it and blew her nose.

"I talked to your father," she said. "He won't help me."

"Are you surprised?"

"More like disappointed." She shifted away from him and stared in his face. "You know I will never forgive you for this."

Murat did know. Marrying Daphne that way had been a calculated risk. But once he had made up his mind, there was no going back. He would face her wrath in the short term to gain her acceptance in the long term.

"Time is a great healer," he said.

"Not in this case. My anger will only grow."

He tucked her hair behind her ear and smiled. "I have seen the new sculpture you have started. I believe it is going to be me falling down the stairs. You have found a way to release your anger."

"It's not enough." Her blue eyes flashed fury. "You had no right to——"

He pressed his fingers against her mouth. "Let us not have that conversation again."

"Then which one do you want to have? The one where I call you a lying bastard? The one where I say that taking away my freedom is an unforgivable act and that you'll never get away with it?"

"They are variations on a theme."

"It's what I want to talk about."

She was so beautiful, he thought. Not just in her fury, but always. There was an intensity about her, and he longed for that energy to be focused on him.

He captured her left hand and held it in his. "You do not wear your ring."

"Why would I?"

"Because it is a symbol of our marriage and your position in my world." He pulled the ring from his pocket and tried to slide it on her finger. She pulled back.

"You are not usually one to act like a child," he said.

"I'm making an exception."

"Very well. I will leave it here until you change your mind." He set the ring on the nightstand.

She drew in a breath. "I'm leaving, Murat. Eventually I'll find a way to escape you and this palace."

"You are not my prisoner."

"Of course I am. I have been from the beginning. I don't suppose you would care to tell me why."

"You have made all the choices, save one."

"Yeah, that last really big one when there was a wedding." She pressed her lips together. "I *will* leave just as soon as I'm sure I'm not pregnant."

Her words crashed into him. He stood and stared at her. "Pregnant?"

She rolled her eyes. "Don't you give me that happy expectant-father face. It's unlikely. We only did it the one time, and let me tell you how much I'm regretting that incident."

Pregnant. Of course. He had been so caught up in making love with Daphne that he had not taken precautions, which was very unlike him. He had always been careful not to be trapped by that particular game.

A child. A son. An heir.

"Stop grinning," she demanded.

"Am I?" He felt as if he could fly.

"There's no baby."

"You don't know that."

"I'm reasonably confident. It was just one time."

"It only takes one time." He cupped her cheek. "You understand the law, Daphne. You know what happens if there is a child."

Despair entered her eyes. "You win. I couldn't leave my baby, and I would never be allowed to take him or her from the country." She shook off his touch. "But know this. I'm not sleeping with you ever again, and as soon as I know I'm not pregnant, I'm leaving."

Strong words, but he doubted she meant them. Not completely. "Would you leave the people of Bahania so soon? You are their future queen."

"They've lived without me this long. I'm sure they can survive into the future."

"You will change your mind."

"I won't." She stood and faced him. "Murat, you think this is a game, but it's very serious. I don't want to be here. I don't want to be married to you."

"I will convince you."

"You can't."

But he could. He knew that. He was Crown Prince Murat of Bahania, and she was a mere woman. Her will could not withstand the pressure of his.

He knew now he should never have let her go all those years ago. It was a mistake he would not repeat again.

"I want to love the man I marry," she told him earnestly. "I don't love you."

"You will."

"How do you figure? You're going to force me to love you?"

"Yes."

"It's not possible."

"Watch me."

Chapter Ten

Cleo sat in the middle of several boxes of shoes and grinned. "So I guess when you're the once and future queen, you don't go to the accessories, the accessories come to you."

Daphne wove her way between nearly a dozen racks of clothes sent over to the palace by boutique owners and fashion designers.

"The clothes, too," she said as she took a cashmere jacket off a rack and studied the light-blue color. "This is overwhelming."

Cleo held up a pair of strappy sandals. "I hate you for not having the same size feet as me. Just so we're all clear. I don't think I've ever seen a shoe this narrow."

"Or as long," Daphne said. "I have big feet."

"But skinny. I, of course, wear a 6 wide." She wiggled her hot-pink painted toes. "Billie's going to have a heart attack when I tell her what she's missed."

Daphne put the jacket back on the rack and returned to the sofa. "Then please don't tell her while she's flying. She only has a couple more weeks until the doctors ground her for the rest of her pregnancy. Besides, as far as I can tell, the clothes-fest is going to go on for several more weeks, so she's welcome anytime."

"Cool." Cleo dropped the shoes back in the box and picked up a leather handbag. "At least I can borrow this. If you're getting it. Are you?"

"I have no idea."

The clothes had started arriving three days ago. At first Daphne had kept the racks in the spare bedroom in their suite, but that space had filled rapidly. She'd finally asked for a large unused conference area and had all the clothes brought down, along with some sofas and several large mirrors. Dressing as the wife of the crown prince was serious business.

"You should be happier," Cleo said. "These are all beautiful."

"I know." Daphne did her best to smile. She wasn't sure she'd been convincing.

The problem was without Calah around to distract her—the baby was currently down for her nap—Cleo was far too observant. Daphne didn't know what to say to her new sister-in-law. That it had been a week and she still felt angry and trapped.

True to her word, she avoided Murat as much as possible and slept in the suite's guest room. He acted as if there was nothing out of the ordinary and insisted on discussing their future in terms of decades.

"Want to talk about it?" Cleo asked.

"I don't know what there is to say." Or how much she was willing to confess.

"I know the marriage happened pretty fast," Cleo said as she stood and walked over to the same sofa and sat at the opposite end. She fingered her short, spiky blond hair. "There was some talk."

"I'll bet. It's just…" She sighed. "I didn't ask for this. I know, I know." She held up both hands. "Boo-hoo for the poor woman who married a prince and will one day be queen. How sad."

Cleo shook her head. "If you're not happy, you're not happy."

"I wish it were that simple." She didn't want to talk about what Murat had done. Somehow she guessed that Cleo wouldn't want the information, nor would she act on it.

"Have you thought about giving the relationship a chance?" Cleo asked. "I know these guys act all imperious, but underneath, they're amazing husbands. You just have to get past the barrier down to their hearts."

"I don't think Murat has a heart."

"Do you really mean that?"

"No." He must have. Somewhere. "I'm finding the situation overwhelming. I'm doing interviews later for my chief of staff. I need someone to help me stay organized. Invitations are pouring in. I don't want to accept any of them, but Murat has to go, which means…"

She still hadn't decided what it meant. Did she go with him? Put on a front and pretend to be the happy bride? Did she refuse? While she wouldn't mind rubbing his face in what he'd done, he wasn't the only one involved. In some ways she felt responsible for the citizens of Bahania. She didn't want them embarrassed by her behavior.

"I don't want to make life easier for him," she admitted, "but my own sense of what is right is on his side. I really hate that."

Cleo leaned close. "You're thinking too much. Just relax and take each day as it comes. These royal things get easier with time. At least you have the advantage of breeding. You should have seen my first few lessons with the etiquette guy. I think I completely scared him."

Daphne stared into Cleo's big blue eyes and easy smile. "I doubt that. I'm sure he was charmed."

"Not when I accidentally poured the hot tea into his lap instead of his fine china cup."

Daphne laughed. "I'll bet that got his attention."

"In more ways than one." She shrugged. "The princes are worth it. That's the best advice I can give you. Know that they're worth every annoyance, every pain. I'm so thankful I met Sadik and fell in love with him. It wasn't easy, but now…" She grinned. "I know this sounds lame, but my life is perfect."

"I'm happy for you," Daphne said, and meant it. Cleo had

grown up in difficult circumstances. She'd more than earned her happy ending.

But not everyone's story was the same. Should Daphne ignore her responsibilities because she was still intent on leaving? Should she play the part while she was here? And if she played it too much, would she become complaisant? She would never forgive herself if she gave in to Murat. Worse, she would have taught him not only was it acceptable to treat her badly, but that there were no consequences. Ignoring everything else, did she want to be married to a man who thought so little of her?

Cleo stood. "Sorry to gush over your clothing and run, but Calah will be waking up soon and I want to be there." She smiled. "Sadik tells me that our nanny has the cushiest job around. Great pay and I never let her do any work."

"Your daughter is lucky."

"I like to think I'm the lucky one." She wiggled her fingers at Daphne and crossed to the door. When she reached it, she turned back. "If you need to talk more, you know where I live."

"Absolutely."

"Good. I'll—" Cleo gave a laugh and turned around "—look who just appeared," she said and dragged Murat into the room. "Your wife needs help," she said. "Too many good clothing choices. Maybe you could talk her into modeling a few things for you."

Murat glanced between the women. "An intriguing proposition. I will consider it."

Cleo left.

Daphne stayed where she was on the sofa while Murat walked through the maze of racks and the boxes of shoes, purses and scarves.

"Have you made sense out of any of this?" he asked.

"Not really. I need a schedule first to figure out what sort of clothing I'll need."

"I see. And you do not want to agree to a schedule because that is too much like giving in."

She shrugged, even though he'd guessed correctly.

"You have time," he said. "No one will expect you to have a full schedule right away."

"And if I don't want one ever?"

He sat down across from her. "There are advantages and disadvantages to any position in life."

"I know your advantages," she said. "You pretty much get whatever you want."

"True, but there is a price to pay."

"Which is?"

"I have much to offer. Favors, knowledge, an interesting circle of acquaintances. Who comes to see me because of who I am and who comes because of what I can do for him?" He loosened his tie. "Now I am aware of the possibilities at the first meeting, but when I was younger, it was not so easy to see those who expected something in return."

Daphne understood exactly what he meant. "I had the same thing, on a much smaller scale. Not so much with friends, but sometimes my teachers were too impressed by my parents to actually pay attention to me."

"Exactly." He shrugged. "Reyhan, Sadik and Jefri were free to roam the city, making trouble, having fun. I was not. While they played, I learned about governments and rulers and history. All in preparation. Each day I was reminded of my responsibility to my people. I did not know who they all were, but sometimes I hated them."

The man sat across from her but she could easily picture the boy. Tired, restless, but forced to stay inside for one more lesson when all he wanted was to go play with his brothers.

Compassion made it difficult for her to want to keep her distance, which meant he was making good on his word to convince her to care about him. Talk about smooth.

"While we are on the subject," he said, "your father called me. He wishes to discuss expanding the family business into Bahania, and from there El Bahar and the Middle East."

Daphne couldn't believe it. Her own father? Heat flared on her cheeks and she had a bad feeling she was blushing.

"I'm sorry," she said. "I'll phone him right away."

Murat leaned back in the sofa and shook his head. "There is no need. As my father-in-law, he is due some consideration. I will put my people on it and he can work through them."

"It's only been a week," she said, angry that after years of ignoring her, her father was now willing to use her situation to his advantage. "He could have waited a little longer."

"Perhaps, but if you allow yourself to get upset over every person who comes looking for something, then you will spend your life in a state of great anxiety. It means nothing, Daphne. Let it go."

Maybe it meant nothing to him, but it meant something to her. Unfortunately, no matter how much she wanted to hate Murat, he was the only person who could understand what she was going through.

She didn't want to live in a world where people used her to get what they wanted, yet that had been his whole life.

"Have you ever been sure about anyone?" she asked. "How do you know if he or she is interested in you or what you can offer?"

"Sometimes the situation is very clear. Those are the people I prefer. When I know what they are after I can decide to give it or not. But when they play the game too well..." He sighed. "I was more easily fooled when I was younger. After college, a few women managed to convince me that their love for me was greater than the universe itself when what they really wanted was the title and money."

She winced. "That couldn't have been fun."

"No. But for every half dozen of them there was someone sincere. A young woman who didn't know or didn't care. You, for example."

She smiled at the memory. "I didn't have a clue."

"I know, and when you found out, I thought you would run so far in the opposite direction that I would never catch you."

Her smile faded. "And when I did run, you didn't come after me."

He stared at her, then dropped his gaze to her left hand. "You still refuse to wear your ring."

"Are you surprised?"

"No. Disappointed."

"Want to talk about what I'm feeling?"

"If you would like."

She narrowed her gaze. "That's new. Since when do you care about my feelings regarding anything?"

"I want you to be happy."

She couldn't believe it. "You kept me prisoner, then married me against my will. Not exactly a recipe for happiness."

"We are husband and wife now. I would like you to make the best of the situation. You may find yourself pleasantly surprised."

She leaned toward him. "Murat, when will you see what you did was wrong? Why won't you at least admit it? I meant what I said. I want out."

"There will be no divorce. The king will not allow it."

Daphne stood, with the thought of escaping, only there wasn't anywhere to go. She glanced around at all the clothes she had to try on, the reminder about her interviews, the stack of books on history and protocol.

"Did it ever occur to you that whatever chance we might have had for happiness is now dead because of what you did?" she asked quietly.

Murat stood and moved close. He touched her cheek. "In time you will let go of the past and look toward the future. I can be patient. I will wait. In the meantime I have a meeting." He glanced at his watch. "For which I am now late."

"Somehow I don't think you'll get a reprimand."

He flashed her a smile. "Probably not." He nodded at the clothes. "Are you truly overwhelmed?"

"Of course. How could I not be?"

"Would you like to leave this all behind for a few days?"

"Is that possible?"

"Yes. Although it requires you getting back on a horse."

"I can do that."

"Good." He tightened his tie. "Be ready, tomorrow at dawn. You'll need to dress traditionally. I will have someone leave the appropriate clothing in our room."

"Where are we going?"

"It's a surprise."

Daphne spent a restless night in the small guest room bed. She couldn't stop thinking about Murat, which wasn't all that uncommon, only this time she wasn't nearly so angry.

Maybe it was because they'd discussed a little of his past. She wouldn't have enjoyed being hampered by so many restrictions. While it might be good to be the king, growing up as the prince sounded less fun.

She appreciated his understanding of what her father had done, but hated that such things were commonplace to him. Who had ever cared about Murat simply for himself? Who had ever loved him?

She didn't mean family, but someone else. A woman. Had there been even one to care about the man more than the position he held?

She opened her eyes and stared into the darkness. Would she have? Ten years ago, if she hadn't run, would she have loved him more than anyone?

Of course, she thought. She already had. She'd wanted to get lost in him and have him get lost in her. She hadn't run because of her feelings, but because of a lack of his. At twenty, she'd needed to be important, an emotional equal. She'd wanted to matter.

Funny how ten years later her goal hadn't changed.

That was what he didn't understand. Of course she was furious about how he'd forced her into marriage. He was wrong and egotistical and he deserved some kind of punishment. But if he'd come to her and even hinted that she mattered, she might have been willing to accept his apology and give things a try. Not that Murat would ever admit he'd done anything wrong, let alone apologize.

While it was her nature to make the best of a bad situation, she believed down to her bones that he had to understand he'd acted selfishly.

She rose and turned off the alarm, then moved into the small bathroom to shower. Every night Murat invited her to share the large, luxurious bedroom and every night she refused. Now, as she stood under the spray of hot water, she found her body remembering what it had been like to make love with him. She wanted to feel his touch again.

"Which only goes to show you're in need of some serious therapy," she muttered as she turned away from the spray.

After drying herself and her hair and applying plenty of lotion to combat the dryness of the desert, she slipped on her bra and panties, then a lightweight T-shirt and jeans. Next came her riding boots, followed by the traditional robes that covered her from shoulder to toes. Last, she slipped on her head covering.

As she stared at herself in the mirror, the only part of her she recognized was her blue eyes. Otherwise, she could have been any other Bahanian woman of the desert. Most women who lived in the city had long abandoned the traditional dress, but she and Murat would be heading into the desert where the old ways were still favored.

She left the bedroom and found Murat waiting for her in the living room.

He wore a loose-fitting white shirt and riding pants. She could see her reflection in his boots.

"I can arrange a Jeep if you would prefer," he said by way of greeting.

"I'd rather ride. I won't go off by myself again. I've learned my lesson."

He nodded, then held out his hand. The diamond wedding band rested on it. "We are married. I will not have my people asking questions."

She stared at the ring, then at him. The internal battle was a short one because she agreed that she did not want others brought into their private battle of wills. She took the ring and slipped it on.

His expression didn't change at all. She'd half expected him to gloat and was pleased when he didn't.

"Shall we go?" he asked.

Murat stepped out of the car into the milling crowd by the stable. Nearly fifty people collected supplies, checked horses, loaded trucks or called out names on the master list. His head of security gave him a thumbs-up, before returning to the conversation he'd been having with his team.

Murat helped Daphne out of the car, then waited while she glanced around.

"Did you say something about roughing it?" she asked in amusement. "I was picturing us on a couple of horses, with a camel carrying a few supplies."

"This is not much more than that."

She laughed. "Of course not. You do know how to travel in style."

"Will you feel better knowing we are to sleep in a tent?"

"Gee, how big will it be?"

"Not large. A few thousand square feet."

"However will we survive?"

"Everyone else is housed elsewhere. There is a kitchen tent, a communication tent and so on."

She shaded her eyes as she stared into the distance. "I'm glad we're going."

As was he. Even shrouded in yards of fabric, she was still beautiful. He had not enjoyed the past week—her anger and silence. He hated that she slept in another bed, although he would not force her into his.

Why did she not understand that what was done was done and now they should get on with their lives? Did she really think that being married to him was such a hardship? She insulted him with her reluctance and sad eyes.

"Daphne," he said, drawing her attention back to him. "About our time in the desert. I would like us to call a truce."

"I'm not sure that's possible when only one of us is fighting," she said. "But I understand what you're saying."

She looked at the horses, then the camels and trucks. "Will we be joined by some of the nomadic tribes?"

"Yes. Word has spread that I will be among my people. They will join us as they can."

She looked back at him. "I agree to the truce, but for your people, not for you."

"As you wish."

For now it was enough. If she spent time with him and forgot to be angry, he knew he could win her over. Then when they returned to the palace, all would be well.

"Come," he said, holding out his hand.

She took it and allowed him to lead her to a snow-white gelding.

"Try not to fall off this one," he said as he helped her mount.

She settled into the saddle and grinned down at him. "Try not to make me angry."

"That is never my goal."

"But you're so good at it."

"I am a man of many talents."

Something flashed in her eyes. Something dark and sensuous that heated his blood and increased his ever-present wanting.

"We're not going there," she said. "Don't think for a moment there's going to be any funny business."

"But you enjoy laughing."

"That's not what I mean and you know it."

"So many rules."

"I mean this one."

"As you wish."

She might mean it but that did not prevent him from changing her mind. The desert was often a place of romance and he intended to use the situation to his advantage. Their tent might be large and well furnished, but there was only one bedroom… and one bed.

"Tell me where we're going," Daphne said after they'd been traveling for about an hour. "Is it a specific route? We're on a road." Sort of. More of a dirt track that cut through the desert.

"Yes. This leads north to the ancient Silk Road. We will not go that far—just into the heart of the desert."

The Silk Road. She'd heard of it, studied it. To think they were so close. There was so much history in Bahania. So many treasures for her to discover.

She shifted slightly in her saddle. After a few minutes of trepidation in finding herself back on a horse, she'd quickly settled into the rhythmic striding and lost her fear. Murat riding close beside her helped.

She supposed it wasn't a good sign that the very man who made her insane also made her feel safe. "Will we be camping by an oasis?" she asked.

"Each night. Eventually we will make our way to—" He hesitated.

"What?" she asked.

"We are going to a place of great mystery. It is not far out of our way, and I thought you would enjoy reacquainting yourself with my sister Sabrina."

Daphne remembered the pretty, intelligent teenager from her previous visit to Bahania. "She lives out here?"

"Yes, with her husband. My sister Zara resides there, as well."

"Zara. Okay, she's the daughter of the dancer. The American who found out she was the king's daughter a few years ago?"

"Exactly. She is married to an American sheik named Rafe. He is the chief of security."

"Of what?"

Murat looked at her. "That is the secret. You must take a solemn vow to never reveal it to anyone." He seemed to be perfectly serious.

"You know I'm still planning to leave," she said.

"We agreed not to speak of such things."

"Not speaking doesn't take away the truth. But I would never betray the people of Bahania. Or you."

He nodded, as if he'd expected no less. "You have heard of the City of Thieves?"

She thought for a second. "It's a myth. Like Atlantis. A beautiful city in the middle of the desert where those who steal find sanctuary. Supposedly some of the most amazing missing treasures are said to reside there. Jewels, paintings, statues, tapestries. If a country has lost something of great value in the last thousand years, it can probably be found in the City of Thieves."

"It is true."

She blinked. "Excuse me?"

"All of it. The city exists."

"You mean like a real city. Buildings. People. Cool stolen stuff?"

"There is a castle built in the twelfth century and a small city surrounding it. An underground spring provides water. The buildings all blend so perfectly with their surroundings that they cannot be seen from any distance or from the sky." He motioned to the large crowd behind them. "We will leave nearly everyone long before we near the city. Prince Kardal will send out his own security forces to escort us in."

"I can't believe it," she breathed. "It's like finding out the Easter bunny is real."

"Sabrina is an expert on the antiquities there. Due to her influence, several pieces have already been returned to some countries. She will take you on a tour if you would like."

"I'd love it. When do we get there?"

He laughed. "Not so fast. First we must ride deep into the desert and find our way to the edge of the world."

"I've never been there," she admitted, more than a little intrigued.

"It is a place worth visiting."

Chapter Eleven

Daphne might hate the way Murat had arranged their marriage and not enjoy being kept in Bahania against her will, but she had to admit that the man knew how to travel and travel well.

Small trucks with large tires kept pace with the group on horse-and-camelback. Several vehicles were designated as moving cafeterias, offering everything from cold water to sandwiches and fresh fruit.

Lunch had been a hit-and-miss affair, eaten while her horse drank and rested, but Murat promised a dinner feast when they reached their camp for the first night.

He had also promised more people would join them, and he was true to his word.

By midafternoon, the number of travelers had tripled. Every hour or so another group appeared on the horizon and moved toward them. There were families with small herds of camels or goats, several young men with carts, and what looked like entire tribes.

Murat's security spoke with them first, inspected a few bags and boxes, then let them join the growing throng. A few of the men rode to the front of the queue and spoke briefly with Murat.

She noticed that those brave enough to do so seemed to focus most of their attention on her.

"Why do they do that?" she asked as a man bowed low in his saddle and returned to his family somewhere behind them. "If they want to meet me, why don't they just ask?"

"It is not our way. First they must speak with me and remind me of their great service to me or my father. Perhaps their connection is through a bloodline or marriage. Once I have acknowledged their place, they retreat. Later, at camp, they will bring their wives and children and introductions will be made."

He glanced at her and smiled. "I do not flatter myself that so many people are interested in traveling with me. I have gone into the desert dozens of times. It is their future queen who sparks their imagination."

Daphne felt both flattered and guilty. She was happy to meet anyone interested in meeting her, but she hated the thought of letting them think her position as Murat's wife was permanent.

"Your eyes betray you," he said. "How tender your feelings for those you have not yet met. Perhaps if you opened your heart to your husband, you would be less troubled."

"Perhaps if my husband had bothered to win my affection instead of forcing something I never wanted, I could open my heart to him."

Instead of looking subdued or chagrined or even slightly guilty, Murat appeared pleased. "You have not called me that before."

"What?"

"Your husband."

How like him to only hear that part of the sentence. "Don't get too excited. I didn't mean it in a good way."

"Nevertheless it is true. We are bound." His gaze dropped to her midsection. "Perhaps by a child growing even now."

"Don't count on it."

She knew that if he had his way, he would will her to be pregnant. And if she had hers…she would be gone by morning.

Daphne breathed in the sweet air of the desert. The sounds delighted her—the laughter of the children, the jingling of the harnesses on the horses and camels, the call of the birds following them overhead.

As always the vastness of the wilderness left her feeling both small and yet very much a part of the world. All right—if truth be told, she would not wish herself away just yet. Perhaps it would be better if she left Murat *after* this trip.

"It has been many years since my people have had a queen to call their own," he said.

"Then you should encourage your father to remarry."

"He has had four wives and several great loves. I think he prefers his various mistresses."

"What man wouldn't?"

Murat's expression hardened. "Is that what you think? Do you resist me because you assume I will not keep my vows? I assure you, I have no interest in being with another woman. You are my wife and I seek solace in your bed alone."

Had things been different, the information would have thrilled her. As it was, she felt a slight flicker in her chest, but she quickly doused it.

"For now," she said.

"For always."

He drew his horse so close, her leg brushed against his.

"I am Crown Prince Murat of Bahania. My word is law. I will honor our vows to my death."

The declaration had the desired effect. She felt bad for doubting him and for the briefest moment wondered if she was being incredibly dumb to resist him. Yes, he'd married her against her will, but it wasn't as if he planned to mistreat her.

Wait! Was that her standard for a happy marriage? Lack of mistreatment? What about love and respect? What about treating each other with dignity? What about the fact that for the rest of their lives together, he would think it was all right to ignore her opinion and desires and simply do what he wanted?

"I plan to release you well before you breathe your last," she said.

His gaze narrowed. "You mock my sincerity."

"You ignore my deepest and most sincere wishes."

"I have not tried to bribe you."

She couldn't help laughing. "And that's a good thing?"

"I knew you would not approve. Nor would jewels and money influence your decision."

"You're right about that." How could he know her so well on the one hand and be such a jerk on the other? "You're very complicated."

He smiled. "Thank you."

"I'm not sure it's a compliment."

"Of course it is. You will not be bored with me."

That was true. "We'd fight a lot."

"Passion is healthy."

"Too much anger can chip away at the foundation of a relationship."

"I would not allow that to happen."

"You don't always get to choose."

"Of course I do. I am—"

She cut him off with a wave of her hand. "Yeah, yeah. Crown prince. Blah, blah, blah. You need some new material."

He stared at her with the shocked expression of a man hearing words from the mouth of a beetle. Both dark eyebrows raised, his mouth parted and she half expected him to stick his finger in his ear and jiggle it around.

"You dare to speak to me that way?"

"What's the problem? I am, for the moment at least, your wife. If I don't, who will?"

"No one. It is not permitted."

"Murat, you seem to be a pretty decent ruler, but you really have to get over yourself."

She half expected him to call down thunder onto her. Instead he stared at her for a long moment, then tossed his head back and began to laugh.

The sound delighted her, even as she realized she'd never heard it before. Oh, he'd laughed, but not like this—unrestrained, uncontrolled. He was not a man who allowed himself to be taken off guard very often.

In that moment she knew she could make a difference for him. She could be the person he trusted above all others, the person he depended upon. She could ease his burden, give him a safe place to rest.

Need filled her. All her life she had longed to be a part of something. She'd always felt out of step with her family, and since leaving home, she'd never found anyone to love that completely. With Murat...

He was a man who took what he wanted. She thought of all the dates she'd had with guys who didn't bother to call when they said they would or who were too intimidated by her family to want a relationship with her. Men who hadn't been strong.

Murat was too strong. They had been too weak. Was there any comfortable place in the middle? And if she had to choose one or the other, which was best?

Strength, she decided. Perhaps there was something to be said for a prince of the desert.

"What do you think?" Murat asked as he passed her a bowl filled with a spicy grain dish.

Daphne smiled. "It's amazing. I feel as if I'm in the middle of a giant movie."

A sea of tents surrounded them. Twilight approached, and in the growing dark, campfires stretched out toward the horizon. The last rays of the sun danced off the dozens of banners flying from tall poles.

Scents of a thousand meals prepared on open flames blended with perfumes and oils and the clean smell of fresh straw.

She and Murat dined alone. The guards were always there,

ever-present shadows who watched for danger. Yet she felt comfortable and at peace. Should the unlikely occur and someone try to attack Murat, the intruder would be laid low long before he reached the center of the camp. The desert tribes were both fierce and loyal.

"While silence is often welcome in a woman," he said, "in your case it troubles me. What are you plotting?"

"I'm thinking about your people. They have a long and proud history."

"It is true. Many have sought to invade our land and none have succeeded. Now we have an air force to protect us from the skies." He picked up his glass of wine. "Why do I know you care more for the fate of my people than you care for me?"

"Because it's true," she said cheerfully before biting into a piece of chicken.

"You think you can say anything to me."

"Pretty much." She reached for her napkin. "What are you going to do to me? I'm the future queen. You can't really lock me up."

"There are other forms of punishment."

He spoke the words in a low voice that grated against her skin like burned velvet.

"Cheap threats," she told him. "I am the future queen. You must honor me."

"I already do."

"Not enough to admit you were sincerely wrong to hold me prisoner and marry me against my will."

"Perhaps we could put that behind us and move forward."

She glanced up toward the stars. "Oh, look. There's a flying camel."

He growled. "You mock me."

"I'm telling you what it will take for me to forgive and forget. It won't happen without you accepting your part in what you did."

"We will speak of something else."

"I had a feeling you'd say that." She reached for another piece of chicken.

The night was cool but pleasant. Murat sat across from her, looking completely at home in the primitive surroundings.

"Did you come out here much when you were younger?" she asked.

"When I could. There were many things for me to do back at the palace. Studies, lessons. I was presented to visiting dignitaries and expected to sit through many meetings. But when time permitted I escaped to the desert."

Where he could just be a boy. She could imagine him riding hard and fast as he played with the other children. For an hour or two he wouldn't be the prince, and how he must have treasured that time.

Daphne shifted on her cushion. She wasn't used to sitting so low on the ground. As she got more comfortable, she noticed a group of people walking toward them. There were maybe seven or eight, both men and women. They took a few steps, stopped, seemed to argue among themselves, then moved forward again.

One of the guards rose and spoke with them. After a few minutes, they were waved forward. The walking, stopping, arguing continued as they got closer.

"I wonder what that's about?" she asked, nodding at them.

Murat followed her gaze. "They are not sure if they should interrupt us," he said. "The men resist, but the women insist. Some men should control their wives better."

"Some men are sensible enough to listen to a more intelligent opinion. What should we do?"

"Greet them."

Murat wiped his hands, then rose and helped her to her feet. They stood by the fire and waited as the small group approached.

Everyone bowed. One of the women elbowed one of the men but he didn't speak. Finally the woman took a step forward and bowed again.

"Greetings, Your Highness," she said, speaking to Daphne. "May the new day find you strong and healthy and blessed with good fortune always."

"May the new day find you equally blessed," Daphne replied. "I fear it will not."

"We should not be here," one of the men said. He looked at Murat. "We are sorry to have troubled you and your bride."

"No!" The woman glared at him. "We are in need."

"How can we help?" Daphne asked.

The woman sighed. "A family who travels with us has a camel in labor. There is trouble of some kind. The man who usually helps with such things did not come with us. We have heard that you are trained with animals. Is it true?"

Daphne took in their robes. While the cloth was clean, it had been mended and patched in several places. She doubted these people could afford to lose a healthy, breeding camel.

The man with her grabbed her arm. "In all this crowd, there must be one other who can assist us. You should not bother the wife of the crown prince."

"There is no time," the woman said. "The mother grows weak." She looked at Daphne. "Please help us."

Daphne wasn't sure of the protocol of the situation. Nor did she know if she could help. "I've never delivered a camel before," she admitted. "I've had a lot of experience with cows and horses. If that is good enough."

The woman sagged with relief. "Yes. Please. A thousand thanks. This way." Then she hurried off.

Daphne started to follow her and wasn't all that surprised when Murat and his guards fell into step.

"You have delivered cows and horses?" he asked. "In Chicago?"

"No. In the country. It's not all that far to the farmlands in the south. I would spend a few months there every summer. Nothing against your father and his hundred or so cats, but it was always a nice change to work on big animals instead of small house pets."

As she walked, she shrugged out of her robes, handing them to Murat who passed them on to a guard. By the time they reached the straw-lined enclosure, she was down to her jeans and a T-shirt. Both of which were going to be pretty yucky by the time this was done. Birth was never tidy.

Three hours later a baby camel teetered on spindly legs. His mother moved close and nudged him until he began to nurse. Daphne leaned against the makeshift fence and smiled. This was the part she liked best—after, when things had gone well.

"Impressive," Murat said, stepping out of the shadows and moving close. "You were very confident."

"All that medical training paid off." She stretched. "I didn't think you'd stick around. It's late."

"I wanted to see what happened." He put an arm around her and led her away from the pen. "While you were working, I spoke with some of the elders of the tribe. The mother has died and the father is ill. There are three boys who tend the family's small herd. They desperately needed this birth."

"I'm glad I didn't know that," she admitted. "I wouldn't have liked the pressure."

"Had the camel died, I would have compensated them, but you were able to give them back their livelihood."

There was pride in his voice, which surprised her. Her parents had never thought much of what she did for a living, why should Murat?

He pulled her close, but she resisted. "I'm pretty stinky," she said. "I don't suppose we have a shower in our tent."

"No, but I can provide you with a bath."

"Really?"

"Of course."

Their massive private tent had still been under construction at dinner so she hadn't had a chance to see the interior. Now she followed Murat inside to a foyer-like opening. They removed their shoes. He held open a flap, and she stepped into an amazing world she hadn't known existed.

The fabric ceiling stretched up at least ten feet. Carpets were piled on top of each other underfoot. Her toes curled into the exquisite patterns and softness.

Low benches and plush chairs provided seating around carved tables. Old-fashioned lamps hung from hooks, providing illumination. The faint but steady rumble of a generator explained the flow of fresh, cool air she felt on her face.

"This way," he said and led her deeper into the tent.

There was a dining area, a huge bed on a dais, and a tub filled with steaming water that nearly made her moan with delight.

She had to resist the urge to dive in headfirst. Instead she tugged off her socks, then glanced down at her filthy T-shirt.

"Good thing I didn't pack light," she said. "I think this one is past recovering."

Murat shrugged out of his robes and left them draped over a low chair. Then, wearing only loose trousers and a white shirt, he moved close and held out his hand.

"What?" she asked.

"Your clothing."

She took a step back. "I'm not getting undressed in front of you."

"You forget. I have seen you bare before."

"That's not the point."

Actually, it was exactly the point. Getting naked with Murat around would only lead to trouble. Even talking about it made her body start to react. Tiny pinpricks of desire nipped at her skin. Her belly felt hollow and hot and an ache took up residence between her thighs.

"I'm perfectly capable of bathing myself," she said.

"I am offering to help." His dark gaze caught her and wouldn't let her go.

"Not necessary."

"Are you afraid?"

"Murat, I'm not playing that game. Now shoo so I can get cleaned up."

Instead of leaving, he moved closer. "I am here to help you with your bath, my most stubborn princess. I give you my word that I will make no attempt to seduce you in your bath. I will not make suggestive remarks or touch you in any inappropriate way. Now, take off your clothes."

Was this how the cobra felt in the face of the snake charmer, she wondered. She didn't want to listen or do as he said, yet she found herself reaching for the hem of her T-shirt and pulling the whole thing off, over her head. She handed it to Murat.

Her jeans were next, leaving her in a bra and panties. Turning her back on him, she unfastened the former and pushed down the latter. They tumbled to the carpeted ground. Then she stepped into the steaming tub and sank down into the water.

The heat soothed aching muscles. She reached up to keep her hair out of the water, but Murat had moved behind the tub and brushed her hands away.

"I will do it," he said as he gently coiled her hair, then took pins from a nearby tray and secured her hair on top of her head. "Here."

He handed her a bar of scented soap and a washcloth. She breathed in the smell of flowers and sandalwood.

The water was clear, which made her feel awkward about being naked. Murat stayed behind her, and there weren't any mirrors, so she tried to tell herself he wasn't really there…watching. Still, as she smoothed the soapy washcloth across her suddenly sensitive breasts, she felt his gaze on her.

She turned only to find him with his back to the tub. He stood by the wooden dresser, opening a drawer and drawing out a nightgown. Okay, so her imagination was putting in some overtime. Obviously he'd meant what he said. This was just a bath.

Being female and completely comfortable supporting two opposite ideas at exactly the same time, her next thought was one of annoyance. Didn't he *notice* that she was naked? Didn't he find her sexually appealing? Wasn't he aroused by the situation? They were married, and a man was supposed to want his wife.

She quickly finished washing and wrung out the cloth. Annoyance made her slosh the water as she stood.

"Could you hand me a towel?" she asked.

Murat reached for one and handed it to her. From what she could tell, he barely looked at her naked, wet body. How perfect. Now that he had her, he didn't want her anymore. Just like a man, she thought as she rubbed herself dry. Fine. She could 'not want' him, too.

She wrapped the towel around herself and stepped out of the tub. He passed her a nightgown. The soft, pale silk was unfamiliar, but at this point she was too much in a temper to care. She let the towel drop to the floor and slid the nightgown over her head.

The see-through fabric left nothing to the imagination. The front dipped down nearly to her stomach, and the back consisted of a few lacy straps and nothing else. Ha! As if Murat would care.

She wanted to kick him. She walked to stalk out into the night and scream her frustration to the heavens. What was wrong with him not to react? And more important, why did she care? She didn't love Murat. Lately she didn't even like him very much. So why did it bother her that he hadn't pounced on her like a cat on catnip?

"I'm going to bed," she said curtly. "Good night."

"You enjoyed your bath?" he asked from his place just behind her.

"It was fine."

"You would consider it finished now?"

She turned until she could look at him. "As I'm out of it, dry and dressed, I would go with yes."

"Good."

A rush of movement followed the word and she found herself caught up against him as he hauled her into his arms and pressed his mouth to hers.

She had no time to think or react or even feel. His hands were everywhere. Her back, her sides, her breasts. He kissed her hotly, ravishing her. Somehow she managed to part her lips, and he swept inside with the purposefulness of a man set on claiming his woman.

Even as he cupped her breast and stroked her hard nipple through the thin fabric of her nightgown, he squeezed her rear and pulled her into him. She felt the pulsing hardness of his arousal.

"You want me," she murmured, her mouth still against his.

He raised his head and stared at her. "Of course. Why would you think otherwise?"

"Because I was naked and you just ignored me."

"I gave you my word I would not bother you while you were in your bath."

Of all the times for him to keep it, this would not have been her first choice.

"You're the most annoying man," she told him.

He bent down and swept her into his arms. "Let me annoy you some more," he said as he carried her to the bed on the other side of the tent.

There were candles hanging everywhere and fresh-cut flowers in vases all over the room. The white linens had been folded back invitingly. Murat knelt on the mattress, then lowered her onto the smooth surface.

She kept her arms around his neck and pulled him close so she could kiss him.

Once again he claimed her with a kiss that marked her as his. She supposed she should protest, or at least not like it so much, but she couldn't help squirming in delight as he nipped on her lower lip, then drew the sensitive curve into his mouth.

He nibbled her jaw and down her throat. Lower and lower until he settled over her tight, aching nipples.

The silk was so thin, he didn't bother pushing it away. Instead he licked and sucked her through the fabric. She ran her fingers through his hair, to touch him as much as to hold him in place. He moved to her other breast, repeating the glorious touching and teasing, until she felt hot and strung far too tightly.

Wanting poured through her. She couldn't seem to keep her legs still, and between her thighs a pulsing hunger began.

"Murat," she breathed as she began to tug at his shirt. "I need you."

"No more than I need you." He took the hint and shrugged out of the garment.

She took advantage of his distraction to pull up her nightgown in a shameless invitation. She knew this wasn't her smartest act of the day, but she couldn't seem to stem the tide of need rushing through her. She might have had other lovers, but she'd never wanted one the way she wanted Murat. Desperation made her reach for his trousers. He had to be in her. Now!

"Impatient?" he asked with a smile as he shed the rest of his clothing, then slipped between her legs. "Let me take the edge off, my sweet."

Instead of filling her with his hardness, he bent low and gently parted her swollen flesh with his fingers. Then he pressed his mouth against her hot, damp center.

She had only a second to brace herself before the impact of the pleasure nearly had her screaming down the tent. Vaguely mindful of their neighbors, she held in her cries of delight as he licked all of her before settling on that one single point of pleasure.

He traced quick circles, making her breathe more quickly. Tension made her dig in her heels and grab on to the covers. She tossed her head from side to side as he gently sucked that one perfect spot.

She rocked her hips in time with his movements, moving

closer and closer to her ultimate release. Every brush of his tongue, every whisper of breath pushed her onward. When she finally clung to the edge, so ready to surrender all to him, he slipped two fingers inside of her.

The combination was too much. She tried to hold back, to enjoy the moment longer, but it wasn't possible. Passion claimed her and she called out Murat's name as she sank into the waves of pleasure.

Fast, at first, then slowing, but not really ever ending. Not even when he raised his head and stared at her with wild, hungry eyes. He continued to move his fingers. Back and forth, back and forth. Mini-waves rippled through her. Climax after climax. As long as he touched her, she came.

She stared at him, unable to control her body's response to his touch.

"Murat," she breathed.

He shifted closer, at last replacing his fingers with his arousal. He thrust into her, filling her until she thought she might shatter.

It was too good. There was too much. She came again and again. Every time he moved into her, she gave herself over to the release. Faster and faster until they were both breathing hard, and then she lost herself again in a violent shuddering that left her both shattered and satisfied down to her bones.

Chapter Twelve

Daphne awoke the next morning with the sense of being one with the world. She could hear the birds outside and the low voices of people in the encampment. The smell of cooking made her mouth water, and the sounds of laughter made her smile. She had a feeling that when she climbed out of bed, there was a very good chance she would float several inches above the carpeted tent floor.

What a night, she thought as she pushed her hair out of her face and sat up. Murat was long gone. She vaguely recalled him kissing her before he'd left their bed sometime after dawn.

They'd continued to make love, each time more passionately than the time before until she'd been afraid she would never be able to recover. Her body ached, but in the best way possible. Her skin seemed to be glowing, and she knew she would be hard-pressed not to spend the entire day grinning like a fool.

Everything had been perfect. Except… She pressed her hands to her flat stomach and wondered if they'd made a baby last night. She and Murat had made love several times without any kind of protection. The thought had never crossed her mind. She knew the price of having his child—she would never be able to leave.

Now, in the soft light of the morning in the beautiful tent, she wondered if perhaps she should make her peace with all that had happened. Was his behavior really that horrible? He'd only—

"Earth to Daphne," she said aloud. "Let's think about this."

Rational thought returned, pushing away the lingering effects of the night of pleasure. Of course she couldn't give in. Even if she wanted to stay married to Murat, she would still need to make him understand that he couldn't have his way in everything. That for their marriage to be a happy and successful union, they both had to make decisions, and he couldn't simply bully his way into what he wanted.

Which meant getting pregnant was a really dumb idea. She was going to have to avoid his bed.

She stood and faced the rumpled sheets. It was a very nice bed and the man who slept in it was nothing short of magical when it came to making love. Still, she had to be strong. At least until she knew if she were pregnant.

She washed using the basin of water on the dresser, then pulled on the garments that had been left out for her. Murat had mentioned something about a tribal council today. He would assemble the leaders from the various tribes and then hear judgments and petitions from the people. She'd agreed to attend.

Intricate embroidery covered her robes. In place of a headdress, a small diamond-and-gold crown sat on a pillow.

Daphne stared at it. While she knew that Murat was the crown prince and that he would one day be king, she never really thought about it all that seriously. But now, staring at the crown, she felt the weight of a thousand years of history pressing on her.

She carefully brushed her long, blond hair until it gleamed, then she set the crown on her head and secured it with two pins. She checked that it was straight, all the while trying not to notice she actually had it on her head, then left for the main part of the tent.

One of Murat's security agents sat waiting for her. When she approached, he stood and bowed.

"Good morning, Princess Daphne," he said. "The judgments are about to begin. If you will follow me."

He led her outside into a beautiful, clear morning. The camp was nearly deserted, but up ahead she saw a huge covering that would easily hold a thousand people. They walked toward it, avoiding the main entrance and instead circling around to the back.

She ducked under a low hanging and found herself behind a dais that held several ornate chairs. Murat approached and took her hand in his.

"We are about to begin," he said with a smile.

He spoke easily, but his eyes sent her another message. One that reminded her of their night together and all that had happened between them.

She wanted to tell him they couldn't do that again. Not until things were straightened out between them, but this was not the time or place.

She followed him up onto the dais and sat in a chair just to the left and slightly behind his. On his right sat the tribal council. In front of them were hundreds of people sitting in rows. A few stood on either side of the room, and an older man with a parchment scroll stood in the center.

He read from the ancient document in a language she didn't recognize. She remembered enough from her previous time in Bahania to know he called all those seeking justice to this place and time. That the prince's word would be final. Judgments against those charged with crimes were covered in the morning, while petitions came in the afternoon.

Several criminals were brought forward. Two charges were dismissed as being brought about by a desire for revenge rather than an actual crime. One man accused of stealing goats was sentenced to six months in a prison and a branding.

Daphne winced at the latter and Murat caught the movement.

"It is an old way," he said, turning toward her. "A man is given three chances. The brand allows the council to know how many times he has been before them."

"But branding?"

"He stole," Murat said. "These are desert people. They exist hundreds and thousands of miles from the world as you know it. If you steal a man's car in the city, he can walk or take a bus. You steal a man's goats or camels in the desert and you sentence him and his family to possible death. They may starve before they can walk out of the desert or to another encampment. They would not be able to carry all their possessions themselves, so they would be discarded. The youngest children might die on the long walk to safety. Stealing is not something we take lightly."

His words made sense. Daphne understood that where life was harsh, punishment must be equally so, but the whole concept made her uncomfortable.

Several more minor cases were brought forward. Then a man in his late twenties was walked in front of the dais.

The guards took his left arm and held it out for all to see. Three brands scarred his skin. Daphne sucked in a breath.

"He is charged with stealing camels," a member of the council told Murat.

"Witnesses?"

Five people stepped behind the men. Two were his accomplices, while the other three—a father and two sons—had owned the camels. The father spoke about the night his camels were taken. He had a herd of twenty, and this man and his friends took all of them. He and his sons went after the thieves only to find that one of the camels had gone lame and the thieves had slit its throat.

The crowd gasped. Daphne knew that to kill such a useful creature because it had gone lame was considered an abomination.

The cohorts spoke of the crime. They had already been

charged and had confessed. Each had a fresh brand—their only brand. But the leader had three.

Murat listened to all the evidence, then turned to the council.

"Death," each of them said.

When it was his turn to speak, he said, "You decided not to end your thieving yourself. We will do it for you."

The criminal dropped his head to his chest. "I have two children and no wife."

Murat nodded for the children to be brought out.

A boy of maybe fourteen stepped forward, holding on to the hand of a much younger girl. The boy fought tears, but the little girl seemed more confused, as if she didn't understand what was happening.

"What of this?" Murat asked the boy. "Do you have a brand on your arm?"

The teenager squared his shoulders. "I do not steal, Prince Murat. I protect my sister and honor the memory of my mother."

"Very well." Murat turned his attention to the crowd. "Two children of the thief."

There was a moment of silence, then a tall man in his early forties stepped toward the dais.

"I will take them," he said.

Murat was silent.

The man nodded. "I give my word that they will be treated well and raised as my own. The boy will be given the opportunity to attend college if he likes."

Daphne glared at the man and raised her eyebrows.

He caught her gaze and took a step back. "Ah, the girl, too."

"Better," she murmured.

"She-wolf," Murat whispered back. But he sounded pleased.

Still Murat did not speak to the man making the offer. At last the man sighed. He called out to the crowd. Several people turned to watch as a young girl of eleven or so stepped out and walked to the man.

"My youngest," he said heavily. "The daughter of my heart.

I give her into your keeping, to ensure the safety of those I take in."

The girl stared up at him. "Papa?"

He patted her head. "All will be well, child."

Murat rose. "I agree," he said. "The children of the thief will enter a new family. Their pasts will be washed clean and they will not carry their father's burden."

He walked to Daphne and held out his hand. She stood and took it, then followed him off the dais, toward the rear of the tent.

"What was all that?" she asked. "Why did that man bring out his daughter?"

"Because she is insurance. We will check on the condition of the two children he is taking in, but here, desert traditions run deep. Should he not treat them well, they will be removed from his care, along with his daughter. She gives him incentive to keep his word."

She'd never heard of such a thing. "An interesting form of foster care."

"It is more than that. He will take those children into his home and treat them as his own. I meant what I said—they will not bear the stigma of their father's crimes." He urged her toward their tent. "It is often this way with the children of criminals. They are taken in and given a good home. I have never heard of one of them being ill treated. I know the man who claimed them. He will be good to them."

She ducked into the tent and found lunch waiting for them. "I guess it really does take a village."

"For us it does."

He held out her chair, then took the seat across from hers. A young woman carried a tray of food toward them.

"What happens this afternoon?" Daphne asked as she served herself some salad. "More criminals?"

"No. The petitions. Anyone may approach me directly and ask me to settle a dispute."

"That must keep you busy."

He smiled. "Not as busy as you would think. My word is law, and I have a reputation of being stern and difficult. Only the truly brave seek my form of justice."

"Are you fair?" she asked.

He shrugged. "The fate of my people rests in my hands. I do not take that responsibility lightly. I do my best to see both sides of the situation and find the best solution for all concerned."

He wasn't what she thought. At first she'd described Murat as being just like her family—friendly and supportive as long as he got his way. But now she questioned that. He wanted to be a good leader. A good man.

How did she reconcile that with what he'd done to her? What was the solution to her dilemma? How did she show him that they had to be honest with each other before they had any hope of a relationship together?

After lunch Murat met with his tribal council, and Daphne went for a walk. She strolled by the makeshift stables and stopped to watch several children play soccer. A young woman approached and bowed.

"Greetings, Princess," she said. "I am Aisha. It is a great honor to meet you."

"The honor is mine," Daphne said with a smile.

The girl was maybe sixteen or seventeen and incredibly beautiful. In the safety of the camp, she left her head uncovered. Her large brown eyes crinkled slightly at the corners as if she found life amusing. Her full mouth curved up at the corners. Jewelry glinted from her ears and caught the sunlight.

"I must confess I sought you out on purpose," Aisha said. "I have a petition for the prince, but I dare not deliver it myself."

"Why?"

The girl ducked her head. "My father has forbidden me."

Daphne didn't like the sound of that. "He forbids you to seek justice?"

She shrugged. "He has offered me in marriage to a man in our tribe. The man is very honorable and wealthy. Instead of my father having to provide me with a dowry, the man will pay *him* the price of five camels."

This would be the part of the old-fashioned desert world Daphne didn't like so much. "Is your potential fiancé much older?"

Aisha nodded. "He is nearly fifty and has many children older than me. He swears he loves me and I am to be his last wife, but…"

"You don't love him."

"I…" The girl swallowed. "I have given my heart to another," she said in a whisper. "I know it's wrong," she added in a rush. "I have defied my father and dishonored my family. I know I should be punished. But marriage to someone so old seems harsh. Please, Princess Daphne, as the wife of the crown prince, you are entitled to plead on my behalf. The prince will listen to you."

Daphne thought about her own recent marriage and the circumstances involved. "I'm not the right person to take this to the prince. You have to believe me."

"You are my only hope." Tears filled Aisha's eyes. "I beg you."

The girl reached for the gold bangles on her wrists. "Take my jewelry. Take everything I have."

"No." Daphne shook her head. "You don't need to pay for my support. I…"

Now what? She felt bad for the girl, but would Murat give his new wife a fair hearing in these circumstances? He had said he took his responsibility very seriously. She would have to trust that…and him.

"I'll do it," she said. "Tell me what you want from the prince."

Murat listened as the woman explained why she was entitled to have her dowry returned to her. Her case was strong and in the end, he agreed. The husband, who had only married her for her dowry, sputtered and complained, but Murat stared him down and he retreated. Murat spoke with the leaders of the woman's tribe to make sure there would be no retribution and gave her permission to contact his office directly if his wishes weren't carried out.

Next two men argued over the use of a small spring deep in the desert. Murat gave his ruling, then watched as a veiled woman approached. By the time she'd taken a second step, he knew it was Daphne.

Why did she seek him so publicly? To petition for her own freedom?

For a moment he considered the possibility. That she would seek to hold him to the fairness he claimed to offer all. A protest rose within him. There were no words, just the sense that she couldn't leave. Then he remembered their night of lovemaking and the one that had occurred nearly three weeks before. She could not go until they were sure she was not with child. More than anyone, she understood the law of the land.

Relief quickly followed, allowing him to relax as she walked toward him. As she reached the dais, she bowed low, then flipped back her head covering to reveal her features. Many in the waiting crowd gasped.

"I seek justice at the hand of Crown Prince Murat," she said, then frowned slightly. "You're not surprised it's me."

"I recognized your walk."

"I was covered."

"A husband knows such things."

Several of the women watching smiled.

He leaned forward. "Why do you seek my justice? For yourself?"

"No. For another. I call forward Aisha."

A young woman no more than sixteen or seventeen moved next to Daphne. Murat held in a groan. He had a bad feeling he knew what had happened. The girl had approached Daphne and had told a sad story about being forced to marry someone she didn't love. Daphne had agreed to petition on her behalf.

Murat looked at the teenager. "Why do you not petition for yourself?" he asked.

The girl, a beauty, with honey-colored skin and hair that hung to her waist, dropped her chin and stared at the ground. "My father forbade me to do so."

Murat shifted back in his chair and waited. Sure enough, someone started pushing through the waiting throng. A man stepped forward and bowed low.

"Prince Murat, a thousand blessings on you and your family."

Murat didn't speak.

The man twisted his hands together, bowed again, then cleared his throat. "She is but a child. A foolish young girl who dreams of the stars."

Murat didn't doubt that, but the law was the law. "Everyone is entitled to petition the prince. Even a foolish young girl."

"Yes. Of course you are correct. I never dreamed she would seek out your most perfect and radiant wife. May you have a hundred sons. May they be long-lived and fruitful. May—"

Murat raised his hand to cut off the frantic praise. No doubt the thought of a hundred sons had sent Daphne into a panic. He looked at her and raised his eyebrows.

"You see what you have started?"

"I seek only what is right."

Murat sighed and turned his attention to the girl. "All right. Aisha. You have the attention of the prince, and your father is not going to stop you from stating your case. What do you want from me?"

It was as he expected. Her father wished her to marry an old man with many children.

"I am the wife he expects to care for him in his waning years," she said in outrage.

"And the man in question?" Murat asked.

There was more movement in the crowd, and a tall, bearded

man stepped forward. He had to be in his late fifties. He bore himself well and had the appearance of prosperity about him.

The man bowed. "I am Farid," he said in a low voice.

"You wish to marry this girl?" Murat asked.

Farid nodded. "She is a good girl and will serve me well."

"Instead of asking for a dowry, he offers me five camels," the father said eagerly. "He has been married before and has lost each wife to illness. Very sad. But all in the village agree the women were well treated."

Murat felt the beginnings of a headache coming on. He looked at the girl.

"There is one more player missing, is there not?"

Aisha nodded slowly. "Barak. The man I love."

Her father gasped in outrage, the fiancé looked patiently indulgent and a steady rumble rose from the crowd.

At last Barak appeared. He was all of twenty-two or twenty-three. Defiant and terrified at the same time. He bowed low before Murat.

"You love Aisha, as well?" Murat asked.

The young man glanced at her, then nodded. "With all my heart. I have been saving money, buying camels. With her dowry, we can buy three more and have a good-sized herd. I can provide for her."

"I will not give her a dowry," her father said. "Not for you. Farid is a good man. A better match."

"Especially for you," Murat said. "To be given camels for your daughter instead of having to pay them makes it a fine match."

The father did not speak.

Murat studied Farid. There was something about the color of the skin around his eyes. A grayness.

"You have sons?" Murat asked the older man.

"Six, Your Highness."

"All married?"

"Two are not."

Murat saw the picture more clearly now. "How long do you have?" he asked Farid.

The man looked surprised by the question, but he recovered quickly. "At most a year."

"What?" the girl's father asked. "What are you talking about?"

Murat shook his head. "It is of no matter." He rose and nodded at his wife. "If you will come with me."

He led her to the rear of the tent.

"What's going on?" Daphne wanted to know. "Can you do this? Stop the hearing or whatever it is in mid-sentence? What about Aisha? Are you going to force her to marry that horrible old man?"

Murat touched her long, blond hair. "That horrible old man is dying. He has less than a year to live."

"Oh. Well, I'm sorry to hear that, but the information means Aisha was right. He's buying her to take care of him in his old age. If he's so rich, why doesn't he just hire a nurse?"

"Because this isn't about his health. It's about his wealth. Farid has six sons. Two are not married. Per our laws, he must leave everything to them equally, which divides his fortune into small pieces. But that is not the best way to maintain wealth in the family. What if the sons do not get along? What if their wives want them to take the inheritance to their own families? If Farid dies married, he can leave forty percent of what he has to his wife. The rest is split among his children. I believe his plan is for one of his unmarried sons to then marry Aisha and together they will run the family business."

Daphne looked outraged. "Great. So she's to be sold, not once but twice? That's pleasant."

"You are missing the point. Farid doesn't want her for himself."

"I get the point exactly. Either way she's been given in marriage to someone she doesn't know or care about. And she's in love with someone else. What about that?"

Why did Daphne refuse to see the sense of the union? "She could be a wealthy widow in her own right in just a few months," he said. "She wouldn't have to marry one of the sons if she didn't want to."

"Are you saying she should agree to this? That in a few months, she could bring in what's his name—"

"Barak."

"Right. She could bring in Barak? That's terrible, too."

Murat shook his head. "Marriage isn't just about love, Daphne. It is about political and financial gain."

"I see that now. What are you going to do?"

"What do you want me to do?"

She raised her eyebrows. "It's my choice?"

"Yes. Consider it a wedding gift."

"I want Aisha to have the choice to follow her heart. I want her to be free to marry Barak."

"Despite what I have told you?"

She stared at him. "Not despite it, but *because* of it."

"And years from now, when she and Barak are struggling to feed their many children, do you not think she will look back on what she could have had and feel regret?"

"Not if she loves him."

"Love does not put food on the table." Love was not practical. Why did women consider it so very important?

"I want her to be with Barak," Daphne insisted.

"As you wish."

He led her back to the dais and took his seat. Aisha had been crying, and her father looked furious. Farid seemed resigned, while the young lover, Barak, attempted to appear confident even as his shaking knees gave him away.

Murat looked at Aisha. "You chose your petitioner well. Daphne is my bride and, as such, I can refuse her nothing. I grant your request, but listen to me well. You are angry that your father would sell you to a man so many years older. You

see only today and tomorrow. There is all of your future to consider. Farid is a man of great honor. Will you not consider him?"

Aisha shook her head. "I love Barak," she said stubbornly.

Murat glanced at the boy and hoped he would be worthy of
her devotion. "Very well. Aisha is free to marry Barak."

Her father started to sputter, but Murat quelled him with a
quick glare.

"I give them three camels in celebration of their marriage.
May their union be long and healthy."

Aisha began to cry. Barak bowed low several times, then
gathered his fiancée in his arms and whispered to her.

Murat turned to the angry father. "I give you three camels,
as well, in compensation for what you have lost in your deal
with Farid."

Murat knew that Farid had offered five camels, but he wasn't
about to give the father more than he gave the couple.

Finally he looked at Farid. "When it is your time, your family may bring you to the mountain of the kings."

The crowd gasped. The honor of being buried in such a place
was unheard of.

Farid bowed low. "I give thanks to the good and wise prince.
I wish that I would live to see you rule as king."

"I wish that, as well. Go in peace, my friend." Murat then
waited as they all left.

"Who is next?" he asked.

Daphne stayed quiet during dinner. Murat seemed tense and
restless. He had been that way since returning to their tent.

When the last plate had been cleared away, she put down
her napkin and smiled. "I want to thank you again for what
you did today."

"I do not wish to speak of it."

"Why not? You made Aisha very happy."

"I granted the wish of a spoiled girl. She is too young to know
her heart. Do you really believe she will love that boy for very

long? And then what? She will be poor and hate her husband. At least her father sought to secure her future."

Daphne couldn't believe Murat actually thought the marriage of a sixteen-year-old to a man four times her age was a good thing.

"Her father wanted to sell her," she said in outrage. "That's pretty horrible."

"I agree, the father's motives were suspect, but Farid was a good man, and she would have had financial security."

"Right. To be sold again into marriage with one of his sons."

"She might have fallen in love with one, as well."

"Or she might not."

Murat stared at her as if she were a complete idiot. "As a widow, she would be free to marry whomever she liked. No one could force her into the marriage."

"Gee, so it's only the one time. That makes it all right."

He turned away. "You do not understand our ways and our customs."

"I don't think it's that, at all. I think you're angry because I petitioned for the girl."

He stood and glared at her. "I am angry because my wife took the side of a foolish young woman and I did as she requested. I am angry because I believe Aisha chose poorly."

He stopped talking, but she sensed there was more. Something much larger than Aisha and her problems. But what?

Murat walked away from the table into the sitting area of the tent. She followed him.

"You gave a woman her freedom, Murat. What is so terrible about that?"

"What is so terrible about our marriage?" he asked. "Why do you seek to escape?"

Was that it? Did he see her in Aisha?

"I'm not in love with anyone else," she told him. "I would have told you if I was."

"I never considered the matter," he said, but she wasn't sure she believed him.

"Being married to you isn't terrible," she said slowly, still not sure what they were arguing about. "My objection is to the way it happened. You never asked."

"I did and you refused."

"Right. And you went ahead and married me, anyway. You can't do that."

"I can and I did."

She couldn't believe it. "You say that like it's a good thing."

"Achieving my goal is always a good thing." He moved toward her. "We are married now. You will accept that."

"I won't."

"And if you carry my child?"

Daphne pressed both hands to her stomach. They should know fairly quickly. "I'm not."

"You are not yet sure." He loomed over her. "Make no mistake. Any child will stay here. You may leave if you like."

"I would never leave my baby behind."

"Then the decision is made for you."

She wanted to scream. She wanted to demand that he understand. Why was he being so stubborn and hateful?

"I won't sleep with you again," she said.

"So you told me before, yet look what happened."

She felt as if he'd slapped her. "Is that all that night meant to you? Was it just a chance to prove me wrong?"

"Your word means very little."

She turned away, both because it hurt to look at him and to keep him from seeing the tears in her eyes.

"I'm sorry I came on this trip with you," she said. "I wish I'd never left the palace."

"If you prefer to be back there, it can be arranged."

"Then go ahead and do it."

Chapter Thirteen

Murat left the tent without looking back. Daphne wasn't sure what to do, so she stayed where she was. Less than forty minutes later she heard the sound of a helicopter approaching. One of the security agents came and got her, and before she could figure out what had happened, she found herself being whisked up into the night sky.

The glow of all the campfires seemed to stretch out for miles. She pressed her fingers against the cool glass window and wished for a second chance to take back the angry words she and Murat had exchanged.

He'd hurt her. She refused to believe he'd spent last night making love with her only to prove a point. Their time together had to have meant something to him, too. But why wouldn't he admit it? And why had he let her go so easily?

Just like before, she thought sadly, when she'd broken their engagement. He'd let her go without trying to stop her then, too.

The trip back to the palace took less than thirty minutes. She made her way to the suite she shared with Murat and let herself inside.

Everything was as she'd left it, except that the man she'd

married was gone. She had no idea when he would return or what they would say to each other when he did.

She wandered through the room, touching pictures and small personal things, his pen or a pair of cuff links. She missed him. How crazy was that?

Something brushed against her leg. She looked down and saw one of the king's cats rubbing against her. She picked up the animal and held it close. The warm body and soft purr comforted her. Still holding the cat, she sank down on the sofa and began to cry.

"So, how was it?" Billie asked the next morning as she threw herself on one of the sofas. "I can't imagine riding through the desert. Flying would get you there much faster."

Cleo sat next to her sister-in-law and swatted her with a pillow. "The journey is the point. When you fly you never get to see anything."

"Yeah, but you get there fast." Billie grinned. "I'm into the whole speed thing."

"And we didn't know that." Cleo fluffed her short, blond hair. "Did you have a good time? I thought you would have been gone longer."

"It was great," Daphne said, hoping the cold compresses she'd used earlier had taken down some of the swelling around her eyes. Crying herself to sleep never made for a pretty morning after. "I enjoyed the riding, and the tent was incredible. Like something out of *Arabian Nights*. There were dozens of rugs underfoot, hanging lights and a really huge bathtub."

Billie smoothed the front of her skirt over her very pregnant belly. "Tubs can be fun. Anything you want to talk about?"

"Not really," Daphne said, trying to keep things light. "The cultural differences were interesting. I enjoyed watching Murat work with the council."

"You weren't gone long enough to get to the City of Thieves, were you?" Cleo asked, then covered her mouth. She winced and dropped her hand. "Tell me Murat told you about it. I *so* don't want to be shot at dawn."

"Not to worry. He did. And, no, I didn't make it there."

She'd been looking forward to it, too. She hadn't really wanted to leave the caravan. She'd acted impulsively in the moment. Why had she reacted so strongly last night? Why had he been so willing to fight with her and let her go?

"I wanted to see Sabrina and meet Zara," she said.

"They're both very cool," Cleo said. "You'll have time later. Or we could plan a lunch. The show-off here can fly us out there in a helicopter."

"Cleo's just jealous because I'm talented," Billie said with a grin.

"It's disgusting," Cleo admitted. "And she brags about it all the time."

"Do not."

"Do, too."

Daphne felt a wave of longing. These women weren't sisters, yet they were closer than Daphne had ever been to anyone in her family. If she stayed, she could be a part of this, as well.

If.

Cleo shifted to the edge of the sofa and laced her hands together. "I'm not sure how to say this delicately, so I'm just going to blurt it out. Something's up. You're obviously unhappy. You're back early and Murat isn't with you. Given how you two came to be married and all, Billie and I were wondering if you wanted to talk. You don't have to, but we're here to listen."

Daphne bit her lower lip. She did want to confide in someone, but... "You're both in very different places."

"Okay." Billie looked confused. "I know you mean more than us sitting on the sofa and you sitting on a chair."

Daphne couldn't help laughing. Cleo stared at Billie and rolled her eyes.

"She means we're in love with our husbands and she's not sure she is." She glanced at Daphne. "Is that right?"

"Yes."

"I knew that," Billie said. "I guess you have a point. But Murat isn't so bad, is he?"

"I don't know."

Daphne realized it was the truth. That while she hated what he'd done to her—how he'd used circumstances and manipulated her to get what he wanted—she wasn't sure how she felt about the man himself.

"There's the whole 'going to be queen thing," Cleo said. "Does that count for anything?"

"Of course it doesn't," Billie said. "Daphne has more depth than that."

Cleo sighed. "I actually wasn't asking you."

"Do you two ever stop arguing?"

"Sure," Cleo said. "When we're not together." She linked arms with her sister-in-law. "Billie and I have fabulous chemistry. I love sniping at her more than almost anything. It's like a sporting event."

Billie nodded. "Jefri and Sadik have gotten used to never getting a word in edgewise when the four of us have dinner."

"Shopping is a complete nightmare for the guys," Cleo said. "We have credit cards and we know how to use them." She disentangled her arm. "How can you not want to be a part of this?"

"You're tempting me."

"More than being queen?"

Daphne curled up in the chair and leaned her head against the back. "I remember when I was here before. I was so young, just twenty, and engaged to Murat. The thought of being queen really terrified me. I was sort of a serious kid, and I knew there would be huge responsibilities. I didn't think I could ever manage."

"And now?" Billie asked.

"I don't know. There's a part of me that thinks I could really help Murat. He doesn't have anyone he can confide in. Not to say anything against his brothers."

Cleo and Billie looked at each other, then at her. "I know what you mean," Cleo said. "Sadik is in meetings with Murat and that kind of thing, but he only has to worry about his own area of expertise. Murat has all the responsibility. King Hassan is handing over more and more of the day-to-day ruling. So a wife he trusted could help lighten the load."

"Maybe. I think I could make a difference. As much as I don't get along with my family, I have to admit I've been raised to be married to a powerful man."

"How nice not to have to learn what fork goes where," Billie grumbled.

Daphne grinned. "It's a skill that has served me well."

"So you're okay with the office of queen, which means the problem lies with Murat himself," Cleo said. "I think you're going to have to solve that one on your own."

Daphne knew she was right. "I appreciate the support."

Billie slipped to the edge of the sofa and leaned close. "I'm about to say something I shouldn't, but I have to because I feel bad about what happened. Cleo, you can't tell anyone. Not Zara or Sadik or anyone."

"I won't. I promise."

Billie nodded and stared at Daphne. "If you want to leave, just tell me. I can get you on a plane and back to the States in five hours."

Daphne thought of the long flight over. "How is that possible?"

Billie grinned. "We'd take a jet. No luggage room, but plenty of speed. I need an hour's notice. That's all. If it gets bad and you need to run, I'll take you."

Daphne felt her eyes start to burn. These women didn't even know her and yet they were willing to offer so much support.

"I appreciate the offer. I doubt things will come to that, but if they do, I know where to find you."

The women left after lunch. Daphne walked into the gardens and admired the bronze artwork there. Her favorite piece stood in the center of a large, shallow pool. A life-size statue of a desert warrior on the back of a stallion. As she studied the power in the horse's flanks and the fierce expression on the warrior's face, her fingers itched to be back in clay. She wanted to make something as wonderful as this.

"If only I had that much talent," she said ruefully. But she still enjoyed the process. She had time for that here. Time for many things she enjoyed.

She sat on a bench and raised her face to the sun. Now that she was alone, she could admit the truth. She missed Murat.

Despite his imperious ways and how he made her crazy, she missed him. She wanted to hear his voice and laughter. She wanted to watch him work and know that his strength would one day be their children's. She wanted his touch on her body and her hands on his.

So when exactly had she stopped hating enough to start caring about him? Or had she ever hated him? What did she do now? Accept what had happened and move on?

Her heart told her no. That giving in would mean a lifetime of never being more than an object in his life. She wanted more than his rules and wishes. She wanted him to care. To woo her. To love her.

She dropped her chin to her chest as the truth washed over her. She wanted him to love her enough to come after her, instead of always letting her go so easily. She wanted to know it was safe to fall in love with him.

But how? How did she convince a man who believed he was invincible that it was all right to be vulnerable once in a while? How did she get him to open up to her? How did she get him to give her his heart?

She touched her stomach. If she was pregnant, she had her lifetime to figure it out. If she wasn't, then time might be very, very short.

Which did she want? If she had to choose right now, which would it be?

* * *

Murat couldn't remember the last time he'd been drunk. He usually didn't allow himself to indulge. As crown prince it was his responsibility to be alert at all times. But tonight he couldn't bring himself to care.

He'd waited all day for Daphne to return, but she had not. Even as he and his people rode deeper into the desert, he watched the sky for a helicopter that did not come.

He should never have ordered the helicopter. He knew that now. If he'd ignored her outburst, she would still be with him. But her reluctance to accept their marriage as something that could not be changed made him furious. How dare she question his authority? He had honored her by marrying her. It was done, and they needed to simply move forward.

But did Daphne see it that way? Was she logical and grateful? No. She constantly fought him, making life difficult, looking at him with accusations in her eyes.

He reached for the bottle of cognac and poured more into his glass. The smooth liquid burned its way down his throat.

Time, he told himself. He had time. Unless she wasn't pregnant. Then she would leave as she had before.

Do not think about that, he told himself. She would not leave again. He wouldn't permit it. Nor would the king.

The sound of muted footsteps forced his gaze from the fire. He watched as several of the tribal elders approached, bowed, then joined him by the fire.

"Will you be attending the camel races tomorrow, Your Highness?" one of the men asked.

Murat shrugged. He had wanted Daphne to see them, but now… "Perhaps. After the morning petitions."

"The council sessions went well today," another said. "Your justice, as always, provides a safe haven for your people."

Murat knew the compliments were just a way to ease into the conversation the old men *really* wanted to have with him. He thought of how Daphne would listen attentively, all the while secretly urging them to get to the point.

She played the games of his office well. She understood the importance of ritual and tradition, even when she didn't agree with it. Unlike many women he had met, she would have patience for tribal councils and diplomatic sessions and negotiations.

"You made an interesting choice with Aisha," the first man said. "To give her to Barak."

He decided to help them cut to the chase. "The decision was a gift to my bride. It was her request that the young lovers be allowed to start a new life."

"Ah." The elders nodded to each other.

"Of course," one of them said, "a woman sees with her heart. It has always been the way. Their tender emotions make them stewards of our households and our children. But when it comes to matters of importance, they know to defer to the man."

Not all of them, Murat thought as he took another drink. He wondered what Daphne would make of being called the steward of his household. The title implied employment and a distance between the parties far greater than in a marriage.

One of the elders cleared his throat. "We could not help but notice the princess has left us. We hope she was not taken ill."

"No. Her health continues to be excellent."

"Good. That is good."

Silence descended. Murat stared into the flames and wished the old men would get to the point, then leave him alone.

"She is American."

"I had noticed that," Murat said dryly.

"Of course, Your Highness. It is just that American women can be strong-willed and stubborn. They do not always understand the subtleties of our ways." The man speaking held up both hands in a gesture of surrender. "Princess Daphne is an angel among women."

"An angel," the others echoed.

"Not the word I would have chosen," Murat muttered. She was more like the devil—always prodding at him. If he wasn't careful, she would soon be leading him around by the nose.

"Have you tried beating her?" one of the men asked.

Murat straightened and glared. The old man shrank back.

"A thousand pardons, Your Highness."

Murat rose and pointed into the darkness. "Go," he commanded. "Go and never darken my path again."

The man gasped. To be an elder and told to never show his face to the prince was unheard of. The old man stood, trembling, then crept away into the night.

Murat sank down by the fire and looked at each of the six remaining men. "Does anyone else wish to suggest I beat my wife?"

No one spoke.

"I know you are here to offer aid and advice," he said. "In the absence of the king, you are my surrogate family. But make no mistake—Princess Daphne is my wife. She is the one I have chosen to be the mother of my children. Her blood will join with mine and our heirs will rule Bahania for a thousand more years. Remember that when you speak of her."

The men nodded.

Murat turned his attention to the fire. As much as Daphne frustrated him, he had never thought to hit her. What would that accomplish? He already knew he was physically stronger. Old fools.

"Do you know why the princess left us?" one of the men asked in a soft, timid voice.

Interesting question. Murat realized he did not know. One minute they had been fighting and the next she was gone.

"She angered me. I spoke in haste," he admitted.

"You could demand her return," a man said.

Murat knew that he could. But to what end? To have her staring at him with anger in her eyes? That was not how he wished to spend his days. Yet to spend them without her was equally unpleasant.

"The prince wishes her to return on her own," another man said.

Murat squinted at him through the flames. He was small and very old. Wizened.

"The elder speaks wisely," he said. "I wish her to return to me of her own accord."

The tiny man nodded. "But she will not. Women are like the night jasmine. They offer sweetness in the shadows, when most of the world slumbers. Other flowers give their scent in the day, when all can enjoy them. A very stubborn flower."

"So now what?" Murat asked.

"Ignore her," one man said. "Give her time to get lonely. She will be so grateful to see you when you do return that she will bend to your will."

An interesting possibility, Murat thought. Although Daphne wasn't the bending type.

"You could take a mistress," another suggested. "One of the young beauties who travel with us. A man does not miss the main course when there are many sweets at the table."

He shook his head. Not only was he not interested in any other woman, he had given his word. He would honor his vows until his death.

"A flower needs tending," the little old man said. "Left alone it grows wild, or withers and dies."

The other elders stared at him. "You wish Prince Murat to go to her? To go after a woman?"

Murat was equally surprised by the advice. "I am Crown Prince Murat of Bahania."

The old man smiled in the darkness. "I do not believe her ignorance about your title and position are at the heart of the problem."

Daphne had said much the same thing.

"The gardener yields to the flower," he continued. "He kneels on the ground and plunges his hands deep in the soil. His reward is a beauty and strength that lasts through the harshest of storms."

The cognac had muddled Murat's brain to the point that the flower analogy wasn't making any sense. "You want me to what?"

"Go to her," the old man said. "Provide her with fertile soil and she will bloom for you."

If Daphne grew anything it would be thorns, and she would use them to stab him.

Go to her? Give in?

Never. He was a prince. A sheik. She was a mere woman.

He reached for the bottle, then stood abruptly and stalked into his tent without saying a word. When he reached the bedroom, he stood in the silence and inhaled the scent of Daphne's perfume.

How he ached for her.

"Go to her," the old man had said.

And then what?

Daphne stood her ground with the servants and basically bullied them into helping her set up her art table and supplies in the garden of the harem.

"But the crown prince said you were not to return here," one of the men said, practically wringing his hands.

"I'm not moving in," she said, trying to be as patient as possible. "I just want to work here. It's quiet, and the light is perfect."

With a combination of prodding, carrying most of the stuff herself and threatening to call the king, she got her supplies in place and finally went to work.

The clay felt good against her bare hands. She had a vision for what she wanted the piece to be, but wasn't sure if her talent could keep pace with her imagination. Sleeplessness made her a little clumsy—she'd spent the past three nights tossing and turning—but she reworked what she had to and kept moving forward with the piece.

The sun had nearly set when she realized she'd had nothing to eat or drink all day. Dizziness made her sink onto the bench in the garden. But the swimming head and gnawing stomach were more than worth it, she thought as she stared at the work she'd accomplished so far. She could—

"I forbade you to come to this place."

The unexpected voice made her jump. She stood and turned, only to see Murat stalking toward her.

"I left specific instructions," he said. "Who allowed you to return to the harem?"

He wore a long cloak over his riding clothes. The fabric billowed out behind him, making him seem even taller and more powerful than she remembered.

She'd missed him. The past seventy-two hours had passed so slowly. Only getting back to her art had kept her sane. She longed to hear him, see him, touch him, but now as he stalked toward her, she wanted to ball up the unused part of her clay and throw it at him.

"I'm not giving you any names," she told him. "And for your information, I'm simply using the garden as my art studio. I can't get the right light in our suite, and the main gardens are too busy. All those people distract me. The harem isn't used, so I'm not in anyone's way."

He glared at her. "You are still living upstairs with me?"

"I was, but I have to tell you, I'm seriously rethinking that decision."

She wiped her hands on a towel and walked away.

Murat watched her go. On the helicopter flight back to the palace, he had thought about all the things he would say to Daphne when he saw her. They had been soft, conciliatory words designed to make her melt into his arms. When she wasn't in their suite, he had gone looking for her, only to be told she was in the harem.

He had thought that meant she had moved back, but he had been wrong. Now what?

He walked out of the garden only to find his father entering the harem. King Hassan shook his head.

"I just passed your wife. She seemed to be very annoyed about something."

"I am aware of that."

His father sighed. "Murat, you are my firstborn. I could not wish for a better heir. You have been born to power and you will lead our people with strength and greatness. But when it comes to Daphne, you seem to stumble at every turn. You must do better. I worked too hard to get her back here and into your life to have you destroy things now."

Chapter Fourteen

Daphne reached the suite she shared with Murat in record time, but once there she didn't know what to do with herself. She wanted to burn off some of the excess energy flowing through her. She wanted to throw something, but everything breakable was far too valuable and beautiful.

After pacing the length of the living room twice, she stopped by the sofa where one of the king's cats slept. Petting a cat or dog was supposed to be calming, she reminded herself. She stroked the animal and scratched under its chin, but still her blood bubbled within her.

"Of all the arrogant, terrible, hard-hearted men on the planet. To think I *missed* him." Talk about stupid.

"Never again," she vowed. "Never ever again will I think one pleasant or kind thought about—"

The door to the suite opened and Murat walked in. She stood and glared at him. "Don't even try to talk to me. I'm furious."

Murat closed the door and walked toward her. "I just spoke with my father."

"Unless you're going to tell me he's agreed to us getting a divorce, I'm not interested."

He unfastened his cloak and draped it across a chair. "He took me to task for annoying you."

"Really? Well, he's a very smart man."

Murat ignored her comment. "He was most disappointed we were not getting along better, especially in light of all his effort to bring us back together."

"I…" She blinked. "What?"

He motioned to the sofa. She sank down next to the cat she'd been petting and waited while Murat sat across from her.

"He told me that he has been waiting a long time for me to pick a bride. When I seemed reluctant, despite the various women in my life, he decided there must be some reason from my past. He made a study of my previous relationships and kept coming back to you and our broken engagement."

"That's right," she said. "Broken and not fixed."

"When he discovered you were unmarried, as well, he decided to bring us back together to see what happened."

"That's not possible." She refused to believe it. "I wasn't brought here for you. I came because of Brittany…"

She felt her mouth drop open and quickly pressed her lips together. Sensible Brittany who, out of the blue, suddenly decided to marry a man she'd never met and move half a world away.

"She was in on it," she breathed.

"Apparently. No one else in your family knew. My father found out that the two of you were close and contacted her. Together they hatched this plan."

"No." Daphne shook her head. "She would never do that to me. She's not that good a liar."

"Apparently she is." He motioned to the phone. "Feel free to check with her."

"I will." She picked up the receiver and punched in the number for her sister's house. When the maid answered, Daphne asked for Brittany.

"Hey, Aunt Daphne, how's it going? College starts in ten days and I'm *so* excited. Mom's still annoyed with you, but she's getting over it. She thinks I should start dating the governor's son. He's okay, I guess, but not really my type. What's up with you?"

Despite Murat's revelation and the possibility that Brittany had been a part of some plan, Daphne couldn't help smiling as she listened to her niece's monologue.

"I'm good," she said. "I've missed you."

"I've missed you, too. Think I could come over there for winter break? We could go shopping and ride a camel. It would be fun. Plus I'd love to finally meet Murat."

"I'll bet you would. Sure. You can come here. But first I need to ask you something. Did the King of Bahania get in touch with you a couple of months ago?"

Brittany sucked in a breath. "What?"

"Did he want you to pretend to be willing to marry Murat to lure me back to Bahania? Brittany, I want the truth. This is very important."

The teenager sighed. "Maybe. Okay, sort of. Yes. He called and we talked. He was really nice. Not at all like I imagined a king would be. He said that the reason you hadn't fallen in love with any other guy was that you still loved Murat but you wouldn't admit it to anyone. Not even to yourself. At first I told him he was crazy, but then I thought about it for a while and I decided he might be right."

"Oh, God."

"So I said I would marry Murat so that you'd get all worried and stuff. Which you did. I felt bad on the plane. I was acting so shallow, but it was important. And then you went to see Murat and I came home."

"Did anyone else know?"

"Are you kidding? Mom would never have agreed. I sort of felt bad about how excited she got over me marrying a prince and all. But, sheesh, how could she take it seriously? He's so old."

"Practically in his dotage."

"But it worked out great. Right?" Brittany sounded slightly unsure of herself. "I mean you married him and everything. You're happy, Aunt Daphne, aren't you? I'd never hurt you for anything. You know that, right?"

"Of course I know that. I love you, Brittany. You'll always be my favorite niece."

Brittany laughed. "I'm still your only niece, but I know what you mean. How did you find out?"

"The king told Murat."

"Was he furious?"

"He was unamused."

"But you're okay."

Daphne thought about the young woman she'd loved for eighteen years. Whatever Brittany had done, she'd acted out of love and concern.

"I'm completely fine. I love you."

"I love you, too. Let's talk soon."

"Absolutely. Bye."

Daphne hung up the phone and looked at her husband. "It's true. Brittany was a part of it from the beginning. She pretended to be interested in marrying you to get me on the plane."

He leaned back in the chair and closed his eyes. "And I played right into my father's hands by losing my temper and locking you in the harem."

Not to mention marrying her against her will, but she didn't say that.

"I'm pretty mad," Daphne admitted. "But I also feel kind of stupid. I can't believe those two were able to trick us like that."

Murat looked sheepish. "It does not say much about our powers of reasoning. I kept telling my father I was not interested in a teenage bride, but he insisted she be brought over for my inspection."

"I got all maternal and demanding," she said. "I was terrified Brittany was throwing away her life." She glanced at him. "Not that life as your wife is so terrible, but it wasn't right for her."

"Believe me, I did not want her, either."

Daphne felt as if she'd shown up for a big party only to find out the celebration had been the previous night. She felt both awkward and let down.

"So, um, now what?" she asked.

He straightened. "I should not have yelled at you before," he said, "when I found you in the garden. As I told you, I thought you had moved out of our rooms."

Had Crown Prince Murat of Bahania just apologized? "I know. I'm sorry. I didn't mean to give that impression. I just wanted to work with my clay."

"As you should. I enjoy the things you create." He smiled. "Even when they mock me."

Something tightened her heart. She felt happy and nervous at the same time. She cleared her throat.

"I didn't really want to leave. Before. Our trip into the desert. All this is so confusing and I reacted to that and what happened with Aisha. I don't always know what I'm feeling. Then we were fighting, and you said I could go and I said I wanted to and then I was here."

He stood and crossed to the sofa, where he sat next to her. He took both her hands in his.

"I missed you, Daphne. So much so that the tribal elders came to offer me advice."

She liked him touching her, but even more than that, she liked the sincerity in his gaze and that he'd missed her.

"What did they say?"

"One suggested I beat you. I sent him away."

"Thank you. I wouldn't respond well to a beating."

"I am many things, but I am not a bully."

"I know." He would never use his position of strength to take advantage of someone physically.

"One thought I should take a mistress."

Her stomach clenched. The sharp pain made her gasp. "What did you decide?"

He pulled one hand free and touched her cheek. "I want no other woman. Even if I chose not to be bound by my vows, I would still be true."

The pain eased.

"Finally, the oldest of the elders told me you were like a flower and that I should tend you in your garden."

She frowned. "What does that mean?"

"I was hoping you could tell me."

"I haven't a clue."

He stared deeply into her eyes as he slid his hand from her cheek to her mouth. He brushed his fingers against her lips. "Stay with me."

She didn't know if he meant that night or for always. Her heart told her to give in, that in time Murat would learn to yield, while her head reminded her that to stay based on an expected change in behavior was foolish.

Could she accept Murat as he was? Could she be with him knowing he would overrule her at will and never let her be an equal in their relationship? It wouldn't take much for her to fall in love with him again, but would he return those feelings? Could a man who thought of her as a mere woman ever give his heart?

"Stay," he repeated, then saved her from answering by kissing her.

She surrendered to his touch, still not sure how far to hold her heart out of reach.

"You can't be serious," Daphne said over dinner, several days later.

"It will never happen. The Americans are not ready to elect a woman president."

"But if they did…"

Murat shrugged. "You expect me to meet with a woman as an equal?"

"Of course. Didn't your father meet with Prime Minister Margaret Thatcher?"

"Perhaps. I am too young to recall." He cut into his meat. "You seem agitated."

"I'm trying to figure out what I should throw at you."

He raised his eyebrows. "Such threats of violence over a

simple discussion. You see why women are not good in politics. There is too much emotion."

She narrowed her gaze, just as she caught the twitch at the
corner of his mouth.

"You're toying with me," she said, both relieved and determined to get him back.

"Perhaps."

"I should have known. You *would* meet with a woman president."

"Of course, but I doubt it will happen during my lifetime.
Perhaps our son will have to deal with the situation."

She was about to say that any son of hers would respect
women and their rights, only to stop herself at the last minute.
Perhaps that wasn't the best conversational tack to take. Not
when the truce between them was so fragile.

It had been three days since Murat had returned from the
desert. Three days in which she'd slept in his bed, made love
with him and toyed with the idea of simply accepting her marriage as permanent.

Her feelings grew, and she knew that the point of no return
was at hand. If she fell in love with him, she wouldn't want to
go, regardless of their past.

"You grow quiet," he said, setting down his knife and fork.
"Are you troubled about some matter?"

"No."

Troubled didn't begin to describe her emotions.

"At the risk of starting another battle between us," he said.
"It has been nearly three weeks since the first time we made
love. You have not started your period."

"I know. I'm late."

She watched him carefully, but his expression didn't change.
She wondered if he was crowing on the inside.

"Do you think you are pregnant?"

She wasn't sure. "I don't feel any different, but I don't know if I
should. I could get a pregnancy test and take it if you would like."

"What would you prefer to do?"

"Wait a few more days. Sometimes stress upsets my cycle."

She'd certainly had her share of that in the past month or so.

She expected him to insist that she find out that very evening. Instead he nodded. "As you wish."

She couldn't help smiling. "Are you unwell?"

"No. Why do you ask?"

"You never give in on anything."

He sighed. "I am doing my best to nurture the flower in my garden. Do you feel nurtured?"

She held in a laugh. He *was* trying hard. "Nearly every minute of every day."

"Ah. Now you mock me again." He carefully put his napkin on the table and rose. "I think my flower needs a good pruning."

He had an evil gleam in his eye. Daphne stood and started to back away.

"Murat, no."

"You do not know what I have in mind."

"I can tell it's going to be bad. Now stop this. Think of your delicate flower. You have to be nice."

He made a noise low in his throat and started toward her. She shrieked and ducked away. In a matter of seconds he caught her.

In truth, she didn't mind being dragged against him. Even as he pressed his mouth to hers, he caught her up in his arms and carried her into their bedroom.

"What about dinner?" she asked when he set her on her feet next to their bed and reached for the zipper at the back of her dress.

"I am hungry for other things."

Murat worked through the messages left for him by his assistant. On the one hand he appreciated his new and warm relationship with Daphne. On the other, he found his workdays long and dull when compared with the nights he spent in her company. While his ministers spoke of the oil reserves and the state of the currency-exchange market, he thought of her body pressing against his and the way she cried out his name when he pleasured her.

Things were as they should be, he thought contentedly. She had made her peace with her situation. Now they would grow together as husband and wife. There would be many children and a long and happy life together.

His assistant knocked on the door.

"Come in," Murat called.

Fouad entered with several folders. "The king wishes to change your lunch meeting to this afternoon. It seems he is to dine with Princess Calah."

Murat smiled at the thought of his father having lunch with the charming toddler. "That is excellent. Have the kitchen send up a second meal to my suite. I will dine with my wife."

"Very good, sir." Fouad set the folders on the desk. "I have had a call from our media office. Princess Daphne turned down an interview request from an American women's magazine. They were surprised, as the publication is known for honest reporting. They were interested in making a connection with her, sir, not doing an exposé."

"Perhaps she is not aware that such interviews are welcome. I will mention it to her."

"Yes, sir."

Fouad completed his business and left. Forty minutes later Murat walked into his suite to find the table set for two.

"This is a surprise," Daphne said as she walked into the living room, then crossed the tile floor to kiss him. "A very pleasant one."

"My father and I were to have lunch, but he chose instead to dine with a very attractive young woman. So I took the opportunity to spend some time with you."

Daphne led him to the table. "Calah?" she asked.

"Of course."

"He loves that little girl."

Murat's gaze dropped to Daphne's flat stomach. Did *his* child grow there? So far she had not gotten her period, nor had she offered to take a pregnancy test. He had decided to let her make the decision. If she was with child, he would soon know.

They sat across from each other and spoke about their morning. As she served them each salad, he mentioned the interview with the American magazine.

"You are welcome to speak with them," he said. "I will not forbid it."

"My flower heart trembles at your generosity," she said in a teasing voice.

He pretended to scowl. "I can see I have been too lenient with you."

"Not to worry, Murat. If I had wanted to give the interview I would have. But I wasn't interested."

"Why not?"

Instead of answering, she mentioned that Billie and Cleo were planning a day trip to the City of Thieves and that she wanted to join them.

"Of course Billie wants to fly us there herself, and the king has said that would not be allowed. She's too far along in her pregnancy."

He watched her as she spoke, noting a slight shadow in her eyes.

"Daphne, why did you refuse the interview?"

"It's not important."

Which meant that it was. "I will not rest until you tell me."

She set down her fork. "If you must know, I didn't know what to say. This was for a big bridal issue they're doing in a few months. They're collecting romantic stories from different couples and they wanted to talk about how we met and fell in love. I didn't think it was a good idea to tell them the truth. That you locked me in the harem then married me against my will while I was unconscious. Rather than having to make up something, I declined the interview."

She continued speaking, changing the subject to the upcoming trip to the City of Thieves, but he could not hear her. The impact of what she had said—a bald statement of a truth he knew well—seemed to render him immobile.

For the first time he understood what she had been trying to tell him all along. That he had held her captive, like a common criminal. Of course the quarters were luxurious and she had not been mistreated in the least, but he had locked her away. Then, knowing she wanted nothing to do with him, he had taken advantage of a medical condition to force her into marriage.

Had he given her the choice, she would have refused him. She would have left. She was not with him because she wanted to be.

The truth sliced through him like a knife. He had always known that she complained about his treatment, but he had told himself it was all simply the meaningless chatter of a woman with too much time on her hands. He had not considered she had cause for her complaints. Had she been a stranger and appeared with her petition while he had been in the desert, he would have freed her from her marriage and locked away the man in question.

The phone rang in the suite. Daphne excused herself to answer it. Murat took advantage of her distraction to leave the table. He indicated he was going back to his office and she nodded. On his way out, he noticed a new clay sculpture on a table.

Two lovers, he thought. Bodies entwined, arms reaching. The sheer passion of the piece took his breath away. It gave him hope. But as he moved closer, he saw the lovers were faceless.

Did she not see him in the role, or did she wish for another man? He knew he pleased her in bed—her body told the tale all too well for him to think otherwise. But was that enough? Did claiming a woman's body mean anything when a man could not lay claim to her mind or her heart?

Chapter Fifteen

Daphne sat alone in the suite and stared out at the perfect view. The light wind had cleared the air enough for her to see all the way to Lucia-Serrat. Two cats dozed next to her on the sofa, their small, warm bodies providing a comforting presence. But it wasn't enough to heal the ache in her heart.

She wasn't pregnant. Proof had arrived an hour before.

She'd suspected, of course. That was why she'd resisted taking a pregnancy test. She hadn't wanted to *know*. She hadn't wanted to have to choose.

Funny how a month ago she would have been delighted with the chance to escape. She would have already had it out with Murat and been busy packing her bags. But now everything was different.

Instead of relief, she felt a bone-crushing disappointment, which told her a truth she'd tried to deny for a long time—she didn't want to go.

Murat wasn't perfect—he would never understand that what he'd done to her was wrong. He would never see her as a partner, but that didn't stop her from loving him. She wanted to be with him, regardless of his faults. She wanted their children to have his strength and stubbornness. She wanted to be a part of his world and his history. She loved Bahania nearly as much as she loved its heir and she didn't want to go.

Since he'd returned from the desert they hadn't discussed their future. No doubt he assumed her silence meant agreement, but that wasn't her way. She wanted to tell him what she'd decided, even if that meant listening to him say how he'd known what was best all along. She wanted to feel his arms around her as he pulled her close and kissed her. She wanted to take him to bed and get started on making their firstborn.

She stood and walked out of the suite with the intent of finding him in his office. But he wasn't there. His assistant said that he had gone for a walk.

Daphne went to the main garden and saw him sitting on one of the stone benches. His shoulders were slumped as he stared at the ground. An air of profound sadness surrounded him.

"Murat?"

He looked toward her and smiled. His expression brightened and the sadness disappeared as if it had never been. In response, her heart fluttered and she wondered how she had ever fooled herself into thinking she didn't love this man with every fiber of her being.

"I've been looking for you," she said as she walked closer.

"You have found me." He shifted to make room for her, then studied her as she sat next to him. He tucked her long hair behind her ear. "As always, your beauty astounds me."

"I'm not all that."

"Yes, you are."

He sounded so serious, she thought, wondering what was going on.

"Unlike many who shine only for a short time," he continued, "you will be beautiful for decades. Even as time steals the luster of your youth, you will gleam like a diamond in the desert."

"That's very poetic and very unlike you." She frowned. "What's going on?"

"I have been sitting here thinking about us. Our marriage."

Her pulse rate increased. "Me, too. I have to tell you something." She paused, not sure how to say it all—that she loved him, that she wanted to stay and make their marriage work. But the words that came out were, "I'm not pregnant."

He didn't react. His gaze never wavered, his hand on her remained still.

"You are sure?" he asked quietly.

"Very." She waited for him to say something else, and when he didn't, she leaned closer. "What's wrong? Shouldn't you tell me you're disappointed? That we'll be trying again soon?"

He drew in a breath. "I would have. Before. Now I know that this is for the best."

She jerked back as if he'd slapped her. "What?"

"It is for the best," he repeated. "A child would complicate things between us."

"How can they be complicated? We're married."

"In law, but not in spirit. I am sorry, Daphne. I did so much without thinking of you, and there is only one way to make that right. I will set you free."

She couldn't think, couldn't breathe. Confused and sure she must be hearing things, she pushed to her feet and walked across the path.

"I don't understand," she whispered.

He stood. "I was wrong to keep you here against your will, and I was wrong to marry you without your consent. I thought you did not mean your protests, but you did. We cannot have a marriage where you are little more than a prisoner in a gilded cage. I cannot take back what I have done in the past, but I can set it right." He nodded at the ring on her left hand. "You need not wear that reminder any longer. I will speak to the king and arrange for our divorce. You are free to leave whenever you like."

He turned and walked a few feet, then paused. With his back still to her he said, "Take what you like. Clothing, jewels. Any artwork. Consider it compensation for the wrong done to you. There will be a settlement, of course. I will be generous."

Then he was gone.

She made her way back to the bench where she collapsed. Tears poured down her cheeks. She wanted to scream out her pain to the world, but she couldn't seem to catch her breath.

This wasn't happening, she told herself. It couldn't be that Murat had finally figured it all out, only to let her go.

"I love you," she said to the quiet garden. "I want to stay and be with you."

But he'd never offered that. Was it because he didn't think she would be interested, or was it because he didn't care enough about her? Had she been little more than a convenient bride, one easily forgotten?

She wasn't sure how long she sat there grieving for what could have been. An hour. Perhaps two. Then she straightened and brushed away her tears. All along she'd allowed circumstances to choose her path for her. It was time for her to act. She would find Murat and talk to him. If after she explained her feelings for him and her thoughts about staying in the marriage he still wasn't interested, then she would leave. But she wasn't going to give up without a fight.

Once again she went to his office, but he was not there. Fouad, his assistant, shook his head when she asked what time he would return.

"Prince Murat has left the country," he said. "On an extended trip. He is not expected to return for several weeks."

She couldn't believe it. "He's gone? Where?"

"I have his itinerary here, if you would like it."

She took the offered sheet of paper and tried to read the various entries, but the print blurred.

"Wh-when was this planned?" she asked.

Fouad looked sympathetic. "He has been working on it for a few days now, Your Highness. I'm terribly sorry to be the one to tell you about it."

The paper fluttered from her fingers, but she didn't try to pick it up.

He couldn't have left. Not so quickly. She'd just spoken to him a few minutes ago.

"I don't understand. When did he pack? He can't have just left."

"I'm sorry," Fouad repeated.

Daphne forced herself to smile. "You've been very kind. Thank you."

She left and made her way to the elevator, then to the suite she was supposed to share with Murat. Only, he was gone and she was no longer his wife.

She stepped inside to find the king waiting for her.

"My child," he said as he walked toward her. "I have spoken with Murat."

"He's gone," she said, still unable to believe the words. "He left. For several weeks. I had a list of where he was going, but I..." She glanced around for the paper, only to remember she'd dropped it in his office. "He said I could leave. Did he tell you that?"

King Hassan nodded. "The divorce will be finalized as quickly as possible. You are free to return to your life in America."

"Right." Her life. The practice she no longer had, the family who would never forgive her, the friends who couldn't possibly understand what she'd been through.

"He is very sorry for what he has done," the king said. "He sees now that he should never have held you against your will."

She drew in a breath. "Perhaps you shouldn't have meddled, either."

"I agree." Murat's father suddenly looked much older than his years. "I thought the two of you were right for each other. That you only needed time together to realize how right you were. I was an old fool and I hurt you both. I am deeply sorry."

She swallowed, then shook her head. "You weren't wrong.

Not completely. I know that Murat isn't interested in me or our marriage, but I…" Her throat tightened. "I love him. I would have stayed." She touched her stomach. "When I told him I wasn't pregnant, he told me to leave."

The king held out his arms, and Daphne rushed into them. She gave in to the tears.

"I could call him back," King Hassan said. "He still has to listen to me."

Temptation called, but she pushed it away.

"Please don't," she said as she straightened and wiped her face. "There has been too much manipulation already. I wouldn't want Murat to be forced into our relationship. I would only want him there because it was what he desired."

"What will you do now?"

"Go back to the States."

The king bent down and kissed her cheek. "Stay as long as you would like. Despite what has happened, you are welcome here."

"I doubt Murat would be thrilled to come home and find me here."

"You never know."

She was pretty sure. He'd let her go without a fight—as he always had.

It took her most of the next day to gather the courage to pack her things and prepare to leave. She only took a few items of the new clothing she'd received since marrying Murat—the things she'd worn in the desert and the nightgowns she'd worn in their bed. She left all the jewelry, including the diamond band that had been her wedding ring.

"Can we do anything?" Billie asked as she hugged Daphne goodbye. "Are you sure you don't want me to fly you home?"

"I think I'll be more comfortable on the king's plane, but thanks."

Cleo moved in for her hug. "I'm sorry Murat is being such

a jerk about all this. Men are so stupid." Tears filled her blue eyes. "What I don't get is I would have sworn he was really crazy about you."

Daphne had thought so, too, but she'd been wrong. About so much.

"Keep in touch," Cleo said.

Daphne nodded even though she knew it would never happen. They might send a card back and forth, but in the end they had nothing in common.

"You've both been terrific," she said. "Please tell Emma goodbye for me. I'm sorry I never had the chance to see Sabrina again, or meet Zara."

The three women hugged again, then Daphne walked out of the suite with them and carefully closed the door behind her.

She rode alone to the airport. Cleo and Billie had offered to come with her, but she wanted to be by herself. She was done with tears and hopes and shattered dreams. She didn't want to feel anything, ever again.

But the burning ache inside of her felt as if it could go on forever. How was she supposed to get over loving Murat? Only now that she had lost him forever did she realize that he had been her heart's desire from the very beginning.

Murat stepped out of the limo and hurried inside the palace. Urgency quickened his steps as he raced up the stairs to the suite he shared with Daphne. He jerked open the door and stepped inside.

"Daphne?"

The large space echoed with silence.

"Daphne? Are you here?"

He walked into their bedroom. She wasn't there. Nor was the book she kept on her nightstand. He moved to the bathroom next and saw her makeup tray was empty. She was gone.

Defeat crashed through him. He had gone away to forget her only to realize that she was with him always. Even knowing that he owed her the choice, he wanted the chance to convince her to stay. But she hadn't even waited two days.

He walked down the hall and into his office. Two things caught his attention at once—a diamond band placed exactly in the center of his desk and the sculpture of the lovers he'd seen before.

He moved forward and picked up the ring. Funny how it still felt warm, as if she had only just removed it. He squeezed it in his hand, then dropped it into his jacket pocket. Then he turned his attention to the clay.

The intense embrace mesmerized him. He followed the graceful line of arms and torso up to the—

His heart froze. No longer were the lovers faceless. She had pressed in features. Just a hint of a nose, a slash for a mouth, but he recognized both of the faces.

Swearing, he picked up the phone and demanded a connection to the airport.

The luxurious jet raced down the runway. Daphne leaned back in the leather seat and closed her eyes. While she doubted she would sleep, she didn't want to watch as Bahania disappeared behind her.

Faster and faster until that moment just before the wheels lifted off. Then the jet suddenly slowed and sharply turned.

"Everything's fine, Your Highness," the pilot said over the intercom. "A signal light came on to tell us the cargo door isn't closed tight. We need to return to the hangar. It will only take a couple of minutes to fix."

She nodded her agreement, then realized the man couldn't see her. "Thanks for letting me know," she said as she pushed the intercom button on the console beside her seat.

She flipped through the stack of magazines left for her and picked out one on interior design. When she returned to Chicago, she either had to join another practice or go out on her own. That had been her plan when she'd left.

Maybe a change in cities would be nice. She'd never lived in the South or the West. She could go to Florida, or perhaps Texas.

She glanced out the window and saw several uniformed crewmen rushing around the plane. Then the main door opened. Daphne looked up in time to see a tall, handsome, imperious man striding on board.

Her heart took a nosedive for her toes. Rational thought left her as hope—foolish hope—bubbled in her stomach.

Murat took the seat opposite hers and leaned toward her.

"How could you leave without telling me you love me?" he demanded.

"I... I didn't think you'd want to know."

He scowled. "Of course I want to know that my wife loves me. It changes everything."

She couldn't think, couldn't breathe, couldn't do anything but drink in the sight of him.

"You told me to leave," she reminded him.

"I thought you were anxious to be gone." He glared at her. "This is your fault for not confessing your feelings." His expression softened. "I am happy to know my love is returned."

She couldn't have been more surprised if he'd told her he was a space alien.

"You l-love me?" she asked breathlessly.

"With all my heart and every part of my being." He took her hands in his. "Ah, my sweet wife. When I realized how badly I had treated you, I did not know how to atone for what I had done. Setting you free seemed only right, even though it was more painful than cutting off my arm. When you accepted my decision without saying anything, I thought you did not care about me."

"I was too shocked to speak," she admitted. "Oh, Murat, I do love you. I have for a long time. Maybe for the past ten years. I'm not sure."

He stood and pulled her to her feet. "You are a part of me.

You are the one I wish to be with for always. I want you to share in my country, my history. I love you, Daphne."

She wasn't sure if he pulled her close or she made the first move. Suddenly she was in his arms and he was kissing her as if his life depended on her embrace.

She clung to him, needing him more than she'd ever needed anyone ever.

He pulled back. "But if you must leave, I will let you," he said.

She couldn't believe it. "But you said—"

He smiled. "You may go, but I am coming with you. I will be next to you always."

She laughed. "I don't want to go anywhere. I love Bahania and I love you."

Right there, in the walkway of a jet, Crown Prince Murat of Bahania dropped to one knee.

"Then stay with me. Be my wife, the mother of my children. Love me, grow old with me and allow me to spend the rest of my life proving how important you are to me."

"Yes," she whispered. "For always."

He stood and reached into his jacket pocket. When he withdrew a ring, she started to shake. Then she realized he wasn't holding the diamond band he'd given her after their marriage. Instead he held a familiar and treasured engagement ring—the one she'd left behind ten years ago.

"My ring," she said breathlessly. "You kept it all this time."

"Yes. In a safe place. I was never sure why, until now. I know I was keeping it for you to wear again." He slid on the ring, then kissed her.

Lost in the passion of his body pressing against hers, she barely heard the crackle of the intercom.

"Prince Murat?" It was the pilot. "Sir, are we still going to America?"

"No," Murat said into the intercom. He sank onto a chair and pulled Daphne onto his lap. "We are not."

"Are we going anywhere?"

Murat leaned close and whispered in her ear. "Do you have any pressing engagements for the rest of the afternoon?"

She shifted so she could straddle him. "What did you have in mind?"

He chuckled, then pressed the intercom button again. "Once around the country."

"Yes, sir."

"Which gives us how long?" she asked.

He reached for the buttons on her blouse.

"A lifetime, my love. A lifetime."

* * * * *

The Christmas Bride

Dear Reader,

I confess, I love Christmas romances. I haunt the bookstores every November and December, buying every one I can find. There's nothing more romantic than falling in love during the holidays.

I also have a soft spot in my heart for the sheik books I write. To me they are pure escapist fun into a world of sexy, dangerous men just ready to be tamed by loving the right woman. *The Sheik and the Christmas Bride* is no exception, and this time there is the added thrill of the holiday season.

Kayleen grew up in an orphanage, so she desperately wants to belong. Prince As'ad grew up with every privilege, but still has an empty place in his heart. Three little girls, unexpected passion and even a Christmas miracle create what I hope is a story that brings the holiday season alive for you.

Happy reading,

Susan Mallery

Prologue

"This is an impossible situation," King Mukhtar of El Deharia announced as he paced the width of his private chambers.

Princess Lina watched her brother, thinking it would be impossible for him to pace the *length* of his chambers—the room was so big, she would probably lose sight of him. Ah, the trials of being king.

Mukhtar spun back unexpectedly, then stalked toward her. "You smile. Do you find this amusing? I have three sons of marriageable age. *Three!* And has even one of them shown interest in choosing a bride and producing heirs? No. They are too busy with their work. How did I produce such industrious sons? Why aren't they out chasing women and getting girls pregnant? At least then we could force a marriage."

Lina laughed. "You're complaining that your sons are too hardworking and that they're not playboys? What else is wrong, my brother? Too much money in the treasury? Do the people love you too much? Is the royal crown too heavy?"

"You mock me," he complained.

"As your sister, it is not just my privilege, it's my duty. Someone needs to mock you."

He glared at her, but she was unimpressed. They had grown

up together. It was hard to find awe in the man when one had seen the boy with chicken pox.

"This is serious," he told her sternly. "What am I to do? I must have heirs. I should have dozens of grandchildren by now and I have not a single one. Qadir spends his time representing our country to the world. As'ad deals with domestic issues so our people have a thriving economy. Kateb lives his life in the desert, celebrating the old ways." Mukhtar grimaced. "The old ways? What is he thinking?"

"Kateb has always been a bit of a black sheep," Lina reminded the king.

Her brother glared at her. "No son of mine is a sheep. He is powerful and cunning like a lion of the desert or a jackal."

"So he is the black jackal of the family."

"Woman, you will not act this way," Mukhtar roared in a fair imitation of a lion.

Lina remained unimpressed. "Do you see me cowering, brother? Have you ever seen me cowering?"

"No, and you are poorer for it."

She covered her mouth as she pretended to yawn.

His gaze narrowed. "You are intent only on your own amusement? You have no advice for me?"

"I do have advice, but I don't know if you'll like it."

He folded his arms across his chest. "I'm listening."

Not according to his body language, Lina thought humorously. But she was used to her brother being imperious. Having him ask for her advice was a big step for him. She should go with it.

"I have been in communication with King Hassan of Bahania," she said.

"Why?"

She sighed. "This will go much faster if you don't interrupt me every thirty seconds."

Mukhtar raised his eyebrows but didn't speak.

She recognized the slightly stubborn expression. He thought

he was being protective and concerned, making sure she was kept safe from the evilness of the world. Right. Because the very handsome king of Bahania was so likely to swoop down and ravish her forty-three-year-old self.

Not that she would say no to a little ravishing, she thought wistfully. Her marriage had ended years before when her beloved husband had died unexpectedly. She'd always meant to remarry and have a family, but somehow that had never happened. She'd been busy being an aunt to Mukhtar's six boys. There had been much to do in the palace. Somehow she'd never found the time…or a man who interested her.

Until Hassan. The widower king was older, but vital and charming. Not to mention, he was the first man who had caught her attention in years. But was he intrigued by her? She just couldn't tell.

"Lina," her brother said impatiently, "how do you know Hassan?"

"What? Oh. He and I spent time together a couple of years ago at a symposium on education." She'd met the king formally at state events dozens of times, but that had been the first occasion she'd had to speak with him for more than five minutes. "He also has sons and he has been very successful in getting them all married."

That got her brother's interest. "What did he do?"

"He meddled."

Mukhtar stared at her. "You're saying…"

"He got involved in their personal lives. He created circumstances that brought his sons together with women he had picked. Sometimes he set up roadblocks, sometimes he facilitated the relationship. It all went well."

Mukhtar lowered his arms to his sides. "I am the king of El Deharia."

"I know that."

"It would be inappropriate for me to behave in such a manner."

Lina held in a smile—she already knew what was coming. "Of course it would."

"However, you do not have my restrictions of rank and power."

"Isn't that amazing."

"You could get involved. You know my sons very well." His gaze narrowed. "You've been thinking about this for some time, haven't you?"

"I've made a few notes about a couple of women I think would be really interesting for my nephews to get to know."

He smiled slowly. "Tell me everything."

Chapter One

Prince As'ad of El Deharia expected his world to run smoothly. He hired his staff with that expectation, and for the most part, they complied. He enjoyed his work at the palace and his responsibilities. The country was growing, expanding, and he oversaw the development of the infrastructure. It was a compelling vocation that took serious thought and dedication.

Some of his friends from university thought he should use his position as a prince and a sheik to enjoy life, but As'ad did not agree. He didn't have time for frivolity. If he had one weakness, it was his affection for his aunt Lina. Which explained why he agreed to see her when she burst into his offices without an appointment. A decision, he would think many weeks later, that caused him nothing but trouble.

"As'ad," Lina said as she hurried into his office, "you must come at once."

As'ad saved his work on the computer before asking, "What is wrong?"

"Everything." His normally calm aunt was flushed and trembling. "There is trouble at the orphan school. A chieftain is in from the desert. He's demanding he be allowed to take three sisters. People are fighting, the girls don't want to go with him, the teachers are getting involved and one of the nuns is threatening to jump from the roof if you don't come and help."

As'ad rose. "Why me?"

"You're a wise and thoughtful leader," Lina said, not quite meeting his gaze. "Your reputation for fairness makes you the obvious choice."

Or his aunt was playing him, As'ad thought, staring at the woman who had been like a mother to him for most of his life. Lina enjoyed getting her way and she wasn't above using drama to make that happen. Was she this time? Although he couldn't imagine why she would need his help at a school.

She bit her lower lip. "There really *is* trouble. Please come."

Theatrics he could ignore, but a genuine request? Not possible. He walked around his desk and took her arm to lead her out of his office. "We will take my car."

Fifteen minutes later As'ad wished he'd been out of the country when his aunt had gone looking for assistance. The school was in an uproar.

Fifteen or so students huddled in groups, crying loudly. Several teachers tried to comfort them, but they, too, were in tears. An elderly chieftain and his men stood by the window, talking heatedly, while a petite woman with hair the color of fire stood in front of three sobbing girls.

As'ad glanced at his aunt. "No one seems to be on the roof."

"I'm sure things have calmed down," she told him. "Regardless of that detail, you can clearly see there *is* a problem."

He returned his gaze to the woman protecting the girls. "She doesn't look like a nun," he murmured, taking in the long, red hair and the stubborn expression on her face.

"Kayleen is a teacher here," his aunt said, "which is very close to being a nun."

"So you lied to me."

Lina brushed away the accusation with a flick of her hand. "I may have exaggerated slightly."

"You are fortunate we have let go of the old ways," he told his aunt. "The ones that defined a woman's conduct."

His aunt smiled. "You love me too much to ever let harm befall me, As'ad."

Which was true, he thought as he walked into the room.

He ignored the women and children and moved over to the tall old man.

"Tahir," he said, nodding his head in a gesture of respect. "You do not often leave the desert for the city. It is an honor to see you here now. Is your stay a long one?"

Tahir was obviously furious, but he knew his place and bowed. "Prince As'ad. At last a voice of reason. I had hoped to make my journey to the city as brief as possible, but this, this *woman*—" he pointed at the redhead still guarding the children "—seeks to interfere. I am here because of duty. I am here to show the hospitality of the desert. Yet she understands nothing and defies me at every turn."

Tahir's voice shook with outrage and fury. He was not used to being denied and certainly not by a mere woman. As'ad held in a sigh. He already knew nothing about this was going to be easy.

"I will defy you with my dying breath, if I have to," the teacher in question said, from her corner of the room. "What you want to do is inhuman. It's cruel and I won't allow it." She turned to As'ad and glared at him. "There's nothing you can say or do to make me."

The three girls huddled close to her. They were obviously sisters, with blond hair and similar features. Pretty girls, As'ad thought absently. They would grow into beauties and be much trouble for their father.

Or would have been, he amended, remembering this was an orphanage and that meant the girls had no parents.

"And you are..." he asked, his voice deliberately imperious. His first job was to establish authority and gain control.

"Kayleen James. I'm a teacher here."

She opened her mouth to continue speaking, but As'ad shook his head.

"I will ask the questions," he told her. "You will answer."

"But—"

He shook his head again. "Ms. James, I am Prince As'ad. Is that name familiar to you?"

The young woman glanced from him to his aunt and back. "Yes," she said quietly. "You're in charge of the country or something."

"Exactly. You are here on a work visa?"

She nodded.

"That work visa comes from my office. I suggest you avoid doing anything to make me rethink your place in my country."

She had dozens of freckles on her nose and cheeks. They became more visible as she paled. "You're threatening me," she breathed. "So what? You'll deport me if I don't let that horrible man have his way with these children? Do you know what he is going to do with them?"

Her eyes were large. More green than blue, he thought until fresh tears filled them. Then the blue seemed more predominant.

As'ad could list a thousand ways he would rather be spending his day. He turned to Tahir.

"My friend," he began, "what brings you to this place?"

Tahir pointed at the girls. "They do. Their father was from my village. He left to go to school and never returned, but he was still one of us. Only recently have we learned of his death. With their mother gone, they have no one. I came to take them back to the village."

Kayleen took a step toward the older man. "Where you plan to separate them and have them grow up to be servants."

Tahir shrugged. "They are girls. Of little value. Yet several families in the village have agreed to take in one of them. We honor the memory of their father." He looked at As'ad. "They will be treated well. They will carry my honor with them."

Kayleen raised her chin. "Never!" she announced. "You will

never take them. It's not right. The girls only have each other. They deserve to be together. They deserve a chance to have a real life."

As'ad thought longingly of his quiet, organized office and the simple problems of bridge design or economic development that awaited him.

"Lina, stay with the girls," he told his aunt. He pointed at Kayleen. "You—come with me."

Kayleen wasn't sure she could go anywhere. Her whole body shook and she couldn't seem to catch her breath. Not that it mattered. She would gladly give her life to protect her girls.

She opened her mouth to tell Prince As'ad that she wasn't interested in a private conversation, when Princess Lina walked toward her and smiled reassuringly.

"Go with As'ad," her friend told her. "I'll stay with the girls. Nothing will happen to them while you're gone." Lina touched her arm. "As'ad is a fair man. He will listen." She smiled faintly. "Speak freely, Kayleen. You are always at your best when you are most passionate."

What?

Before Kayleen could figure out what Lina meant, As'ad was moving and she found herself hurrying after him. They went across the hall, into an empty classroom. He closed the door behind them, folded his arms across his chest and stared at her intently.

"Start at the beginning," he told her. "What happened here today?"

She blinked. Until this moment, she hadn't really seen As'ad. But standing in front of him meant she had to tip her head back to meet his gaze. He was tall and broad-shouldered, a big, dark-haired man who made her nervous. Kayleen had had little to do with men and she preferred it that way.

"I was teaching," she said slowly, finding it oddly difficult to look into As'ad's nearly black eyes and equally hard to look away. "Pepper—she's the youngest—came running into my classroom to say there was a bad man who wanted to take her away. I found the chieftain holding Dana and Nadine in the hallway." Indignation gave her strength. "He was really holding them. One by each arm. When he saw Pepper, he handed Dana off to one of his henchmen and grabbed her. She's barely eight years old. The girls were crying and struggling. Then he started dragging them away. He said something about taking them to his village."

The rest of it was a blur. Kayleen drew in a breath. "I started yelling, too. Then I sort of got between the chieftain and the stairway. I might have attacked him." Shame filled her. To act in such a way went against everything she believed. How many times had she been told she must accept life as it was and attempt change through prayer and conversation and demonstrating a better way herself?

Kayleen desperately wanted to believe that, but sometimes a quick kick in the shin worked, too.

One corner of As'ad's mouth twitched. "You hit Tahir?"

"I kicked him."

"What happened then?"

"His men came after me and grabbed me. Which I didn't like, but it was okay because the girls were released. They were screaming and I was screaming and the other teachers came into the hall. It was a mess."

She squared her shoulders, knowing she had to make As'ad understand why that man couldn't take the girls away.

"You can't let him do this," she said. "It's wrong on every level. They've lost both their parents. They need each other. They need me."

"You're just their teacher."

"In name, but we're close. I live here, too. I read to them every night, I talk to them." They were like her family, which made them matter more than anything. "They're so young. Dana, the oldest, is only eleven. She's bright and funny and she wants to be a doctor. Nadine is nine. She's a gifted dancer.

She's athletic and caring. Little Pepper can barely remember her mother. She needs her sisters around her. They *need* to be together."

"They would be in the same village," As'ad said.

"But not the same house." She *had* to make him understand. "Tahir talks about how people in the village are *willing* to take in the girls. As if they would be a hardship. Isn't it better to leave them here where they have friends and are loved? Where they can grow up with a connection to each other and their past? Do you know what he would do to them?"

"Nothing," As'ad said flatly, in a voice that warned her not to insult his people. "He has given them his honor. They would be protected. Anyone who attacked them would pay with his life."

Okay, that made her feel better, but it wasn't enough. "What about the fact that they won't be educated? They won't have a chance. Their mother was American."

"Their father was born here, in El Deharia. He, too, was an orphan and Tahir's village raised him. They honor his memory by taking in his three daughters."

"To be servants."

As'ad hesitated. "It is their likely fate."

"Then he can't have them."

"The decision is not yours to make."

"Then you make it," she told him, wanting to give him a quick kick to the shins, as well. She loved El Deharia. The beautiful country took her breath away every time she went into the desert. She loved the people, the kindness, the impossible blue of the skies. But there was still an expectation that men knew better. "Do you have children, Prince As'ad?"

"No."

"Sisters?"

"Five brothers."

"If you had a sister, would you want her to be taken away and made a servant? Would you have wanted one of your brothers ripped from his family?"

"These are not your siblings," he told her.

"I know. They're more like my children. They've only been here a few months. Their mother died a year ago and their father brought them back here. When he was killed, they entered the orphanage. I'm the one who sat with them night after night as they sobbed out their pain. I'm the one who held them through the nightmares, who coaxed them to eat, who promised things would get better."

She drew herself up to her full five feet three inches and squared her shoulders. "You talk of Tahir's honor. Well, I gave my word that they would have a good life. If you allow that man to take them away, my word means nothing. I mean nothing. Are you so heartless that you would shatter the hopes and dreams of three little girls who have already lost both their parents?"

As'ad could feel a headache coming on.

Kayleen James stated her case well. Under other circumstances, he would have allowed her to keep the children at the school and be done with it. But this was not a simple case.

"Tahir is a powerful chieftain," he said. "To offend him over such a small matter is foolish."

"Small matter? Because they're girls? Is that it? If these were boys, the matter would be large?"

"The gender of the children is immaterial. The point is Tahir has made a generous gesture from what he considers a position of honor. To have that thrown in his face could have political consequences."

"We're talking about children's *lives*. What is politics when compared with that?"

The door to the classroom opened and Lina stepped inside. Kayleen gasped. "He has the girls?"

"Of course not. They've gone back to their rooms while Tahir and his men take tea with the director." Lina looked at As'ad. "What have you decided?"

"That I should not allow you into my office when you do not have an appointment."

Lina smiled. "You could never refuse me, As'ad. Just as I could never send you away."

He held in a groan. So his aunt had taken sides. Why was he not surprised? She had always been soft-hearted and loving—something he had appreciated after the death of his own mother. But now, he found the trait inconvenient.

"Tahir is powerful. To offend him over this makes no sense," he said.

Lina surprised him by saying, "I agree."

Kayleen shrieked. "Princess Lina, no! You know these girls. They deserve more."

Lina touched her arm. "They shall have more. As'ad is right. Tahir should not leave feeling as if his generous offer has been snubbed. Kayleen, you may not agree with what he's trying to do, but believe me, his motives are pure."

Kayleen looked anything but convinced, yet she nodded slowly.

Lina turned to As'ad. "The only way Tahir can save face in this is to have the children taken by someone more powerful who is willing to raise them and honor the memory of their father."

"Agreed," As'ad said absently. "But who would—"

"You."

He stared at his aunt. "You would have me take three orphan girls as my own?" It was unbelievable. It was impossible. It was just like Lina.

"As'ad, the palace has hundreds of rooms. What would it matter if three girls occupied a suite? You wouldn't have to deal with them. They would have your protection as they grew. If nothing else, the king might be momentarily distracted by the presence of three almost-grandchildren."

The idea had merit, As'ad thought. His father's attempts to marry off his sons had become unbearable. There were constant parades of eligible young women. An excuse to avoid the events was worth much.

As'ad knew it was his duty to marry and produce heirs, yet he had always resisted any emotional involvement. Perhaps because he knew emotion made a man weak. His father had told him as much the night the queen had died. When As'ad had asked why the king did not cry, his father explained that to give in to feelings was to be less of a man.

As'ad had tried to learn the lesson as well as he could. As a marriage of convenience had never appealed to him, he was left with the annoyance of dealing with an angry monarch who wanted heirs.

"But who would care for the girls?" he asked. "The children can't raise themselves."

"Hire a nanny. Hire Kayleen." Lina shrugged. "She already has a relationship with the girls. They care for her and she cares for them."

"Wait a minute," Kayleen said. "I have a job. I'm a teacher here."

Lina looked at her. "Did you or did you not give the girls your word that their life would get better? What are you willing to do to keep your word? You would still be a teacher, but on a smaller scale. With three students. Perhaps there would even be time for you to teach a few classes here."

The last thing As'ad wanted was to adopt three children he knew nothing about. While he'd always planned on a family, the idea was vague, in the future, and it included sons. Still, it was a solution. Tahir would not stand in the way of a prince taking the children. And as Lina had pointed out, it would buy time with his father. He could not be expected to find a bride while adjusting to a new family.

He looked at Kayleen. "You would have to be solely responsible for the girls. You would be given all the resources you require, but I have no interest in their day-to-day lives."

"I haven't even agreed to this," she told him.

"Yet you were the one willing to do anything to keep the sisters together."

"It would be a wonderful arrangement," Lina told Kayleen. "Just think. The girls would be raised in a palace. There would be so many opportunities for them. Dana could go to the best university. Nadine would have access to wonderful dance teachers. And little Pepper wouldn't have to cry herself to sleep every night."

Kayleen bit her lower lip. "It sounds good." She turned to As'ad. "You'd have to give your word that they would never be turned out or made into servants or married off for political gain."

"You insult me with your mistrust." The audacity of her statements was right in keeping with what he'd seen of her personality, but it was important to establish control before things began.

"I don't know you," she said.

"I am Prince As'ad of El Deharia. That is all you need to know."

Lina smiled at her. "As'ad is a good man, Kayleen."

As'ad resented that his aunt felt the need to speak for his character. Women, he thought with mild annoyance. They were nothing but trouble.

Kayleen looked him in the eye. "You have to give your word that you'll be a good father, caring more for their welfare than your own. You'll love them and listen to them and not marry them off to anyone *they* don't love."

What was it with women and love? he wondered. They worried too much about a fleeting emotion that had no value.

"I will be a good father," he said. "I will care for them and see that they are raised with all the privileges that go with being the daughter of a prince."

Kayleen frowned. "That wasn't what I asked."

"It is what I offer."

Kayleen hesitated. "You have to promise not to marry them off to someone they don't care about."

Such foolish worries, he thought, then nodded. "They may pick their own husbands."

"And go to college and not be servants."

"I have said they will be as my daughters, Ms. James. You test my patience."

She stared at him. "I'm not afraid of you." She considered for a second.

"I can see that. You will be responsible for them. Do as you see fit with them." He glanced at his aunt. "Are we finished here?"

She smiled, her eyes twinkling in a way that made him wonder what else she had planned for him. "I'm not sure, As'ad," she told him. "In a way I think we're just beginning."

Chapter Two

Kayleen wouldn't have thought it was possible for her life to change so quickly. That morning she'd awakened in her narrow bed in a small room at the orphanage. If she stood in the right place and leaned all the way over, she could see a bit of garden out of her tiny window, but mostly the view was a stone wall. Now she followed Princess Lina into an impossibly large suite in a palace that overlooked the Arabian Sea.

"This can't be right," Kayleen murmured as she turned in a slow circle, taking in the three sofas, the carved dining table, the ornate decorations, the wide French doors leading out to a balcony and the view of the water beyond. "These rooms are too nice."

Lina smiled. "It's a palace, my dear. Did you think we had ugly rooms?"

"Obviously not." Kayleen glanced at the three girls huddled together. "But this stuff is *really* nice. Kids can be hard on furniture."

"I assure you, these pieces have seen far more than you can imagine. All will be well. Come this way. I have a delightful surprise."

Kayleen doubted any surprise could beat a return address

sticker that said El Deharian Royal Palace but she was willing to be wrong. She gently pushed the girls in front of her as they moved down the hallway.

Lina paused in front of a massive door, then pushed it open. "I didn't have much time to get things in order, so it's not complete just yet. But it's a start."

The "start" was a room the size of a small airport, with soaring ceilings and big windows that let in the light. Three double beds didn't begin to fill the space. There were armoires and desks and comforters in pretty pastels. Big, fluffy stuffed animals sat on each bed, along with a robe, nightgowns and slippers. Each of the girls' school backpacks sat at the foot of her bed.

"Laptop computers are on order for the girls," Lina said. "There's a big TV back in the living room, behind the cabinet doors. There are a few DVDs for the girls, but we'll get more. In time, we can move you to a different suite, one with a bedroom for each of the girls, but for now I thought they'd be more comfortable together."

Kayleen couldn't believe it. The room was perfect. Bright and cheerful, filled with color. There was an air of welcome, as if the space had been hoping for three girls to fill it.

Dana turned around and stared at her. "Really? This is for us?"

Kayleen laughed. "You'd better take it, because if you don't want it, I'll move in."

It was the permission they needed. The three girls went running around the room, examining everything. Every few seconds one of them yelled, "Look at this," because there was so much to see.

A ballerina lamp for Nadine, a throw covered with teddy bears for Pepper. Dana's bed had a bookcase next to it. Kayleen turned to Princess Lina.

"You're amazing."

"I have resources and I'm not afraid to use them," her friend told her. "This was fun. I don't get to act imperious very often and send servants scuttling to do my bidding. Besides, we all enjoyed pulling this together in a couple of hours. Come on. Let's go see where you'll sleep."

Kayleen followed Lina past a large bathroom with a tub big enough to swim in, to a short hallway that ended in a beautiful room done in shades of green and pale yellow.

The furniture was delicately carved and feminine. The bed-covering was a botanical print that suited her much better than ruffles and frills. The attached bathroom was more luxurious than any she'd ever seen.

"It's silk," she whispered, fingering the luxurious drapes. "What if I spill something?"

"Then the cleaners will be called," Lina told her. "Relax. You'll adjust. This is your home now that you're a part of As'ad's life."

Something else that just plain wasn't right, Kayleen thought. How could she be a part of a sheik's life? Make that a sheik *prince?*

"Not a happy part," she murmured. "He didn't want to help."

"But he did and isn't that what matters?"

Kayleen nodded, but her head was spinning. There was too much to think about. Too much had happened too quickly.

"Our bags! Kayleen, hurry! Our bags are here."

Kayleen and Lina returned to the main room to watch as their suitcases were unloaded. The pile had looked so huge at the orphanage, but here it seemed small and shabby.

Lina lightly touched her arm. "Get settled. I'll have dinner sent up. Things will look better in the morning."

"They look fine now," Kayleen told her, almost meaning it. "We live in a palace. What's not to like?"

Lina laughed. "Good attitude." She held out her arms and the sisters rushed to her for a hug. "I will see all of you in the morning. Welcome to the palace."

With that, she was gone. As the door to their suite closed

behind her, Kayleen felt a whisper of unease. A palace? How could that be home?

She glanced at the girls and saw fear and apprehension in their eyes. It was one thing for her to worry, but they shouldn't have to. They'd already been through so much.

She glanced at her watch, then looked back at the girls. "I think we need to give the new TV a test drive. Here's the deal. Whoever gets unpacked first, and that means putting things neatly in the armoire, not just throwing them, gets to pick the movie. Start in five, four, three, two, one. Go!"

All three sisters shrieked and raced for their bedroom.

"I can go fastest," Pepper yelled as she crouched down in front of her suitcase and opened it.

"No way," Dana told her. "I'm going to win because you'll pick a stupid cartoon. I'm too old for that."

Kayleen smiled at the familiar argument, then her smile faded. Dana was all of eleven and in such a hurry to grow up. Kayleen suspected the reason had a whole lot to do with being able to take care of her sisters.

"That's going to change," she whispered, then returned to her room to unpack her own suitcases. Lina had promised that Prince As'ad could be trusted. He'd given his word that he would raise the girls as his own. That meant they were safe. But, after all they'd been through, how long would it take them to feel that way?

The evening passed quickly. Dinner was sent up on an elegant rolling table and contained plenty of comfort foods for lost, lonely children. Kayleen piled everyone on the largest sofa and they watched *The Princess Diaries,* then compared the differences in the movie castle and the real-live palace they'd moved into. By nine all three of them were asleep and Kayleen found herself alone as she wandered the length of the beautiful suite.

She paused by the French doors leading onto the balcony, then stepped out into the warm night.

Lights from the shoreline allowed her to see the movement

of the waves as they rolled onto the beach. The inky darkness of the water stretched to the horizon. The air was warm and salty, the night unexpectedly still.

She leaned against the railing and stared into the sky. What was she doing here? This wasn't her world. She could never in a million years have imagined—

The sound of a door opening caused her to turn. She saw a shadow move and take the shape of a man. Fear gripped her then, as quickly as it had come, faded. But she *should* be afraid, she told herself. He could be anyone.

But he wasn't, she realized as he stepped into the light. He was Prince As'ad.

He was as tall and broad as she remembered. Handsome, in a distant sort of way. The kind of man who intimidated without trying. She wondered if she should slip back into her own rooms before he saw her. Perhaps she wasn't supposed to be out here. Then his dark gaze found her.

"Good evening," he said. "You and the girls are settled?"

She nodded. "Thank you. The rooms are great. Your aunt thought of everything to make us feel at home." She looked up at the imposing structure of the palace. "Sort of."

He moved toward her. "It's just a really big house, Kayleen. Do not let the size or history intimidate you."

"As long as none of the statuary comes alive in the night and tries to chase us out."

"I assure you, our statuary is most well-behaved."

She smiled. "Thanks for the reassurance. No offense, but I doubt I'll sleep well for the next couple of nights."

"I hope that changes quickly." He shrugged out of his suit jacket. "If you find my aunt forgot something, let someone on the staff know."

"Sure." Because every palace had a staff. And a king. And princes. "What do we call you? The girls and I. Your Highness? Prince As'ad?"

"You may all use my first name."

"Really? And they won't chop off my head for that?"

One corner of his mouth twitched. "Not for many years now." He loosened his tie, then pulled it free.

Kayleen watched for a second, then looked away. He wasn't undressing, she told herself. The man had the right to get comfortable after a long day of...of...being a prince. This was his balcony. She was the one who didn't belong.

"You are uneasy," he said.

She blinked. "How did you figure that out?"

"You are not difficult to read."

Great. She had the sudden thought she wanted to be mysterious and interesting. Mostly interesting. Like *that* was going to happen.

"A lot has changed in a short period of time," she told him. "This morning I woke up in my usual bed in the orphanage. Tonight I'm here."

"And before you lived in El Deharia? Where did you sleep?"

She smiled. "In the Midwest. It's very different. No ocean. No sand. It's a lot colder. It's already November. Back home the leaves would be gone and we'd be bracing for the first snowfall. Here, it's lovely."

"One of the great pleasures of the most perfect place on earth."

"You think El Deharia is perfect?"

"Don't you think the same of your birthplace?"

Not really, she thought. But they came from very different circumstances. "I guess," she murmured, then felt awkward. "I was a teacher there, too," she added, to change the subject. "I've always loved children."

"Which makes your employment more enjoyable," he said. "I would imagine a teacher who dislikes children would have a difficult time."

Was he being funny? She thought he might be, but wasn't sure. Did princes have a sense of humor? She'd assumed being royal meant being serious all the time.

"Yes, that was a joke," he said, proving she was as readable as he said. "You are allowed to laugh in my presence. Although I would suggest you are sure I'm being humorous. To laugh at the wrong time is a grave mistake most people only make once."

"And we're back to the head-chopping. You're not like anyone I've ever met."

"Not many princes in the Midwest?"

"No. Not even rock stars, which in my country are practically the same thing."

"I have never been fond of leather pants on a man."

That did make her laugh. "You could be considered fashion forward."

"Or foolish."

"You wouldn't like that," she said without thinking, then covered her mouth. Oops.

Something flickered in his gaze. He folded his arms. "Perhaps a safer topic would be the three sisters you insisted I adopt."

"What about them?" Had he changed his mind? She would hold him to his promise, no matter how nervous he made her.

"They will have to change schools. The orphanage is too far away. The American School is closer."

"Oh. You're right." She hadn't thought that part through. "I'll get them registered in the morning." She hesitated. "What do I tell the administrator?"

"The truth. They are my adopted daughters and are to be treated as such."

"Bowing and scraping?"

He studied her. "You're an interesting combination of rabbit and desert cat. Fearful and fearless."

She liked the sound of that. "I'm working to be all fearless. I still have a ways to go."

He reached out and before she realized what he intended, he touched a strand of her hair. "There is fire in your blood."

"Because I'm a redhead? I think that's just an old wives'

tale." She'd always wanted to be a cool blonde, or a sexy brunette. Well, maybe not sexy. That wasn't her style.

"I know many old wives who are wise," he murmured, then released her. "You will be responsible for the girls when they are not in school."

She nodded, wishing they were still talking about her being brave and that he was still touching her hair. Which was strange. Prince As'ad was nothing more to her than her employer. A very handsome, *powerful* employer who could trace his lineage back a few thousand years. She didn't even know who her father was.

"What are you thinking?" he asked.

She told him the truth.

"And your mother?"

Kayleen regretted the change in topic. "I, um, don't really remember her. She left me with my grandmother when I was a baby. She took care of me for a few years, then left me at an orphanage." She gave a little shrug as if the rejection hadn't mattered. "She was older and I was a handful."

In the darkness it was difficult to read As'ad's expression. She reminded herself there was no reason to be ashamed of her past—she hadn't been able to control it. Yet she felt as if she were being judged and found wanting.

"Is that the reason you defended the girls so fiercely?" he asked. "Your own past?"

"Maybe."

He nodded slowly. "They live here now. As do you. You are all to consider the palace your home."

If only. "Easier said than done," she murmured.

"It will be an adjustment. Although it would be best if they did not roller-skate down the hallways."

"I'll make sure of that."

"Good. You will want to learn about the palace. There is much interesting history here. Perhaps you and the girls should take one of the daily tours."

She stared at him. "Tours? People come here and take tours?"

"Only of the public rooms. The private quarters are off-limits. There are security people on duty. You are safe here."

She wasn't worried about being safe. It was the idea of living somewhere grand enough to have tours that made her mouth go dry.

"What does your family think of this?" she asked. "Will anyone be angry?"

He seemed to grow taller. "I am Prince As'ad of El Deharia. No one questions my actions."

"Not even the king?" she asked.

"My father will be pleased to see me settling down. He is anxious for his sons to start a family."

Kayleen had a feeling adopting three American sisters wasn't exactly what King Mukhtar had in mind.

"You said you have brothers," she said.

"I am one of six," he said. "They are in and out of the palace. Kateb lives in the desert, but the others keep rooms here."

Six princes, one princess, one king and her. What was wrong with this picture?

"You will be fine," he said.

"Would you stop knowing what I'm thinking? It's not fair."

He shrugged. "I am gifted. It can't be helped."

"Apparently not." He also seemed to have no problems with his ego. What would it be like to grow up so confident, so sure about everything, including his place in the world?

"Kayleen, you are here because of me," he said, his voice low and mesmerizing. "My name is all the protection you require. It can be used as a shield or a weapon, however you prefer."

"I can't imagine using it as either," she admitted.

"It is there for you. Know that. Know no harm can befall you while you are under my care." He looked at her. "Good night."

Then he turned and was gone.

Kayleen stared after him, feeling as if she'd just had a close encounter with a character from a book or a movie. Who said things like "My name is all the protection you require"? Yet, he was telling the truth. She believed that down to her bones.

No one had ever taken care of her before. No one had ever protected her.

Oh, sure, the nuns had always made sure their charges were safe, but that was different. This was specific.

She hugged her arms across her chest, as if feeling the comforting weight of his protection. As if feeling the strength of the man himself.

It felt good.

As'ad walked into the king's offices the next day and nodded at Robert, his personal assistant.

"Go right in, sir," Robert said with a smile. "The king is expecting you."

As'ad walked through the double doors and greeted his father.

"I hear you have taken in a family," his father said from his seat behind his impressive desk. "Lina tells me you are to adopt three orphans. I did not know you cared for such causes."

As'ad took one of the chairs opposite the desk and shook his head. "It is all Lina's doing. She insisted I go to the orphanage to prevent a nun from jumping off a roof."

"A what from what?"

"Never mind. There was no nun. Only a teacher."

A small kitten who had spit in fury and outrage. He smiled at the memory of Kayleen's determination.

"Three American girls were there," he said. "Their father was born here. When their mother died, he brought them back and then he was killed. Tahir heard of their situation and wanted to take them back to his village."

"Admirable," the king said. "Three orphaned girls would be of no value. Tahir is a good man."

"Yes, well, their teacher didn't share your admiration. She insisted the girls could not be separated, nor could they give up their education to be servants."

"Without family, what choice did the girls have? Tahir would have given them the honor of his name."

"I agree," As'ad said. "Yet that, too, was lost on their teacher. She attacked Tahir."

The king's eyebrows rose. "She lives?"

"She's small and apparently did him no harm."

"She is lucky he didn't insist on punishing her."

"I suspect he was pleased to find a way out of the situation."

"So you solved the problem by taking the girls."

"Yes, and their teacher, who will be responsible for them." He looked at his father. "They are charming girls," he said, hoping it was true. "Almost like granddaughters for you."

The king stroked his beard. "Then I will visit them and their teacher. As'ad, you did the right thing. This pleases me. Obviously you are settling down as you grow older. Well done."

"Thank you, Father."

As'ad kept his voice respectful. Lina was right. Now As'ad would be spared the royal matchmaking for a while.

"What is she like, this teacher?" the king asked. "Is she of good character?"

"Lina thinks so." He was nearly convinced himself. Her sad history could have made her hard or bitter. Instead she led with her heart.

"Have you any interest in her yourself?"

As'ad stared at his father. "In what way?"

"As a wife. We already know she likes children and is willing to face a chieftain to protect her charges. Is she pretty? Would she do for one of your brothers?"

As'ad frowned. Pretty? Kayleen? "She is not unattractive," he said slowly, remembering how she'd looked the previous night with her long hair glowing like fire. "There is a spark in her. A pureness."

Pureness? Where had *that* thought come from?

"I wonder what she thinks of the desert," the king mused. "Perhaps she would do for Kateb."

"She would not," As'ad said sharply, suddenly irritated, although he could not say why. "Besides, I need her to care for my daughters. Find my brothers' brides elsewhere."

"As you wish," the king said easily. "As you wish."

As'ad stared at the three bridge proposals in front of him. While each provided the necessary access, they couldn't be more different. The cheapest bid offered a utilitarian design while the other two had an architectural element that would add to the beauty of the city. There were—

His phone buzzed. He stared at it a second, then pushed the intercom. "I said I was not to be disturbed."

"I understand, sir. Your orders were very clear." His normally calm assistant sounded...flustered. "It's just, there's someone here to see you. A young woman. Kayleen James. She says she is the nanny for your children?"

The slight rise in Neil's voice probably came from the fact that he wasn't aware As'ad *had* any children.

"I'll explain it all later," As'ad told him. "Send her in."

Seconds later Kayleen walked into his office. As she moved across the open space, he took in the plain brown dress that covered her from the neck to down past her knees, and the flat, sensible shoes. She'd pulled her hair back in a braid. Her pale skin looked bare, and although her eyes were large, she did nothing to enhance her features. Even her earrings, tiny gold crosses, provided little adornment.

He was used to women who took the time and made the effort to be as beautiful as possible. Women who dressed in silk, who showed skin, who smelled of enticing perfumes and glittered with diamonds. Did Kayleen not care for such adornments or had she not had the opportunity to dress that way?

She could, he acknowledged, easily transform herself into a beauty. The basics were already in place—the perfect bone structure in her face, the large eyes, the full mouth.

Without meaning to, he imagined her wearing nothing at all.

Pale and soft, covered only by her long hair, a naked temptress who—

"Thank you for seeing me," Kayleen said, interrupting the erotic image that had no place in his head. "I guess I should have made an appointment."

"Not at all," he said as he came to his feet and motioned toward a sofa in the corner. "How can I help you?"

She sat down. "You're very polite."

"Thank you."

She smoothed the front of her dress. "The palace is really big. I got lost twice and had to ask directions."

"I can get you a map."

She smiled. "For real or are you teasing?"

"Both. There is a map of the palace. Would you like one?"

"I think I need it. And maybe a computer chip implant so security can find me." She looked uneasy as she glanced around the room. "This is nice. Big, but I guess that comes with being a prince."

He couldn't tell if she was just nervous or stalling. "Kayleen, is there a reason for your visit?"

"What? Oh. Right. I enrolled the girls in the American School this morning. It all went well. I used your name."

He smiled. "Bowing and scraping?"

"Some. Everyone was very eager to help. And to have me tell you they helped. That part is weird. You're probably used to it."

"I am."

"The school is great. Big and modern with a real focus on academics. Not that the orphan school is terrible. If they had more funding..." She sighed. "Asking about that is probably inappropriate."

"Will knowing that stop you from asking?"

She considered for a second. "Not really."

"I will see if funds can be made available."

Her eyes widened. "Just like that?"

"I have made no promises. But I'm sure a few dollars could be found."

"That would be great. We're not working with a big budget over there, so anything would help. Most of the teachers live in, which means the salaries aren't huge."

He doubted they would ever be huge. Teachers didn't choose their profession in an effort to amass a personal fortune. He frowned.

"Why did *you* become a teacher?" he asked.

"Because I couldn't be a nun."

An answer he never would have expected. "Did you want to be a nun?"

Kayleen nodded slowly. "Very much. The orphanage my grandmother took me to was run by nuns. They were wonderful to me. I wanted to be just like them. But I don't really have the right personality."

"Too outspoken?"

"Too…everything. I'm opinionated, I have a temper, I have trouble with the rules sometimes."

She seemed so quiet and mousy in her baggy brown dress, but there was something in her eyes, a spark that told him she was telling the truth. After all, she had attacked Tahir.

He'd never met an almost-nun before. Why would a pretty woman want to lock herself away from the world?

"Our Mother Superior suggested I go into teaching," Kayleen continued. "It was a great idea. I love it. I love the children. I wanted to take a permanent position there, but she insisted I first see the world. That's how I ended up here. Eventually, I'll go back."

"To the convent school?"

She nodded.

"What about a husband and a family?"

Kayleen ducked her head, but not before he saw her blush. "I don't really expect that to happen to me. I don't date. Men are… They don't think of me that way."

He recalled his earlier fantasy about seeing her naked. "You would be surprised," he murmured.

She looked up. "I don't think so."

"So there has never been anyone special?"

"A boyfriend?" She shook her head. "No."

She was in her midtwenties. How was that possible? Did such innocence truly exist? Yet why would she lie about such a thing?

He found himself wanting to show her the world she'd been avoiding. To take her places.

Ridiculous, he told himself. She was nothing to him. Only the children's nanny.

Chapter Three

Kayleen backed out of the kitchen, her hands up in front of her, palms out. "No really. I mean it. Everything we have is terrific. I love the food. I've gained three pounds."

When she could no longer see the head chef's furious expression, she turned and hurried to the closest staircase, then ran up to a safer floor.

She'd only been offering to help, she told herself. But her offer of assistance had been taken as an insult.

With the girls gone all day and a kindly worded but clear letter from the orphan school saying it would be too awkward to have her teaching there, now that she was under Prince As'ad's "protection," Kayleen had nothing to do with her time. Sitting around was boring. She needed to keep busy with *something*. She couldn't clean the suite she and the girls lived in. There wasn't even a vacuum in the closet.

She wandered down the main hallway, then paused to figure out where she was. The wide doorways looked familiar. Still, what would it hurt to have a few "you are here" maps to guide newcomers?

She turned another corner and recognized the official royal

offices. In a matter of minutes she was standing in front of As'ad's assistant, Neil.

"I really need to see him," she said.

"You do not have an appointment."

"I'm his nanny." It was a bluff. She was staff and she had a feeling that all staff needed an appointment.

"I'm aware of who you are, Ms. James. But Prince As'ad is very particular about his schedule."

Neil was British, so the word sounded like "shed-ule."

The door to As'ad's office opened. "Neil, I need you to find—" He saw Kayleen. "How convenient. You're the one I'm looking for."

Guilt flooded her. "Is it the chef? I didn't mean to insult him. I was only trying to help."

His gaze narrowed. "What did you do?"

She tucked her hands behind her back. "Nothing."

"Why don't I believe you? Come inside, Kayleen. Start at the beginning and leave nothing out."

She glanced longingly at the exit, but followed As'ad into his office. When they were both seated, he looked at her expectantly.

She sucked in a breath. "I went down to the kitchen. I thought I could maybe help out there. I didn't mean anything by it. I'm bored. I need to do *something*."

She stopped talking and pressed her lips together to hold in a sudden rush of emotion. *Need*—there was the word that mattered. She had to be needed.

"You have your three charges," he said. "Many would find that enough."

"Oh, please. They're in school for hours at a time. Someone else cooks, cleans and I'm guessing does our laundry. So what do I do the rest of the time?"

"Shop?"

"With what? Are you paying me? We never discussed a salary. Are there benefits? Do I have a dental plan? One minute

I was minding my own business, doing my job, and the next I was here. It's not an easy adjustment."

One corner of his mouth twitched. "If I remember correctly, you assaulted a chieftain. Not exactly minding your own business."

She didn't want to talk about that. "You know what I mean."

"I do. Tell me, Kayleen. What did you teach?"

"Math," she said absently as she stood up and crossed to the window. As'ad's view was of a beautiful garden. She didn't know anything about plants, but she could learn. Maybe the gardener needed some help.

"Advanced?"

"Some."

"You're comfortable with statistical analysis?"

"Uh-huh." What were the pink flowers? They were stunning.

"Then I have a project for you."

She turned. "You want me to do your taxes?"

"No. I want you to work with the education minister. While many girls from the rural villages are graduating from high school and going on to college, the number is not as great as we would like. For El Deharia to grow as a nation, we must have all our citizens educated and productive. I want you to find out which villages are sending the most girls to college, then figure out what they're doing right so we can use that information to help the other villages. Does that interest you?"

She crossed back to the sofa. "You're serious? You're not just offering me this to keep me busy?"

"You have my word. This is vital information. I trust you to get it right."

He spoke with a low, steady voice that seemed to pull her closer. There was something in his eyes that made her want to believe him.

Excitement grew inside of her. It was a project she could throw herself into, and still have plenty of time for the girls. It would be challenging and interesting and meaningful.

She rushed toward him. "I'd love to do it. Thank you."

She leaned forward impulsively, then stopped herself. What was the plan? To hug him? One did not idly hug a prince and she didn't go around hugging men.

She straightened and took a step back, not sure if she should apologize or pretend it never happened. As'ad rose and crossed to his desk. Apparently he was going to ignore what she'd almost done. Or he hadn't noticed.

"Then we are agreed," he said. "You'll report your progress to me in weekly meetings." He opened a desk drawer and pulled out a credit card. "Use this to get yourself a laptop and printer. Your suite already has Internet access."

She hesitated before taking the card. No one had ever offered her a credit card before. She fingered the slim plastic. "I'll, um, make sure I get a bargain."

"You don't have to. Kayleen, do you have any idea how wealthy I am?"

"Not really," she admitted.

"You don't need to shop for a bargain."

But she would. She would be responsible with his money, even if he didn't care.

"Okay. I'll get right on ordering one."

He studied her for a moment. "You may also use that to shop for yourself and the girls."

"We don't need anything."

"You will. Clothes wear out. Even my limited knowledge of children tells me they grow and require new clothes."

"You're right." She stared at the card. "You're also very kind."

"I am not. My daughters deserve the best because of who I am."

"You don't have a self-esteem crisis, do you?" she asked, both amused and envious.

"No. I am clear on my place in the world."

Must be nice, she thought longingly.

"You belong here, as well," he told her.

Because he was once again reading her mind? "Not really."

"If I say it is so, it is."

"Thank you" seemed the right response. He was being kind. The truth was, she didn't belong here at all. She was just staff and easily replaceable.

She turned to leave, but he called her back.

"I'll get you information on your salary and benefits," he said. "I should have taken care of that before."

She smiled. "You're a prince. I guess you're not into details."

"You're very understanding. Thank you."

"You're welcome."

His dark gaze caught hers. She told herself it was okay to go now, that they were done. But she couldn't seem to pull away. She felt a powerful need to move closer, to…to… She wasn't sure what, but *something*.

The phone rang. He glanced down and she was able to move again. As much as she wanted to stay, she forced herself to walk out of the office.

"We're making progress," Lina said as she curled up on her bed and held the phone close.

"There is no 'we,'" Hassan told her. "You are in this on your own."

"That's not true. This was all your idea. You're in this as deeply as I am."

"You're a very difficult woman."

"I know." She smiled. "It's part of my charm."

"You *are* charming."

She squeezed her eyes shut and did her best not to scream. Not only wasn't it fitting her position, but she was forty-three. Forty-three-year-old women didn't go around screaming because a handsome man flirted with them on the phone. Even if that handsome man was the king of Bahania.

"Kayleen really likes As'ad," she continued. "She's having a little trouble adjusting to the palace, but who wouldn't? Still, she's doing well. He came and talked to me about making sure she had a salary and benefits. He wants to be generous. That's something."

"You may be reading too much into what he says."

"I hope not. She would be good for him. He always holds back his emotions. I blame his father for that."

"How refreshing," Hassan said dryly. "One usually blames the mother."

She laughed. "Speaking as a woman, I would say that needs to change."

"This is my favorite part of our conversations. The sound of your laughter."

Her heartbeat went from normal to hyperdrive in two seconds. Good thing she was lying down—otherwise, she would have fallen.

"It is as beautiful as the rest of you." He paused. "Have I startled you with my confession?"

"Um, no. It's fine. I mean, thank you."

He sighed. "How much of this awkwardness is because I am a king and how much of it is because I am so much older?"

"None of it is because you're the king," she said without thinking.

His short "I see" had her backpedaling.

"No, no. It's not about your age. I just wasn't sure… We've never really talked about… I thought we were friends."

"We are. Do you wish us to be more?"

Oh, my. Talk about putting it all out there.

Lina clutched the phone and told herself to keep breathing. She was terrified to tell the truth, to admit that she thought about him a whole lot more than she should. What if he wanted to know so he could let her down gently?

"Hassan," she began, then stopped.

"I would like us to be more than friends," he said. "Does that information make things easier or harder for you?"

She exhaled. "Easier. A lot easier. I want that, too."

"Good. I did not expect to find you, Lina. You are a gift for which I will always be grateful."

"Thank you," she whispered, not sure what else to say. "I'm intrigued, as well."

"Intrigued," he repeated. "An interesting choice of words. Perhaps we should explore all the possibilities."

As'ad walked into his suite at his usual time in the early evening. But instead of quiet, dark rooms, he found the living area bright and loud. Dana and Pepper were stretched out on the floor, watching a show on his large television. Nadine swirled and danced by the window and Kayleen stood at the dining room table, arranging flowers.

She looked up when he entered. "Oh, good. You're here. I called Neil to ask him what time you'd be home. He didn't want to tell me." She wrinkled her nose. "I don't think he likes me."

"Perhaps he is just trying to protect me."

"From us?" She asked the question as if it were a ridiculous possibility. "I wanted to have dinner ready, which it is. I have to say, this calling down to the kitchen and ordering food is really fun. We each picked a dish. Which may not have been a good idea. The menu is fairly eclectic."

She paused for breath, then smiled. "We wanted to have dinner with you."

She wore another dress that was ugly enough to be offensive. The dull gray fabric sucked the life from her face and the bulky style hid any hint of curve. Yet when she smiled, he found his mood lifting. He wanted to smile back. He wanted to pull her close and discover the body hidden beneath.

Heat stirred, reminding him how long he had lived only for his work.

He ignored the need and the wanting, the heat that forced blood south, and set down his briefcase. He even ignored that, given her past, Kayleen had probably never been with a man, and instead focused on the fact that she and the girls were in his room.

He had made himself extremely clear. She was to keep the children away from him. They had their own suite and everything they could possibly want or need. He had only taken the sisters to keep them from a less desirable fate. Yet when he started to remind Kayleen of that, he could not seem to bring himself to say the words.

Perhaps because she looked so hopeful as she smiled at him. He did not want to squash the light in her eyes.

"I'll get some wine," he said, moving to the small wine rack tucked in a cabinet. Something stronger might make the evening go more quickly, but he only had wine in his rooms. He did not, as a rule, drink here. Of course he did not, as a rule, have a woman and three children to contend with.

Nadine danced over to him. "Hi, As'ad," she said, her eyes bright with happiness, her mouth smiling. "Did you have a good day? I got every word on my spelling test except one and it was really hard. My new teacher says I'm a good speller. I'm good in all my subjects, except math, and Kayleen is gonna help me with that."

Pepper ran over and pushed in front of Nadine. "Hi! I'm in school, too, and I'm good at math." She stuck out her tongue at her sister, then smiled back at him. "I made a picture and I brought it for you, but you don't have a 'frigerator, so where are we gonna put it?"

Dana stood and joined them. "He doesn't want your picture," she said, then sighed, as only an older sibling can. "She's not a very good artist."

Pepper stomped her foot. "I'm an *excellent* artist. You're just a butthead."

Dana gasped, Nadine looked worried and Pepper slapped her hand over her mouth. Terror darkened her blue eyes and she glanced between him and Kayleen. Apparently saying "butthead" was not allowed.

As'ad rubbed his temple.

Kayleen walked over and looked at Pepper. "You know that's wrong."

Pepper nodded frantically, her hand still over her mouth.

"You need to apologize to Dana."

Pepper, a tiny girl with long, curly blond hair, turned to her big sister. "I'm sorry I called you that."

Dana put her hands on her hips. "That's not good enough. You always call people—"

Kayleen cleared her throat. Dana hunched her shoulders.

"Thank you for apologizing," she grumbled.

Kayleen touched Pepper's shoulder. "Now you help me think of a suitable punishment. What is appropriate for what you did?"

Pepper's eyes filled with tears. "No story tonight?" she asked in a whisper.

Kayleen considered. "That's a little harsh. What if you have to give up your choice on movie night? Dana gets two choices instead."

Pepper shivered slightly, then nodded. "Okay."

"Good." Kayleen smiled at As'ad. "We're healed. You ready to eat?"

He opened the bottle of wine and joined them at the table. When he was seated, before he could pour, Kayleen reached for Pepper's hand and his. He stared at her.

Pepper leaned toward him. "We have to say grace."

"Of course."

He took Kayleen's hand and Nadine's, then lowered his head while Kayleen offered brief thanks for their meal. While she served, he poured two glasses of wine and passed her one.

Kayleen handed him a plate. "I've never been much of a drinker."

"Neither have I." Although under the circumstances, he just might be starting.

This was too much, he thought. More than he'd expected or wanted. There were children at his table. And a woman he did not know and was not going to sleep with, and having sex with her would be the only acceptable reason to have her here. Yet he saw no easy way to escape.

"We go around the table and talk about our day," Kayleen said as she passed Dana her plate. "Everyone has to say one good thing that happened. I hope that's okay."

And if it was not?

He glanced down at the plate in front of him. Lasagna, mashed potatoes, macaroni and cheese and a salad.

"Perhaps some kind of menu would be helpful," he told Kayleen.

"I know. I'll get one made up. But the girls really wanted to order you their favorites."

Dana talked about how she'd finished her homework early and had found a collection of medical texts in the palace's main library. Nadine mentioned her dance class and how well she'd done.

"I hit a boy," Pepper announced cheerfully. "He was teasing these three girls. He's kinda big, but I wasn't scared. So I hit him. The teacher didn't like it but because I'm new, she said she was going to let it go this one time. I heard this other teacher saying that boy needed a good beating and maybe I'm the one to give it to him." She beamed. "That was fun."

Kayleen quickly covered her mouth with her napkin. As'ad saw the humor in her eyes and knew she was hiding a smile. He took a sip of wine to keep from laughing. He liked Pepper—she had the heart of a lion.

"Perhaps hitting boys is not the best plan," he said as he set the glass down. "One day one of them might hit you back."

"I'm tough," she said.

"Still. Violence is a poor strategy."

"What's a better one?"

He hesitated, not sure what to say.

Kayleen grinned. "We're all waiting to be dazzled by your strategy."

"Perhaps you would like to offer a suggestion?" he asked.

"Not really. Go ahead."

Privately he agreed with Pepper's approach, but he doubted it would be successful as she grew.

"We'll talk later," Kayleen said, rescuing him. "I know hitting a bully seems like a good idea, but it's going to get you into a lot of trouble. Not only with the teachers and with me, but as As'ad mentioned, you could get hurt."

"All right," Pepper grumbled. "But sometimes boys are really stupid."

Dana looked at As'ad. "What good thing happened to you?"

"I decided on a bridge. There is to be a new one over the river. After much planning and discussion, a choice was made. I am pleased."

All three girls stared at him. "You're going to build a bridge?" Nadine asked.

"No. I have given my approval and told them what to do. Now they will do it."

"Cool," Dana breathed. "What else can you tell people to do?"

"Can you throw them in the dungeon?" Pepper asked. "Can I see the dungeon?"

"One day."

Her eyes widened. "There's a real one? Here? In the palace?"

"Yes, and sometimes children who do not behave are sent to it."

They all went silent.

He chuckled. "So, Kayleen, what was your one good thing for today?"

This, Kayleen thought as she tried not to stare at the handsome man at the head of the table. This dinner, this moment, with the girls having fun and As'ad acting like they were all part of the same family.

It wasn't real—she knew that. But all her life she'd wanted to be a part of something special, and here it was.

Still, she had to say something. "There are stables nearby," she told the girls. "I found them when I was out walking."

All three of them turned to him. "Horses? You have horses?" Dana asked.

"We love horses," Nadine told him.

"I can ride." Pepper paused, as if waiting for As'ad to be impressed. "I've had lessons."

He turned to Kayleen. "At the orphanage?"

"A former student left several horses to the school, along with the money to pay for them. Many of the children ride."

"Do you?"

There was something about his dark eyes, she thought, knowing she could stare into them for hours and never grow tired of the effect of the changing light.

"Badly," she admitted. "The horse and I never figured out how to talk to each other."

"That's because horses don't talk," Pepper told her, then turned to As'ad. "Kayleen falls off a lot. I try not to laugh, because I don't want her to hurt herself, but it's kinda funny."

"For you," Kayleen murmured.

The main door to the suite opened and a tall, gray-haired man strode into the suite.

"As'ad. There you are. Oh. You're having dinner with your family."

"Father," As'ad said as he rose.

Father? Something nagged at the back of Kayleen's mind, before bursting free. Father? As in the king?

She jumped to her feet and motioned for the girls to do the same. Once they were standing she didn't know what to do next. Bow? Curtsy?

As'ad glanced at her, then the girls. "Father, this is Kayleen, the girls' nanny." Then he introduced each of the sisters. "Ladies, this is my father, King Mukhtar."

Three mouths dropped open. Kayleen kept hers shut by sheer force of will.

The king nodded graciously. "I am delighted to meet all of you. Welcome to the royal palace of El Deharia. May you live long, with happiness and health in abundance. May these strong walls always protect you and provide solace."

Kayleen swallowed. As greetings went, it was a really good one.

"Thank you so much for your hospitality," she murmured, still trying to accept the fact that she was in the presence of a real live king. Which meant As'ad really was a prince.

She knew he held the title, but she didn't think of him as royal or powerful. Yet he was.

The king motioned to the table. "May I?"

Kayleen felt her eyes widen. "Of course, Your Highness. Please. We weren't expecting you, so the meal isn't exactly... traditional."

The king took a seat. As'ad motioned for them to resume theirs. Mukhtar studied the various serving bowls, then scooped some macaroni and cheese onto a plate.

"I haven't had this in years."

"It was my pick," Pepper told him. "It's my favorite. They make it really good here. Sometimes, at the orphanage, Kayleen would sneak us into the kitchen and make the kind in a box. That's good, too."

The king smiled. "So my chef has competition."

"Not really," Kayleen told him. "His food is amazing. I'm honored just to eat it."

As'ad looked at his father. "In an effort to fill her day, Kayleen went down to the kitchen and offered to help. It did not go well."

Kayleen felt herself flush. "He was a little insulted. There was a crash. I'm guessing he threw stuff."

"Was that the night my soufflé was burned?" the king asked.

"I hope not," Kayleen told him.

He smiled. "So what conversation did I interrupt?" he asked.

"We were talking about horses," Nadine told him. "We rode and took lessons at the orphanage."

The king looked at his son. "Horses. I believe we have a stable, do we not?"

As'ad glanced at the girls. "The king is teasing. The palace stables are world famous."

Dana leaned toward him. "Do you have horses that go fast?"

"Faster than would be safe for a novice rider."

She wrinkled her nose. "If we took more lessons, we would be experts."

"Exactly," As'ad told her.

The king nodded. "I agree. All young princesses should know how to ride. I will speak to the head groom myself and arrange lessons." He glanced at Kayleen. "For all of you."

"Thank you," she murmured, because it was expected.

"You do not look excited," As'ad whispered to her.

"Pepper wasn't kidding about me falling. It happens all the time."

"Perhaps you need more personal instruction."

She stared into his eyes as he spoke and found herself getting lost in his gaze. It was as if he had an energy field that pulled her closer. She had the oddest feeling he was going to touch her—and she was going to like him touching her.

"Riding is an enjoyable way to get exercise," the king said.

"Has anyone asked the horse about that?"

She spoke without thinking—something that had often gotten her in trouble back at the convent. There was a moment of silence, then the king laughed.

"Very good," he said. "Excellent. I like her, As'ad. This one may stay."

"I agree," As'ad said, still looking at her in a way that made her thighs feel distinctly weak. "She will stay."

Would she? Kayleen wasn't so sure. She still had her life

plan to fulfill and that included leaving El Deharia in a matter of months. A situation complicated by As'ad and her promise to the girls.

Chapter Four

After the king left and dinner was finished, Kayleen sent the girls back to their suite while she lingered behind to speak with As'ad.

"There are just a couple of things I need to discuss with you," she told him when they were alone.

"I'm learning that with you, there always are."

She wasn't sure what he meant by that, so decided to ignore the comment. "It's only about six weeks until Christmas," she said. "We have to start planning. I don't know what happens here at the palace, but this is the girls' first Christmas without either of their parents. We have to do something."

He studied her for a long time. "El Deharia is a very open country. All faiths are celebrated here. No one will object if you wish to set up a tree in your suite."

"It's more than that," she said, telling herself there was no reason to be afraid, even though As'ad was much taller than her and having to look up to meet his gaze gave her a crick in her neck. "You need to participate."

He looked shocked. "I do not."

She'd had a feeling he would be difficult.

"You've always had family," she pointed out. "Your brothers, your aunt, your father. These girls have no one. The holidays are going to be sad and scary and they're going to feel so alone."

Kayleen spoke from experience. She still remembered waking up on Christmas morning and feeling an ache in her chest. No matter how many presents had been donated to the orphanage, no matter how the nuns tried, there hadn't been *family*.

She hadn't even had the dream that a wonderful couple would find her and want to adopt her. She had plenty of relatives—just no one who wanted her.

"They need traditions, both old and new," she continued. "They need to feel welcome and loved."

His expression tightened. "Then you will take care of that."

"But you're their father now."

"I am someone who agreed to let them live here. Kayleen, these girls are your responsibility, not mine. Do not cross this line with me."

"I don't understand. You were so great with them at dinner. Are you telling me that was just an act? That you don't care?"

"I have compassion. I have honor. That will be enough."

Was he kidding? "That's not enough. It will never be enough. We're talking about children, As'ad. Lost, lonely children. They deserve more. They deserve to be loved." She wasn't just talking about the children—she was talking about herself. The difference was she'd already given up her dreams.

"Then they will have to find that love in you."

She took a step back. Her throat tightened and her cheeks were hot. "You're saying you don't plan to love them?"

He might as well have said he was going to kill them in their sleep!

"I will honor my responsibilities. In doing so, it is necessary for me to be strong. Emotion is weakness. You are a woman—I don't expect you to understand. Just trust me, it is so. I will see to the girls' needs. You can take care of their hearts."

She didn't know what to say or where to begin to argue with him. "That's the craziest thing I've ever heard," she told him.

"Love isn't weakness. It's strength and power. The ability to give means you can be more, not less."

He actually smiled at her. "Your passion is a testament to your caring. That's excellent."

"So it's okay for me to have emotions, but not you? Because you're a man?"

"More than a man," he reminded her. "A prince. I have responsibilities for others. It is my duty to stay strong, to not be swayed by something as changeable as feelings."

"Without compassion, there can be no judgment," she snapped. "Without feelings, you're only a machine. A good ruler feels for his people."

"You cannot understand."

"And you can't mean this."

"I assure you, I do." He took her arm and walked her to the door. "Celebrate Christmas however you wish. You have my permission."

"Can I have your head on a stick instead?" she muttered as she jerked free and walked out into the hallway.

Of all the stupid, annoying things she'd ever heard. He wasn't going to feel anything because he was a prince? But it was okay for her because she was a woman?

"No way," she told herself as she headed back to her own rooms. "Something is going to change around here and it isn't going to be me."

"It's so egotistical," Kayleen ranted the next morning as she paced the length of her living room. "So two hundred years ago. He gets to be in charge because he's a man? What does that make the rest of us? Chattel? I'm so angry, I want to throw him in the dungeon until he begs. I'm smart. I'm capable. And I have a heart. Why can't he see that emotions give us depth? They define us. Are all men so stupid? I have to tell you, Lina, the more I see of the world, the more I long for the convent."

Her friend smiled at her. "Is it possible your energy and intensity on this topic is one of the reasons you *weren't* called to serve in that way?"

"That's what I was always told when I was growing up. I was too passionate about things. Too willing to go my own way. It's just when I see an injustice, I can't stop to think. I act."

"As you did with Tahir."

Kayleen remembered the tall chieftain who had wanted to take the girls. "Exactly."

"Life does not always move on your timetable," Lina said. "You need to be patient."

"Don't act impulsively," Kayleen said, knowing she'd heard the same advice a thousand times before.

"Exactly." Lina patted the seat next to her. "As'ad is a product of his world. His father taught all his sons to avoid emotion. To think logically. While my brother grieved after his wife died, he chose not to show that to the boys. In front of them, he went on, as if unmoved by her passing. In my opinion it was the wrong lesson."

Kayleen agreed. "Because of that, As'ad won't care?" She didn't wait for an answer. "He's not stupid. Why can't he see the truth all around him?"

"He has been trained for a specific purpose. His is a life of service, in a way, but with ultimate power and ego. You haven't met his brothers, but they are all like him. Strong, determined men who see little virtue in love. It's probably why none of them have married."

"But love is strength and a great gift," Kayleen said as she sat on the sofa. "He has to love the girls. They need that. They deserve it. He would be better because of it. Happier. Besides, there's a ticking clock here."

Lina frowned. "You're still leaving?"

"I can go back on my twenty-fifth birthday. That's less than four months away."

"But you have the girls now."

"I know." Kayleen hadn't worked that part out. "They'll get settled and then As'ad can bring in someone else."

She spoke bravely, but the words sounded a little feeble, even to her.

"I'm surprised," Lina admitted. "When you asked As'ad to adopt the girls, I thought you were taking on the responsibility with him. This isn't like you, Kayleen. To retreat from the world."

"The world isn't always a fun place. I want to go back to where I belong." Where she'd grown up. It was the only home she'd ever known. "I can teach there." That was the deal. She had to stay away until she was twenty-five. Then she could return to the convent school forever.

"You can be a mother here."

"Not really. It's just a game. When the girls are older, As'ad will have no use for me. Besides, if he doesn't want to get involved, maybe I can take them with me."

"I assume my nephew doesn't know about your plan to leave."

"I haven't mentioned it."

"When will you?"

"Soon. It's not as if he'll miss me or anything."

Kayleen had always wondered what it would be like to be missed by someone. By a man. To be cared for. Loved, even.

"Things change," Lina told her. "You have a responsibility to the girls."

"I know."

"Would you walk away from them so easily?"

Kayleen shook her head. "No. It won't be easy. Sometimes I do think about staying." She didn't know what was right. Her plan had always been to go back. Being here with the three sisters had changed everything.

Was Lina right? Did she, Kayleen, have a responsibility to the children? Should she give up her dreams for them? Could she go back later? When the girls were older?

Three weeks ago, she'd known all the answers and now she

knew none. Her instinct was to go talk to As'ad about all this. But that made no sense. He was a man who didn't listen to his heart and she had always believed the truth could be found there.

"My head is spinning. Enough about this. Let's change the subject."

"All right." Lina smiled slowly. "Hassan is coming here."

Kayleen stared at her friend. "The king of Bahania? The one you've been talking to all this time?"

"I can't believe it, either. I just… We were talking and he said he liked the sound of my laughter and now he's coming here."

Kayleen hugged her. "That's wonderful. I'm so happy. You've been shut up in this palace for years. Good for you."

"I'm scared," Lina admitted. "I thought my life was all planned out. I helped my brother raise his sons, I have my charity work. I was waiting to be a great-aunt. Suddenly there's this wonderful man offering me something I thought I'd lost. There are possibilities. Am I too old for possibilities?"

"Never," Kayleen said fiercely. "The heart is never too old. At least it isn't in all those romantic movies."

"I hope not. I married young and I was so in love. Then he was killed and I never planned to love again. I'm the sister to the king. It's difficult to date. After a while, I stopped wanting to. Then Hassan and I started talking and suddenly I'm alive again." Lina took Kayleen's hands. "I want this for you. I at least experienced falling in love when I was young, but you've never had that."

Kayleen squirmed. "I'm not good with men."

"You don't try. How many dates did you go on before you gave up? Five? Six?"

Kayleen cleared her throat, then pulled her hands free. "One and a half."

"You're too young to lock yourself away in that convent school of yours."

"Because I would meet so many men here at the palace?"

"You'd meet some. More than you would there. There are

many young men in the palace. I would be happy to introduce you to one or two of them."

"I don't know.... I work for As'ad. As nanny to his children."

"Why would he mind you dating?"

"He wouldn't." Not that she enjoyed admitting that truth.

"Then think about what I said. Wouldn't it be wonderful to fall in love?"

As'ad looked up as his brother Qadir walked into his office. "I must speak with Neil about keeping out people who don't have appointments."

Qadir ignored that. "I am back from Paris, where the city is still beautiful, as are the women. You should have come with me. You have been locked up here working for far too long."

As'ad had spent two sleepless nights unable to rest for the need burning inside. Worse, when he closed his eyes, the woman he saw satisfying his ache was Kayleen. An impossible situation. The nanny and a virgin?

"You are right, my brother," he said as he rose and greeted Qadir. "I should have gone with you. There have been changes since you were last here."

"I heard." Qadir settled on a corner of his desk. "Three daughters? What were you thinking?"

"That I had been placed in an impossible situation and this was the easiest way out."

"I find that hard to believe. There had to be another solution."

"None was presented."

Qadir shook his head. "To raise children that are not your own. At least they are girls."

"There is the added advantage of our father now believing I am occupied with my new family and therefore cannot be expected to look for a wife."

"Lucky bastard."

"Indeed. Perhaps now he will focus more of his attention on you."

"He has already begun," Qadir grumbled. "There is to be a state function in a few weeks. Several likely candidates are to be paraded before me, like very attractive cattle."

As'ad grinned. "I, of course, will be busy with my family."

As'ad turned the corner to walk to his rooms and saw all three girls huddled by his door. They wore riding clothes and boots. When they saw him they ran to him.

"You have to help!" Dana told him.

"It's terrible. Please!" Nadine begged.

Pepper simply cried.

He stared at the three of them. "What happened?"

"We went riding," Dana told him, her blue eyes wide and filled with fear and guilt. "We might have been gone longer than we were supposed to, but we were fine. We were only a little late. But Kayleen got worried and came after us, even though we had a groom with us. She went out by herself and she's not back yet."

Pepper brushed her hand across her face as she tugged on the bottom of his suit jacket. "She's not a very good rider. She gets thrown a lot. What if she's hurt and it's all our fault?"

As'ad's first thought was that he regretted that whoever had let Kayleen go out by herself could not be flogged. Sometimes he missed the old ways. His second was the low-grade worry at the thought of a defenseless young woman alone in the desert. It was not a place to be traveled lightly.

The girls crowded close, as if seeking comfort from him. Although he had no time for this, he resisted the urge to push them away and instead awkwardly patted them on their shoulders.

"All will be well," he told them. "I will find Kayleen and return her to you."

"Promise?" Pepper asked, her lashes spiky from her tears.

He crouched down until he could look her in the eye. "I am Prince As'ad of El Deharia. My word is law."

Pepper sniffed. "Promise?"

He gave her a slight smile. "I promise."

Ten minutes later the girls were settled with Lina and he was in the garage, sliding into an open Jeep. The desert was a vast space and in theory, Kayleen could be anywhere. But in truth, an inexperienced rider would stick to trails and not get far. Unless she had been thrown.

He did not allow himself to consider that option. He would find her and if she were hurt, he would deal with the situation as it arose.

He found the riding trail easily. He had been taking it all his life. As it bent to the left, he considered how far Kayleen might have traveled, then accelerated. A mere ten miles into the desert was the permanent outpost of a local tribe. If Kayleen kept to the trail, she would end up there.

He drove slowly, checking the area for signs of any accident, or a woman walking without a horse, but found nothing. At the outskirts of the outpost he saw a cluster of people gathered around a petite woman with flaming red hair. She was holding on to a horse and gesturing wildly.

As'ad eased the Jeep to a stop and picked up the satellite phone. When he was connected with his aunt, he informed her he had found Kayleen and that she appeared fine.

"Will you be coming right back?" Lina asked.

As'ad considered. "I believe we'll stay for dinner."

"That's fine. I'll put the girls to bed. Thanks for letting me know. They were worried."

He disconnected the call and parked, then walked toward the crowd.

Kayleen saw him and excused herself from the group, then raced toward him. When she was close enough, she launched herself at him.

He caught her and held her against him as she trembled in his embrace.

"You came," she breathed. "It's the girls. They're gone. They were late and we had no way to get in touch with them and I was so worried, so I took a horse out myself. I found this village, but no one speaks English and I can't tell if they've seen the girls. What if something happened to them? I'll never forgive myself."

She was distraught and panicked and surprisingly beautiful. Her hazel eyes darkened with emotion and her cheeks were flushed. Impulsively, he bent down and lightly brushed her mouth with his.

"They're fine," he told her. "All three of them returned unharmed. You are the one who is missing."

"What?" She drew in a breath. "They're all right?"

"Perfectly fine, although suffering from guilt for causing you distress. Kayleen, the girls are good riders. The head groom took them out himself to confirm that. They also had someone with them. Why did you feel it necessary to go rescue them yourself?"

"I don't know. I was worried and I acted."

"Impulsively."

She glanced down. "Yes, well, that's an ongoing problem."

"So it seems."

She looked around and noticed the villagers gathered close. "Oh." She pulled back.

As'ad let her go, but only reluctantly. She had felt good in his arms. He wanted to kiss her again—but thoroughly and without an audience. He wanted to push aside her unattractive clothing and touch the soft skin beneath. Instead he stepped back and turned to greet Sharif, the village chieftain.

"She is your woman?" Sharif asked.

Kayleen spun toward the old man. "You speak English? You stood there, pretending not to understand and you speak *English?*"

"They don't know you," As'ad told her. "They were being cautious."

"What about desert hospitality? What about claiming sanctuary or asylum or something?"

"Did you?" he asked.

Kayleen pressed her lips together. "No. I was asking if they'd seen the girls. They wouldn't answer and they weren't speaking English."

As'ad glanced at Sharif. "She is mine."

"Then you are both welcome. You will stay and eat with us?"

"It is an honor."

"Arrangements will be made."

"Arrangements?" Kayleen asked. "What arrangements? And what's all this about being your woman? I'm your nanny. There's a really big difference."

He took her by the elbow and led her to the Jeep. "It makes things easier if they think you belong to me. Otherwise you would be fair game for every man here. You're very exotic. They would find that tempting."

Kayleen didn't know what to say to that. She was so far from exotic that if they put her picture on that page in the dictionary, it would have a circle with a line drawn through it over her face. She couldn't imagine a man ever being tempted by her.

It was the hair, she thought with a sigh. Bright red hair tended to call attention to itself.

"Fear not," As'ad told her. "I have claimed you. You are safe."

She shivered slightly, but not in fear. It was more from the memory of the brief kiss he'd given her when he'd first arrived. An unexpected and warm touch of his lips on hers. She'd been shocked by the contact, but not in a scary way. More surprised, but pleased.

"We're staying for dinner," he said.

"I got that."

"It's the polite thing to do."

She looked around at the tidy camp. "I don't mind. I like it here, out in the desert. Although it would be nice if they didn't pretend not to understand me."

"They are private people. You rode in from nowhere, babbling about missing children. They were cautious."

She narrowed her gaze. "I do *not* babble."

He raised an eyebrow.

"Not often," she amended. "I was scared. I thought the girls were lost."

"You were not equipped to find them, yet you went after them."

"Someone had to."

"Perhaps one of the grooms. Or you could have called me."

Oh. Right. "I didn't think of that. I'm not used to having resources."

"Perhaps next time you will consider that you do."

It would take some getting used to. "You came after me yourself," she said. "*You* could have sent one of the grooms."

"The girls were most distressed to think they were the cause of your being gone. Coming after you myself seemed the quickest way to allay their fears."

"It was a little impulsive. You have resources, too."

"You mock me?"

"Maybe."

"A dangerous path."

"I'm not afraid."

Something flashed in his eyes. Something dark and primitive that made her heart flutter. She didn't know if she should throw herself at him or run into the desert, so she stood her ground.

"So what do you think is for dinner?"

The women of the village prepared a rich stew with lots of vegetables and a flat bread that smelled so good it made Kayleen's mouth water. She did her best to be friendly and polite, helping with the cooking as much as the women in the camp would let her.

Zarina, Sharif's oldest daughter, was the only one who would speak to her in English.

"Am I really that scary?" Kayleen asked quietly as she stirred the stew.

"You are different. From the city and from another country. You do not know our ways."

"I could learn."

Zarina, a dark-haired beauty with a flashing smile, laughed. "Give up your comforts to roam the desert? I do not think so."

"Comforts don't matter to me," Kayleen told her. She would give up many things to belong somewhere.

"Yet you live in the palace with the prince."

"It's a long story and I don't live with him. I take care of..." She shook her head. "It's a really long story."

Zarina glanced at As'ad where he sat with the leaders of the tribe. "The prince is handsome. If I were not happily married, I might try to steal him from you."

Kayleen started to say he wasn't hers to steal, but figured there was no point. "He's nice."

Zarina laughed. "Not nice. No man worth having is nice. As'ad is a desert warrior. He takes what he wants, but then he protects those he claims. He is a strong man. A powerful husband. You have chosen well."

A lion of the desert? As'ad? He was strong and powerful and he did seem to take care of those around him. His presence here was proof of that. But a dangerous animal? She didn't believe that. As for her choosing him...as if.

He looked up and met her gaze, then rose and approached. "What troubles you, Kayleen?"

"Nothing. I was just thinking. Zarina says it's good she's happily married, otherwise she would steal you from me."

He laughed. "She is a beautiful woman."

Kayleen didn't like that answer. "You and I don't have that kind of relationship."

"So you would not mind if she and I..."

"No," Kayleen said carefully, even as a knot formed in her stomach. It was hard and hot and made her feel uncomfortable. "You have a family now. You should be with someone."

"You suggest Zarina?"

"She's already married."

"I am Prince As'ad of El Deharia. I can have whomever I choose."

How annoyingly arrogant. "I don't think so. You're just a man. There are women who would say no to you."

He moved closer. "Who would that be?"

She stood at straight as she could, tilted her head back and glared at him. "Me, for one. I'm not interested."

His smile was slow, sexy and confident beyond measure. "You think so."

"Absolutely."

"I see."

He reached toward her. Before she knew what he intended, he pulled her close and kissed her.

Chapter Five

Kayleen had almost been kissed once in her life, on a date with a young man in college. He had been nice enough, but she was so inexperienced that just being around him had made her nervous. At the end of their awkward evening, he'd moved in for a kiss and she'd bolted for the safety of her dorm room.

But there was no bolting from As'ad. With his arms around her, she had nowhere to go. Not to mention the fact that she didn't want to run.

She'd wondered about kissing, had wondered if she was the last innocent in a world where even twelve-year-olds seemed to know more about men and sex than she did. She'd wondered how it was possible to enjoy someone being so close, pressing his mouth against hers. Worse, using his tongue in some intimate way.

Would she feel trapped, uncomfortable, violated?

The short answer was no, she thought as As'ad moved his mouth gently against hers, teasing, caressing, but not taking. Even though his arms were around her, she didn't feel trapped. Instead she felt protected and wanted.

The wanting was new, as was the odd hungry sensation inside of her. She needed to be closer, although she couldn't say why.

She put her hands on his shoulders, feeling the strength and heat of him. As'ad would keep all in his world safe, she thought, distracted by the pressure of his lips. It would be nice to feel safe.

She inhaled the masculine scent of him, liking the fragrance. She enjoyed the feel of his body so close to hers. She grew bolder and slipped her arms around his neck, bringing her front in contact with his.

He increased the pressure of his mouth on hers. His strong hands traveled up and down her back. When he stroked his tongue against her bottom lip she gasped in shock, then felt the soft, erotic touch of his tongue against hers.

Fire shot through her. The unexpected heat made her tremble as she almost expected to go up in flames. Sensations exploded everywhere, especially in places that were usually without them. Her breasts ached in a way they never had before. Her legs felt funny—trembly and weak. She stood frozen, unsure, awkward, yet willing him to keep on kissing her.

Fortunately As'ad seemed more than capable of reading her mind. He explored her mouth with his tongue, making her tingle and want to lean into him. She ached, but couldn't say for what. She clung to him, and at last, tentatively, slowly, carefully, touched her tongue to his.

A low, masculine groan burst from him. The sound filled her with a sense of sensual power she'd never experienced before. She touched his tongue again and felt a reaction in her own body. A clenching. A wanting. A hunger.

She let herself get lost in the touching, the intimate kiss. It was heaven. She could do this for hours. She liked how her body turned to liquid. She liked everything about kissing him.

But instead of reading her mind again, he put his hands on her shoulders and eased her away from him.

"What?" she breathed.

"Perhaps another time," he said calmly. "When we are alone."

Alone? What was he…

Kayleen bit her lower lip and turned her head. While much of the village had gone about their business, there were still several obviously interested people observing their kiss. As she looked at them, they grinned. A couple waved. A few of the women laughed knowingly.

"Now no one will question that you are mine," he told her.

They arrived back at the palace shortly after ten. Kayleen met Lina in the suite she, Kayleen, shared with the girls.

"We're back," she said. "Thanks for staying with them."

"It was fun," Lina told her. "So how was your evening?"

Kayleen did her best not to blush, although she could feel heat on her cheeks. "It was fine. Good. I really liked meeting everyone in the village. They're wonderful people. Dinner was good. They let me help a little with the cooking. Everyone was friendly." She realized she was babbling and pressed her lips together, then blurted, "Nothing happened."

Lina slowly raised her eyebrows. "Excuse me?"

"Nothing happened. With As'ad. In case you were, you know, wondering. Nothing happened."

"I see." Lina smiled. "You're protesting an awful lot, especially when you consider I never asked if anything happened."

"Oh." Kayleen shifted. She needed to stop talking now or Lina would find out about the kiss. Not that Kayleen regretted it—on the contrary, it was a delicious secret she wanted to keep to herself.

Lina waited another few seconds, then walked to the door. "I'll see you later, then."

"Uh-huh. Thanks again for staying with the girls."

"Anytime," Lina said, and then left.

When she was alone, Kayleen tiptoed into the girls' bedroom. All three of them were asleep. She smoothed covers, adjusted the nightlight, then went into her own room. When she had shut the door behind her, she sighed with happiness, spun in a slow circle, then sank onto the bed.

She'd been kissed. Really kissed and it had been wonderful. Better than she could have imagined.

She'd liked everything about kissing As'ad...the taste of him, the heat, the way he'd held her. She wanted to kiss and be kissed again. Unfortunately, it wasn't the sort of thing she could simply ask him to do. Worse, she wasn't sure *why* he'd kissed her. Had he wanted to, or had he just been proving a point in the village? And why did it suddenly matter which?

Several days later As'ad returned to his rooms to find Kayleen sitting at his dining table in front of a sewing machine. Fabric covered every available surface. She'd pulled over a floor lamp for additional light and didn't notice his arrival.

His reaction was as powerful as it was instantaneous. Not about the fact that she'd once again ignored his request that she take care of all things involving the girls. Instead his body recognized the woman who had most recently brought him to his knees with a single kiss.

A virgin's kiss, he reminded himself, still annoyed and aroused at the sight of her. What should have been meaningless, done only to prove a point, had instead started a fire within him that still burned hot and strong. He'd been hungry before kissing her—now he was starved.

He hadn't been able to sleep for wanting Kayleen. The kiss had shown him potential where he'd seen very little. She'd felt right in his arms—all soft curves and innocence. Yet there had been heat in her, an instinctive passion that had matched his own.

The event should have meant nothing. He should have been able to walk away without thinking of it again. Instead it was all he could do not to cross the room, pull her to her feet and kiss her over and over until she surrendered. He wanted her wet, naked and begging. He wanted all of her.

She looked and saw him. "As'ad." She smiled. "You're back." She stood and held up both hands. "I know what you're going to say. This is a big mess. I'm sorry. I meant to get it cleaned up before you got home. I lost track of time."

Her mouth. He couldn't seem to look away from it. The shape, the hint of white teeth and nimble tongue. His brother Qadir was right—he *should* have gone to Paris and spent the week mindless in an unknown woman's bed. Now the opportunity was lost. He had a bad feeling it would be some time before he could use someone else to forget the appeal of Kayleen.

"What are you doing?" he asked, pleased his voice was so calm. Nothing of his turmoil must show.

"Making costumes for the Christmas pageant. All three girls are in it. I want the costumes to be a surprise."

"The school will not provide them?"

"I suppose they could. They asked if some of the parents could help out. I said I would. Lina found this machine for me. It's fabulous and practically sews on its own. You should see the instruction manual—it's as thick as a dictionary. But I'll figure it out."

He fingered a length of fabric. "I am sure there are employees in the palace who could do this for you."

She looked as if he'd slapped her. "But I like sewing. Besides, it'll matter more if I make the costumes for the girls."

"As you wish."

"I'm going to guess you're not into crafts."

He allowed himself a slight smile. "No."

"I learned to sew in the orphanage. I could make more clothes for a lot less. You probably don't do anything like that here."

"We do not."

She tilted her head and her long, red hair tumbled over her shoulders. His fingers curled toward his palms as he ached to touch her hair, to feel it in his hand, dragging along his chest, across his thighs.

"Did your mother sew?" Kayleen asked, jerking him back to the present.

"I don't know. She died when I was very young. I don't remember her."

The light faded from her eyes. "Oh. I'm sorry. I knew she was gone. I didn't know how old you were when it happened. I didn't mean to remind you of that."

"It is of no consequence."

"But it's sad."

"How can it be sad if the memory is gone?"

She frowned. "That is the loss of what should have been."

"I am not wounded, Kayleen. Share your concerns with someone who needs them."

"Because you feel nothing?" she asked. "Isn't that what you told me? Emotion makes you weak?"

"Exactly." Any emotion. Even passion. His current condition proved that.

"What about trust?" she asked.

"Trust must be earned."

"So many rules. So many chances to turn people away. It must be nice to have so many people in your life that there are extras."

She sounded wistful as she spoke, which made him want to pull her close and offer comfort.

Kayleen, who wanted to belong, he thought, realizing her concern for the girls came from having lived in an orphanage herself. She was all heart and would bruise easily in a harsh world. Their backgrounds couldn't be more different.

"It is a matter of control," he told her. "To need no one is to remain in charge."

She shook her head. "To need no one is to be desperately alone."

"That is not how I see it."

"That doesn't make it any less true. There's nothing worse than being alone," she told him. "I'll get this cleaned up now, and get out of your way."

* * *

Kayleen walked through the palace gardens. While she loved the beauty of the rooms inside, they were nothing when compared with the opulence of the lush gardens that beckoned just beyond her windows.

She chose a new path that twisted and turned, and once again reminded herself that she wanted to find a book on flowers in the palace library. She'd grown up gardening, but in the convent, all extra space had been taken up with vegetables. With money tight and children to feed, the nuns had not wasted precious earth on flowers.

Kayleen plucked a perfect rose and inhaled the sweet scent, then settled on a stone bench warm from the sun. She needed a moment to close her eyes and be still. Maybe then the world would stop turning so quickly.

So much had happened in such a short time. Meeting As'ad, moving here with the girls, getting ready for the holidays, kissing As'ad.

The latter made her both sigh and smile. She longed for another kiss from him, but so far there had been no opportunity. Which made her wonder if the kiss had been as interesting and appealing to him. Maybe he'd found her inexperience disgusting. Maybe he'd been disappointed.

Did it matter? There shouldn't be any more kissing between them. She had her life plan and As'ad had his. They wanted opposite things—she needed to connect and he claimed connection didn't matter. She just wasn't sure she believed him.

She heard footsteps on the path and turned toward the sound. She expected to see one of the many gardeners. What she got instead was the king.

"Oh!" Kayleen sprang to her feet, then paused, not sure what she was supposed to do.

King Mukhtar smiled. "Good afternoon, Kayleen. I see you are enjoying my garden."

"I enjoy wandering," she said with a slight bob she hoped

would pass for a curtsy and/or bow. "Have I stepped into off-limits space?"

"Not at all. I welcome the company. Come, child. Walk with me."

It didn't sound like a request.

Kayleen fell into step beside the king and waited for him to start the conversation. She was just starting to sweat the silence when he said, "Are you settled into the palace? Does it feel like home?"

She laughed. "I'm settled, but I'm not sure anywhere this magnificent will ever feel like home."

"A very politically correct answer," he told her. "Where did you grow up?"

"In an orphanage in the Midwest."

"I see. You lost your parents at an early age?"

She shrugged. "I don't know anything about my father. My mother had me when she was really young. She couldn't handle a baby so she left me with her mother. When that didn't work out, I went to the Catholic orphanage, which turned out to be a great place to grow up."

She was used to telling the story in a upbeat way that avoided making anyone feel awkward. There was no reason for the king to know that her mother had abandoned her and that her grandmother hadn't wanted to be stuck with another child to raise. No reason to talk about what it had felt like to be left on the doorstep of an orphanage on her fifth birthday, knowing no one in her family wanted anything to do with her. King Mukhtar wouldn't know what it felt like to never belong anywhere.

"So you don't remember your mother at all?" he asked.

"No." Which was fine with Kayleen.

"Perhaps you'll meet again one day," the king said.

"I would like that very much," Kayleen lied, knowing it was what the king wanted to hear.

Growing up, she'd been taught that it was her duty to forgive her mother and grandmother for abandoning her. She'd made peace with what had happened, but that didn't mean she wanted to be close now. Perhaps there *were* circumstances that, if explained, would help her understand. In truth, she wasn't interested enough to find out.

"So your past is the reason you were so against the three sisters being split up," the king said.

"Absolutely. They only have each other. They need to stay together."

"Because of you, they will."

She smiled. "Actually As'ad gets all the credit. He's the one who saved them. I'll always be grateful to him."

The king glanced at her. "I heard you rode into the desert and met with some of the villagers who live there."

"I did. I liked them a lot. It's an interesting way of life. Carrying one's roots wherever one goes."

"Most young women would be more interested in the elegant shops on our boulevards than in the desert."

She wrinkled her nose. "I'm not much into shopping." She'd never had the money for it to be serious sport and she doubted the stores the king spoke of had much in the way of bargains.

"Perhaps As'ad will take you one day," the king said.

"That would be fun, but it's not necessary. He's given me so much already."

"So you like my son?"

"Of course. He's a wonderful man. Charming and kind and patient." And a great kisser, but she wasn't going to mention *that* to the king.

"I am pleased to hear you are getting along," King Mukhtar told her. "Very pleased."

Chapter Six

Kayleen waved at Neil, As'ad's assistant, and when the man didn't lunge for her, walked past him and into the prince's office.

As'ad glanced up from his computer. "You have so intimidated my assistant that he has given up trying to stop you."

She laughed. "If only that were true. I won't stay long, I just..." She walked to the desk, started to sit down, then stopped. "I spoke with the king."

As'ad looked at her as if waiting for her point.

"Your father is a king," she said.

"Yes, I know."

"I don't. I can't be speaking with a king. That sort of thing doesn't happen to people like me. It doesn't happen to anyone. It's not normal."

"You live in the royal palace. What did you expect?"

"Not to be living here," she admitted. "It's too crazy. You're a prince."

"Again, information I have already obtained."

She sighed and sank into a chair. "You're not taking me seriously."

"You have given me no reason to. My father and I are who we have always been."

She nodded slowly. He'd grown up this way. It was impossible for him to grasp the incredibleness of the situation for her.

"I shouldn't have made you take the girls," she told him. "I didn't think the whole thing through. How they would change things for you."

He rose and walked around the desk until he was standing in front of her and she had to look way, way up to meet his gaze.

"You did not *make* me do anything."

She waved that away. "You know what I mean."

"Indeed, I do not. I was aware that adopting three American sisters would make things different and still I went forward."

Which made her wonder why he hadn't just dismissed her like an annoying gnat. Isn't that what princes did?

"I don't belong here," she told him. "I'm not used to this sort of thing."

He took her hand and pulled her to her feet. "I say who belongs and who does not."

"Off with my head?"

"That is not what I had in mind."

She knew he was going to kiss her even before he bent toward her and brushed his mouth against hers. She couldn't say how she knew, only that anticipation tightened her stomach and she forgot to breathe. Nothing else mattered but the feel of his lips on hers and the nearness of his body. He put his arms around her and drew her close.

It was like going home. The sense of belonging and safety. She'd never experienced that before and the sensation was so sweet, so perfect, she never wanted to be anywhere else. Then his mouth was moving on hers and she got lost in the kiss, the feel of his hands moving up and down her back. The heat of them. The way they pressed against each other, her body melting into his.

She put her hands on his upper arms and explored his muscled strength. When the pressure on her lips increased, she parted and was rewarded by the sensual sweep of his tongue across hers.

Somewhere along the way she must have remembered to breathe again because she moaned low in her throat. She felt tense and relaxed at the same time. She wanted this to never stop and she wanted more.

Without thinking, she rose on tiptoe, so she could press herself against him more fully. She tilted her head and kissed him back, teasing his tongue with hers.

His hands moved more urgently. One slipped to her rear, where he squeezed her curves. The contact shocked her, but excited her, too. Instinctively she arched forward, bringing her lower body in contact with his. He squeezed again, then moved his other hand to her waist before sliding it higher.

Anticipation chased away any hint of apprehension. His large hand settled on her breast with a confidence that allowed her not to be afraid. She broke the kiss so she could lean her forehead against his shoulder while he cupped her breast in his hand.

His touch was gentle and slow, but more wonderful than anything she'd ever experienced before. It was as if he knew the best way to touch her, to stroke her. When he moved his fingers across her nipple, she gasped and clung to him.

He moved his free hand to her chin, raised her head, then kissed her again. She held on to him as the room began to spin faster and faster. When he finally stepped back, she wasn't sure she could stay standing.

His eyes were dark as night, but bright with a fire that burned as hot as the one flaring inside of her. She'd never seen sexual need on a man's face before, but she recognized it now. Recognized it and knew that somehow she had caused it.

He wanted her. It was magic and filled her with delight and wonder and a sense of feminine power. Now if only she knew what to do with it.

"Kayleen."

He'd spoken her name dozens of times before, but never with

his voice so heavy and rumbling. She wanted this, she thought happily. She wanted this and so much more.

Somewhere in the distance she heard people talking. She remembered they were in his office and she had interrupted his day. The realization made her unsure of what to do next.

"I should, ah, probably go," she told him, wondering if he would ask her to stay.

"Do not worry about the king," he said instead. "My father is very pleased with you."

"How do you know? Have you talked to him?"

"I have no need. You are exactly what he wants you to be."

What? But before she could ask for an explanation, As'ad's phone rang. He glanced at his watch. "A teleconference with the British foreign minister."

"Right. Okay. I'll see you later."

She walked back to her room, wondering what it all meant. The kiss, the intimate touch, As'ad's comment that she was what the king wanted her to be. Did that mean a good nanny? A tidy guest?

Yet more reminders that this was a foreign world and not one she was likely to be comfortable in. She should be eager to escape. Yet there was a part of her that wouldn't mind staying for a very long time.

"You summoned me?" Lina asked as she breezed into the room. "And don't say you didn't. There was a definite command in your message."

"I won't deny it," As'ad told her, motioning to the sofa in the corner and joining her there.

"Am I to be punished?" she asked, a twinkle in her eye.

"You are my aunt and the woman who raised me. I have great respect for you."

"So I'm in *serious* trouble."

She didn't sound worried, but then why should she? He would never do anything to hurt her. Despite what she'd done, he had trouble being angry with her. Not that he would let *her* know that.

If he was annoyed with anyone, it was with himself for being too blind to see what was happening. It had been obvious from the beginning and he hadn't noticed.

"Shall you go first or shall I?" Lina asked.

"I called you here."

"I know, but that doesn't mean I don't have an agenda."

He nodded. "Please. Begin."

"I spoke with Zarina the other day. You claimed Kayleen as your own."

"For the moment. She created a stir in the village. I did not wish things to get awkward."

"You kissed her."

That damn kiss, he thought grimly. It had created nothing but trouble. The second kiss had been worse. Now he knew the passion between them had not been brought on by too many nights alone. It flared as bright and hot as the sun. He ached to claim Kayleen's body. But her innocence and position in his household made the situation complicated.

"To make a point," he said with a casualness he didn't feel.

"So that explains it," Lina murmured. "You have no feelings for her yourself."

None that he would admit to. "No."

"So if I wanted to introduce her to a pleasant young man, you would be agreeable?"

"I would," he lied, picturing himself ripping off the man's head. "But it will not be an issue."

"You're saying I don't know any young men, but you are wrong. I know several. One is an American. I mentioned Kayleen to him and he thought he would like to meet her. Did you know it's nearly Thanksgiving?"

"Nearly what?"

"Thanksgiving. It's an American holiday. I had forgotten myself, but the young man in question mentioned getting together with Kayleen that evening. They would both be missing home and could connect over that."

Missing home. Kayleen would, he thought, and so would the girls. They would miss the traditional dinner.

"I will arrange it," he told his aunt.

"Kayleen's date?"

"Of course not. Thanksgiving dinner for her and the girls. A traditional meal. I'll speak with the head chef right away." He turned his attention back to his aunt. "As for your young American, I doubt he exists."

"Of course he does."

"Perhaps, but he is not intended for Kayleen. You have other plans for her."

"I have no idea what you're talking about. But while we're on the subject, Kayleen is lovely, isn't she? I met her the first time I volunteered at the orphanage. She'd been here all of two weeks and yet had already settled in. I was impressed by her intelligence and her dedication to the children. She has many fine qualities."

"I will not marry her."

Lina narrowed her gaze. "No one has asked you to." Her voice was level enough, but he saw the temper in her eyes.

"You would not ask," he told her. "But you have gone out of your way to throw her in my path. Tell me, was Tahir a part of your plan? Did you arrange for him to come to the orphanage and set the events in motion?"

"I have no idea what you're talking about, but if I did, I would point out Kayleen would be a good mother. Her sons would be strong. You have to marry someone. Why not her?"

Why indeed? A case could be made for his aunt's logic. Kayleen may not have been born royal, but sometimes that was an advantage. She had an inner strength he respected—it was her heart that made him wary.

"She cares too much," he told his aunt. "She is too emotional."

"She's a woman."

"She leads with her heart. She deserves someone who can appreciate that."

Lina studied him for several seconds, then nodded. "All right. That's the one answer I can respect. It's too bad. I think she would have been good for you. Then we'll just have to find her someone else."

"She is the children's nanny."

"She deserves more than just a job. You were right, there's no young American man, but I'll find her someone." She rose and smiled. "Don't worry, As'ad. While I'm finding Kayleen a husband, I'll find you another nanny. You won't be inconvenienced."

Those should have been the words he wanted to hear, but something about them bothered him. Something he couldn't define but that created a knot in the middle of his chest.

"What is it?" As'ad asked, staring at the thick, flat cutout.

Dana grinned. "It's a turkey."

He eyed the layers of paper. "It is a turkey that has met with some unfortunate circumstances."

She giggled, then pulled the top over, creating a three-dimensional paper turkey. "It's a decoration," she told him. "They delivered a whole box of 'em. We can put them on the table and hang them from the ceiling." She glanced up at the curved, fifteen-foot ceiling. "Okay, maybe not the ceiling. But we'll put them all around."

"This is tradition?" he asked.

"Uh-huh. Along with the leaves."

The box with the flat paper turkeys had also included festive garlands in fall colors, along with silk leaves in red, brown and gold.

Pepper leaned over and grabbed a handful of leaves. "I'll put these on the table. We can make a line down the center of the tablecloth. It'll be pretty."

Nadine trailed after her younger sister, picking up the leaves that drifted to the floor. As'ad took a length of garland and followed them to the table.

"This will go on top of the leaves?" he asked.

Pepper grinned. "Uh-huh. And we need to have candles. Really tall ones. They're the prettiest." She set down her leaves, put her hands on her hips and looked at him. "How come you don't know this?"

"We don't celebrate Thanksgiving here."

Her blue eyes widened. "But you have to."

"They weren't discovered by pilgrims," Nadine told her. "America was the new world. It had to be found."

"It was lost?" Pepper asked.

"In a manner of speaking," As'ad said. "It's a celebration unique to your country. Although I believe the Canadians also celebrate Thanksgiving, but on a different day."

He waited while the two girls straightened out the leaves, then he set the garland on top. It was attractive, he thought. Very festive. Kayleen would like it. The surprise would make her happy.

He imagined her throwing herself at him, and him pulling her close. Then the vision shifted and changed so they were both naked and he was pushing his way inside of her as they—

"As'ad, what traditions do you have here?" Dana asked.

He forced his attention back to the present. This was not the time to explore sexual fantasies with the girls' nanny.

"We have many celebrations. There is the day the El Deharian armies defeated the Ottoman Empire. We also celebrate Christmas, although it is not as big a holiday here as it would have been for you back in the States."

Pepped sighed. "I worry about Santa being able to find us here."

"He'll find you and he'll enjoy the large fireplace in your room," As'ad told her. "It won't be so hard for him to get inside."

Her eyes widened. "Santa comes to the palace?"

"Of course."

"So I can write him a letter? I've been very, very good this year."

"Yes. You can write a letter. We'll arrange to have it sent through the royal post office, so it gets priority treatment."

The little girl beamed at him.

"Will there be snow at Christmas?" Dana asked as she set yet another paper turkey on the bookcase.

"We do not get snow here."

"I didn't think so." She shrugged. "I miss snow. We grew up in Michigan and we always had a white Christmas. We used to made snowmen and snow angels. Mom always had hot chocolate and cookies waiting."

"I don't remember her much," Pepper said in a whisper.

"Sure you do," Nadine told her. "She was tall and pretty, with blond hair."

There was a wistful, sad quality to her voice. It tugged at something in As'ad. Like Pepper, he had minimal memories of his mother. Perhaps his older brothers had more. He had never asked. Instead he'd been raised by a series of nannies when he'd been young and tutors when he was older. Then he'd been sent away to school. It was the expected life of a prince.

"I don't remember her," Pepper insisted, her eyes filling with tears.

He crouched in front of her. "You remember snow, don't you?"

She nodded slowly. "It's cold and white and it makes my nose red. I want snow for Christmas."

"It seems unlikely," he told her. "We live in the desert, on the edge of the ocean. This is not a cold climate. But it can still be very beautiful."

"We'll be fine," Dana told him bravely. "You'll see. It's just the change. Change is hard. For all of us."

"Agreed, but you are here now. This is where you will stay. Didn't Kayleen tell you?"

The girls exchanged glances, then looked at him.

"We don't know what we're going to do," Pepper told him. "We're supposed to stay here, with you, but what happens when Kayleen leaves?"

He straightened. "What are you talking about? She's not going anywhere."

"Yes, she is. She told us a long time ago." Dana drew in a breath. "She'll be twenty-five soon. When she's twenty-five she gets to go back to teach at the convent school where she grew up. It's what she always wanted. What we don't know is if we go with her or stay here with you."

Lina hovered by the front of the palace, not an easy thing to do when there were tour groups lining up, official visitors arriving and she was well recognized. She supposed it would make more sense to wait in her rooms until she was notified that King Hassan was in residence. But she couldn't stand the thought of being confined right now. It was far easier to walk the length of the entryway—a distance of about two hundred feet—than walk back. If nothing else, she was getting her exercise for the day.

Part of the problem was she hadn't slept for a week. She'd barely dozed the previous night and had been wide awake at four in the morning. It had taken nearly a half hour with chilled gel packs on her eyes to reduce the puffiness. Then there had been the issue of what to wear.

She'd gone through her considerable wardrobe more than once over the past few days. A dress seemed too formal, slacks too casual. In the end she'd settled on a black skirt and a silk blouse. She'd fussed over her makeup, her hair, her jewelry. It was like being sixteen again, but with all the baggage that comes with middle age. It was exhausting.

As she paced, smiled at visitors and did her best not to be recognized by the tour group moving into the palace, she told herself it was ridiculous to be so nervous. Officially she'd known

King Hassan for years. But this was the first time he was coming to El Deharia to see *her*.

"It's not a date," she murmured to herself, grateful the vast entryway was finally almost empty. "It's a…a…" She sucked in a breath, not sure what his visit was.

A large SUV drove into the courtyard, followed by a dark Mercedes. Another SUV parked behind it.

Guards stepped out, looking stern in their business suits and sunglasses. One of them moved to the rear of the Mercedes and opened the passenger-side door.

Lina walked toward the car, telling herself to be calm, to smile and speak with at least the pretense of intelligence. King Hassan stepped out into the afternoon.

He was a man of medium height and strong build. His hair was gray, as was his neatly trimmed beard. He had handsome features and an air of confidence and power about him. There were no outward symbols of his rank, yet just looking at him, it was easy to guess he wasn't like everyone else.

Lina hesitated. Normally she curtseyed when she greeted a monarch, yet that now seemed strange. Still, protocol and her upbringing won out.

But before she could offer the gesture of respect, Hassan stepped toward her, took both her hands in his and smiled at her.

"My dear Lina. You are more beautiful than I remember."

He gazed into her eyes. She stared back, seeing pleasure and humor, along with something very much like interest. Her stomach continued to flop around, but the reason changed from nerves to anticipation. A warmth stole through her and she smiled.

"Welcome, sir. All of El Deharia is pleased at your visit. Me, most of all."

He pulled her close and tucked her hand into the crook of his arm. "Hassan," he said. "You must call me Hassan. Do you forget how you mocked me in your e-mails? You can't be formal now."

They walked into the palace. "I never mocked you," she told him, liking the feel of being next to him, close to him.

"You called me a crazy old man who was too concerned about his cats."

She laughed. "I did not. You're making that up."

"Perhaps."

He smiled at her, making her heart beat wildly and her throat get dry. It had been so long since any man had affected her, she thought happily. So long since she'd let herself notice a smile, a voice, a touch.

They walked along the main corridor, toward the elevators that would take them up to the guest floors.

"How is your first project coming?" he asked. "Has As'ad noticed the lovely Kayleen?"

"Absolutely." Lina grinned. "She got lost in the desert and ended up with some local tribesmen. As'ad went after her and claimed her for his own. He says it was to keep her safe, but I think there was more to it than that. When they got back, Kayleen specifically told me nothing had happened. She was so intent on telling me that, I knew something had."

"So you are a success."

"Not yet, but I hope to be soon."

They rode up three floors and exited onto a wide, open hallway.

"Your suite is just down here," Lina told him. "It is the one you stayed in before."

When they reached the double doors, she opened one and led the way in. The rooms were large, elegantly furnished and only used for kings and heads of state.

Fresh flowers filled several vases and a large fruit basket sat on the dining room table.

"I thought we could go out to dinner tonight," she said. "There are a couple of really nice restaurants in the city with private rooms. I can give the names to your head of security so he can check them out in advance. There are a few plays we could take in and a visiting European symphony, depending on what interests you most. My brother would be delighted if you would care to ride any of his horses and I—"

Hassan crossed to her and pressed his finger to her mouth. "You can stop talking now."

She drew in a breath, then pressed her lips together. "All right."

"I am not here to be entertained or to go riding. I am here to spend time with you. You have charmed me, Lina. I had not thought that would happen again in my lifetime and I am delighted to be wrong. I sense many possibilities."

Oh, my. The man had simply put it out there. Of course, he was a king and that could have something to do with his confidence level. If only she could say the same about herself.

"I, ah…" She swallowed. "Me, too."

He laughed, then pulled her close. "So let us see where this all leads."

And then he kissed her.

Chapter Seven

As'ad watched as several members of the kitchen staff set up the dinner. There was a large turkey, along with dishes of stuffing, yams, vegetables, mashed potatoes, gravy and several pies.

"I'm starving," Pepper whispered to Dana. "Can I have just a bite?"

"No," her sister told her. "We're waiting for Kayleen, remember? It'll just be a few more minutes."

Kayleen had phoned to say she'd received the message telling her to come to As'ad's room for dinner and would be right up.

As'ad did his best to focus on the girls, on how Pepper kept sniffing the air and how Nadine gracefully danced from foot to foot in impatience.

His plan had worked perfectly—the room was decorated, the meal prepared and Kayleen would be able to celebrate her country's holiday. Yet despite the success, he couldn't shake the deep sense of outrage that stirred within him.

She was leaving in a few months? Just like that? She hadn't said anything to him, hadn't hinted. He had hired her to be nanny to the three girls *she* had insisted he adopt and now she was going to disappear?

Equally insulting was the fact that Dana said she didn't know if the sisters were staying or going. As if it was their decision to make. He was Prince As'ad of El Deharia. *He* decided who would stay and who would leave. How dare Kayleen think she could simply walk away without speaking to him.

He took out his anger on the bottle of Chardonnay he'd chosen for their dinner, jerking out the cork with more force than necessary.

Did Kayleen think it was acceptable to leave the girls so soon after bringing them to the palace? Did she think they could bear another upheaval in their lives? What about him? Was he to raise them on his own?

He didn't know what annoyed him more—the fact that she'd been making plans without consulting him or the reality that she'd been considering leaving in the first place. Not that he personally cared if she went. His outrage was all for the girls, and perhaps for the violation of her position. She was the nanny. She reported to *him*.

Apparently she was not impressed enough with his position and power. Obviously he needed to show her what it meant to deal with someone in the royal family.

He poured himself a glass of wine and drank it down. Even more annoying was her desire to cut herself off from the world. She did not belong in drab clothes, teaching at a convent school. What would happen to her there? Her bright spirit and fresh beauty would wither and die. She would grow old before her time.

It was up to him to change that. As her employer, he had a duty to protect Kayleen, even from herself. He knew best. At least here, in the palace, she would *live* her life. So how to convince her that she must stay, must serve him and be nanny to the girls?

He could order her, he thought as he poured a second glass of wine, then dismissed the idea as quickly as it formed. It pained him to admit the truth, but Kayleen was not one to take orders well, even from a prince. So he must convince her another way. He must make her see that there was more to her future than the high walls of a convent school. That there was much she would miss.

It would be one thing if she wanted to leave to live, he told himself. Perhaps to marry, although the idea of her with another man was irritating. Who would be good enough for her? Who would be patient with the unexpected virgin? Who would teach her the—

The thought formed. A solution. Perhaps unorthodox, but workable. He considered the possibilities and knew that it would be successful. A sacrifice, he thought, but not a hardship.

In time, she would thank him.

Kayleen walked into As'ad's rooms with her mind still on her work. She'd been making a lot of progress on the report he'd requested and had found out a lot of interesting information about the various reasons why some villages sent a lot of young women to college and some didn't. She wanted to discuss it all over dinner after they—

She paused, noting the room was especially dark, which didn't make sense. There had been lights in the corridor. Had she accidentally gone into the wrong room?

She reached for a switch on the wall, only to have all the lights come on, the three girls jump out from behind furniture and yell, "Surprise!"

Kayleen took a step back. "What are you up to? What's the surprise?"

And then she saw the paper turkeys covering every surface in the room. The festive fall garland, the leaves decorating the perfectly set table.

"It's Thanksgiving," Pepper said, rushing up and grabbing her hand. "We're having a real Thanksgiving dinner."

As'ad appeared. "The kitchen staff have done their best. They have never had a Thanksgiving dinner, so they apologize in advance if they didn't get everything exactly as you would have it."

Thanksgiving? Here? She'd willed herself not to think about the holiday, but it had been difficult and much of the day she'd felt sad. To walk into this was more than she could have imagined.

Dana and Nadine moved next to her. Kayleen crouched down to hug all three girls. Still holding them close, she looked up at As'ad.

"Thank you," she said, delighted by the surprise and feeling oddly emotional. "You're very thoughtful."

"I cannot take all the credit. Lina reminded me of the holiday and the girls helped with the preparations. Are you pleased?"

She rose and smiled at him. "Very. Thank you."

She'd never expected the gesture. As'ad wasn't who or what she'd expected. There was a kindness in him, a caring and sensitivity she hadn't thought possible. He was the classic handsome prince, yet he wasn't indifferent or selfish. He could have chosen to spend his life going to parties and hanging out with models and stars. Instead he worked hard and took in orphans.

It occurred to her that he was a good man, the sort of man she admired. The kind of man the Mother Superior had told her to look for when she left for college. Kayleen hadn't found anyone remotely fitting that description during her four years away. How odd she should find him now...here in El Deharia.

As'ad poured her a glass of wine as the girls dragged her to the table. "What are you thinking?" he asked, passing her the glass.

"That you're very unexpected."

"I could say the same about you."

His low voice made her insides quiver.

They served themselves from the buffet and then settled at the table. Kayleen said grace, then took her first bite of turkey.

"It's delicious. Dana, what do you think?" She looked at the girl and was surprised to see tears in her eyes. "What's wrong?"

"Nothing. This is nice. Thank you." A tear rolled down her cheek.

Pepper was crying, as well, and Nadine was sniffing into her napkin.

"I miss my mom and dad," Nadine whimpered. "I want to go home and be with them."

"Me, too," Dana said, and turned her gaze to As'ad. "You're the prince. Can't you do something?"

Kayleen felt helpless. What could she possibly say to make the situation better? She felt awful for the girls, because she understood what they were going through. Holidays were always a mixed blessing—she'd loved the specialness of the day, but it had also reminded her of how alone she was. How she had no family, no one who loved her best.

As'ad put his arm around Dana, then kissed the top of her head. "If only I could," he said quietly. "I know your pain and can tell you with time, it will get better."

"You can't know that," the preteen told him, her voice thick with bitterness. "You can't know anything about it."

"I lost my mother when I was very young. Kayleen grew up with no family. We understand exactly what you are feeling."

Dana seemed to deflate. "That doesn't help. I know it should, but it doesn't. I want to go home."

As'ad stared at her for a long moment, then said, "When I was about your age, I ran away. I was angry at my father for not recognizing that I was growing up, practically a man. I was tired of being sent away to school every year, of being different. A prince. You'll find that out as you grow. To be royal defines one."

"I'm not royal," Dana told him.

He smiled at her. "You are now. You are my daughter."

Dana fiddled with her fork. "What happened when you ran away?"

"I decided to become a camel dealer."

All three of the girls stared at him. Kayleen tried not to laugh. "Really?" she asked.

"Yes. I thought I could make a good living selling camels. I took several from the royal stable, thinking I would use them to start my business."

Her lips twitched, but she was determined to be serious. "There's a royal camel stable?"

His dark gaze settled on her, seeming to caress her with a warm, tender touch. "Of course. There is a royal everything."

Pepper took a bite of turkey and chewed. "Can I see the royal camels?"

"Certainly."

"Do they look different than regular camels?" Nadine asked.

"They wear very small crowns."

Dana grinned. "They do not."

As'ad laughed. "You're right. But they are a special breed. And they are extremely stubborn. I did not know this when I first took them, but soon they were leading *me* into the desert, rather than the other way around."

Nadine giggled. Dana joined in. "What happened?" she asked.

As'ad wove a funny tale about a boy and four stubborn, angry camels, a lost night in the desert and many disasters. By the time he was done, all three sisters had finished their dinner, gotten seconds and were eyeing the pie. The tears were gone, as were the bad memories.

This is what they would remember about their first Thanksgiving in El Deharia, Kayleen thought as she tucked them in and kissed them good-night. As'ad's story would be a part of their history and they would remember it and him for the rest of their lives.

He'd escorted them down to their suite and had waited while they got ready for bed. As she walked back into her living room, she saw he'd started a fire in the fireplace and made himself at home on the large sofa across from the flickering flames.

"It's not exactly chilly outside," she told him, knowing it made sense to sit next to him, but suddenly feeling shy.

"I thought you would appreciate the ambience. More memories of home, but happy ones I hope."

She walked over to the sofa and sat down at the far end. "There are a lot of happy ones," she said, then turned to him. "Thank you for tonight. For the surprise and for helping the girls through a difficult time. This is their first holiday season without their parents and it's going to be hard for them."

"They will need both of us to get through," he said.

"I agree." She was a little surprised that he saw it that way, though. "I didn't think you wanted much to do with them."

"They are charming girls with much potential. I find I enjoy spending time with them."

"I'm glad."

"And you?" he asked, his dark gaze seeming to see into her soul. "What do you think of them?"

"I adore them. Why do you ask?"

"Because you plan to leave them."

She opened her mouth, then closed it. Embarrassment made her stare at the fire. She battled guilt, as if she'd done something wrong. She knew she should have talked to him before—so he learned of her plans from her and not someone else. But she'd been afraid of what he would think of her.

"They told you," she murmured.

"Dana said you planned to return home on your twenty-fifth birthday. That you would lock yourself away and teach at the convent school."

When he said it, her dreams seemed small and pointless. "As you say, it's my home."

"A place we cannot always return to. What of your commitment to the girls?"

"I don't know," she admitted. "I haven't really thought anything through. This was planned a long time ago. I didn't expect to be their nanny."

"You are the one who insisted I adopt them. You *are* the most stable adult presence in their lives. Would you subject them to more upheaval by leaving them so soon after they came to be here? Are they nothing to you?"

"No. Of course not." She hated what he was saying. "I don't know what I was going to do. Of course I'd help you hire someone else. Someone to replace me."

"Would you? Or was your plan to take them with you?"

She ducked her head. "I thought of that, too."

"Did you think that would be allowed? This is El Deharia. No one may take royal children from the country without their parents' permission. I will not give it."

Kayleen could only stare at him. Of course. Thanks to her, he *was* their father and his rules applied. She hadn't thought that part through, either.

"It's all a mess."

"No decision has to be made now," he said. "We will find a solution together. Do you have any other secrets you are keeping from me?"

"What? No. Never. And I would have told you about leaving." She leaned toward him. "As'ad, I wasn't trying to trick you about anything. I was desperate for Tahir not to take the girls back to his village."

Somehow he wasn't at the far end of the sofa anymore, she thought as he reached out and lightly stroked her cheek. "I believe you."

"Good, because it's true. I just…" She had a hard time stringing words together. His touch was very distracting. "I love your country. It's beautiful. I love the modern city and the wildness of the desert. I love your people, the kindness of them. You were right about Tahir only wanting to do the right thing, even if I don't agree with him. I've been learning so much about the villages while researching my project for you. This is an amazing place."

"But it is not home?"

She shook her head slowly. "I feel safe at the convent. That probably sounds stupid to a man like you."

"Feeling safe is important, especially when one did not grow up with that benefit. But there is so much more for you to experience than what you will find behind the convent walls."

"I like the convent walls."

"They lock you in."

"They shelter you."

He smiled gently. "From life. That is not a good thing."

Getting back had been her goal from the moment she'd been told she must leave and live in the world. Those words had broken her heart. It was like being thrown out of her home.

"Those walls protect me," she told him.

He looked at her intently. "*I* will protect you."

Then he leaned in and kissed her.

It was as if she'd been waiting for his kiss all her life. The second his mouth touched her, she felt both relief and an odd tension.

His lips were warm and firm, asking rather than taking, making her want to give all that he asked and more. He brushed against her, exploring, remembering perhaps. She remembered everything about their heated kiss in the desert. The feel of his body against hers, the hard planes and strength of him. The way he'd held her so tenderly, the taste and heat of him.

Those memories combined with the wonder of his kiss to make her strain forward, as she eagerly waited to experience it again. She parted without being asked and was rewarded when he licked her bottom lip before slipping inside.

He kissed her deeply, exploring all of her. She put her hands on his shoulders, as much to steady herself as to touch him, then kissed him back, stroking, dueling, dancing. It was magical, something more wondrous than she'd ever imagined. It was as if she were melting from the inside out.

Again and again he kissed her, taking his time, making her feel as if the magic could go on forever. He stroked her back, moving up and down. Oddly, that touch made her want to squirm in place. If only he would touch her breasts again, she thought hazily. If only he would put his hands there, like he had before.

And because that's what she wanted and because she trusted him fully, she let him ease her onto the sofa, until she was nearly lying down.

He pulled back and stared into her eyes. "You are so beautiful," he murmured before kissing her cheekbones, her nose, her forehead, then her jaw.

Beautiful? Her? She'd seen her reflection a thousand times. Sometimes she thought she might be pretty, but other times, she knew she was just like everyone else.

"Your skin is so soft and pale," he continued as he nibbled his way down her jaw to her neck. It both tickled and aroused, so she stayed very still, wanting him to continue forever.

"Then you blush and the fiery color delights me."

"I'm a redhead," she whispered. "Blushing comes with the package."

"It is a glorious package." He touched her hair. "So cool to the touch. I have fantasies about your hair."

"Seriously?"

"Seriously."

He kissed her again and she kissed him back, but all the while she was wondering what fantasies he could have about her hair? It was just hair, wasn't it? Long and wavy and very red.

He kissed her chin, then trailed down her neck. She'd never thought about a man's lips on her neck and was unprepared for the electric sensations that shot through her, making her toes curl and her insides tighten.

He put his hand on her belly. Even through the layers of clothing, she felt the warmth and each individual finger. He moved up slowly, so slowly. Her breath caught in anticipation.

Touch me there, she whispered to herself, closing her eyes and waiting until he finally settled his palm on her breast.

The feeling was exquisite. She wanted more of that, but didn't know how to ask. He kissed her ear, which was a distraction, then nipped her earlobe, which was delicious. Everything felt so good that she barely noticed when he unbuttoned the front of her dress and eased the fabric open.

She supposed her first instinct should have been to cover herself, but she didn't want to. She wanted to know what it would feel like to have his hand there, on her breast, with only her bra between them.

And then she knew. He touched her gently, almost teasing, fingers lightly brushing her skin. He moved against her tight nipple. She groaned. It wasn't a sound she'd ever made before and she wanted desperately to have reason to make it again.

He explored both breasts, then reached behind her to unfasten her bra. He eased his hand under the cup and touched her again. This time bare skin on bare skin.

It was amazing, she thought, her body practically shaking. She hadn't known she was capable of such sensations. More. She wanted more. More touching, more naked, more kissing, more everything.

As'ad drew back and stood. She opened her eyes and wondered what she'd done wrong. Why was he stopping? Then he bent down and picked her up in his arms. He cradled her against him and kissed her, even as he began to walk across the rug toward the bedroom.

It was the most romantic moment of her life. As they stepped into the darkness of her bedroom, she knew that she wanted to be with him, to experience making love with him. Perhaps there should have been questions or fears, but her mind was free of both. She only knew that her body seemed to recognize him and welcome him. He made her tremble and feel and she wanted more of that.

He lowered her to her feet, then closed the door behind them and turned on a bedside lamp. The light was dim, which was probably better, because as much as she wanted more, she was a little nervous about being naked. People did get naked when they made love, didn't they?

She thought about asking, but then he was kissing her again and speaking seemed really unimportant. His hands were everywhere, gently easing her dress from her shoulders so it puddled at her feet, then removing her bra.

Even as he stroked her tongue with his, he put both his hands on her breasts, cupping the curves and teasing her nipples with his thumbs. It was good—better than good. It was amazing.

Her body was suddenly a great unknown to her. She didn't have any idea about what she would experience next, but she wanted it all.

When he bent his head down and took her breast in his mouth, she gasped, then grabbed him to help herself stay standing. Fire roared through her, settling between her legs where the heat grew.

She knew the mechanics of what went on between a man and a woman, but she'd never imagined it could be so *good*. He moved back and forth between her breasts, licking them with his tongue, sucking until she wanted to scream. It was amazing and arousing and intriguing.

When he moved them to the bed, she went eagerly, wanting to know what else there could be, what other experiences she could have. He removed the rest of her clothes and she shocked herself by not minding that she was naked. Not when he stared down at her with a fire even she could see in his eyes.

"I want you," he breathed. "All of you. Kayleen, I want to touch you and taste you and be inside of you. But I will not take what isn't offered."

He had her at "I want you." She reached out to touch his hand, then gently tugged until he knelt next to her.

"You are eager?" he asked quietly.

"I'm shameless. I want you to touch me." She couldn't say the other stuff, but she was thinking it. She wanted to know what it was like to be with a man—to be with *him*.

He removed his shoes and socks, then shrugged out of his shirt. His chest was broad and muscled, with a light dusting of hair she itched to touch. Then he stretched out next to her and smiled.

"I will go slowly," he told her, tracing the shape of her mouth with his finger. "Tell me if anything frightens you or hurts you and I will stop."

"I know it's going to hurt when you, um, well, you know."

His smile faded. "It will, for a moment. Do you wish to stop?"

She shook her head.

"Good. Neither do I."

He took her hand in his and brought it below his waist. She felt the hard thickness of him.

"This is what you do to me," he told her. "This is what touching you does to me."

His words and his arousal filled her with a feminine power she'd never experienced before. It hadn't occurred to her that a man could *want* her that way. Or any way. A shiver raced through her as desire and anticipation both grew.

He leaned in and kissed her again. His hand settled on her stomach, an unfamiliar weight. She told herself not to think about it, but then he was moving down her belly to the apex of her thighs.

His touch was light and gentle, more teasing than insisting. When he reached the curls only slightly darker than her hair color, she wasn't sure what to do.

A single finger eased between the curls. It explored her, which was really sort of nice. She wouldn't mind him touching her more if he—

He brushed against the very center of her. She'd heard about that place, of course, but had wondered how she would ever know if she was touched there. Stupid question, she thought happily as delicious, erotic fire raced through her. She knew. How could she not know?

He moved against that place again and her legs fell open of their own accord. She found it difficult to breathe.

He continued to touch her there, moving lightly across that

single spot, rubbing it, circling it, making her body tremble and heat and strain. She barely noticed when he stopped kissing her because his touch was so exquisite. She closed her eyes and let herself get lost in the sensation.

Around and around. He moved against her, going faster now. She found herself pulsing her hips in time with his touch. She strained but wasn't sure toward what. He bent down and took her nipple in his mouth. The combination of sensations made her gasp.

It was too much. A direct connection between her legs and her breasts. She grabbed at the sheets, trying to push herself toward…toward…

Her body tensed. She felt every muscle clench, which probably wasn't a good thing, but what he was doing felt too good for her to stop. Then time seemed to pause as she hovered on the brink of—

The wave of sensation caught her off guard. It was unlike anything she'd experienced before. Liquid pleasure poured through her as her muscles contracted. It was frenzied and amazing and she was terrified if she did anything at all, it would end suddenly.

But the moment went on and she lost herself in what she realized was her first orgasm. She allowed herself to breathe and the bliss continued. Tension faded, muscles relaxed, until she felt content and satisfied and more than a little shocked such a thing was possible.

As'ad moved his fingers away. She opened her eyes and stared up at him.

"I want to do that again," she told him.

He laughed. "So you enjoy the lovemaking?"

"Who wouldn't? Can that happen again? Can it happen now?"

He rose onto his hands and knees. "As you wish, Kayleen. We will try another game. But a gentle one. I don't want you to hurt later."

Later was a long time away, she thought as he settled between her legs and gently parted her curls.

It was obvious he was going to kiss her *there,* which was shocking and something she probably should refuse. Except what he'd done before had been so amazing. Could this be as good?

She sank back onto the bed and closed her eyes. A soft whisper of breath was her only warning, then his mouth pressed against her and his tongue touched her more intimately than she'd ever thought possible.

It was like kissing, but a billion times better, she thought as all the air rushed from her lungs. The steady flick of his tongue was impossible to resist. She gave herself over to the sensation, to the tension that quickly tightened all her muscles. Despite the awkwardness of the position and her lack of experience, she found herself pushing toward the pleasure goal.

She wanted that experience again. She wanted the waves, but this time from his tongue. She wanted him to push her higher and closer and she wanted it now!

She found herself digging her heels into the bed as she pushed her body against him. Impatience battled with arousal. The journey was exquisite, but the destination was—

He slipped a finger inside of her. The action was shocking enough to make her gasp. She waited for pain or pressure, but there was only the need to push down on that finger, to have him fill her.

He continued to lick her, making her body tense more. Then he moved his finger in and out, matching the rhythm of his tongue, taking her up and up and up until she had no choice but to crash back to earth.

The second journey down was even better than the first. She felt herself cry out and tried to stifle the noise. Her body shuddered as her release filled every cell and pleasured every nerve. It was too much. She hadn't known that anything like this was possible.

As'ad straightened, then moved next to her. He touched her all over, caressing, but perhaps reassuring. She stared into his dark eyes.

"I didn't know," she whispered.

"There is more."

That made her laugh. "Not possible."

"I will show you."

Would he? Could they explore this together? "I'd like that."

He stroked her face. "What is your wish, Kayleen? For me to leave now? You remain an innocent."

"Technically," she murmured, although she knew a whole lot more than she had an hour ago. She gathered her courage and put her hand on his bare chest. His skin was smooth, his muscles hard. "Be in me."

"You are sure?"

She smiled. "Very."

He pulled her into a sitting position, then stood beside the bed. After removing his slacks and briefs, he stood in front of her.

She'd never seen a man naked before. Art really didn't count. He was bigger than she'd expected.

She stroked the length of him, liking the velvety smoothness of the skin and the way he felt like a rock underneath.

"You're not going to fit," she told him as she wondered if women did to men what he had done to her. Touching with their mouths. Would that be nice?

He chuckled and reached for his slacks. "It will fit."

He removed a square of plastic, then sat on the bed. She was going to ask what he was doing, then remembered that the act itself had consequences. He was making sure she had nothing to worry about.

She was about to ask him why he had a condom in his pocket, then he eased her onto her back and slipped between her legs.

The position felt a little strange and she didn't know what to do with her feet or her hands. Did she just lie there? Was she supposed to move? Should she keep quiet or did people talk?

"This will hurt a little," he warned. "You are prepared?"

She nodded and braced herself.

He smiled. "Perhaps you could pretend you are excited."

"What? Oh, sorry. I'm just nervous."

"Perhaps I can distract you."

He reached between her legs and began to rub her again. She immediately relaxed as the familiar tension started. If he kept that up for very long, she would come again.

But before she could get far along the path, he stopped and she felt something hard pushing against her. She took a deep breath as he slowly, slowly filled her.

The pressure was unfamiliar and a little uncomfortable, but not bad. There was more and more until at last he said, "I am in."

She opened her eyes and smiled at him. "I'm wild now."

He smiled in return. "It will take a little more for you to be wild, but this is a start. I would like you to touch me."

Oh. "All right," she murmured, not sure where or how.

She stroked the length of his arms, then put her hands on his back. He withdrew and pushed in again. This time she tilted her hips slightly, taking him more easily.

By the fifth time, she didn't have to think about the touching—it just happened on her own. And there was a subtle tension between her legs. Different from what happened before, but still compelling.

She closed her eyes and lost herself in the rhythm of him making love to her, filling her, pushing deep inside of her, making her ache and want. He moved faster and his breathing increased. More and more until he groaned and was still.

He murmured her name as he held her. She wrapped her arms around him, feeling the weight of him, a stretch in her hips, and knew that everything had changed forever.

Chapter Eight

Kayleen spent the following morning not sure what to think. Her evening with As'ad played over and over in her mind like a very naughty movie. Every time she remembered him touching her, she felt all squishy inside.

She hadn't expected to sleep, but after he'd gone back to his room, she'd fallen into her bed and the next thing she knew it was morning. She'd awakened happy and sore and just a little out of sorts. She didn't regret what had happened, but she certainly felt...different.

As'ad had been so great, she thought as she waved to the girls as they climbed into the Town Car that took them to school each day. He'd been gentle and patient and funny and sexy. He'd been everything she could have imagined a man being. More, she reminded herself. He was *better* than anything—or anyone— she could have imagined.

And the whole being together thing had been amazing. Who had thought that up? Why hadn't she understood before? Was this what her Mother Superior had meant about getting out in the world?

Kayleen covered her mouth. She doubted that was exactly what the other woman had meant. Still, she understood now that there were possibilities. Things she'd never known about. Did she want to give up that kind of a relationship forever? Did she want to get married and have a family? Did she—

"Good morning, Kayleen. How are you?"

She looked up and saw Lina walking toward her. Kayleen had the sudden thought that the other woman knew. That everyone knew. It had to be obvious, didn't it? Could they tell? Was her appearance different? Was there something in her eyes?

The crash of guilt was as powerful as it was unexpected. Yes, her night with As'ad had been wonderful and exciting, but what was she thinking, giving herself to a man like that? They weren't in love. She wasn't sure she knew what being in love with a man felt like. So she'd just given herself to him? Why? Because he'd made her feel good? Would she give herself to anyone who asked?

"Kayleen?" Lina frowned. "What's wrong? Are you ill?"

"I'm fine," she said, trying to act normal, which was difficult. She suddenly couldn't remember what normal was.

"What happened? You're flushed. Are you sure you feel all right?"

Kayleen ducked her head. Guilt quickly turned to shame as she realized she was not the person she'd always thought. "I'm not sick. It's nothing. I just... I can't... I have to go. Please excuse me."

She turned and ran, but no matter how fast she went, she couldn't escape herself.

As'ad finished with his tie and reached for his jacket. The door to his suite burst open and Lina stepped inside. He raised his eyebrows.

"I did not hear you knock," he said mildly, in too good a mood to mind the intrusion. Last night he had shown Kayleen the possibilities. She would quickly realize that returning to the convent school was not the right path for her. She would want to stay in the world—in *his* world. All would be well and very shortly she would come and thank him.

Perhaps they could continue to be lovers, he thought absently. He had enjoyed his time in her bed. She had been passionate and responsive. Just thinking about her soft cries made him want her again. They could pleasure each other and—

"I can't believe it," Lina said, stepping in front of him, her expression stern. "I can't believe you did it."

He shrugged into his jacket. "Did what?"

"You slept with Kayleen."

He shrugged. "It is not for you to criticize."

"What?" Her voice was high-pitched and carried a tone that warned him there was danger ahead.

He decided to change tactics. "Kayleen is nearly twenty-five. While it is very kind of you to be concerned about her welfare, she is more than capable of taking care of herself."

Lina put her hands on her hips. "Are you kidding me? That's it? That's all you have to say? As'ad, you are a prince. You defiled a virgin under the king's roof. You don't get to escape by telling me she's an adult and therefore responsible for her decisions."

Defiled a virgin? Did she have to say it like that? He shifted uncomfortably. "I did not take anything that wasn't offered."

"Oh, there's an excuse."

"Lina, you will not speak to me this way."

"Of course I will." She glared at him, her outrage clear. "As'ad, I am Kayleen's friend. I brought her into this house. I'm responsible for her."

"You wanted me to marry her."

"I considered it a possibility. I thought you would be a good match. You weren't supposed to take her virginity. She was raised by nuns. She's nearly twenty-five and has had what, a dozen dates?"

He refused to feel guilty. He was Prince As'ad and because of that, whatever he chose to do was the right thing. And yet there was a nagging voice in the back of his head that pointed out he hadn't thought things through.

"She planned to return to the convent school," he told Lina. "She was going to bury herself there."

"So you decided to change that? If you don't want her, who are you to destroy her life?"

"Her life is not destroyed." He resented the implication. "I honored her."

"Oh, please. It was never for you to decide what she did with her life. It was never for you to judge. You took the one thing she would want to give her husband. Now she can't go back to the convent school and you'll have no use for her. Then what? She's ruined, As'ad, and you did it. Kayleen isn't the type to take that lightly. She had choices before. You've taken them away from her."

He turned from his aunt and walked to the French doors leading to the balcony. While Lina made things more dramatic than they needed to be, he understood her point.

He'd wanted Kayleen and he'd taken her. It had happened before—dozens of times. Hundreds. Women were always delighted to be with him. But there was a large difference between them and Kayleen. The women he enjoyed were experienced. They understood how the game was played. Kayleen didn't even know there was a game.

She had given herself eagerly, sensually. She'd enjoyed their lovemaking. He'd opened her eyes to the possibilities, but he had also taken something that couldn't be returned.

His aunt's words echoed in his head. That he had defiled a virgin under the roof of the king. There was a time when, prince or not, such an offense would result in his death. Virginity was a prize to be given to a husband. It was a gift of honor. Something she had no more.

He turned back to Lina, intent on explaining, once again, that he'd only had Kayleen's best interests in mind. That it was important that she not lock herself away and ignore the world. But was that his only motivation?

Had there been some part of him that had wanted to be her first time? Some part of him that had wanted to claim her for himself because he knew he could?

"I will marry her," he said firmly, the words surprising him. He paused, waiting for the sense of being trapped to rise up inside of him. Waiting for the protests he must feel, but there was nothing.

It occurred to him that because he did not plan to love his wife, Kayleen was an excellent choice. As good as any other he could think of. He already liked her. She was spirited and beautiful, he enjoyed her company. She was good with children and had a sharp mind. While she knew nothing of the lifestyle of a royal bride, she would learn quickly. She would provide him with strong sons. And just as important, she was not the type to make unreasonable demands. She would be grateful for his proposal and treat him with respect.

Lina stared at him. "You'll what?"

"I will marry her. I accept my responsibility in what has occurred. Kayleen deserves more than having her gift taken in a thoughtless manner. While she gave herself to me willingly, I do not believe she had thought through the ramifications of our night together."

"That's why they call it 'swept away,'" Lina murmured, then nodded slowly. "You are sure?"

"I will speak to her this morning. I have a meeting in fifteen minutes, but after that I will explain what has to be done. She is a sensible woman. She will understand the great honor I bestow upon her and be pleased."

"How I wish I could be there for that conversation."

"Why do you say that?" he asked.

His aunt smiled at him. "I would tell you to phrase things differently, but you won't listen. For what it's worth, I think you have chosen well, As'ad. I hope things work out the way you want them to."

"They will. I am asking Kayleen to marry me. What more could she want?"

Lina's smile widened. "I can't think of a single thing."

Kayleen ran and ran until she found herself outside. The bright, sunny morning seemed to be mocking her as she wandered through the curving paths. How could everything here be so beautiful when she felt so awful inside?

What had she done? How could she have slept with As'ad? A few kisses and she'd given in? What did that make her?

She found a bench and sat down. The stone was warm to her touch, almost as if it were trying to offer comfort. Her eyes burned as she longed for someone to talk to. Someone to advise her. But who? She didn't feel comfortable discussing something so personal with the other teachers she'd worked with. Especially after moving to the palace. She was too ashamed to call her Mother Superior back home. Normally she would go to Lina, but how to explain to her what she'd done? As'ad was Lina's nephew.

Besides, Kayleen couldn't bear to see disappointment in her friend's eyes.

All the regrets she'd been so happy not to feel seemed to crash in on her. Not regret for what she'd done, but for the consequences, which made her horribly weak. Her regrets were about her future, not her past.

How could she return home now? How could she walk into that place where she'd grown up and had longed to return, knowing she had given in to the first man who asked? It wasn't that she feared punishment, it was that she didn't know who she was anymore.

She stood abruptly and started walking. An odd sound caught her attention.

She turned toward it and saw a large cage filled with doves.

They were beautiful, so white and lovely in the sunlight. She watched them hop from perch to perch.

Her dream was gone, she thought. Her plans, her hopes. Now she was trapped here. Nanny to the girls until they were too old to need her or until As'ad replaced her. She was at his mercy. And then what? Another job? Where? Doing what?

She didn't know who she was anymore. What she wanted. What she should do.

Impulsively she leaned toward the cage and opened the door. The doves chirped in excitement, then in a rush, flew out and up, disappearing into the brilliant blue sky.

"Fly away," she whispered. "Fly and be free."

"I do that myself."

Kayleen jumped and turned toward the speaker. She was stunned to find the king standing on the path.

Horror swept through her. She'd just set free royal doves.

"I... I..."

King Mukhtar smiled kindly. "Don't worry, child. It's difficult to resist setting them loose. There is no need for concern. They always return. It is their nature. This is their home. They can't escape their destiny."

She knew he meant the words to be reassuring, but they cut through her. Yesterday she had known her own destiny, but today she was less sure. What was her place? Where did she belong? What happened now?

"Are you enjoying living at the palace?" the king asked. "You are treated well?"

His question nearly made her laugh. But she was afraid that if she started to laugh, she wouldn't stop and then she would start crying. Hysterics would lead to a lot of questions she didn't want to answer.

"Everything is lovely," she said, doing her best to keep her emotions in check. "The palace is beautiful. I've been studying the history of the building and of your people. There is a long tradition of bravery in battle."

"The desert runs in our blood. We were warriors long before we were rulers."

"It must be difficult to leave the desert," she told him. "The beauty, the wildness, the tradition. The nomads live as they always have."

"With few modern conveniences," he said with a smile. "Much can be endured if one has excellent plumbing."

She gave a little giggle, which seemed to take a sharp turn at the end. She swallowed the sound. "But to walk in the steps of those who have gone before would be a fair compensation."

"So says the woman who has not experienced desert life. Spend a week with my people and then we will have this conversation again."

She nodded. "I would like that."

She spoke the truth. There was something appealing about simplicity right now. About having the rules of one's life spelled out. Too many choices could be complicated.

If she had never left the convent school in the first place, she wouldn't have met As'ad and none of this would have happened. Yet was it equally wrong to hide from the world? To take the safe and, therefore, easy road? To never test herself? Is that what she'd been supposed to learn?

"I just don't know," she said.

The king looked quizzical. "What troubles you, child?"

"Nothing." She felt tears burning in her eyes. "I... I'm sorry. I don't feel well. Please excuse me."

She gave a little bow, then hurried away. When she'd taken a turn in the path and knew she was out of sight, she began to run. The only problem was there was nowhere else to go.

As'ad walked to Kayleen's suite, knocked, then en-tered. He found her in her room, curled up on the bed, sobbing as if her heart was broken.

He stared at her for a moment, feeling both compassion and a sense of certainty that his good news would erase her tears.

He allowed himself to anticipate her sweet kisses when he proposed. How she would be so excited and grateful. Perhaps they would make love again. He was more than ready, although he would have to be careful so that he did not hurt her. She was new to the sensual world and too much attention in too short a time would leave her sore.

He walked to the side of the bed. "Kayleen."

"Go away."

"I will not. Sit up. I wish to speak to you."

"No. I don't want to talk. This isn't your problem."

"Of course it is. I caused it."

She continued to cry, which surprised him. She'd seemed fine when he'd left her last night. A woman should not be left alone with her thoughts. It only created trouble.

"Kayleen—"

"Go *away*."

He considered the situation, then sat on the edge of the bed and pulled her upright. She ducked her head, refusing to look at him. He drew her against him.

"It is not as bad as all that."

"Of course it is." Her body shook with the force of her sobs. "I have betrayed everything I believe in. I'm not the person I thought. I gave myself to you without thinking it through. I barely know you. I don't love you. You're just some guy. What does that say about me?"

Some guy? He was Prince As'ad of El Deharia. He was royal and a sheik. Women *begged* him to claim them for just a single night.

"I honored you," he told her curtly.

"It wasn't an honor to me."

What? He pushed away his annoyance. She was emotional, he told himself. She wasn't thinking clearly.

"Kayleen, we share a connection with the girls. You see me as a friend and someone you can trust. It is natural you would turn to me easily."

She looked at him, her eyes swollen and red. "It's not natural to me. I'm supposed to wait until I'm in love and married."

"Sometimes it is difficult to resist the pull of sensual need."

She hiccuped. "You're saying I gave in because I wanted to do it and you just happened to be there? That's supposed to make me feel better?"

Why was she deliberately misunderstanding him? "Not at all," he said through gritted teeth. "I'm saying that I am an experienced man. I know what to do to awaken that part of a woman."

"So you tricked me? While I appreciate the effort, it's not working. I have a responsibility in this. I have to deal with what happened, what I did and what it says about me."

"I did not trick you."

She shifted away and stood. "Whatever. You can go now."

"I am not leaving," he said as he rose to his feet. "Kayleen, you are missing the point of my visit."

She wiped her cheeks with her fingers. "What's the point?"

Not exactly the opening he'd imagined. He cleared his throat. "It occurs to me that you were not in a position to consider the ramifications of what happened to us. You were lost in the moment, not realizing that by giving in to me you were destroying your most precious gift and—"

Fresh tears filled her eyes. "How could you?" she breathed and ran into the bathroom, slamming the door behind her.

He stared in disbelief. She'd walked away from him?

He followed her to the closed door. "Kayleen, please come out here at once."

"Go away. I have to figure this out and you're not helping."

He opened the door and stepped into the bathroom. "You will listen to me. I am here to make this better. I am here to fix your problem."

She shook her head. "You can't fix anything. I've lost everything I wanted."

"You have lost nothing. You are not a woman to be locked

away. You deserve more than that and I am going to give it to you. Think of being married, of having a family to fill your day, children of your own." He paused to give her a chance to brace herself for the honor he would bestow upon her.

"Kayleen, I will marry you."

He smiled at her, waiting for her tears to dry. Instead more fell. Perhaps she did not understand.

"You will be my wife. You will live here, with me. In the palace. I have taken your virginity, therefore I will return your honor to you by marrying you. You will carry my name."

He waited, but she said nothing. She didn't even look at him.

"All right. I see you are having trouble understanding all this. It is unlikely you ever allowed yourself to dream of such a life. In time you will be able to believe this has truly happened. Until then, you can thank me and accept. That is enough."

She raised her gaze to stare at him. Something hot and bright burned in her eyes, but it wasn't happiness or gratitude.

"Thank you?" she repeated, her voice high and shrill. "*Thank you?* I'm not going to thank you. I wouldn't marry you if you were the last man alive."

He was so stunned that when she shoved him, he took a step back. The bathroom door slammed shut in his face and he heard the bolt shoot home.

Chapter Nine

"Take another drink of tea," Lina said soothingly.

Kayleen wrinkled her nose. The brew was a nasty herbal concoction that tasted like wet carpet smelled, but her friend assured her it would help. At this point, Kayleen was open to any suggestions.

She finished the mug and set it on the table, then grabbed a cookie she didn't want to get the taste out of her mouth.

"Better?" Lina asked.

Kayleen nodded because it was expected. In truth she didn't feel better, she felt awful. She still couldn't get herself to understand what had happened or how she'd so quickly and easily lost her moral compass. Yes, As'ad was handsome and charming and an amazing kisser, but she should have been stronger than that.

Lina sighed. "I can see by the look on your face that you're still beating yourself up. You need to let it go. Men like my nephew have been tempting women since the beginning of time."

"It's not that I don't appreciate the information," Kayleen murmured. "It's just..."

"It doesn't help," Lina said kindly.

"Sort of. I feel so stupid and inexperienced."

"At least you're more experienced than you were."

Despite everything, Kayleen smiled. "That's true. I won't fall for that again. Next time, I'll resist."

Assuming there was a next time. Her last meeting with As'ad had ended badly. He had to be furious.

"He was serious about marrying you," Lina told her. "Don't dismiss that."

"I didn't have a choice. He didn't propose—he commanded, then he expected me to be grateful. I know he's part of your family and you love him, but that wasn't a proposal, Lina. He's just so…"

"Imperious?"

"Among other things."

And it hurt, Kayleen admitted to herself. That he would talk to her that way. If he'd come to her with compassion, truly understanding what she was going through, she would have been appreciative of what he offered. She might have been tempted to say yes. At least then her world would have been set right. But to act the way he did?

"I understand," Lina said. "As'ad is like most princes—used to being impressive. He handled the situation badly and violated your romantic fantasy at the same time."

Kayleen frowned. "I don't have a romantic fantasy."

"Don't you?"

An interesting question. She'd never really thought about getting married and having a family, so she'd never really thought about a proposal. But if she had, it would have been different. Flowers and candlelight and a man promising to love her forever.

The image was clear enough to touch, she thought ruefully.

"Okay, maybe I did. Maybe I didn't allow myself to believe it would ever happen, but deep down inside, I wanted more than instructions and an order to feel grateful."

Lina winced. "That bad?"

"Oh, yeah. The only good news is I slammed the bathroom door in his face. I don't think that happens to As'ad very much."

She touched her stomach, as if she could rub away the knot that had formed inside. If As'ad was angry enough, he could send her away and she might never see the girls again. "How mad is he?"

"He's less angry and more confused. From his perspective, he did a wonderful thing."

Kayleen resisted the need to roll her eyes. "I'll write a thank-you note later."

"His world is a different place," Lina said quietly. "Like his brothers, he has been raised to know that he will be expected to serve his country, that his life, while privileged, comes with a price. Growing up it was difficult for him to know who truly wanted to be friends because they liked him, and who wanted to be friends with a prince. He made mistakes and slowly learned whom he could and could not trust."

Kayleen could relate to the pain of not having real friends, of wanting to find a place that was safe.

"But he had his brothers."

"Yes, and that helped. Still, as he got older, there were many girls, then women, willing to do anything to make him fall in love with them. Or at least sleep with them."

Kayleen felt heat on her cheeks. "Like me."

"Not like you at all. You didn't throw yourself at him or pretend to be interested. You were caught up in circumstances. As'ad shares blame in what happened. I'm simply saying he has a different perspective. While his proposal was meant to be the right thing, he handled it badly. As'ad isn't skilled in dealing with emotion. His father saw to that. He was taught that emotions make a man weak. He avoids them."

Kayleen had heard that from him and still found it hard to believe anyone could think of love as a weakness. Love gave a person infinite power and strength.

"Is there any part of you that wants to marry As'ad?" Lina asked.

The question was unexpected. Kayleen considered her reply. "It seems the easy way out."

"Which does not give me an answer."

Did she want to marry As'ad? In truth, the idea wasn't horrible. He was a nice man and the thought of spending every night in his bed was thrilling beyond words, which probably meant she was in even worse shape than she'd first thought.

But there was more to marriage than the physical, she thought. There was a lifetime of connection. Did she want to have children with As'ad? Be a true mother to the three girls? Live in El Deharia forever?

The swell of longing surprised her. The need to belong—to have roots and a home—swept over her until it was difficult to breathe. She'd been on the outside looking in all her life. To be inside now was more than she'd ever dreamed. But to marry without love?

"I'm tempted," she admitted. "Marrying As'ad would give me so much. But I'm not in love with him."

"Practical marriages are a time-honored tradition," Lina reminded her.

"I'm not royal. He's a prince. Doesn't that matter?"

"The old ways have changed. Now a prince may pick his bride. You have qualities such as honor, intelligence and kindness that make you everything I could want for As'ad."

The gentle praise made Kayleen want to cry again. "Thank you," she whispered.

"There is more to consider," Lina said. "As the wife of a prince, you would be in a position to do good on a grand scale, both here and in the world. You could devote yourself to many worthwhile causes, assuming you have time after you and As'ad start to have children."

Lina painted a picture that was difficult to resist. "Allow me to use some of the intelligence you claim I have to point out you're manipulating me."

Lina smiled. "Perhaps a little, but not as much as I could. If I truly wanted to convince you against your will, I would tell you that As'ad needs you. He needs someone who will love him unconditionally and teach him how important love is."

"I don't love him."

Lina's smile never wavered. "Perhaps you are right, but I'm not convinced. I know you, Kayleen. You wouldn't give yourself lightly to a man. I think you have feelings for As'ad and it won't take much for them to grow. Everyone deserves love. Give him his and in time, he will give you yours."

The idea of being loved was much more powerful than the fantasy of being a princess. Yes, the palace was lovely, but Kayleen would be content to live in a trailer at the ends of the earth if she could be with a man who truly loved her.

Was Lina right? Did she, Kayleen, have feelings for As'ad? Did he need her to care for him?

"What are you thinking?" Lina asked.

"That I don't know what to do."

"Then we are in a good place to start finding that out."

Kayleen forced herself to go to As'ad's office because it was the right thing to do. She knew that he had only been trying to help and the fact that he'd done it so badly didn't excuse her behavior or take away his intent. Still, it was embarrassing to face him again after her emotional outburst. She'd slammed a door in his face, both figuratively and literally. He might not be so happy to see her.

She walked into his office. Neil, his assistant, didn't immediately throw her out, which she considered a good sign.

"Is he available?" she asked.

"Perhaps. Just a moment." Neil buzzed As'ad and announced her. There was a pause before Neil said, "You may go in."

Kayleen nodded, then braced herself and opened the door.

The prince rose as she entered. He wore a suit, which was typical, yet everything about him seemed different.

Maybe it was because she *knew* him. She'd touched his bare skin, had been as intimate with him as it was possible to be. She knew his heat, his taste, his sound. She knew what he could do to her and how she could make him react. Nothing was as it had been and she wondered if it would ever be the same again.

"Kayleen."

His voice was low, his dark eyes unreadable.

Their last meeting was a blur. She'd been beyond upset, still reeling from the reality of what she'd done. While she'd tried to explain that her feelings were about herself and not him, she wasn't sure he'd understood or believed her. Oddly, she didn't want him to feel bad.

She crossed her arms over her chest, then dropped her hands to her sides. The silence stretched between them. It occurred to her that he might be feeling a little awkward after the way she'd rejected him.

Was that possible? Did a prince get upset when his proposal of marriage was thrown back in his face? She couldn't decide if As'ad was too arrogant to feel rejection or if the lack of it in his life left him unprepared for the sensation.

"I'm sorry," she told him, meeting his gaze. "You came to me in good faith and made a generous offer. I handled the situation badly. I know you meant well and I should have acknowledged that. You were trying to do the right thing."

"I was," he agreed. "But I have blame, as well. I could have phrased things differently and not been so…"

"Imperious?" she offered.

"That is not the word I would have chosen."

"And yet it fits perfectly."

His gaze narrowed slightly. "Your apology seems to be lacking humility."

"Humility has never been a strength for me. Yet another flaw."

"You have much to recommend yourself, Kayleen. That is what I should have told you before."

Had he always been so good-looking? she wondered as she got caught up in his eyes. His features were perfectly balanced and his mouth…just looking at it made her remember kissing him over and over again.

Weakness invaded her legs, making it suddenly difficult to stand. Fortunately As'ad took her arm and led her to the sofa at the far end of his large office. When she was seated, he settled next to her.

He smiled. "You challenge me."

"Not right now."

"True, but let's give it a minute. You have done well with the girls."

"They mean a lot to me."

He touched her cheek. "I do not want to see you lock yourself behind convent walls. In my arrogance, I chose to make that decision for you. I chose to seduce you so that you couldn't return. It was wrong of me and I apologize."

She opened her mouth, then closed it. He'd planned it? All of it? "You slept with me on purpose? You weren't caught up in the moment?" The information stunned her and hurt quite a bit.

"I was more than caught up," he told her. "You bewitched me."

"I don't think so."

He cupped her chin, forcing her to look at him. "I assure you, my desire for you remains as fiery as ever."

There was a light in his eyes, a need she recognized. Her insides clenched and she found herself wanting to be with him again. The hurt faded.

"I took away your choices," he told her. "I decided for you and that is wrong."

"An apology is enough," she muttered, wishing she could look away from his intense gaze.

"It is not."

"Marriage is a pretty high price to pay for poor judgment."

One corner of his mouth lifted. "I said I was wrong to decide *for* you. I never said there was anything wrong with my judgment."

"What?"

He released her chin only to take her hand in his. "Kayleen, I am a man in need of a wife. I need someone who understands what it is to give with her whole heart, who will love the girls and El Deharia and my people. I need someone who cares more about what is right than the latest fashions or how many pieces of jewelry she has in her possession. A woman I can respect, who will stand up to me and yet be by my side. I need *you*."

She heard the words. Her heart was still beating, she could hear that, too, and feel his hand on hers. And yet it was like she'd left her body and was watching the moment from somewhere else. Because there was no way this was really happening to her. Princes didn't propose to her. Normal guys didn't even want to *date* her.

"But…"

"Do you doubt my sincerity?" he asked. "I cannot promise to be the most perfect husband, but I will try to be all you wish me to be. I need you, Kayleen. Only you."

Need. The word was magic. To be needed meant to never be abandoned. She would have a home, a husband, a family. As Lina had pointed out, she could help people and make a difference in the world. Her—some no-name kid whose only family had dumped her on the steps of an orphanage and left her forever.

"I can't be a princess," she blurted without thinking. "I don't even know who my father is. What if he's in prison or worse? I told you about my mother. She abandoned me. My grandmother didn't want me, either. What if there's something hideously wrong with me?"

"There is not. There never could be." As'ad drew her hand to his mouth and kissed her fingers. "I know *you*," he told her. "That is enough. I know your character and you are more than I could ever wish for. I would be proud to have you as my wife. Marry me, Kayleen. Marry me and adopt the girls. We will be a family together. We need you."

There was only one answer, she thought as her eyes filled with tears. Happy tears, she reminded herself as she nodded.

"Yes," she whispered. "Yes, I'll marry you."

"I am pleased."

He leaned in and kissed her. She started to respond, but then he straightened and removed something from his jacket pocket. Seconds later, he slipped a massive diamond ring onto her finger.

She stared down at the center stone. It was nearly as big as a dinner plate. It glittered and shimmered and was unlike anything she had ever seen.

"Do you like it?" he asked.

"I don't know if I can live up to it," she admitted. "I think the ring is a little too smug for me. What if it calls me names behind my back?"

He chuckled. "This is why you delight me."

"Seriously, As'ad. I own two pairs of earrings, a cross necklace and a watch. I don't think I can wear this."

"What if I told you I picked that stone specifically and had it set for you? The diamond belonged to an ancestor of mine. A queen known for speaking her mind and ruling both her people and her husband with wisdom and love. She was admired by all. She lived a long time and saw many grandsons born. I think she would have liked you very much."

As he spoke, the ring seemed to glow a little brighter. The last of Kayleen's fears faded and she knew she had finally found the place she was supposed to be.

As planned, As'ad went to Kayleen's suite after work that evening. She and the girls were waiting, although only Kayleen knew the nature of the announcement.

He walked in to a domestic scene, with Dana and Nadine both absorbed in their homework and Pepper on Kayleen's lap. The little girl read aloud.

As'ad took in the moment, thinking how it looked like a

styled photograph. They were his responsibility now—all
of them.

His gaze settled on the woman he would marry. Over the
years he hadn't given much thought to his bride and he never
would have imagined someone like Kayleen. But now that
she was here—in his life—he knew he had made an excellent
choice. She would suit him very well.

As for the sisters—he had grown fond of them. With Kayleen he would have sons, but the girls would always be special,
for they had come first.

He smiled as he imagined facing Dana's first boyfriend. It
would not be easy to meet a prince on a first date, but having
to deal with him would be an excellent test of character for any
young man.

Kayleen looked up first. "As'ad, you're here."

"So I am."

She took the book from Pepper, then set the girl on the sofa
next to her. After she rose, she paused, as if not sure what to do.
They were engaged now—some greeting was required. Obviously she did not know what.

He crossed the room to her and pulled her close, then kissed
her. Behind him, he heard the girls murmuring. They were not
used to such displays of affection, but they would become accustomed to them. He enjoyed being with a woman and having
Kayleen in his bed would be one of the perks of married life.

When he stepped back, he kept his arm around her.

"We have something to tell you," he said.

All three girls huddled together, their eyes wide and apprehensive.

Kayleen smiled. "It's a good thing. Don't worry."

"Kayleen and I are to be married," As'ad said. "Nothing has
been formally announced so you'll need to keep the information a secret for now, but I wanted you to know."

The girls stared at each other, then back at him. "What about
us?" Dana asked, sounding worried.

Kayleen knelt down and held out her arms. "You're staying right here. With us. We'll both adopt you. This will be your home forever."

Nadine and Pepper ran into her embrace. Dana looked at him. Her smile was bright and happy, her eyes wide with excitement.

"I'd hoped this would happen," she admitted. "I wanted you to figure out you were in love with Kayleen. You look at her the way Daddy used to look at Mommy."

Love? Not possible, As'ad thought, dismissing the very idea. Kayleen kept her head down. Dana rushed to her.

"Do you have a ring?" the girl asked.

Kayleen removed it from her pocket and slipped it on her fingers. The girls gasped.

"That's really, really big," Pepper said. "Is it heavy?"

"I'm getting used to it."

As'ad watched in contentment. All had turned out well, thanks to his aunt. She had given him advice on the best way to approach Kayleen. While he didn't usually agree with taking advice from a woman, in this case she was the acknowledged expert.

She had told him about Kayleen's desire to be needed. It was a position he could respect. Having a place to belong was far better than worrying about a fleeting emotion like love.

Kayleen stood. The girls rushed at him and he found himself embracing them all. He bent down and gathered Pepper into his arms, then straightened and settled her on his hip.

"I'm a real princess now," she said. "I want a crown."

"A princess wears a tiara," he told her.

"Then one of those. Does this mean the next time I hit a bully I won't get into trouble?"

"Hitting anyone is never a good idea," Kayleen told her.

Pepper sighed and looked into his eyes. "But you're the *prince*. Can't you change that?"

She was delightful, as were her sisters. He smiled. "I will see what I can do."

"You shouldn't encourage her," Kayleen told him.

Perhaps not, but he suddenly wanted all that was possible for the girls. He wanted to give them everything, show them everything, and always keep them safe.

An odd pressure tightened in his chest. It was a feeling he didn't recognize, so he ignored it. But it was there.

Fayza St. John arrived the next morning exactly on time for her prearranged meeting with Kayleen. She was a fifteen-year veteran of the protocol office, something she shared with Kayleen immediately upon their meeting.

"I'll be in charge of the wedding," Fayza said as she stretched her thin lips into what Kayleen hoped was a smile.

Everything about the woman was thin—her body, her face, her legs, her hair. She was well-dressed, but more than a little scary-looking, although elegant. Kayleen had the feeling that the other woman already knew her dress had been bought at sixty percent off at a discount outlet and that the patch pockets had been added after the fact to cover a stain that wouldn't come out.

"You're our first bride in decades," Fayza went on. "Princess Lina was the last, of course. With the princes getting older, we knew it was just a matter of time, so we've been doing a lot of prep work, just in case. Now you'll have to deal with a lot of decisions yourself, but much of the wedding will be handled out of my office. You can request things like colors, but everything will have to be vetted. While this is your happy day, it is also a state occasion." She paused. "Any questions?"

Kayleen shook her head. A question would require a functioning brain, which she didn't have at the moment. Marrying As'ad was unexpected enough, but to find out the event would be a state occasion?

"Obviously no serious work can get done until we have a date," Fayza continued. "The king mentioned a spring wedding."

"Uh-huh."

"With a formal announcement right after the holidays?"

Kayleen nodded.

"All right. That gives us time, which, believe me, we won't have enough of. You'll start working with one of our people right away. She'll help you learn the culture and traditions of El Deharia. You'll need instruction in the language, deportment, current events, etiquette and a hundred other things I can't even think of right now. Oh, I'll need your personal list for the announcements and the wedding. What family are you inviting?"

Kayleen had to consciously not grab her head to keep it from spinning. This wasn't anything she'd imagined. All she wanted was to marry As'ad and get on with her life.

"Does it have to be like this?" she asked. "Can we just go away and get married quietly?"

Fayza laughed. "He's a prince, dear. And the first one to marry. You're going to be on the cover of *People* magazine."

The idea made her want to throw up. "What if I don't want to be?"

"Sorry—this will be the social event of the spring. We'll try to keep the number of guests down. Anything over five hundred is a nightmare."

F-five hundred? Five? As in five hundred?

Kayleen stood and walked to the window. The need to run was as powerful as her instinct to keep breathing. None of this felt right, probably because it wasn't. Not for her. But this was As'ad's world. This was what he expected. If she was to be his wife, she would have to learn his ways. He believed in her and she wouldn't let him down.

"Your family? About how many?" Fayza asked again.

What family? Not her own—they had abandoned her. Why would she want them at her wedding? Would any of the nuns she knew back home make the journey?

"I'm not sure I have any," she admitted.

"Something we'll deal with later. Now, you're going to have to be a little more careful when you go out. You must be escorted, either by Prince As'ad or Princess Lina. If neither of them are available, you'll have a security person with you. You already have one in the car when the girls go to and from school, so that helps. You will not be allowed to be alone with a man who is not attached to the palace. No friends even. Brothers are fine, cousins squeak in."

"That won't be a problem," Kayleen told her as she stared down into the garden.

She wanted to marry As'ad, she thought. She wanted to be with him, his wife, the girls' mother. But like this? Why couldn't he be a regular man? Even the camel dealer he had joked about on Thanksgiving.

She told herself she was being ungrateful. That her hardships were nothing when compared with those in the world who truly suffered. She should be grateful.

"We won't be making an announcement for a few months," Fayza continued. "It's unlikely there will be any media leaks, but it would be best if you didn't wear your engagement ring outside the palace. Just to keep things quiet."

Kayleen nodded, but she wasn't really listening anymore. Instead she stared at the cage in the garden. The one that had held all the doves. Even though the door was open, the space was full again. They had all returned home.

Products of their destiny, she thought. Trapped. Just like her.

Chapter Ten

"**I**'m not sleeping at all," Lina complained as she sat on the stone bench in the garden.

"Thank you."

It took her a moment to realize what Hassan meant. She laughed. "All right. Yes, you're a part of my exhaustion, but not the only part. Playing matchmaker is hard work. I feel guilty in a way. I started all this. I brought them together."

"You introduced them and then removed yourself from the situation. You did not lock them in a room together and insist they become intimate. They chose that course themselves."

"I agree, in theory. But I planned this from the beginning. I thought Kayleen would be good for As'ad and that she secretly longed for more than teaching at the convent school. But what if I was wrong? What if I messed up both their lives?"

Hassan leaned in and kissed her. "You worry too much."

"I'm very good at it."

"Perhaps it is not a gift one should cultivate."

She smiled. "You don't actually expect me to change, do you?"

"Not really."

"Good." Her smile faded. "I just wish I knew I'd done the right thing."

"Why would it be otherwise? As'ad proposed and Kayleen agreed. Now they will be thrown together even more. Who knows what might happen."

He was so confident the outcome would be positive, but Lina wasn't so sure. What if As'ad couldn't open his heart to Kayleen? What if she stopped falling in love with him?

"I can see I do not have your full attention," Hassan complained. "I forbid it to be so."

She laughed. "You are not king here, sir. You are my guest."

His dark eyes brightened with humor. "I have enjoyed being your guest. Spending time with you makes it difficult for me to consider going home. But I must."

She didn't want to think about that. "You have many sons to rule in your place."

"For a time, but the ultimate responsibility is mine. I must also consider my people. I do not want them to believe I have abandoned them."

"I know." She didn't want to think about that. She didn't want Hassan to leave, but couldn't ask him to stay. She looked at him. "I will miss you."

"As I will miss you." He squeezed her hand. "I suppose it would be presumptuous to ask that you could come with me to Bahania."

She steeled herself against hope. "As a visit?"

He smiled. "No, my love. Not as a visit. It has been so long, I'm doing this badly." He kissed her. "Lina, you are an unexpected treasure in my life. I did not think I would find love again. I certainly never expected to find such a beautiful, enticing woman such as yourself. Your physical perfection is only matched by the gloriousness of your spirit and your mind. You have bewitched me and I wish to be with you always. I love you and would be most honored if you would consider becoming my wife."

Kayleen stood frozen on the garden path. She'd been walking as she did each morning, only to accidentally stumble into a personal moment.

At first she'd only heard the low rumble of voices and had thought nothing of them. There were often other people in the garden. Then she'd heard King Hassan say something about his people. The next thing she knew, he'd proposed.

Now she held her breath and looked desperately for a way to escape so they could be alone. She turned slowly, intent on creeping away, when Hassan spoke again.

"Tears are unexpected, Lina."

"They're happy tears. I love you so much. I never dreamed, either, that I could fall in love."

"So you will be my queen."

"Oh, dear. A queen. I never thought of that."

"My people will adore you nearly as much I do. I have the added delight of knowing every part of you."

There was a soft giggle and silence. Kayleen took advantage of their attention to each other and quietly moved away.

So Lina and the king had fallen in love. She was happy for them. The thought of her friend moving to Bahania was a little sad, but also exciting. Kayleen had never known a queen before.

She made her way back to her suite. As she climbed the wide staircase leading to the second floor, she paused, remembering the king's emotional proposal and how happy Lina had been. Even from several feet away, Kayleen had felt the love they shared.

"I want to be in love," Kayleen whispered. "With As'ad."

She wanted to love the man she would marry and she wanted him to love her back. Could it happen? Was it possible? Or was she like a child, hoping to catch the moon?

As'ad walked into the suite Saturday morning. "Are you ready?" he asked.

The girls all called out that they were, while Kayleen hovered behind them. For some reason, she felt shy with As'ad. How strange. She'd never felt awkward with him before. Perhaps it was because they were engaged now. Everything was different, yet it was oddly the same.

"You never said what we were going to do," Dana told him.

"I know. It's a surprise."

He crossed to Kayleen and smiled at her. "You are quiet."

"I'm caught up in the moment."

"You don't know what the moment will be."

"I'm sure it will be wonderful."

"Such faith." He captured her hand in his, then glanced down. "You do not wear my ring."

She pulled her hand free and hid it behind her back. "I, um, thought it was best. After talking to Fayza and all."

"Who is Fayza?"

"From the protocol office. I think that's where she's from. She wanted to talk to me about the wedding and how to behave, now that I'm going to be, you know, a princess."

She could speak the word, but it was hardly real to her. It was the same as saying she was going to wake up an aardvark. A princess? Her? Not possible.

"I see," As'ad murmured. "What were her instructions?"

Kayleen tried to remember them all. "I shouldn't go out by myself. I shouldn't talk to any man who isn't staff or a member of the royal family. I shouldn't wear my ring until the engagement is officially announced. I shouldn't talk to the press, dress inappropriately." She paused. "There's more. I wrote it all down."

He touched her cheek, then lightly kissed her. "It seems there are many things you should not do. Perhaps it would have been easier to give you a list of what is allowed."

"That's what I thought."

His dark gaze settled on her face. "Kayleen, you may do whatever pleases you. In all things. I would ask that you not travel outside of the palace walls without a bodyguard, but you may come and go as you wish. You are my fiancée, not my slave."

She liked the sound of that. "But Fayza was very insistent."

"I assure you, she will not be again. Would it please you to wear your engagement ring?"

She nodded. Somehow wearing the ring made her feel as if she belonged.

"I would like you to wear it, as well."

She went into her bedroom and slipped on the ring. When she turned, she found As'ad behind her. He pulled her close and settled his mouth on hers.

His kiss was warm and insistent, with just enough passion to make her breath catch. She liked the feel of him next to her, the way he held her as if he would never let her go. She liked the taste and scent of him, the fire that burst to life inside of her.

"What are they doing?" Nadine asked in what Kayleen guessed was supposed to be a whisper.

"They're kissin'," Pepper told her.

As'ad straightened. "There are issues with children I would not have guessed," he told her. "Such as privacy."

She smiled. "It's because they're excited about the surprise. You never said what it was."

"You're right. I did not." He led her back into the living room and faced the girls. "We are going shopping. All three of you need new wardrobes, now that you are to be my daughters."

Nadine spun in place. "Pretty dresses and party shoes?"

"Of course. Riding clothes, as well. Play clothes and whatever else Kayleen thinks you require."

"I want a crown," Pepper announced.

As'ad laughed. "I am not sure the store carries crowns, but we will ask."

Kayleen laughed. "Maybe we can make one here." She turned to him. "Thank you. The girls will love getting new things. They're all growing so quickly."

"You will be shopping, as well," he told her.

"What? I'm fine."

"You need a wardrobe that befits your new position." He shook his head. "What you have will not do."

She felt herself flush and tried to tell herself that it made sense a prince wouldn't be impressed by her plain, inexpensive wardrobe.

"I've never been much of a shopper," she admitted. Growing up, she'd made do with hand-me-downs and donations. When she started working, she'd never made a lot of money and her clothing budget had been modest at best.

"You will have to learn," he told her. "You are a beautiful woman and you deserve to wear beautiful things. Silks and lace with jewels that glitter. You will sparkle like the stars in the sky."

She'd never heard him talk like this before, she thought happily. She liked it.

The store was like nothing she'd ever seen before. It was on a quiet street with pale buildings that had striped awnings at all the windows. There was no sign overhead. Just discreet gold lettering on the door.

"I have called ahead," As'ad told her as they got out of the limo. "Wardrobes have been collected for each of the girls."

"How did you know the sizes?" she asked, wishing she'd had something nicer to wear into the store. She felt frumpy.

"Neil phoned the laundry and asked them to check. A selection has been made for each of them but the final decision is yours. If something has been forgotten, it will be ordered."

Kayleen had a feeling this was going to be a different experience than the sixty-percent-off sales at the discount stores she usually frequented.

A tall, slender woman greeted them graciously. She was beautifully dressed and smiled as she bowed to Prince As'ad.

"Sir, you are always welcome here. How delighted we are to be of service."

"Glenda, this is Kayleen James, my fiancée. These three

young ladies are my daughters. Dana, Nadine and Pepper, this is Miss Glenda."

The girls smiled shyly and stayed close to him.

"A perfect family," Glenda told him. "Although a son would be a lovely addition."

"You speak as my father does," As'ad told her. "You are prepared?"

"We have dozens of things to show everyone. I think you will be pleased." She turned to the girls. "Come on. I'll show you." Glenda took Dana's hand and introduced her to the clerks who were hovering. Each gathered a girl and led her off. Then Glenda turned to Kayleen.

"Such beautiful hair," she said with a sigh. "And a natural color." She slowly walked around Kayleen. "Good structure, excellent posture, clear skin. Prince As'ad, you're a fortunate man."

"I think so."

"All right. Let the fun begin. The dressing rooms are this way." She glanced back at As'ad. "You will find magazines, drinks and a television waiting for you."

"Thanks." He smiled at Kayleen. "Enjoy yourself."

Kayleen nodded because she couldn't speak. Nothing about this experience was real to her. None of it had any basis in reality. In her world, boutique owners didn't act this way. They weren't so accommodating or friendly. At least, Kayleen thought the woman was being friendly. She could have just been acting nice because of the money that would be spent, but Kayleen hoped not.

She followed Glenda to the dressing room where the girls were giddily trying on clothes.

"I have socks with kittens!" Pepper yelled. "Can I have socks with puppies?"

"Yes," the woman helping her said with a laugh. "We even have giraffes."

"I *love* giraffes."

For Nadine there were dance clothes and frilly dresses, for Dana, clothes that were slightly less girly, but still pretty. Pepper ran to Kayleen and thrust kitten socks in her hand.

"Aren't they the best?" she asked breathlessly.

"They are."

"I love shopping!"

"So you're starting them young," Glenda murmured.

"Apparently."

She was taken into her own dressing room where dozens of items hung. There were dresses and jeans and blouses and skirts and suits. In the corner, three towers of shoe boxes stood nearly four feet high.

"We'll start with the basics," Glenda told her. "The prince mentioned you didn't have much of an appropriate wardrobe." She laughed. "Hardly something he had to mention. Not many of us have clothing fit for royal duty. Of course you'd be starting over. And isn't that the best place to be?"

Kayleen fingered her plain dress. "I've never been into fashion before."

"That is about to change. Fortunately you can learn a lot fairly quickly. Pay attention to what looks good on you rather than what's in style, go with classics and coordinates. And expect to be tortured by pretty shoes on formal evenings. All right, dear, let's see what you've got."

Glenda waited patiently until Kayleen figured out she was expected to undress.

Kayleen reluctantly unzipped her dress and stepped out of it. Glenda nodded.

"Excellent. Not too curvy, so you can dazzle in evening wear. That's good. No offense, dear, but you have very ugly underwear. If you're going to marry a prince, you need sexy and pretty. You want to keep him interested."

She began making notes, then motioned to the rack on the right. "We'll start there."

An hour later Kayleen realized she'd underestimated women

who shopped for sport. It was exhausting. Trying on, walking out for As'ad's approval, then getting pinned and poked so everything fit perfectly, finding the right shoes, walking around in them, getting another nod from As'ad, then starting the whole thing over with a different dress.

She was zipping up a simple day dress when Dana walked into the dressing room.

"We're finished," she said. "As'ad said to tell you Aunt Lina is coming by to take us to the movies."

Kayleen smiled. "Are you as tired as I am?"

Dana nodded. "It was fun, but work."

"I didn't get to see half of what any of you bought. We'll have to have a fashion show when the clothes are delivered."

But instead of agreeing, Dana moved close, put her arms around Kayleen's waist and started to cry.

Kayleen sat down and pulled the girl onto her lap. "What's wrong?"

"I miss my mom and my dad," she said as she cried. "I know it's wrong, but I do."

Kayleen hugged her tight. "It's not wrong to miss them. Of course you do. This is all new and different. You want to share what's happening and you want the comfort of what's familiar. I don't blame you at all. You've been so brave, sometimes I forget you're not all grown-up."

"I get scared."

"Because all this is different?"

Dana buried her face in Kayleen's shoulder. "We don't want you to go away."

"I won't."

"Promise? Not ever? No matter what?"

"We will always be together. As'ad and I are getting married. We're going to be a family."

Dana looked at her. "If you leave him, you'll take us with you?"

Kayleen smiled. "I'm not leaving."

"You could. People leave."

"I won't, but if something happens and I do, I'll take all three of you with me. I promise."

Dana wiped her face. "Okay. I trust you."

"Good, because I love you."

Dana sniffed. "Really?"

"Really. You and Nadine and Pepper. I love you all so much. I always wanted girls and now I have three."

Dana hugged her hard. Kayleen held her, willing her to feel safe, to know she, Kayleen, would always protect her. At last Dana straightened.

"I'm better," she said as she slid to her feet.

"I'm glad. I'm always here, if you need to talk or anything. Just tell me. Okay?"

Dana nodded and left. Kayleen stood and smoothed the front of the dress. "We know it wrinkles," she said to herself.

As'ad stepped into the dressing room. He stood behind her and put his hands on her shoulders.

"I heard your conversation with Dana," he told her, meeting her gaze in the mirror.

"Do you disapprove?" she asked.

"Not at all. You reassured her and she will reassure her sisters." One corner of his mouth turned up. "Perhaps you could have hesitated before agreeing you would probably leave me."

"I never said that. I won't. Marriage is forever for me."

"As it is for me," he told her, then turned her to face him. "You are an excellent mother. That pleases me. For the girls and the sons to follow."

"You do realize that you're technically responsible for the gender of any children we have. That if I have girls, it's your fault?"

He smiled. "Yes, I know. Although I would remind you I am one of six brothers. So the odds are in my favor."

She wanted to mention that a healthy child should be enough, regardless of gender. But what was the point? As'ad was a prince and a sheik. He was arrogant, but he was also kind and charming and she didn't want to change anything about him.

"Are you enjoying shopping?" he asked.

"It's a lot of work. I'm not really used to this level of service."

"You will become accustomed to it."

"Maybe. Do I really need all these clothes? It seems excessive."

"You are my wife."

"I get that, but still…"

"You represent El Deharia. The people have expectations."

Oh. Right. How long would *that* take to get used to? "Then it's fine," she told him.

"So you will do what is necessary for my people but not for me."

"Pretty much."

He bent down and kissed the side of her neck. Her insides clenched in response.

"I see I have to teach you to respect me," he murmured, his mouth moving against her skin.

He wrapped his arms around her waist and drew her back against him. He was warm and hard and she loved the feel of him so close.

She wanted this to be real—all of it. The girls as her family and As'ad as the man she loved more than anyone else. She wanted him to feel the same way. She wanted to make him weak at the knees and be all to him. If only…

He turned her to face him. "When we return to the palace I wish to discuss finances with you," he told her. "You and the girls will always be taken care of. Even if something should happen to me, you will be financially secure. The palace will always be your home, but should you wish to live elsewhere, money would be made available."

He didn't have to do that. She wasn't marrying him for the money. "I don't want anything to happen to you."

"Neither do I. Regardless, you are protected. Now that we are engaged, I have opened a bank account for you. As you spend money, more will be provided. I will give you credit cards, as well." He touched her face. "I want you to be happy, Kayleen. Go shopping as you like."

"I don't need much."

"Then you will be embarrassed by your excesses. Life is different now. You are different."

He kissed her, his mouth moving lazily over hers. When she parted, he slipped his tongue inside, teasing hers until she couldn't catch her breath.

She wanted him to touch her everywhere. She wanted them to make love. She wanted to know the wonder of a release, his body so close to hers, their hearts beating together.

He pulled back slightly. "Although I would prefer you didn't change too much," he whispered as he lowered the zipper on her dress.

She felt his hands on her bare skin. He pulled the dress down to her waist, then moved aside the cup of her bra. His fingers were warm on her breast. He brushed against her hard nipple, making her gasp, then lowered his head and sucked on her.

Aware they were in a dressing room with a very flimsy door, she did her best to keep quiet, but it was difficult as his tongue circled her. Heat blossomed between her legs. Heat and an ache that made her squirm for more.

"So impatient," he whispered, then unfastened her bra.

She pushed the scrap of lace away and ran her hands across his head, then his shoulders. More. She needed more.

He chuckled before moving to her other breast and teasing it until her breath came in pants.

She felt one of his hands on her leg. The material of her dress was drawn up and up, then he moved between her legs.

She knew she should stop him. The girls were gone, but there were other people out there. Clerks and Glenda and maybe customers. They couldn't do this.

Except she didn't want him to stop. Not when he pushed down her panties and urged her to step out of them. Especially not when he slipped his hand between her thighs and began to rub.

He found her center immediately. Back and forth, back and forth, the steady pressure of his fingers on her slick flesh. She was so ready, she thought as she held in another groan. He eased her backward, then raised her leg until her foot rested on the bench.

"Lean on me," he whispered.

She did as he asked because to do otherwise was to risk him stopping. He supported her with one arm around her waist and eased the other under her dress, back between her legs.

She clung to him as he carried her higher and higher. The pleasure was so intense, she could think of nothing else. He knew exactly how to touch her, how to push her closer and closer until her release was in sight.

She felt the tension in every part of her body. She began to shake, holding on to him to keep from falling. Her breath came in pants. Suddenly she was there…on the edge and aching for him to push her over.

He circled her once, twice, and then she was coming and coming and it was as intense and glorious as she remembered. He leaned in and kissed her, silencing her gasps. He continued to touch her, flying with her, down and down, as the ripples of release eased through her. She was still shuddering in after-shocks when he swore softly and let her go.

"What's wrong?" she whispered.

"This was supposed to be for you," he muttered as he bent down and grabbed her bra. "Here. Put this on."

"I don't understand."

He looked at her, passion flaring in his eyes. "I must take you back to the palace at once. To my bed. We will finish the shopping later."

She smiled. "That's a good plan."

* * *

It was nearly midnight when Kayleen dialed the familiar number and, when the call connected, ask to speak to the woman in charge.

"Kayleen? Is that you?"

Kayleen smiled. "Yes. It's been too long since I last called. I'm sorry."

"If you've been off having adventures, I forgive you at once. How are you? How is life at the palace? You must tell me everything."

The familiar voice, rich with affection and a life energy that inspired those around her, made Kayleen wish to be back in the convent, sitting in the room with her Mother Superior, instead of half a world away.

"I'm well. Very busy. I... The girls are adjusting well." She'd already called and talked about As'ad adopting the girls and her becoming their nanny.

"I worry about them. There have been so many upheavals. So much pain for those so young. You're with them and that must help."

"I hope so." Kayleen cleared her throat. "I have something to tell you. I'm not sure what you'll think." She drew in a deep breath. "It's about Prince As'ad. He arranged for us to have a Thanksgiving dinner a few weeks ago. It was lovely. But then..."

The Mother said nothing. Kayleen suspected she had long ago learned that silence was powerful motivation for the other person to keep talking.

"It was late and we were alone," Kayleen said, then told her everything. When she'd finished explaining about the proposal, she paused, waiting for whatever judgment might follow.

"He is a good man?" the other woman asked at last.

It wasn't the question Kayleen had expected. "Um, yes. A very good man. A little too used to getting his way, but that must come with being royal."

"He takes care of you and the girls?"

"Yes. Very well."

"Can you love him?"

An interesting question. "Yes, I can. I want to."

"Then I am pleased. I always wanted a husband and a family for you, Kayleen. I know you longed to return here, to the familiar, but sometimes we find our happiness in unexpected places. To love and be loved is a great blessing. Enjoy what you have and know I am always thinking of you."

"Thank you," Kayleen whispered, feeling the words wash over her like a blessing.

"Follow your heart and you will never be led astray. Follow your heart, child."

Kayleen nodded. She could already feel her heart drawing her toward As'ad. As he was the man she would marry, it was a journey she longed to make. To a place where she would finally belong.

Chapter Eleven

Kayleen looked at all the designs spread out on the large dining room table. "You're kidding," she said.

"This is only from today's mail," Lina told her with a sigh. "I never thought anything I did would make designers notice me. I certainly buy nice clothes, but I'm not that into fashion. Besides, I gave up being trendy years ago. But the second Hassan announced our engagement, I started getting calls." She flipped through the sketches of wedding gowns. "He was supposed to wait, you know. He promised." She sounded more exasperated than actually annoyed.

"He said he couldn't stand to keep his happy news a secret," Kayleen told her with a smile. "I saw the news conference. He was giddy."

Lina grinned. "Don't tell him that. He'll explain that a king is never giddy."

"He was this one time. I'm glad you're so happy."

"Me, too." Lina sighed. "I've really liked my life. I've been blessed. Even though I lost my husband so early, I had my brother's sons to fill the void. I was okay with that. I was going to grow old taking care of their children. Now, suddenly, I'm in love and engaged. I still can't believe it."

Kayleen glanced at Lina's ring—the diamonds glittering on the platinum band made her engagement ring look like a tiny toy. "You're going to have to start exercising more if you're going to carry that around all day."

Lina laughed. "I know. It's huge. So not my taste, but if you'd seen the look on Hassan's face when he put it on my finger. He was so proud. How am I supposed to tell him I'd like something smaller than a mountain?"

"If it doesn't really matter to you, you don't."

"You're right." Lina picked up a design and studied it. "You're going to have to go through all this as soon as your wedding is announced."

"Hopefully on a much smaller scale," Kayleen told her, knowing being royal was going to take a lot of getting used to. "I only ever wanted to belong to a family. Now I have a whole country."

"There are perks."

"I'm not that interested in the perks."

"Which is why I'm glad As'ad picked you," Lina told her. "I know you're not in it for the money." She set down the design and picked up another. "I'll admit I'm hoping you'll fall in love with him."

Kayleen felt herself blush. "I've thought about it," she admitted. "He's a good man. Thoughtful and kind. He really cares about the girls. He takes care of things. He makes me feel safe. I know I like him, but love? What does that feel like?"

"Like you can hold the stars in the palm of your hand," Lina said, then laughed. "I sound foolish."

"You sound happy."

"I am. Hassan is my world. Oh, I know that will change, we'll settle into something more normal. But for now, I'm enjoying the magic. The way my heart beats faster when he walks in a room. The way he can take my breath away with a simple kiss. I only want to be with him."

"So I'm boring you?" Kayleen teased.

Lina laughed. "Not exactly. But I think about him all the

time. It was different before. When I was young. I loved my husband, but I didn't appreciate what I had. Now that I'm older, I understand how precious love is. How rare." She turned to Kayleen. "I think you already know that, because of how you grew up."

"I know it's something I want. It's important to me. I want to love As'ad. I already love the girls."

"Then you're halfway there. Just give things time."

"We have that," Kayleen murmured.

"You have your life. After you're married, you can start having children of your own."

Kayleen touched her stomach. A baby. It had always been her secret dream. The one she wouldn't allow herself to think of very often.

Lina sighed. "I'd love to get pregnant. I'm a little old, but I'm going to try."

"Really?"

The princess nodded. "I always wanted children. While my nephews have been a source of endless delight, I confess I still have the fantasy of my own child. Hassan is willing to try. We'll see. If it is meant to be, then it will happen. If not, I still have the man of my dreams."

"I'm nervous," Kayleen told As'ad as they walked into the auditorium at the American School. "I've been working with the girls. I know in my head they'll be fine, but I'm still terrified."

"Yet they are the ones performing."

"I want them to do well so they'll be happy," she said. "I don't want them to feel bad."

"Then you should have faith in them. They have practiced. They are ready."

"You make it sound so logical."

"Is it not?"

"No, it's not. It's horrible. I think I'm going to throw up."

As'ad laughed and pulled her close. "Ah, Kayleen, you delight me."

"By vomiting? Imagine how excited you'll be when I get a fever." She grumbled, but in truth she enjoyed the feel of his arm around her and the heat of his body next to hers. Not only for the tingle that shot through her, but because the sensation was familiar. She'd leaned against him enough to know it was him. She would be able to pick him out blindfolded—by touch or scent alone. She'd never been able to think that before.

They took seats toward the front, by the aisle. Kayleen was vaguely aware that people were looking at them, but she was too nervous for the girls to notice or feel uncomfortable. A thousand horrible scenarios ran through her mind. What if Dana forgot her lines or Nadine tripped or Pepper decided to teach some bully a lesson?

As'ad took her hand and squeezed her fingers. "You must breathe. Slowly. Relax. All will be well."

"You don't *know* that."

"I know that your panic will in no way influence the outcome and it will only make you more uncomfortable."

"Again with the logic. It's really annoying."

She glanced at him and he smiled. She smiled back and felt something tug at her belly. Something that felt a lot like a connection. It startled her and made the rest of the room fade away. In that moment, there was only As'ad and she didn't want anyone or anything else.

A few minutes later, the orchestra began and the curtains parted. The pageant went from the youngest students to the oldest, so it wasn't long before Pepper appeared on stage with her class. They did a skit about a frog family snowed in for the holidays. Pepper was the mother frog.

Kayleen mouthed the girl's lines along with her, only relaxing when she left the stage at the end of the skit.

"A flawless performance," As'ad murmured. "You worry for nothing."

"Maybe my worrying is what made it perfect."

"You do not have that much power. Nadine is next. I believe she will dance. That will be enjoyable to watch."

Sure enough, Nadine and several of her classmates danced to music from *The Nutcracker*. Kayleen willed her to hold her positions exactly long enough and exhaled when the music ended and the girls were still.

"You will wear yourself out," As'ad told her.

"I can't help it. I love them."

He looked into her eyes. "Do you?"

"Of course. How could I not?"

Something flashed through his eyes—something she couldn't read. "I was most fortunate to find you. Not that I can take total credit." He smiled. "We must send Tahir, the desert chieftain, a gift of thanks."

"Maybe a fruit basket."

"I was thinking more of a camel."

"That can be tricky," she told him. "Don't you hate it when all you get in a year is camels?"

"You mock me."

"Mostly I'm mocking the camel."

Another class took the stage, then Dana's group appeared. Once again Kayleen held her breath, willing the preteen to get through all the lines without messing up.

Partway through the performance, As'ad took her hand in his. "You may squeeze my fingers, if that helps."

She did and felt a little better. When Dana finally left the stage, Kayleen slumped back in exhaustion.

"I'm glad we only have to do that a few times a year," she said. "I couldn't stand it."

"You will grow more used to this as the girls are in more performances."

"I don't want to think about it. I'm not sure my heart could take it."

"Then brace yourself. There is one more surprise yet to come."

She turned to him. "What are you talking about?"

"You'll see. All will be revealed when we leave here."

Kayleen really wanted to whine that she wanted to know *now,* but managed to keep quiet. She fidgeted until the last song ended, then followed As'ad out of the auditorium. Only to step into an impossible-to-imagine scene of snow.

It fell from the sky, cold and wet and delightful. The children were already outside, running and screaming. Kayleen held out her hands, then laughed as the snow landed on her palms.

"It's real," she said.

As'ad shrugged. "Dana mentioned missing snow, as did the other girls. I thought they would enjoy this."

It was only then that Kayleen noticed the roar of the large snow-making machine off to the side of the parking lot.

"You arranged it?" she asked, stunned by the thoughtful gift.

"Neil arranged it. I simply gave the order."

It wasn't just simple, she thought. As'ad had thought about the girls, about how this time of year would be difficult for them, and he'd done his best to make it better.

Dana came running up to them. "It's snowing! I can't believe it."

She flung herself at As'ad, who caught her and held her. Then Nadine was there and Pepper and he was holding all of them.

Kayleen watched them, her eyes filling with happy tears. It was a perfect moment, she thought.

Her chest ached, but not in a scary way. Instead it seemed that her heart had grown too big to hold all her emotions. Light filled her until she was sure it poured from her body.

The world around them shrank until there was only As'ad and the children he held. She wanted to hold that moment forever, to never forget the image or the feelings.

The director of the school came up to greet them and the spell was broken. Dana crossed to Kayleen and hugged her.

"Isn't this the best?"

"It's wonderful," Kayleen told her. "All of it. You did really well. I was scared, but you didn't seem nervous at all."

"It was fun," Dana said. "I've never been in a play before. I like it. I think I want to go into drama next year." She raised her face to the snow. "Can you believe this?"

Kayleen looked at the tall, handsome prince who had asked her to marry him. The man who spoke of their life together, of children and who made it snow in the desert because it brought a smile to a child's face.

"No, I can't," she admitted, even as she realized she now knew exactly what it felt like to be in love.

As'ad watched the children play in the snow and was pleased with his gift. All was going well. Lina had told him to pay attention to the females in his life—that for a small amount of effort, he would receive much in return. She had been right.

He heard Kayleen's laughter and found her in the crowd. With her hair like fire and her hazel eyes, she was a brightly colored flamingo in a flock of crows. He was proud to have her as his bride. She would provide him with strong, healthy sons and serve the people of his country well. She would keep him satisfied at night and, if the emotions he'd seen in her eyes earlier told the truth, love him.

He knew it was important for a woman to love her husband. That life was much easier for them both when her heart was engaged. He had hoped Kayleen would come around and she had. She would be content in their marriage, as would he. He could not ask for more.

"I'm exhausted," Kayleen said as she slumped in the back of the limo. "All that worrying, then the snowball fight. If this keeps up much more, I'm going to have to start working out."

"I do not wish you to change anything about yourself," As'ad told her.

Words to make her heart beat faster, she thought as he pulled her into his arms and kissed her.

At the first brush of his mouth, her entire body stirred in anticipation. She was eager to taste him, touch him, be with him. Unfortunately the trip back to the palace was only a few minutes.

"Perhaps later," he murmured, kissing her mouth, her cheeks, her jaw.

"Yes," she whispered. "I am very available."

"An excellent quality."

Far too soon, they arrived at the palace. A royal guard opened the passenger door and As'ad stepped out. He held out his hand to her. As she took it, she saw King Mukhtar in the courtyard. He seemed very pleased with himself as he spoke with a woman Kayleen had never seen before.

"Who is that?" she asked.

"I do not know."

The woman was of average height, with platinum-blond hair teased and sprayed into a curly mass. Heavy makeup covered her face, almost blurring her features. She wore a too-tight sweater and jeans tucked into high-heeled boots. Inappropriate clothing for someone visiting a palace.

Kayleen had never seen her before but as she walked toward the king and his guest, she got an uneasy feeling in the pit of her stomach.

King Mukhtar saw her and beamed. "My dear, you are back. Excellent. I have a surprise." He put his hand on his companion's back and urged her forward. "Do you remember when we were walking in the garden shortly after you arrived? You mentioned your family. Specifically how you did not remember your mother and did not know her whereabouts."

Kayleen jerked her attention back to the badly dressed woman and wanted to be anywhere but here. It wasn't possible. Nothing that horrible could really be happening.

"I have found her," the king said proudly. "Here she is. Kayleen, this is your mother. Darlene Dubois."

The woman smiled broadly. "Hi, baby. Why, Kayleen, you're just so pretty. I knew you would be. Let me look at you. You're all grown up. How old are you now? Nineteen? Twenty?"

"Twenty-five."

"Oh, my. Well, don't go telling people that. They'll think I'm getting old. Although I was only sixteen when you were born." She held out her arms. "Come on, now. I've missed you so much! Give your mama a hug."

Trapped by the manners instilled in her by caring nuns, Kayleen moved forward reluctantly and found herself hugged and patted by the stranger.

Could this woman really be her mother? If so, shouldn't she feel a connection or be excited? Why was her only emotion dread?

"Isn't this fabulous?" Darlene asked as she stepped back, then linked arms with Kayleen. "After all these years. You won't believe how shocked I was when that nice man on the king's staff called and invited me to El Deharia. I confess I had to look it up on a map." She smiled at the king. "I had to leave high school when I got pregnant. Since then, I've been pursuing a career in show business. It hasn't left much time for higher education."

Or contact with her family, Kayleen thought bitterly, remembering standing alone on the steps of the orphanage while her grandmother told her that no one wanted her and that she would have to stay with the nuns.

"But what about my mommy?" Kayleen had cried.

"You think she cares? She dumped you with me when you were a baby. You're just lucky I put up with you all these years. I've done my duty. Now you're on your own. You'll grow up right with those nuns looking after you. Now stop your crying. And don't try to find me or your mama again. You hear?"

The memory was so clear, Kayleen could feel the rain hitting her cheeks. She knew it was rain because it was cold, unlike the tears that burned their way down her skin.

"Kayleen, would you like to show your mother to her rooms?" the king asked. "She is on the same floor as you and the girls. The suite next to yours. I knew you would want to be close."

Kayleen was happy that one of them was sure of something. She felt sick to her stomach and caught by circumstances. She looked at As'ad, who watched her carefully.

"What girls?" Darlene asked. "Do you have babies of your own?"

Darlene sounded delighted, but for some reason Kayleen didn't believe her. The other woman didn't seem the type to be excited about being a grandmother.

"They're adopted," As'ad told her. "My children."

Kayleen introduced them, using the chance to disentangle herself from her mother.

"A prince?" Darlene cooed. "My baby marrying a prince. Does that just beat all." She smiled at the king. "You have very handsome sons, sir. They take after you."

Mukhtar smiled. "I like to think so."

Kayleen couldn't believe this was happening. It didn't feel real. She looked at As'ad and found him watching her. There was something quizzical in his expression, as if he'd never seen her before.

What was he thinking? Was he looking at her mother and searching for similarities? Was he uncomfortable with the living reminder that she didn't come from a socially connected family? That she would be of no use to him that way?

"Your mother must be tired from her journey," the king said. "Let us keep you no longer."

"I'll arrange to have your luggage sent up," As'ad told the other woman. "Kayleen, I'll see you later."

She nodded because she had no idea what to say. Both the king and As'ad left, abandoning Kayleen to a stranger with greedy eyes.

"Well, look at you," Darlene drawled when they were alone. "Who would have thought my baby girl would grow up and land herself a prince. I'm so happy for you, honey." She grabbed a strand of Kayleen's hair and rubbed it between her fingers. "God, I hate that color. Mine's exactly the same. It costs a fortune to keep it bleached, but it's worth every penny. Men prefer blondes. Although you're carrying the color off great and the prince obviously likes it." She looked Kayleen up and down. "You could pass for Vivian's twin."

"Who's Vivian?"

"My sister. Your aunt. You had to have met her before, when you were living with my mama." She looked around at the vast entrance hall. "Did you get lucky or what? I couldn't believe it when that guy who works for the king called and asked if you were my daughter. After all this time, I had no idea what had happened to you." She smiled. "Imagine my surprise to see what you've become. My little girl. Come on. Show me what life is like in the palace."

Kayleen led her down the hallway. Her head hurt. This couldn't be happening. Not after all these years. Not *now,* when she was engaged to As'ad.

Then she scolded herself for not being happier to see her mother. The woman had given birth to her, after all. Then abandoned her. But shouldn't she be able to forgive that?

Rather than try to decide now, Kayleen talked about the history of the palace. She took Darlene to the room next to hers and walked inside.

The other woman followed, then breathed a sigh of sheer pleasure as she took in the view of the Arabian Sea and the elegant furnishings filling the large space.

"Oh, I like living like this," Darlene said. "How did you get from that convent to here?"

Kayleen looked at her, trying not to notice that under the layers of makeup, they had the same eyes. "You knew about that? Where they sent me?"

"Sure. Mama kept complaining about how much trouble you were. I got tired of hearing it and told her to take you there. I knew, ah, you'd be cared for real well. So how'd you get here?"

"I took a teaching job at the convent school here. I'm a teacher."

Darlene looked amused. "Seriously? You teach children? Interesting."

Kayleen watched her move around the room. "Your last name is Dubois?"

Darlene nodded without looking at her. She lifted up a small Waterford clock, as if checking the weight and the value.

"Is that my last name?"

Darlene glanced at her. "What are you talking about?"

"I never knew. When my grandmother dropped me off at the orphanage, I didn't know my last name. Everyone in the house had a different one. Grandmother wouldn't say which was mine. I had to make one up."

Darlene grinned. "I made mine up, too. What did you pick?"

"James. From the King James Bible."

"I prefer Tennessee Williams myself." Darlene started opening cabinets. "Can you drink in this place?"

"Yes. Right there." Kayleen pointed to the carved doors hiding the fully stocked wet bar.

Darlene found the ice and fixed herself a vodka tonic, then took a long drink. "Better," she said with a sigh. She walked to the sofa and sat down, then patted the seat next to her. "You're going to start at the beginning and tell me everything."

Kayleen stayed where she was. "About what?"

"The story here. You're really engaged to that prince?"

"Yes. There will be a formal announcement in a few weeks and a wedding in the spring."

Darlene took another drink. "So you're not pregnant. I'd wondered if you were."

Kayleen tried not to be insulted. "I didn't have to trick As'ad into marrying me."

"Of course not. I didn't mean to imply you would. Still, you have to be sensible. Do you have a prenuptial agreement? How many millions is he offering? Do you have an attorney? I wonder if you could get one to fly out and help."

Kayleen took a step back. "I don't need an attorney. As'ad has promised the girls and I will be taken care of."

"And you believe him? You're lucky I'm here."

Kayleen doubted that. "Why *are* you here?"

"Because I finally found my long-lost daughter."

"You knew I was in the convent all those years. That's hardly lost."

Darlene shrugged. "You're much more interesting now, honey."

"Because of As'ad." It wasn't a question.

"Partly. Oh, Kayleen, life was hard for me when you were young. I couldn't take care of a baby, I was just a baby myself. You're grown-up. You can see that. Then I lost track of you. But now we're together."

Kayleen found it difficult to believe she would have been so hard to find.

Darlene stood. "I'm your mother. I want what's best for you. If you really expect this prince to marry you, you're going to have to keep him interested. I can help you with that. Otherwise, some rich socialite will steal him away. We don't want that, do we?"

"I find it hard to believe you care anything about me," Kayleen said, feeling both anger and guilt. What was she supposed to believe? "You never did before."

"Don't say that. Of course I cared. But I had a career. You were better off with those nuns. They took real good care of you."

"How would you know?"

"It's the kind of people they are. Am I wrong?"

"No," Kayleen told her. "They're exactly who you'd think they would be."

"Then you should thank me." She walked to the bar and fixed a second drink. "I'm not leaving, Kayleen. The king thinks he's done you a big favor, finding me and bringing me here. I, for one, agree with him. You're my baby girl and that means something to me. We're going to get to know each other, you and I. Now run along. I need to rest. We'll talk about this more later."

Kayleen left. Not because she'd been told to, but because she couldn't stand to be there anymore.

She didn't know what to think about Darlene. She'd never really allowed herself to imagine what her mother was like—it hurt too much to think about all she'd lost. But this woman wasn't anyone's fantasy.

Then Kayleen thought about what the Mother Superior would say about judging someone so quickly. Maybe Darlene *was* sorry about their lost relationship. Maybe they could at least learn to be friends. Didn't Kayleen owe her to give her a chance to prove herself?

Chapter Twelve

Kayleen returned to her suite, but she couldn't seem to settle down. Not with her mother so close. Just a wall away.

It was her own fault for lying, she reminded herself. If she'd told King Mukhtar the truth, none of this would have happened. But she hated talking about how her mother didn't want her and her grandmother abandoned her. It sounded sad and pathetic. So she'd made up a more comfortable version and now she was stuck with it.

She walked to the French doors and started to open them, then remembered her mother was right next door. She didn't want another run-in with her. She turned back to pace the room when someone knocked.

Kayleen froze, afraid of who would be there. The door opened and As'ad stepped inside.

Without thinking, she ran to him. She wrapped her arms around him, wanting to feel the warmth of him, the safety that came from being close.

"That bad?" he asked as he hugged her.

She nodded.

"I take it my father's surprise was not a pleasant one."

She looked at him. "I don't know," she admitted. "I don't

know what to think or what I feel. She's not like mothers on television."

"Few are." He touched her cheek. "Are you all right?"

She sighed. "I will be. It's just strange. I don't know her. I've never known her and now she's here and we're related and I can't figure out what it all means."

"I should probably tell you that getting to know her will take time, that it will get easier, but I am not sure that is true." He smiled at her. "So perhaps I bring you good news."

"Which is?"

"Do you remember your unexpected visit to the desert? Sharif, the chieftain there, has heard of our engagement and invites us to join him and his people for dinner."

"I thought the engagement was supposed to be a secret."

"There are those who find a way to know everything. He is one of them."

"He probably saw light reflecting off my diamond ring. It's like a beacon."

As'ad chuckled. "Perhaps. I have spoken with Lina. She is pleased to take the girls if you would like to go."

Kayleen bit her lower lip. "Is it too rude to leave my mother on her first night here?"

"I think she will be exhausted from her journey. Perhaps you can leave a message on her phone and see her another time."

Kayleen was more than up for that. She left the message, then changed into a comfortable dress for her evening in the desert and met As'ad downstairs.

They walked out front where a Jeep was waiting. "You will need to learn to ride," he told her. "Eventually you will want to go into the desert with the girls."

"I know." She settled in beside him and fastened her seat belt. "Maybe I'd do better on a camel. Horses and I don't get along."

"A camel is not a comfortable ride. Trust me. You would much prefer to be on a horse."

"Maybe." She would have to try a camel first.

It was late afternoon. The sun sat in the west, giving every-thing a rosy, golden glow. The air was warm with the promise of a cool night to follow.

"I wonder what it's like to live in the desert," she said as she stared out the window. "Traveling with a tribe, connected to the land."

"No plumbing, no heat or air-conditioning, no closet."

She laughed. "I can't see you worrying about a closet."

"I would not, but what about you?"

"I like plumbing and closets." She didn't have a lot of things, but she did like to have her few treasures around her.

"My brother Kateb lives in the desert," he said. "He has al-ways preferred the old ways, when life was simple and a man lived by his wits and his sword."

"You're serious? He's a nomad?"

"It is how he prefers it. When each of us reached the age of thirteen, my brothers and I were sent into the desert for a sum-mer. It is considered a rite of passage—a test of manhood. The tribes were not cruel, but we were shown no preference be-cause of our stature. I enjoyed my time, but had no interest in changing my future because of the experience. No so Kateb. He spoke of nothing else when he returned. Our father insisted he complete his education and Kateb agreed. But when he grad-uated from university in England, he returned here and went into the desert."

It sounded romantic, Kayleen thought, if she didn't think about the reality of the life. Weren't there sand fleas? And the heat in summer would be devastating. Still, the wilderness had some appeal. Not answering to anyone. Except one would have to answer to the tribe. There would have to be rules for the greater good.

"Will I meet him?" she asked.

"Not tonight. Kateb lives deep in the desert. Once or twice a year he returns to the palace, to meet with our father."

As'ad watched as Kayleen stared out into the desert. "It's all so beautiful," she said. "I can see why your brother would want to make it his home. Even without running water."

She spoke almost wistfully, as if she meant what she said, which she most likely did. He had learned that Kayleen's word was truth—an unusual trait in a woman. But then Kayleen was not like other women he'd known.

Now that she had a wardrobe of designer clothes, she dressed more like someone engaged to a prince, but there was still an air of…freshness about her. She blushed, she looked him in the eye when she spoke, she never considered hiding her emotions. All things he liked about her. He hoped she would not develop a hard edge of sophistication. He enjoyed her candor and down-to-earth ways.

A surprise, he thought, knowing he had always preferred women of the world. Of course, those women had been companions for his bed, not anyone he would consider to be the mother to his children. He remembered a conversation he'd had years ago with his aunt. Lina had told him that there were different women in this world. That he should have his fun but save his heart for someone unlike his playthings.

She had been right—not that he would give her the satisfaction of telling her. At least about marriage. His heart remained carefully unengaged, as it should in situations as important as these.

He pulled up by the edge of the camp and parked. Kayleen drew in a deep breath.

"They are so going to laugh at me," she murmured.

"Why would they do that?"

She looked at him and said, "Good evening. Blessings to you and your family," in the old tongue of El Deharia. Then added in English, "My pronunciation is horrible."

"You are learning our language?"

"It seemed the right thing to do. Plus, last time almost no one would talk to me in English. It's their country, right? One of the maids is teaching me on her lunch hour. She's taking night classes and I'm helping her with her calculus."

He stared at the hazel-eyed beauty who sat next to him. In a few months, they would be married and she would be a princess for the rest of her life. Her blood would mingle with his and their children would be able to trace their lineage back a thousand years.

She had a vault of jewels to wear whenever she liked, a bank account that never emptied; she lived in a palace. Yet did she expect humble people of the desert to speak her language? Did she hire a tutor? Have a linguistic specialist summoned? Not Kayleen. She bartered with a maid and learned an ancient speech not spoken outside the desert.

In that moment, as he stared into her eyes and saw their future, he felt something. A faint tightness in his chest. A need to thank her or give her something. The feeling was fleeting and unfamiliar, therefore he ignored it.

Or tried to.

There could be no softer emotions. With them came weakness, and strength was all. But he could be grateful that she had stumbled into his life and changed everything.

He reached for her hand. "I am glad we are to be married," he told her.

Happiness brightened her eyes and her whole face took on a glow. Love, he thought with satisfaction, knowing all would be well.

"I am, too," she whispered.

Sharif and Zarina greeted them as they arrived, then the other woman pulled Kayleen aside.

"I see you managed to keep him all to yourself," Zarina teased as she picked up Kayleen's left hand and stared at the ring there. "You have chosen well."

"I think so."

Zarina laughed. "I recognize that smile. You are pleased with As'ad."

"He's wonderful."

"What every bride should think about her groom."

She led Kayleen toward a group of women and introduced her. Kayleen recognized a few of them from her last visit and greeted them in their native language. There were looks of surprise, then two of them started talking to her, speaking so quickly she caught about every tenth word.

"I have no idea what you're saying," she admitted in English. "I'm still learning."

"But you are trying," Zarina said, sounding pleased. "You honor us with your effort."

"I was hoping we could be friends," Kayleen told her.

Zarina smiled. "We are. But we will have to remember our places. Once you are a princess, things will change."

"Not for me." Kayleen wasn't interested in position or money. She wanted more important things.

"Then we will be good friends," Zarina told her. "Come. We are fixing dinner. You can keep us company. We will teach you new words. Perhaps words of love to impress your future husband."

"I'd like that."

Kayleen settled in the open cooking area. The women gathered there, talking and laughing. She couldn't follow many of the conversations, but that was all right. She would get more fluent with time.

She liked the way the women all worked together, with no obvious hierarchy. How the children came and went, dashing to a parent when they felt the need for attention. How easily they were picked up and hugged, how quick the smiles.

The tribe was an extended family—in some ways similar to her experiences in the orphanage. The group pulled together for the greater good. The difference was one would always belong to the tribe.

Roots, she thought enviously. Roots that traveled along. What would that be like?

She thought about her mother, back at the palace. They were supposed to be family, but Darlene was a stranger to her. Kayleen only had vague memories of her aunts and her grandmother, but then she'd forgotten on purpose. What was the point of remembering long days of being left alone, of being hungry and frightened?

She heard giggles and saw Zarina whispering to one of the young women. There were gestures and the next thing Kayleen knew, she was being pulled into a tent.

"We don't do this very much," Zarina told her. "It is only to be used on special occasions. With power comes responsibility."

"I have no idea what you're talking about."

Zarina opened a trunk and dug around, then pulled out several lengths of sheer veil.

"The trick is to maintain the mystery," Zarina told her as she passed over the fabric. "It's about confidence, not talent. No man can resist a woman who dances for him. So you can't feel self-conscious or worry about how you look. You must know in your heart that he wants you with a desperation that leaves him weak. You are in charge. You decide. He begs and you give in."

Kayleen took a step back. "If you're saying what I think you're saying…"

"After dinner, we will send As'ad to a private tent. You will be there. You will dance for him." Zarina smiled. "It's a memory he'll hold on to for the rest of his life."

As much as Kayleen wanted to be accepted by the women of the tribe, she was terrified at the thought of trying to seduce As'ad.

"I don't know how to dance. I'm not good at this."

"You are the woman he wishes to marry. You know all you need to. As for the dancing…it is easy. Come, I will show you."

Zarina tossed the fabric onto a pile of pillows, then shrugged out of her robes. Underneath she wore a sleeveless tank top and cropped pants. A simple, modern outfit that would work perfectly in the desert.

"Lower your center of gravity while keeping your back straight. Rock your hips until you feel the movement, then begin to rotate them."

Zarina demonstrated, making it look easy. Kayleen tried to do as she said, but felt awkward.

But she didn't give up and after a few minutes, she had the hip movement down. Next she learned to hold her arms out to the side, moving them gracefully.

"Very good," Zarina told her. "Now turn slowly. You want to dance for a minute or two, turn, then remove one of the veils."

Kayleen skidded to a stop. "I can't dance naked."

"You won't have to. No man can resist the dance of the veils. You will remove two, maybe three, then he will remove the rest."

"What if he thinks I look stupid?"

"He won't. He'll think he's the luckiest man alive. Now let us prepare you for the evening."

Unsure she was really going to be able to do this, Kayleen followed Zarina to another tent where there were several women waiting. She was stripped down to her underwear and sat patiently as henna was applied to her hands and feet.

"It's the temporary kind," Zarina told her. "A sugar-based dye that will wash off in a week or so."

Kayleen stared at the intricate design and knew she wouldn't mind if it lasted longer.

Next she was "dressed" in layers of veils. They were wound around her, woven together until they appeared to be a seamless garment. They were sheer, but in enough volume to only hint at what was below.

Zarina applied makeup, using a dark pencil to outline Kayleen's eyes and a red stain on her lips.

"Better than lipstick," the other woman told her. "It won't come off."

Her hair was pulled back and up through a beaded headpiece. Dozens of bracelets fit on each wrist. The final touch was a pair of dangling earrings that nearly touched her shoulders.

When they were finished, Zarina led her to a mirror. Kayleen stared at the image, knowing it couldn't possibly be her. She looked *exotic*. She'd never been exotic in her life. She also looked sexy and mysterious.

"I will leave you here for a few minutes to practice, then come for you," Zarina told her. "Believe in yourself. With this dance, you can snare As'ad's heart so that he can never be free again. What wife doesn't want that?"

Good question, Kayleen thought when she was alone. Nerves writhed in her stomach, but she ignored them. Having As'ad respect her wasn't enough. She wanted more—she wanted him to love her.

He had to see she was more than just someone to take care of the girls or an innocent he'd slept with. Their engagement might have begun due to circumstances other than love, but it didn't have to stay that way.

She'd already given him her heart—now she had to claim his. Which meant being equal to a prince.

Could she? Kayleen had spent her whole life in the shadows, lurking in the background, not making waves, desperate for what she wanted, but afraid to step up and take it. It was time to be different. If she wanted to love a prince, she would have to claim him. She would have to show him she was so much more than he imagined. Her upbringing had given her an inner strength. She would use that power to achieve her heart's desire.

With a last look at herself, she walked to the front of the tent to wait for Zarina. She wasn't afraid. She was going to bring As'ad to his knees and make him beg. And that was just for starters.

While As'ad enjoyed the company of Sharif, he was disappointed in the evening. He'd brought Kayleen to the desert so they could share the experience. But she had been whisked away and a polite guest did not ask why.

As the strong coffee was served at the end of the meal, he glanced at his watch and calculated how long he would have to wait until they could politely take their leave. Perhaps he and Kayleen could go into town for a couple of hours. There were a few nightclubs that were intimate and had small, crowded dance floors. He liked the idea of holding her close.

Zarina approached and bowed. "Prince As'ad, would you please come with me?"

As'ad looked at his host. "Do I trust your daughter?"

Sharif laughed. "As if I know her plans. Zarina, what do you want with the prince?"

"Nothing that will displease him."

As'ad excused himself and followed her. Night had fallen and the stars hung low in the sky. He thought briefly of his brother Kateb, and wondered when he would next return to the palace. If he came in time, he could attend the wedding. As'ad would like to have all his brothers there for the ceremony. And to point out that he would no longer have to listen to their father's complaints that they had yet to all find brides.

Zarina wove her way through the tents, pausing at one in the back, almost on its own.

"In here, sir," she said, holding open the flap. "I wish you a good evening."

As'ad ducked inside. The tent was dim, with only a few lights. There was an open space covered with rugs, and a pile of cushions in front of him.

"If you will please be seated."

The request came from a dark corner. He recognized Kayleen's voice. A quiet tent, seclusion and the company of a beautiful woman, he thought as he lowered himself to the cushions. The evening had improved considerably.

Music began. The melody was more traditional than contemporary, as were the instruments. An interesting choice, he thought, as Kayleen stepped out of the shadows. It was his last rational thought for a very long time.

She wore veils. Dozens and dozens of sheer lengths of fabric covered her body. Yet there were flashes of skin—her waist, her legs, a bit of arm.

Her face looked the same, yet different, with her eyes suddenly dark and intriguing. Jewels glittered from her wrists and her ears; her skin shimmered in the dim light. She was the woman he knew yet a woman he had never known. Even before she began to move, he wanted her.

She moved her arms gracefully. He saw the henna on her skin and dropped his gaze to her bare feet. It was there, as well. The patterns were oddly erotic on her fair skin.

She moved her hips back and forth, turned and a single veil dropped to the rug.

It showed him nothing more. She was too well-wrapped. But when it hit, his chest tightened. Blood heated and raced through him, heading to his groin, where it settled impatiently. The desire was instant, powerful and pulsing.

He knew of the dance, had heard it described, but had never experienced it himself. He'd heard men talk of the power of being seduced in such a way by a woman and had privately thought them weak. But now, as Kayleen danced in time with the music, he knew he had been wrong. There was something primal in her movements, something that called only him.

She turned again and another veil fell.

It was all he could do to stay seated. He wanted to jump to his feet, pull her close and take her. He wanted to be inside of her, feeling her heat, pleasuring them both. Heat grew until he burned. And still she danced.

Her hips moved back and forth, her arms fluttered. This time when she turned, he knew the veil would fall, anticipated it, looked greedily to see more of her. A tug and it fluttered to the ground.

She turned back. He saw a hint of curve, the lace of her bra, and he was lost. He sprang to his feet and crossed to her. After he grabbed her around the waist, he pulled her against him and kissed her.

He told himself to hold back, that she wouldn't appreciate his passion, but despite his forceful kiss, she met him with the same intensity. She plunged her tongue into his mouth, taking as much as she gave.

Kayleen was shaking, both from nerves and from need. Zarina had been right. Despite her uncertainty, she'd managed to bring a prince to his knees. Or at least his feet, which was just as good.

She'd seen the need in As'ad's eyes, had watched him get aroused. He was already hard and straining. Even as they kissed, he pulled at the veils covering her, swearing with impatience when one tangled and would not budge.

"How many are there?" he asked, his voice thick with frustration and sexual arousal.

"A lot."

She reached for his shirt and began to unbutton that.

"Too slow," he told her and ripped the shirt open, then shrugged out of it. Seconds later he'd removed the rest of his clothes. Then he was naked and reaching for her.

His eagerness thrilled her. She was already damp and swollen, ready to be taken. To show him, she reached between them and stroked his arousal. He groaned as his maleness flexed in her hand.

"I want you," he breathed in her ear. "I want you now."

His words turned her to liquid. "Then take me."

He stared into her eyes. "Kayleen."

"I am to be your wife, As'ad. Take me."

He lowered her to the cushions and pushed the veils aside. After pulling down her panties, he slid his fingers between her legs.

"You want me," he told her as he rubbed against her swollen center.

"Always."

He smiled, then continued to touch her. She pushed his hand away.

"Be in me," she told him. "Claim me."

His breath caught, then he did as she asked. He settled between her knees and pushed inside of her.

She always forgot how large he was, how he filled her and made her ache with need. Normally he was slow and gentle, but tonight he pushed inside as if driven. The passion excited her.

He thrust deeply, groaning, his arousal moving her in a way she'd never experienced before. Her muscles began to tense and she closed her eyes to enjoy the ride.

He took her hard and fast, as if daring her to keep up. She accepted him easily, letting each plunging, rubbing pulse take her higher and higher. She pulled her knees back, then locked her legs around his hips, drawing him in deeper.

Faster and more, pushing and straining until her release was only a heartbeat away.

He spoke her name. She looked up and saw him watching her. "You are mine."

Three simple words, but they were enough to send her spiraling out of control. She lost herself in her release, screaming as the pleasure claimed her. He pushed in twice more, then groaned the end of his journey.

The waves of their pleasure joined them and they clung to each other until the earth stopped moving and their bodies were finally at rest.

Kayleen let herself into her suite shortly after midnight. She felt happy and content and as if she could float. Or do the whole veil dance again!

Rather than turn on a light, she crossed to the balcony and stepped out into the night. The air had a slight chill, but she didn't care. All she had to do was think about how much As'ad had wanted her and she got all hot inside.

The evening had been magical and she didn't want to forget any part of it. If there were—

The sound of a chair moving caught her attention. She turned and saw something sitting in the shadows. The light from a cigarette glowed briefly.

"Well, well, aren't you a bit of surprise." Her mother's voice was low and tight with something Kayleen didn't recognize. "I thought you were just a silly girl who'd gotten lucky, but I was wrong. You just have a different game you play."

Kayleen faced her. "I don't know what you're talking about."

"That innocent, country-mouse act is a good one. I'll bet your prince fell for it in a heartbeat."

"I'm not acting. All of this is real."

Darlene laughed. "Don't try to play me. I invented the game. I'm saying I respect your tactics. They wouldn't work for me, but they obviously work."

"I have no idea what you're talking about. It's late. I'm going to bed."

"You've already been to bed. What you're going to do this time is sleep. Am I wrong?"

"I'm not discussing this with you." She wouldn't allow the other woman to turn her amazing evening into something ugly.

"You made one mistake, though. Falling in love with him makes you vulnerable and that means you can make a wrong move. It's better to stay detached. Safer."

"I'm marrying As'ad. I'm supposed to love him."

Her mother laughed again. "Just don't go expecting him to love you back. Men like him don't. Ever." She inhaled on her cigarette. "That's my motherly advice to you. A little late, but no less valuable."

"Good night," Kayleen told her and walked back into her room.

Her good mood had faded, which she hated, but worse were the doubts. Was her mother right about As'ad? Kayleen needed him to love her. She hadn't realized it mattered, but it did. And if he couldn't…

She walked into her bedroom and sank onto the mattress. If he couldn't, how could she marry him?

Chapter Thirteen

Kayleen huddled in the chair in Lina's living room and did her best to keep breathing. She'd recently discovered that terror and anxiety tended to make her hold her breath. Then she ended up gasping, which was not attractive or likely to make herself feel better.

"She's hideous," she moaned. "Isn't it enough that she abandoned me when I was a baby? Does she have to show up now?"

Lina patted her hand. "I am so sorry. My brother thought he was helping. Truly."

"I know. I've already mentally flogged myself for not telling the truth, but I just hate talking about my biological family. It's pathetic to be abandoned twice. What does that say about me?"

"That you rose above your circumstances. That you have great character and inner strength. That we are lucky to have you marrying into our family."

Kayleen smiled. "You're good."

"Thank you. It's a gift. Now about your mother..."

Kayleen's smile faded. "I don't want to think about her, but I have to. She's everywhere. Lurking. She constantly shows up without warning. She has totally terrified the girls. Last night she made Pepper cry when she told her she was going to have to be smart in life because she wasn't that pretty. Pepper wanted to hit her and I almost let her. Who says that to a little girl? Pepper's adorable. I can forgive her being mean to me, but to little kids? Never."

"Do you want me to tell her to leave the country?" Lina asked. "I will. I can be very imperious. We can ship her back on the next plane."

Kayleen was tempted. Very tempted. "I can't tell you how much I want to say yes. It's just…she's my mother. Shouldn't I try to have a relationship with her? Don't I owe her?"

"Only you can answer that. Although I must ask what you owe her for. Giving birth? You didn't ask to be born. That was her choice. And with having a child, comes responsibility. If she didn't want to be bothered, she should have given you up for adoption."

"I wonder why she didn't," Kayleen said. What would her life have been like if she'd been raised by a couple who wanted a child? She couldn't begin to imagine.

"Who knows. Perhaps the paperwork was too complicated for her tiny brain."

Kayleen grinned. "I like that. But it still leaves me with the issue of what to do with her. While I appreciate your offer to get rid of her, that doesn't feel right to me. I think I have to try and make a real connection with her, no matter how different we are. I'll deal with her for another week. If we can't find some common ground and she's still acting awful, then I'll take you up on your offer."

"You're giving her more chances than I would, but you have a kinder heart."

"Or more guilt." She sighed. "You don't suppose As'ad thinks I'm anything like her, do you?"

"Of course not. We can't pick our relatives. Don't worry— he doesn't blame you for your mother."

"I hope not." She rose. "All right. I need to go make good on my word and try to spend time with Darlene."

"Let me know how it goes."

"I will."

Kayleen walked down a flight of stairs to her suite. She paused at the door, then moved to the next one and knocked.

"Come in."

She walked into her mother's suite and found her at the dining room table, sipping coffee. There was a plate of toast and some fruit in a bowl.

Breakfast, she thought, trying not to judge. It was after eleven.

"Oh, there you are," Darlene said by way of greeting. "I just received the most delightful note from the king. I'm invited to a formal party. Something diplomatic. It sounds fabulous. I'll need something to wear. Can you take care of that?"

Kayleen sat across from her at the table. "Sure. One of the boutiques is sending over some dresses. If you give me your size information, I'll have them send over some for you."

Darlene smiled. "I like the service here."

Despite the fact that she hadn't been up very long, Darlene was perfectly made-up, with her hair styled. She wore a silk robe that clung to her curves. She looked beautiful, in a brittle sort of way.

"I thought maybe we could spend some time together," Kayleen told her. "Get to know each other. Catch up."

Darlene raised her eyebrows. "What do you want to know? I got pregnant at sixteen, left you with my mother and took off for Hollywood. I landed a few guest spots on soaps and a few prime-time shows, which paid the bills. Then I met a guy who took me to Las Vegas. You can make a lot more money there. Which I did. But time isn't a woman's friend. I need to secure my future. I wasn't sure how that was going to happen, when I heard from your king. Now I'm here."

Kayleen leaned toward her. "I'm your daughter. Don't you want to at least be friends?"

Darlene studied her for a long time. "You have a very soft heart, don't you?"

"I've never thought about it."

"You took in those girls. Now you're adopting them. You're going to be exactly the kind of wife As'ad wants."

"I love him. I want him to be happy."

Darlene nodded slowly. "You like it here? In El Deharia?"

"Of course. It's beautiful. Not just the city, but out in the desert. I'm learning the language, the customs. I want to fit in."

Darlene lit a cigarette. Her gaze was sharp, as if she were trying to figure something out. "The king is nice."

"He's very kind and understanding."

"Interesting. Those aren't the words I would have used." Her mother sipped her coffee. "Yes, Kayleen, I *would* like us to be friends. I just showed up here, which had to have been a shock. I've only been thinking of myself. I'm sorry for that."

"Really?" Kayleen was surprised, but pleased to hear the words. "That's okay. You've had a difficult life."

"So have you. But a better one than you would have had if you'd gotten stuck with my family. I know you probably don't believe that, but it's true." She rose. "Let me shower and get dressed. Then, if you have time, you can take me on a tour of the palace. It's a beautiful building."

"It is. I've been studying the history. I want to know everything about As'ad and his people."

Darlene's expression tightened. "I'm sure he appreciates that."

As'ad took Kayleen's hand in his and kissed her fingers. "What troubles you?"

They were having lunch together in his office. She smiled at him. "Nothing. I'm just thinking."

"Obviously not about how you consider yourself blessed above all women for being engaged to me."

She laughed. "No. Not that. I'm thinking about my mother."

"I see."

She looked at him. "You don't approve of her?"

"I do not know her. What matters to me is your feelings."

"I'm not sure of anything," she admitted, wondering when everything had gotten so complicated. "I told her I thought we should get to know each other and try to be friends."

"And?"

"It's better," she said slowly. "I just don't know if I believe her. Then I feel horrible for saying that. I asked, she agreed and now I'm questioning that? Shouldn't I trust her?"

"Trust must be earned. You have a biological connection, but you don't know this woman."

"You're right. I'm so uncomfortable about everything." Especially Darlene's statements that she was in El Deharia to find a rich man to secure her future. Kayleen was torn between keeping her emotional distance and wanting to have family.

She'd always been taught to see the best in people, to believe they would come through in the end. So thinking her mother was using her violated what she knew to be right and what she felt in her heart. But assuming all was well violated her common sense.

She glanced at him. "You know I'm not like her, right?"

He smiled. "Yes, I know."

"Good."

Darlene hummed as she flipped through the dresses on the rack. "I could so get used to this," she murmured as she picked out a low-cut black gown that glittered with scattered beads. "The work is incredible. The details are hand-done. Have you looked at these prices? Twenty-three thousand dollars. Just like that." She put the black dress in front of her and turned to the full-length mirror set up in Kayleen's living room. "What do you think?"

"It's beautiful." Kayleen thought the dress lacked subtlety, but what did she know about fashion?

Darlene laughed. "Not your thing?"

"Not exactly."

"You're young. You'll grow into black." She carried the dress over to the tray of jewelry on the dining room table. "I'm thinking the sapphire-and-diamond-drop earrings and that matching pendant. Or the bracelet. As much as I want to wear both, less is more. Are you wearing that?"

Kayleen held up a strapless emerald-colored dress. The style was simple, yet elegant. It wasn't especially low-cut, but it was more daring than anything she'd ever worn. Still, she wanted to be beautiful for As'ad.

"I love it," she admitted. "But it makes me nervous."

"It's all in the boning. That dress is couture. It should have the support built right in. Don't worry—you'll stay covered." Darlene put her dress back on the rack, then returned to the jewelry tray. "Something surprising. Young, but sophisticated. Let's see."

She picked up an earring, then put it down. She handed another to Kayleen. "Here."

Kayleen took the piece and studied the curving shape. The free-form design was open and sparkled with white and champagne diamonds.

"Really? Not the emeralds?"

"Too expected with the dress," Darlene told her. "And just the earrings. No necklace or bracelet. You're young and beautiful. Go with it. When you start to fade, you can add the sparkle. Someone's going to do your hair, right? You'll want it up, with long curls down your back. And you don't wear enough makeup. It's a party. Use eyeliner."

Kayleen put in the earring, then held her hair away from her face. "You're right."

"Thanks. I've been around a long time and I know what men like. Now let's see how I look in this black dress."

She stripped down to her lingerie and then stepped into the black gown. Kayleen helped with the zipper.

"Perfect," Darlene said as she stared at herself in the mirror.

"I've already met the Spanish ambassador earlier in the garden. He's very charming. A little older, but that's good. I can be his prize."

Kayleen didn't know what to say to that. "Have you ever been married?"

Darlene held her hair up, as if considering the right style. "Once, years ago. I was eighteen. He was nobody. But I was in love and I told myself money didn't matter. Then the marriage ended and I had nothing. I learned my lesson. Something you should learn."

"What are you talking about?"

"As'ad. You get starry-eyed when he's around. It's embarrassing for all of us."

Kayleen flushed. "We're engaged."

"I don't see how that matters." Darlene stepped out of the dress and put it back on the hanger, then reached for her own clothes. "I know this sounds harsh, but believe me, I have your best interests in mind. Men like As'ad don't have to bother with love. You're setting yourself up for heartache. Take what you can get and move on."

"So no one matters. No one touches your heart."

"Life is easier that way," her mother told her.

"You're wrong," Kayleen said. "Life is emptier that way. We are more than the sum of our experiences. We are defined by our relationships. The people we love and those who love us in return. In the end, that matters more than money."

"So speaks the girl who has never been hungry and without a home."

Kayleen stiffened. "I *have* been without a home. My grandmother dumped me at an orphanage because she couldn't be bothered. But then why should she when my own mother walked out on me?"

Darlene pulled on her shirt and buttoned it. "Here we go," she said, sounding bored. "Poor you. Nobody loves you. Get over it. Life is hard, so make the best of it."

"You mean use other people to get what you want."

"If necessary." Darlene seemed untouched by the comment. "Maybe it seems cruel to be tossed aside, but sometimes it's worse to be kept. Your grandmother wasn't exactly a loving parent. There's a reason I left."

"I was your daughter. You should have taken me with you."

"You would have only dragged me down."

"So you left me to the same fate?"

Darlene shrugged. "You got lucky. She didn't bother with you. Trust me, if she had, it would have been a whole lot worse."

Kayleen didn't want to believe the words, but it was impossible not to. "You don't care about me at all."

"I'm proud of what you've accomplished."

"Catching a rich man?"

"Every woman's dream."

"Not mine," Kayleen told her. "I only wanted to belong."

"Then consider the irony. You have what I want and I've turned down a thousand of what you want. Life sure has a sense of humor."

The battle between Kayleen's head and her heart ended. She walked over to the tray of jewelry and shook it. "This is why you're here. This is why you're pretending we can be friends. Let me guess—if you land the Spanish ambassador, you'll be gone and I'll never hear from you again. Until you need something."

Darlene shrugged. "I didn't come looking for you, honey. I was living my life, minding my own business. You're the one who set all this in motion. I'm just taking advantage of the ride."

Kayleen had always tried to hate her mother. It had been easier than being disappointed and heartbroken over being thrown away. But it was impossible to hate someone so flawed and unhappy.

"It won't matter if you end up with the Spanish ambassador," Kayleen told her mother. "You'll never feel like you have enough. There's not enough money in the world to fill that hole inside of you. It's going to take more. It's going to take giving your heart."

"Spare me." Darlene waved her hand dismissively.

"I can't. You can only spare yourself. But you won't listen to me because you think you already know everything you need to. You can't use me anymore. You can stay for the party, but then you have to leave."

Her mother glared at her. "Who the hell are you to tell me whether or not I can stay?"

Kayleen drew herself up to her full height. "I'm As'ad's fiancée."

Kayleen was determined to enjoy her first formal event despite feeling uneasy about her mother. Darlene had been friendly, as if nothing had happened. As if she wasn't planning on leaving. Kayleen was determined to handle the situation herself, so she didn't mention anything to As'ad.

He came to her door a little past seven, looking tall and handsome in a black tuxedo and white shirt.

Dana let him in after insisting Kayleen needed to make an entrance.

"You're so pretty," the girl told her. "He needs to see all of you at once."

Kayleen did her best not to fidget as As'ad walked toward her, his dark eyes unreadable. He paused in front of her.

"You are perfection," he murmured as he lightly kissed her. "I will have to keep you close or you will be stolen away."

"Not likely," she told him with a laugh. She turned in a slow circle. "You like the dress?"

"Yes, but I adore the woman who wears it."

Her heart fluttered.

She'd taken Darlene's advice on her hair, asking the stylist to put the top part up and leave the rest in long curls. The gown fit snugly and seemed secure enough for her to relax. She wore the champagne-and-white-diamond earrings, along with a simple diamond bracelet. Her high-heeled sandals gave her an extra four inches and would be excruciating by the end of the evening, but they looked fabulous.

"When do *we* get to go to formal state parties?" Pepper asked with a whine. "I want a new dress and fancy hair."

"When you are thirteen."

"But that's forever away."

He touched her nose. "You will get there soon enough."

"I only have to wait a year and a half," Dana said happily. "Then I can go."

"Three pretty girls," As'ad told Kayleen. "We're going to have to watch them closely. There will be boys at these parties."

"Am I pretty, too?" Pepper asked. Her eyes were big and she sounded doubtful, as if expecting a negative answer.

Kayleen remembered Darlene's harsh assessment and wanted to bonk her mother on the head for it.

As'ad crouched in front of the little girl. "You are more than pretty. You are a classic beauty. Never doubt yourself. You are to be a princess."

Pepper smiled widely. "When I'm a princess can I chop off people's heads if they're mean to me?"

As'ad choked back a laugh and straightened. "No, but you will have other powers." He took Kayleen's hand. "We must leave. Be good tonight."

"We will," Nadine told him.

Kayleen waved as they left. This being a palace, there was always someone to babysit.

They walked the length of the long corridor, then went down a flight of stairs. Once on the main floor, they joined the milling crowd walking toward the ballroom.

While Kayleen had toured the palace many times, she'd never seen the ballroom anything but empty. She was unprepared for the thousands of lights glittering from dozens of massive chandeliers or perfectly set tables set around a large dance floor.

The room was like something out of a movie. Well-dressed

couples chatted and danced and sipped champagne. She'd never seen so many jewels in her life. Each dress was more beautiful than the one before, each man more handsome. As they walked into the ballroom, she waited for the sense of not belonging to sweep over her. She waited to feel awkward or out of place. Instead there was only contentment and the knowledge that she belonged here.

The burst of confidence bubbled inside of her, as if she'd already had too much champagne. She enjoyed the sensation, knowing this was her world now. She would marry a wonderful man and together they would adopt the girls. In time she would have children of her own.

As'ad led her to the dance floor, then pulled her into his arms. "Now what are you thinking?" he asked.

"That I'm Cinderella and I've finally arrived at the ball."

"So you leave me at midnight?"

She stared into his eyes. "I'll never leave you."

He stared back. "Good. I do not wish you to go. I need you, Kayleen. I will always need you."

Happiness filled her until she felt as if she could float. The music was perfect, as was the night. They danced until the king arrived, then As'ad led her around and introduced her to several of the guests.

The sound of loud laughter caught her attention. She turned and saw Darlene leaning against a much older, heavyset man. The man's attention seemed locked on her barely covered chest.

"The Spanish ambassador?" Kayleen asked As'ad.

"Yes. Do you wish to meet him?"

"Not especially."

He watched Darlene. "So that is who she has chosen?"

"Apparently."

"He's very rich, but alas, he is married. His wife does not accompany him when he travels."

Married? Kayleen looked at her mother. Did Darlene know?

"I should tell her," she said.

He frowned. "Why?"

"Because she's looking for security in her old age and he's obviously not the way to find it."

"Do you care what happens to her?"

"She's my mother. I can't not care." Which didn't mean she'd changed her mind. She still wanted her mother gone. Not that she'd figured out how to make her go.

"I think it is time I dance with my new sister."

Kayleen turned and saw Qadir, As'ad's brother, standing next to her.

"Assuming you don't mind," Qadir told As'ad.

"One dance and don't flirt."

Qadir laughed. "I flirt as easily as I breathe. Are you so worried that I will steal her away?"

"A man always guards what is precious to him."

Kayleen held in a sigh. "Flirt away," she told Qadir. "My heart belongs to your brother."

"Then he is a lucky man." Qadir led her to the dance floor. "You are beautiful tonight."

"Just tonight? Am I usually a troll?"

He laughed. "So this is what has charmed my brother. There's a brain."

"I have all my organs. Unusual, but there we are."

He laughed again. They chatted about the party and the guests. Qadir told her outrageous stories about several people, including a rumor about an English duchess who complained about not being allowed to bring her dog to the event.

When the dance was finished, Kayleen excused herself. Qadir was nice enough, but not the person she wanted to spend the evening with.

She walked around the edge of the room, and saw As'ad speaking with her mother.

"That can't be good," she muttered to herself and crossed the room to where they were standing.

"You will leave," As'ad said as Kayleen approached.

"I'm not so sure about that," Darlene told him. "The girl is my daughter. Who are you to come between her and her family?"

"A man who is willing to pay you to leave."

Kayleen caught her breath. No. As'ad couldn't do that. It wasn't right. She moved forward, but neither of them noticed her.

"You will not see her again," he continued. "If she contacts you herself, that is fine, but you will not have contact with her directly without her permission."

"So many rules." Darlene smiled. "That'll cost you."

"I would think a million dollars would be enough."

"Oh, please. Not even close. I want five."

"Three."

"I'll take four and you'll consider it a bargain."

The room went still. Oh, sure, people were dancing and talking and Kayleen was confident the orchestra kept playing, but she couldn't hear anything except the conversation of the two people in front of her.

"I'll wire the money as soon as you get me an account number," he said.

"I can give it to you tonight." Darlene patted his arm. "You really care for her. That's sweet."

"She is to be my wife."

"So I hear. You know she's in love with you."

Kayleen's breath caught.

"I know." As'ad spoke quietly, confidently.

"I'll bet that makes things real easy for you," Darlene said.

"It does."

Her mother tilted her head. "You think she's foolish enough to think you love her back?"

"You are not to tell her otherwise."

"Of course not." Darlene smiled again. "But I think I should be allowed to keep the dress and the jewelry then. As a token of goodwill."

"As you wish."

"Then she'll never hear the truth from me."

Chapter Fourteen

Kayleen didn't remember leaving the party, but she must have. When she finally looked around, she was in the garden—the one place she always seemed to retreat to. It was mostly in shadow, with lights illuminating the path. She wandered around, her body aching, her eyes burning, neither of which compared to the pain in her heart.

As'ad didn't love her. While he'd never specifically said he cared, she'd allowed herself to believe.

"I'm a fool," she said aloud.

He'd dismissed feelings as nothing more than a convenience. He'd admitted that their marriage would be easier for him, because of her feelings. He was using her. Nothing about their engagement mattered to him. *She* didn't matter to him.

She hurt. Her whole body ached. Each breath was an effort. She wanted to cry, but she was too stunned.

Her hopes and dreams continued to crumble around her, leaving her standing in a pile of dusty "what could have been." She'd thought she'd found where she belonged, where she could matter and make a difference. She'd thought so many things. But in As'ad's mind, she was little more than a comfy ottoman, where he could rest his feet. Useful, but not of any great interest.

She turned, trying to figure out where to go, what to do. Light caught her engagement ring and made it sparkle. She'd been such a fool, she thought bitterly. So stupidly innocent and naive about everything. Her mother had been right—why on earth would a man like As'ad be interested in a country mouse like herself? She'd wrapped herself in the fantasy because it was what she wanted to believe. Because it was easier than accepting the truth.

She heard a sound and looked up. One of the doves shifted in its cage. Willingly trapped because they either didn't understand they could be free or weren't interested. They took the easy way out, too.

Anger joined a sadness so profound, she knew it would scar her forever. Because whatever mistakes she'd made, she truly did love As'ad. She always would. But she didn't belong here. She couldn't stay and marry a man who didn't love her.

That decided, she made her way into the palace. Her mother's door stood partially open. Kayleen stepped inside without knocking to find her mother supervising two maids who were packing her suitcases. Darlene had already changed out of her evening gown into an elegant pantsuit. When she saw her daughter, she smiled.

"Oh, good. You stopped by. That saves me writing a note. Look, I'm leaving—just like you said I should. I've had a great time. I'm sorry we didn't get a chance to get to know each other better. Next time you're back in the States, you'll need to look me up."

Everything about her was false, Kayleen thought emotionlessly. From her bleached hair to her fake smiles.

"You're leaving because As'ad is paying you four million dollars," Kayleen told her. "I heard the conversation."

"Then you know I got what I came for. A secure future. It's not a fortune, but I know how to invest. I'll live well enough and maybe find someone to supplement my excesses. It doesn't compare with your haul, of course, but we can't all be that lucky."

Lucky. Right. To fall in love with a man who didn't care about her.

"When do you leave?" Kayleen asked.

"There's a plane waiting at the airport. I love the truly rich." Darlene frowned. "You're not going to want an emotional good-bye, are you?"

"No. I don't want anything from you."

With that, she left and returned to her own suite. The baby-sitter greeted her.

"They were all so good tonight," the young woman said.

"I'm glad. Thank you."

The other woman left and Kayleen was alone.

Despite the pain, she felt almost at peace. Maybe it was finally seeing the world as it was, and not as she wanted it to be. Maybe it was knowing the truth.

The truth was she would never have the kind of relationship with her biological family that she wanted. She could keep trying and maybe in time, things would improve, but there was no rescue there. There was no happy ending.

The same was true with As'ad. He'd proposed out of duty and maybe with the belief that she would be a good wife. He'd told her he didn't believe in love and she hadn't listened. She'd created a different story because it was what she wanted to believe.

But he didn't love her and he had no intention of loving her. So her choices were clear. She could stay and marry him, live life as a princess, or she could walk away. Darlene would tell her the money, the prestige, the palace, were worth nearly everything. But Kayleen remembered reading once that when a woman marries for money, she earns every penny.

She didn't want to marry for money—she wanted to marry for love. She wasn't like the doves—trapped even though the door was open, she was free to leave.

After looking in on the girls, she returned to her own room. She undressed and pulled on a robe, then sat in a chair by the French doors and stared out at the night.

The only part of leaving that bothered her was knowing how much she would miss As'ad. Despite everything, she loved him. Would she ever be able to love anyone else?

Because that's what she wanted. A real life, with a family and a man who cared. She wasn't going to run back to the convent school. She was going to make her way in the world. She was strong—she could do it.

As'ad found Kayleen in her suite. She'd changed out of her ball gown and pulled on a robe. She sat in the living room, a pad of paper on her lap.

He walked in and stared at her. "You left the party. I looked everywhere and you were gone."

She glanced up at him. "I didn't want to stay any longer."

That didn't sound right, he thought warily. She'd left without talking to him? "Are you ill?"

"I'm fine."

"You came back here to make notes?"

"Apparently." She set the paper and pen on the coffee table, then stood. "Have you transferred the money to my mother?"

He swore silently. "You spoke with her?"

"Not about that. Don't worry. She didn't tell me anything, so she gets to keep the dress and jewelry, right? I mean, that *was* the deal. Along with the four million. A generous offer. I'd already told her to leave, but you didn't know that. She made out well."

"I do not care about the money," he said, trying to remember exactly what he and Darlene had discussed. Obviously Kayleen had been in a position to overhear their conversation.

He felt badly—he guessed she was hurt and his intent had been to avoid that.

"I know," Kayleen said. "But she does, so it works out well for both of you."

He tried to read her expression, but he had no idea what she was thinking. Was she angry?

"Once she is gone, all will be well," he said, willing it to be so.

"I'm not as sure." She stared into his eyes. "This is just a marriage of convenience for you. I'm surprised you'd pick me. I'm sure there are women with better pedigrees out there. Women who understand what it's like to be a princess and who won't have foolish expectations."

"I am pleased to be marrying you. I want you to be the mother of my sons. I respect you, Kayleen. Isn't respect and admiration more important, more lasting, than a fleeting emotion like love? I will honor you above all women. That must have value."

"It does. But love has value, too. Maybe it's a peasant thing."

She was calm and he didn't like it. Screaming and crying he could understand, but not this quiet conversation. What did she want from him?

"I take a lot of the blame," she said, her gaze steady. "I took the easy way out. You told me that after we slept together, and you were right. I want to hide, first at the convent school and then here, with you. I was never willing to really strike out on my own. I was afraid and I let that fear rule me. I thought by staying close to what I knew, I would be safe and belong. Even when I went halfway around the world to your country, I huddled in the orphan school, terrified to take a step."

Her reasoning sounded correct, but he had a bad feeling about what she was saying.

"Now you have chosen a different path," he pointed out. "So you are making changes. That is as it should be."

"I am making changes, As'ad. Big ones." She removed her engagement ring and held it out to him.

"No," he told her, shocked by her actions. "You have agreed to marry me. Changing your mind is not permitted."

"*You* don't get to decide that. I won't marry a man who doesn't love me. I'm worth more. I deserve more. And so do you. I know you believe love makes you weak, but you're wrong.

Love makes you strong. It is powerful and the reason we're here. To love and be loved. You need that, As'ad. I love you, but that's not enough. You have to be willing to love me back. Maybe I'm not the one. Maybe there's someone else you can love."

She gulped in a breath and tried to smile. Her lips trembled. "It hurts to say that. It hurts to think of you with someone else. But I can't make you love me."

She didn't mean this, he told himself. It was the emotion of the moment. She would get over it.

"I will not accept the ring back."

"That's your choice." She put it on the coffee table. "Either way, I'm leaving."

"You cannot go. I won't permit it. Besides…" He prepared to say the one thing that would change her mind. "I need you."

She nodded slowly. "You do. More than you realize. But that's not enough."

He frowned. It had worked before. Lina had told him Kayleen wanted to be needed above all. "I need you," he repeated.

"Maybe, but you can't have me." She sighed. "It's late, and you should go."

Somehow he found himself moving to the door. Then he was in the hallway. He stood there a long time, fighting the strangest feeling that he'd just lost something precious.

No, he told himself. Kayleen wouldn't leave him. She couldn't. She belonged here. To him and the girls. She would be fine. In the morning they would talk again. He would make her understand that she belonged here. With him. It was what he wanted. And he was Prince As'ad of El Deharia. He always got what he wanted.

As'ad gave Kayleen plenty of time to think about what she was considering, which turned out to be the one flaw in his plan. For when he returned to her suite close to midday, she and the girls were gone.

Their closets were empty, the toys missing, the dining room

swept clean of homework and books. The only thing lying there was the engagement ring he'd given her.

He had expected a fight or tears or even an apology, but not the silence. Not the absence of life. It was as if they'd never been there at all.

He walked through the rooms, not truly accepting the truth of it. She had left him.

Him! A prince. After all he'd done for her, all he'd given her. He'd rescued her and the children, started the adoption process for the girls. He'd given them a home, had proposed to Kayleen. What more did she want?

He burst into his aunt's office and glared at her. "This is all your fault," he told her sternly. "You created the problem and you will fix it."

Lina's office was small and feminine, overlooking the garden. Normally he would tease her about the frills and ruffles, but not today. Not now when she had ruined everything.

Lina poured herself some tea from a pot on a silver tray. "I have no idea what you're talking about."

"Of course you do. Kayleen is gone. She left and took the girls. Those are my children. El Deharian law states royal children cannot be taken from the country without their royal parent's permission."

"You're not the royal parent yet. Your petition for adoption has not been approved, nor is it likely to be. Custody will be given solely to Kayleen. She's already spoken to the king."

As'ad stared at her, unable to believe what she was saying. "That is not possible."

"It's very possible. You only took the girls because I suggested it as a way to solve the problem with Tahir. You never actually wanted them."

This was *not* happening, he told himself. "I did not know them. I know them now and they are my daughters."

"Not really. Kayleen is the one who loves them."

"I provided snow for their pageant."

"Which was great and I know they enjoyed it. I'm not saying you didn't care about them, As'ad. But love? You don't believe in it. You've told me yourself. Your father understands completely. Don't forget, these aren't royal children who grew up like you did. They expect their parents to love them. Kayleen will. They're leaving El Deharia. All four of them."

Leaving? Permanently?

"I will not allow it," he told her. "I insist they stay."

"They will through the holidays, then Kayleen is taking the girls back to the States. It will be easier for them to start over. Your father has offered to help financially. Kayleen is being her usual sacrificing self. She will allow him to help her with the girls until she gets established, but then she'll handle things. She's going to let him pay for college, though. Especially for Dana. Apparently she wants to be a doctor."

"I know that," As'ad said through ground teeth. "And Nadine will dance and Pepper has yet to decide, but she's only eight and why should she? This is ridiculous. My father will not support my children. It is my responsibility and my right. You have meddled, Lina. You have ruined everything."

"Actually, you did that all yourself. Kayleen is a wonderful woman. She adored you and would have made you very happy. She was yours to lose and you did. But don't worry. She'll find someone else. I'm a little more worried about you."

He wanted to rant and yell. He wanted to throw her antique desk through the large window. He wanted to crush her teapot with his bare hands.

"None of this is acceptable," he growled.

"I'm sorry you see it that way, but I think it's for the best. Kayleen deserves a man who will love her. Or don't you agree?"

He glared at his aunt. "You seek to trap me with your words."

"I seek to make you understand that you don't deserve a woman like Kayleen."

Her words cut him in a way no words had before. He stared at her for a long moment as the truth settled into the wound.

She was right—he did not deserve Kayleen. All this time he had assumed he was doing her a favor when, in truth, the situation was reversed.

He left Lina's office and retreated to his own. He told Neil he would not be disturbed. Then he stood alone in the silence and wondered what had gone wrong.

Two days later he understood the real meaning of the words *living in hell*. Only there was no living for him, only reminders of what he had lost.

He had always enjoyed life in the palace, but now every room, every corridor, was a reminder of what was missing. He turned, expecting to see one of the girls. But they weren't there. He thought of a thousand things he should tell Kayleen, but she wasn't around to listen. He ached to hold her, touch her, kiss her, and there was no one.

She had left him. Willingly, easily. She had walked away and not come back. She, who had claimed to love him.

While he knew in his heart her affection for him had not had time to fade, in his mind he grew angry. But she was not there to fight with.

He spent the night in her rooms, wandering, sitting, waiting, remembering. He arranged to go to Paris to forget her, then canceled his plans. He, who had never allowed himself to care, to need, to love, had been broken. Prince As'ad of El Deharia reduced to a shell of a man because his woman had left.

He hated that. Hated to be weak. Hated to need.

He hurried to see his father, walking in on the king without knocking. His father looked up from his morning paper. "As'ad, what is wrong? You do not look well."

"I am fine. Kayleen has left."

"Yes, I know."

"You must not give her permission to leave the country, or take the girls with her. Those are my children. The law is clearly on my side."

His father frowned. "Kayleen said you did not love the girls. That they would be better off with her. Was she wrong? What do you wish?"

Love. Why did it always come back to that? As'ad walked to the window and stared out at the horizon.

What *did* he wish?

"I want her back," he said quietly. "I want her here, with me. I want the girls to return. I want…"

He wanted Kayleen smiling at him, laughing with him, close to him. He wanted to see her stomach swell with their baby, he wanted to ease her discomfort when she was sick. He wanted to see the girls grow and learn and prepare for college. He wanted to walk each of them down the aisle, only after terrifying any young man who would claim one of them as he had claimed Kayleen.

What if Dana was in a love with a man who did not love her back? What would he do?

Kill him, he told himself. He would kill the suitor in question, then take his daughter home where she belonged. He would insist she not be with anyone who did not love her desperately. Because that was what she deserved. What they all deserved. He could not let them go under any other circumstances.

Didn't Kayleen deserve the same?

He already knew the answer. He believed it. But if it was true, then shouldn't he let her go to find such a man?

No!

The roar came from deep within him. He faced his father. "No. She is to have no one but me. I am the one who first claimed her and I will not let her go."

His father sighed. "We have let go of the old ways. You will not be allowed to claim a bride who is not interested in marrying you."

"I will convince her."

"How?"

"By giving her the one thing she wants."

The king looked doubtful. "Do you know what that is?"

As'ad finally did. "Where is she?"

Mukhtar hesitated. "I am not sure…"

"I am. Where is she? I know she has not left the country. Lina told me. Where is she hiding?"

And then he knew that, as well. "Never mind. I'll find her myself."

Kayleen did her best to smile. The puppy was adorable, as was Pepper as the two of them tumbled together on the rug by the fire. Dana and Nadine were off with the older girls. Despite the sudden change from a palace to a desert camp, the sisters had adjusted well. They thought they were on a fun adventure.

Kayleen wished she could share their excitement and flexibility. While she appreciated that Sharif and Zarina had taken them in, she longed to be back at the palace. While life under the stars offered a level of freedom she'd never experienced before, it was difficult to even breathe without thinking of As'ad.

She ached for him every minute of every day. She knew she had to stay strong and she was determined not to give in to the need to see him, but there were times when the pain overwhelmed her.

Zarina hadn't asked any questions when Kayleen had shown up with the girls. Instead she'd offered a comfortable tent and acceptance by the villagers. But it was a temporary situation—in a few days the tribe would return to the desert and Kayleen would have to find temporary housing until she could leave El Deharia.

Perhaps in the city somewhere. A small house. Lina had promised it would only take a couple of weeks for her paperwork to be pushed through the legal channels. There were advantages to a royal connection.

Thank goodness As'ad hadn't been interested in hurrying the adoption. If he had she wouldn't have been able to leave.

Royal children could not be taken from El Deharia without the royal parent's permission.

She touched her belly and remembered the last time they'd made love. If she was pregnant, she would be trapped forever. Imagine the irony if she at last had the baby she'd long desired.

"I will not think of that," she whispered to herself. "I will stay strong."

She might not know the future, but she was confident she could handle whatever life threw at her. She'd stood up for what she believed, she'd faced As'ad and turned down the half life he'd offered. She'd been willing to lose everything to gain her heart's desire. There was some peace in knowing she'd been true to herself. Unfortunately peace did not seem to ease pain.

She stood and walked to the fire, where tea always boiled. After pouring herself a mug she stared up at the clear sky. Only two days until Christmas. They would celebrate out here, under the stars, then return to the city.

She turned back to the tent, only to stop when she saw a man riding toward the camp. For a moment her heart jumped in her chest, but then she realized he wore traditional clothes. One of the young men who came and went, she thought, looking away. Someone's husband.

Several of the tribespeople called out to each other. Kayleen tried to figure out what they were saying, but they were speaking quickly, yelling and pointing. Was there a problem?

Then she looked back at the man and recognized him. As'ad. But he was unlike she'd ever seen him before. He looked determined, primal. This was no prince in a suit—this was a sheik.

She stood her ground, reminding herself she had nothing to fear. He couldn't hurt her worse than he had when he'd admitted he didn't love her and that her love for him was a well-timed convenience. She shook out her long hair, then raised her chin. Pride and determination stiffened her spine. She didn't move, not even when he rode his horse right up to her.

Their eyes locked. She had no idea what he was thinking.

Despite everything, she was happy to see him, happy to drink in the male beauty of his hard features. She wanted to touch him and kiss him and give herself to him. So much for being strong.

"I have claimed you," he told her sternly. "You cannot escape me."

"You can't hold me against my will. I'm not your prisoner."

He dismounted and handed the horse off to one of the young boys who had run up. Then he stalked over to her.

"You're right, my heart. I am yours."

She blinked. What had he called her? And what did he mean that he was her prisoner? What?

He touched her face with his fingertips. "I have missed you. Every second of every day since you left me has been empty and dark."

She swallowed. "I don't understand."

"Nor do I. My course was set—the plan clear. I would marry appropriately, father sons, perhaps a daughter or two, serve my people and live my life. It was arranged. It was my destiny. Then one day, I met a woman who leads with her heart, who is fearless and giving and kind and who bewitched me."

She couldn't breathe, but that didn't seem to be such a big deal. This was all good, right? He was saying good things. Maybe, just maybe, she could hope.

"Kayleen, I was wrong," he told her. "Wrong to think I knew so much more, that I was in charge. You swept into my life and nothing was the same. It was better—so much better. I miss you desperately. You and the girls. I need to see you smile every day. All of you. I need to hear your voices, your laughter. You cannot take my daughters from me and you cannot take yourself."

She ached for him. Giving in seemed the only option. But how could she?

"I won't live in a loveless marriage," she told him, fighting tears, fighting the need to surrender. "I deserve more."

"Yes, you do. I was wrong to suggest such a thing before.

You deserve to be loved, to be worshiped. To be the best part of your husband's life."

He took her hands in his and kissed her knuckles, then turned her wrists and kissed her palms.

"Let me be that man," he said quietly. "Let me show you all the ways I love you. Let me prove myself again and again, then, when you are sure, continue to test me." He stared into her eyes. "I will not fail, my heart. I will never fail. Because I love you. Only you. I did not think it was possible, yet here I stand. Humbled. Needing. In love. Can you find it in your heart to forgive me? To give me another chance?"

"Say yes."

The words were whispered from behind her. She sensed all three of the girls standing there, willing her to give As'ad the second chance he asked for.

"Yes," she whispered, then threw herself into his arms.

He caught her and pulled her close, saying her name over and over, then kissed her and held her as if he would never let her go.

He felt so right, next to her, she thought, nearly bursting with happiness. Then there were more arms and he pulled back only to let the girls into their circle of love.

He picked up Pepper and put his arm around Nadine. Kayleen pulled Dana against her and they held on to each other... a family at last.

"I'm so happy," Kayleen told him.

"As am I. Perhaps not as quick a learner as you would like."

"You figured it out."

"Only because you had the strength to leave me. You will always do the right thing, won't you?"

"I'll try."

He kissed her again, then frowned. "Why do you cry?"

"I'm not."

She touched her cheek and felt wetness. But it was cold, not warm and wasn't a tear.

Pepper shrieked. "It's snowing. As'ad, you brought the snow machine to the desert!"

"I did not. There is no way to power it out here."

Kayleen looked up. Snow fell from a clear sky. Perfect snow. Miracle snow. Christmas snow.

He set Pepper on the ground. She joined her sisters and the other children, running around, trying to catch snowflakes in their hands and on their tongues. As'ad pulled Kayleen close.

"You must promise to never leave me again," he said. "I would not survive it."

"As you will never leave me."

He laughed. "Where else would I want to be? I have you."

"For always," she told him.

"Yes," he promised. "For always."

Love burned hot and bright in his eyes. Love that filled the empty space inside of her and told her she had finally, *finally* found her way home.

* * * * *

Keep reading for an excerpt of
The Venetian One-Night Baby
by Melanie Milburne.
Find it in the
Irresistible Italians: A Dangerous Deal anthology,
out now!

CHAPTER ONE

SABRINA WAS HOPING she wouldn't run into Max Firbank again after The Kiss. He wasn't an easy man to avoid since he was her parents' favourite godson and was invited to just about every Midhurst family gathering. Birthdays, Christmas, New Year's Eve, parties and anniversaries he would spend on the fringes of the room, a twenty-first-century reincarnation of Jane Austen's taciturn Mr Darcy. He'd look down his aristocratic nose at everyone else having fun.

Sabrina made sure she had extra fun just to annoy him. She danced with everyone who asked her, chatting and working the room like she was the star student from Social Butterfly School. Max occasionally wouldn't show, and then she would spend the whole evening wondering why the energy in the room wasn't the same. But she refused to acknowledge it had anything to do with his absence.

This weekend she was in Venice to exhibit two of her designs at her first wedding expo. She felt safe from running into him—or she would have if the hotel receptionist could find her booking.

Sabrina leaned closer to the hotel reception counter. 'I can assure you the reservation was made weeks ago.'

'What name did you say it was booked under?' the young male receptionist asked.

'Midhurst, Sabrina Jane. My assistant booked it for me.'

'Do you have any documentation with you? The confirmation email?'

Had her new assistant Harriet forwarded it to her? Sabrina remembered printing out the wedding expo programme but had she printed out the accommodation details? She searched for it in her tote bag, sweat beading between her breasts, her stomach pitching with panic. She couldn't turn up flustered to her first wedding expo as an exhibitor. That's why she'd recently employed an assistant to help her with this sort of stuff. Booking flights and accommodation, sorting out her diary, making sure she didn't double book or miss appointments.

Sabrina put her lipgloss, paper diary, passport and phone on the counter, plus three pens, a small packet of tissues, some breath mints and her brand-new business cards. She left her tampons in the side pocket of her bag—there was only so much embarrassment she could handle at any one time. The only bits of paper she found were a shopping list and a receipt from her favourite shoe store.

She began to put all the items back in her bag, but her lipgloss fell off the counter, dropped to the floor, rolled across the lobby and was stopped by a large Italian-leather-clad foot.

Sabrina's gaze travelled up the long length of the expertly tailored charcoal-grey trousers and finally came to rest on Max Firbank's smoky grey-blue gaze.

'Sabrina.' His tone was less of a greeting and more of a grim *not you again*.

Sabrina gave him a tight, no-teeth-showing smile. 'Fancy seeing you here. I wouldn't have thought wedding expos were your thing.'

His eyes glanced at her mouth and something in her stomach dropped like a book tumbling off a shelf. *Kerplunk*. He blinked as if to clear his vision and bent down to pick up her lipgloss.

He handed it to her, his expression as unreadable as cryptic code. 'I'm seeing a client about a project. I always stay at this hotel when I come to Venice.'

Sabrina took the lipgloss and slipped it into her bag, trying to ignore the tingling in her fingers where his had touched hers. She could feel the heat storming into her cheeks in a hot crimson tide. What sort of weird coincidence was *this*? Of all the hotels in Venice why did he have to be at *this* one? And on *this* weekend? She narrowed her gaze to the size of buttonholes. 'Did my parents tell you I was going to be here this weekend?'

Nothing on his face changed except for a brief elevation of one of his dark eyebrows. 'No. Did mine tell you I was going to be in Venice?'

Sabrina raised her chin. 'Oh, didn't you know? I zone out when your parents tell me things about you. I mentally plug my ears and sing *la-de-da* in my head until they change the subject of how amazingly brilliant you are.'

There was a flicker of movement across his lips that could have been loosely described as a smile. 'I'll have to remember to do that next time your parents bang on about you to me.'

Sabrina flicked a wayward strand of hair out of her face. Why did she always have to look like she'd been through a wind tunnel whenever she saw him? She dared not look at his mouth but kept her eyes trained on his inscrutable gaze. Was he thinking about The Kiss? The clashing of mouths that had morphed into a passionate explosion that had made a mockery of every other kiss she'd ever received? Could he still recall the taste and texture of her mouth? Did he lie in bed at night and fantasise about kissing her again?

And not just kissing, but...

'*Signorina?*' The hotel receptionist jolted Sabrina out of her reverie. 'We have no booking under the name Midhurst. Could it have been another hotel you selected online?'

Sabrina suppressed a frustrated sigh. 'No. I asked my assistant to book me into this one. This is where the fashion show is being held. I have to stay here.'

'What's the problem?' Max asked in a calm, *leave it to me* tone.

Sabrina turned to face him. 'I've got a new assistant and somehow she must've got the booking wrong or it didn't process or something.' She bit her lip, trying to stem the panic punching against her heart. *Poomf. Poomf. Poomf.*

'I can put you on the cancellation list, but we're busy at this time of year so I can't guarantee anything,' the receptionist said.

Sabrina's hand crept up to her mouth and she started nibbling on her thumbnail. Too bad about her new manicure. A bit of nail chewing was all she had to soothe her rising dread. She wanted to be settled into her hotel, not left waiting on standby. What if no other hotel could take her? She needed to be close to the convention venue because she had two dresses in the fashion parade. This was her big break to get her designs on the international stage.

She. Could. Not. Fail.

'Miss Midhurst will be joining me,' Max said. 'Have the concierge bring her luggage to my room. Thank you.'

Sabrina's gaze flew to his. 'What?'

Max handed her a card key, his expression still as inscrutable as that of an MI5 spy. 'I checked in this morning. There are two beds in my suite. I only need one.'

She did *not* want to think about him and a bed in the same sentence. She'd spent the last three weeks thinking about him in a bed with her in a tangle of sweaty sex-sated limbs. Which was frankly kind of weird because she'd spent most of her life deliberately *not* thinking about him. Max was her parents' godson and almost from the moment when she'd been born six years later and become his parents' adored goddaughter, both sets of parents had decided how perfect they were for each other. It was the long-wished-for dream of both families that Max and Sabrina would fall in love, get married and have gorgeous babies together.

As if. In spite of both families' hopes, Sabrina had never got on with Max. She found him brooding and distant and arrogant. And he made it no secret he found her equally annoying…which kind of made her wonder why he'd kissed her…

But she was *not* going to think about The Kiss.

She glanced at the clock over Reception, another fist of panic pummelling her heart. She needed to shower and change and do her hair and makeup. She needed to get her head in order. It wouldn't do to turn up flustered and nervous. What sort of impression would she make?

Sabrina took the key from him but her fingers brushed his and a tingle travelled from her fingers to her armpit. 'Maybe I should try and see if I can get in somewhere else…'

'What time does your convention start?'

'There's a cocktail party at six-thirty.'

Max led the way to the bank of lifts. 'I'll take you up to settle you in before I meet my client for a drink.'

Sabrina entered the brass embossed lift with him and the doors whispered shut behind them. The mirrored interior reflected Max's features from every angle. His tall and lean and athletic build. The well-cut dark brown hair with a hint of a wave. The generously lashed eyes the colour of storm clouds. The faint hollow below the cheekbones that gave him a chiselled-from-marble look that was far more attractive than it had any right to be. The aristocratic cut of nostril and upper lip, the small cleft in his chin, the square jaw that hinted at arrogance and a tendency to insist on his own way.

'Is your client female?' The question was out before Sabrina could monitor her wayward tongue.

'Yes.' His brusque one-word answer was a verbal Keep Out sign.

Sabrina had always been a little intrigued by his love life. He had been jilted by his fiancée Lydia a few days before their wedding six years ago. He had never spoken of why his fiancée had called off the wedding but Sabrina had heard a whisper that it had been because Lydia had wanted children and he didn't. Max wasn't one to brandish his subsequent lovers about in public but she knew he had them from time to time. Now thirty-four, he was a virile man in his sexual prime. And she had tasted a hint of that potency when his mouth had come down on hers and sent her senses into a tailspin from which they had not yet recovered—if they ever would.

The lift stopped on Max's floor and he indicated for her to alight before him. She moved past him and breathed in the sharp citrus scent of his aftershave—lemon and lime and something else that was as mysterious and unknowable as his personality.

He led the way along the carpeted corridor and came to a suite that overlooked the Grand Canal. Sabrina stepped over the threshold and, pointedly ignoring the twin king-sized beds, went straight to the windows to check out the magnificent view. Even if her booking had been processed correctly, she would never have been able to afford a room such as this.

'Wow…' She breathed out a sigh of wonder. 'Venice never fails to take my breath away. The light. The colours. The history.' She turned to face him, doing her best to not glance at the beds that dominated the room. He still had his spy face on but she could sense an inner tension in the way he held himself. 'Erm… I'd appreciate it if you didn't tell anyone about this…'

The mocking arch of his eyebrow made her cheeks burn. 'This?'

At this rate, she'd have to ramp up the air-conditioning to counter the heat she was giving off from her burning cheeks. 'Me…sharing your room.'

'I wouldn't dream of it.'

'I mean, it could get really embarrassing if either of our parents thought we were—'

'We're not.' The blunt edge to his voice was a slap down to her ego.

There was a knock at the door.

Max opened the door and stepped aside as the hotel employee brought in Sabrina's luggage. Max gave the young man a tip and closed the door, locking his gaze on hers. 'Don't even think about it.'

Sabrina raised her eyebrows so high she thought they would fly off her face. 'You think I'm attracted to *you*? Dream on, buddy.'

The edge of his mouth lifted—the closest he got to a smile, or at least one he'd ever sent her way. 'I could have had you that night three weeks ago and you damn well know it.'

'*Had* me?' She glared at him. 'That kiss was…was a knee-jerk thing. It just…erm…happened. And you gave me stubble rash. I had to put on cover-up for a week.'

His eyes went to her mouth as if he was remembering the explosive passion they'd shared. He drew in an uneven breath and sent a hand through the thick pelt of his hair, a frown pulling at his forehead. 'I'm sorry. It wasn't my intention to hurt you.' His voice had a deep gravelly edge she'd never heard in it before.

Sabrina folded her arms. She wasn't ready to forgive him. She wasn't ready to forgive herself for responding to him. She wasn't ready to admit how much she'd enjoyed that kiss and how she had encouraged it by grabbing the front of his shirt and pulling his head down. Argh. Why had she done that? Neither was she ready to admit how much she wanted him to kiss her again. 'I can think of no one I would less like to "have me".'

Even repeating the coarse words he'd used turned her on. Damn him. She couldn't stop thinking about what it would be like to be *had by him*. Her sex life was practically non-existent. The only sex she'd had in the last few years had been with herself and even that hadn't been all that spectacular. She kept hoping she'd find the perfect partner to help her with her issues with physical intimacy but so far no such luck. She rarely dated anyone more than two or three times before she decided having sex with them was out of the question. Her first and only experience of sex at the age of eighteen—*had it really been ten years ago?*—had been an ego-smashing disappointment, one she was in no hurry to repeat.

'Good. Because we're not going there,' Max said.

Sabrina inched up her chin. 'You were the one who kissed me first that night. I might have returned the kiss but only because I got caught off guard.' It was big fat lie but no way was she going to admit it. Every non-verbal signal in her repertoire had been on duty that night all but begging him to kiss her. And when he finally had, she even recalled moaning at one point. Yes, moaning with pleasure as his lips and tongue had worked their magic. *Geez*. How was she going to live *that* down?

His eyes pulsed with something she couldn't quite identify. Suppressed anger or locked-down lust or both? 'You were spoiling for a fight all through that dinner party and during the trip when I gave you a lift home.'

'So? We always argue. It doesn't mean I want you to kiss me.'

His eyes held hers in a smouldering lock that made the backs of her knees fizz. 'Are we arguing now?' His tone had a silky edge that played havoc with her senses.

Sabrina took a step back, one of her hands coming up her neck where her heart was beating like a panicked pigeon stuck in a pipe. 'I need to get ready for the c-cocktail party...' Why, oh, why did she have to sound so breathless?

He gave a soft rumble of a laugh. 'Your virtue is safe, Sabrina.' He walked to the door of the suite and turned to look at her again. 'Don't wait up. I'll be late.'

Sabrina gave him a haughty look that would have done a Regency spinster proud. 'Going to *have* your client, are you?'

He left without another word, which, annoyingly, left her with the painful echo of hers.

Max closed the door of his suite and let out a breath. Why had he done the knight in shining armour thing? Why should he care if she couldn't get herself organised enough to book a damn hotel? She would have found somewhere to stay, surely. But no. He had to do the decent thing. Nothing about how he felt about Sabrina was decent—especially after that kiss. He'd lost count of how many women he'd kissed. He wasn't a man whore, but he enjoyed sex for the physical release it gave.

But he couldn't get *that* kiss out of his mind.

Max had always avoided Sabrina in the past. He hadn't wanted to encourage his and her parents from their sick little fantasy of them getting it on. He got it on with women he chose and he made sure his choices were simple and straightforward—sex without strings.

Sabrina was off limits because she was the poster girl for the happily-ever-after fairytale. She was looking for Mr Right to sweep her off her feet and park her behind a white picket fence with a double pram with a couple of chubby-cheeked progeny tucked inside.

Max had nothing against marriage, but he no longer wanted it for himself. Six years ago, his fiancée had called off their wedding, informing him she had fallen in love with someone else, with someone who wanted children—the children Max refused to give her. Prior to that, Lydia had been adamant she was fine with his decision not to have kids. He'd thought everything was ticking along well enough in their relationship. He'd been more annoyed than upset at Lydia calling off their relationship. It had irritated him that he hadn't seen it coming.

But it had taught him a valuable lesson. A lesson he was determined he would never have to learn again. He wasn't cut out for long-term relationships. He didn't have what it took to handle commitment and all its responsibilities.

He knew marriage worked for some people—his parents and Sabrina's had solid relationships that had been tried and tested and triumphed over tragedy, especially his parents. The loss of his baby brother Daniel at the age of four months had devastated them, of course.

Max had been seven years old and while his parents had done

all they could to shield him from the tragedy, he still carried his share of guilt. In spite of the coroner's verdict of Sudden Infant Death Syndrome, Max could never get it out of his mind that he had been the last person to see his baby brother alive. There wasn't a day that went by when he didn't think of his brother, of all the years Daniel had missed out on. The milestones he would never meet.

Max walked out of his hotel and followed the Grand Canal, almost oblivious to the crowds of tourists that flocked to Venice at this time of year. Whenever he thought of Daniel, a tiny worm of guilt burrowed its way into his mind. Was there something he could have done to save his brother? Why hadn't he noticed something? Why hadn't he checked him more thoroughly? The lingering guilt he felt about Daniel was something he was almost used to now. He was almost used to feeling the lurch of dread in his gut whenever he saw a small baby. Almost.

Max stepped out of the way of a laughing couple that were walking arm in arm, carrying the colourful Venetian masks they'd bought from one of the many vendors along the canal. Why hadn't he thought to book a room at another hotel for Sabrina? It wasn't as if he couldn't afford it. He'd made plenty of money as a world-acclaimed architect, and he knew things were a little tight with her financially as she was still building up her wedding-dress design business and stubbornly refusing any help from her doctor parents, who had made it no secret that they would have preferred her to study medicine like them and Sabrina's two older brothers.

Had he *wanted* her in his room? Had he instinctively seized at the chance to have her to himself so he could kiss her again?

Maybe do more than kiss her?

Max pulled away from the thought like he was stepping back from a too-hot fire. But that's exactly what Sabrina was—hot. Too hot. She made him hot and bothered and horny as hell. The way she picked fights with him just to get under his skin never failed to get his blood pumping. Her cornflower-blue eyes would flash and sparkle, and her soft and supple mouth would fling cutting retorts his way, and it would make him feel alive in a way he hadn't in years.

Alive and energised.

But no. No. No. No. No.

He must *not* think about Sabrina like that. He had to keep his distance. He had to. She wasn't the sex without strings type. She wasn't a fling girl; she was a fairytale girl. And she was his parents' idea of his ideal match—his soul mate or something. Nothing against his parents, but they were wrong. Dead wrong. Sabrina was spontaneous and creative and disorganised. He was logical, responsible and organised to the point of pedantic. How could anyone think they were an ideal couple? It was crazy. He only had to spend a few minutes with her and she drove him nuts.

How was he going to get through a whole weekend with her?

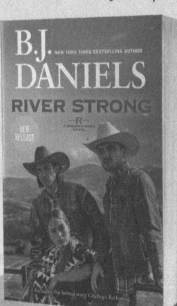